THE WORST YEARS OF YOUR LIFE

Stories for the Geeked-Out, Angst-Ridden,
Lust-Addled, and Deeply Misunderstood
Adolescent in All of Us

Edited by
Mark Jude Poirier

Simon & Schuster Paperbacks
New York London Toronto Sydney

Simon & Schuster Paperbacks
1230 Avenue of the Americas
New York, NY 10020

Copyright © 2007 by Mark Jude Poirier

First Simon & Schuster trade paperback edition August 2007

SIMON & SCHUSTER PAPERBACKS and colophon are registered trademarks
of Simon & Schuster, Inc.

For information about special discounts for bulk purchases,
please contact Simon & Schuster Special Sales at 1-800-456-6798
or business@simonandschuster.com

Designed by Davina Mock-Maniscalco

Manufactured in the United States of America

10 9 8 7 6 5 4 3 2 1

Library of Congress Cataloging-in-Publication Data

The worst years of your life / edited by Mark Jude Poirier.
p.cm.
1. Adolescence—Fiction. 2. Maturation (Psychology)—Fiction. 3. Teenagers—
Fiction. 4. Youth—Fiction. 5. Short stories, American. I. Poirier, Mark Jude.
PS648.A34W67 2007
813'.0108354—dc22
2007019352

ISBN-13: 978-1-4165-4926-0

Contents

Introduction   vii

GEORGE SAUNDERS   Bohemians   1

JENNIFER EGAN   Sisters of the Moon   12

VICTOR D. LAVALLE   Class Trip   24

JULIE ORRINGER   Note to Sixth-Grade Self   36

JOHN BARTH   Lost in the Funhouse   52

RATTAWUT LAPCHAROENSAP At the Café Lovely   81

STANLEY ELKIN   A Poetics for Bullies   106

STACEY RICHTER   The Beauty Treatment   128

JIM SHEPARD   Spending the Night with
                             the Poor   143

contents

ALICIA ERIAN | Alcatraz | 156

A.M. HOMES | A Real Doll | 175

ROBERT BOSWELL | Brilliant Mistake | 198

KEVIN CANTY | Pretty Judy | 203

MARK JUDE POIRIER | Thunderbird | 222

AMBER DERMONT | Lyndon | 241

NATHAN ENGLANDER | How We Avenged the Blums | 262

MALINDA MCCOLLUM | Good Monks | 282

CHRIS ADRIAN | A Child's Book of Sickness and Death | 302

ELIZABETH STUCKEY-FRENCH | Junior | 330

HOLIDAY REINHORN | Charlotte | 355

Contributors | 377

Permissions | 381

vi

Introduction

A T AGE TWENTY-SIX—BROKE, UNPUBLISHED, AND HAVING recently finished a second master's degree of doubtful utility—I took a job at a private school in Phoenix, to teach eighth-grade English to fifty (mostly) rich kids. Developing the curriculum, grading stacks of papers, and lecturing on the use of semicolons was unpleasant in its own inimitable way, but it was nothing compared to the stress I felt being a part of the chaos of middle-school culture again—even at this tony little academy in the shadow of Camelback Mountain.

Most of the eighth-grade girls could have passed for college coeds: tall, already curvy, and dressed in the same clothes that women wore down the road at Arizona State. They were only slightly uncomfortable in their new bodies, and many already knew how to use them. They were evil girls. Really evil. They turned on each other like starving coyotes, and it was difficult to know from day to day who was leading the snarling pack.

The boys were all dorks. Most of them were short and baby-faced, and the few who were tall were gangly messes of raging hormones. Some had vague smudges of mustaches, and all of them were obsessed with sex. With no other publicly appropriate outlets for the sexual energy coursing through their bodies, the boys spent their free time shoving and hitting each other, or grunting along to gangster rap that seemed utterly irrelevant to their privileged lives of private school, tennis lessons, and back-yard pool parties.

Couples would form and pubescent hearts would be broken, but for the most part, the girls failed to recognize their own value and continued to have crushes on their unwieldy male class-mates—despite my advice to shop for dates across the arroyo in the upper school.

And there I was, in the swirling center of it all, with the same clenched feeling in my gut that I'd had when I was a skinny spaz in eighth grade. I actually worried once again about wearing the right clothes, if the students would laugh at my jokes, if I had offended the queen bees, if the students could tell I was gay—I was deep in the closet at the time. I found myself at the mall, making sure I bought the correct Doc Martens or low-top Converse One Stars—the shoes of choice for the middle school set in 1994. I knew who was "going with" whom, which liquor store in Scottsdale sold porno to the boys, and what had happened at Michael K's bar mitz-vah. This was wrong. I was reliving the worst years of my life.

As an eighth-grade teacher, I was given a time-traveling mir-ror to look back at myself in middle school, and what I saw was gruesome. My actual pubescent years were full of mindless Atari video games, biweekly trips to Tucson Mall, skateboarding, then roller-skating, then skateboarding again, seething hatred toward my father for wearing poly-blend slacks, furtive reading of the sex scenes in my mother's Jackie Collins novels, headache-inducing afternoon reruns of *M*A*S*H* and *Barney Miller,* and masturbation, lots of masturbation—including a committed relationship with the water filter jets in our swimming pool. I spent whatever money I had on Donkey Kong and Ralph Lauren Polo shirts, and I went from being an avid reader, excellent student, and amateur herpetologist to a lazy, sarcastic asshole who did his homework right before class, if at all. I gauged my self-worth (and others') with high scores in the arcade and brand-name clothing.

My friend, whose oldest son just entered middle school, can barely stand to talk about her life at his age. She's embarrassed, but mainly frightened for her twelve-year-old son, who only recently stopped believing in Santa Claus. At age twelve, my friend had already learned why bongs were better than standard ceramic pipes, and had hitchhiked all over suburban Boston in a bikini top and cut-off Levi's that she rolled up to make shorter. Alcohol, shoplifting, lesbian experimentation . . . you name it, she was doing it. And now her basketball-obsessed son, who gets straight As and whose only vice is eavesdropping, is off to middle school, off to face legions of kids my friend can only pray are nothing like she was.

Most people agree that these years, somewhere between ages eleven and fifteen, are when people are at their worst physically, socially, morally. "That awkward age" is merely a euphemism for "the worst years of your life." "Growing pains" is a euphemism for "horrible behavior." So why is it that so many writers are drawn to this time for material? And why is it that so much good fiction sprouts from it?

Susan Sontag once said, "The best emotions to write out of are anger and fear or dread,"* and I trust that notion. Our awkward years are full of anger and fear and dread. The only emotion missing from Sontag's list that applies to the years around middle

*Susan Sontag, taped conversation (1980). From "On Writing," *With William Burroughs: A Report from the Bunker* (1981), by Victor Bockris.

school is lust. From ages eleven to fifteen, I know my predominant emotions were fear, anger, dread, and lust. At school I was afraid of being exposed as not as rich as my classmates, or gay, or studious, or smart, or stupid, or ignorant. For a while, I carried *The Preppy Handbook* around like a bible, consulting it for everything from what to wear to what to say. At age thirteen, *The Preppy Handbook* was my safety net—until I decided (or more likely someone else decided) that it was no longer cool, and I threw out my Lacoste shirts and bought a skateboard.

During the same interview, Sontag went on to say, "The least energizing emotion to write out of is admiration." I certainly can't think of anyone I admired during my adolescence, except for maybe Tom Selleck (which was admiration wrapped deeply in unmitigated lust) and the regulars at Skate Country who could do elaborate tricks like "shoot the duck" or "drop the bomb." Using Sontag's guidelines, this time in life is the ripest time from which writers can draw.

The stories in this anthology don't stem from nostalgia for video games, fashion trends, or other pop culture detritus; they stem more likely, I believe, from nostalgia for the intense and sometimes confusing emotions that we all experienced at this time in our lives. It's this intensity of feeling that makes the worst years of your life the source of some great fiction.

The idea for this anthology came to me while I was preparing another anthology, one that focused on something I called "unsafe text"—fiction unlike the quiet, overly crafted, unassuming work that was lauded at the Iowa Writers' Workshop while I was a student there. Kevin Canty's collection, *A Stranger in this World,* as well as Jennifer Egan's *Emerald City: Stories,* were two books I turned to when I was being told my fiction was too dark, that I should try to write something "nice." The stories in Canty's and Egan's collections weren't nice. They weren't quiet and unassuming. They were provocative and evocative. The characters were faced with challenging, awkward, scary, and messy situations, and that's where the stories shined for me. As I looked over the list of stories for this unsafe-text anthology, I realized that many of them focused on protagonists in middle school, around the ages of eleven through fifteen. I dropped unsafe text, and the anthology idea evolved into something more uncomfortably entertaining: *The Worst Years of Your Life.*

I'm excited that it became more specific because it prompted me to dig a little deeper into my favorite collections of short fiction and solicit suggestions from friends. In the process, I discovered many amazing stories, stories that reminded me why I write fiction, stories I might never have read had I not decided to focus the anthology in this new way. On the suggestion of Amber Dermont, whose story "Lyndon" won me over on the first line and appears in this anthology, I picked up Rattawut Lapcharoensap's *Sightseeing* and Alicia Erian's *The Brutal Language of Love.* Not only did each of these books contain stories ideally suited for *The Worst Years of Your Life,* but each book reinforced my idea that fiction does not have to be quiet and unassuming to be good. These writers, and the other writers in this anthology, seem to understand Sontag's ideas about dread and anger, but they all also understand that sometimes, if you care to look hard enough, you can find beauty in ugliness.

Mark Jude Poirier

THE WORST YEARS
OF YOUR LIFE

Bohemians

George Saunders

I N A LOVELY URBAN COINCIDENCE, THE LAST TWO HOUSES ON
our block were both occupied by widows who had lost their
husbands in Eastern European pogroms. Dad called them
the Bohemians. He called anyone white with an accent a Bohemian. Whenever he saw one of the Bohemians, he greeted her
by mispronouncing the Czech word for "door." Neither Bohemian was Czech, but both were polite, so when Dad said
"door" to them they answered cordially, as if he weren't perenni-
ally schlockered.

Mrs. Poltoi, the stouter Bohemian, had spent the war in a
crawl space, splitting a daily potato with five cousins. Conse-
quently she was bitter and claustrophobic and loved food. If you
ate something while standing near her, she stared at it going into
your mouth. She wore only black. She said the Catholic Church
was a jeweled harlot drinking the blood of the poor. She said
America was a spoiled child ignorant of grief. When our ball

1

rolled onto her property, she seized it and waddled into her backyard and pitched it into the quarry.

Mrs. Hopanlitski, on the other hand, was thin and joyfully made pipe-cleaner animals. When I brought home one of her crude dogs in top hats, Mom said, "Take over your Mold-A-Hero. To her, it will seem like the toy of a king." To Mom, the camps, massacres, and railroad sidings of twenty years before were as unreal as covered wagons. When Mrs. H. claimed her family had once owned serfs, Mom's attention wandered. She had a tract house in mind. No way was she getting one. We were renting a remodeled garage behind the Giancarlos, and Dad was basically drinking up the sporting goods store. His NFL helmets were years out of date. I'd stop by after school and find the store closed and Dad getting sloshed among the fake legs with Bennie Delmonico at Prosthetics World.

Using the Mold-A-Hero, I cast Mrs. H. a plastic Lafayette, and she said she'd keep it forever on her sill. Within a week, she'd given it to Elizabeth the Raccoon. I didn't mind. Raccoon, an only child like me, had nothing. The Kletz brothers called her Raccoon for the bags she had under her eyes from never sleeping. Her parents fought nonstop. They fought over breakfast. They fought in the yard in their underwear. At dusk they stood on their porch whacking each other with lengths of weather stripping. Raccoon practically had spinal curvature from spending so much time slumped over with misery. When the Kletz brothers called her Raccoon, she indulged them by rubbing her hands together ferally. The nickname was the most attention she'd ever had. Sometimes she'd wish to be hit by a car so she could come back as a true raccoon and track down the Kletzes and give them rabies.

"Never wish harm on yourself or others," Mrs. H. said. "You are a lovely child." Her English was flat and clear, almost like ours.

"Raccoon, you mean," Raccoon said. "A lovely raccoon."

"A lovely child of God," Mrs. H. said.

"Yeah, right," Raccoon said. "Tell again about the prince."

So Mrs. H. told again how she'd stood rapt in her yard watching an actual prince powder his birthmark to invisibility. She remembered the smell of burning compost from the fields and men in colorful leggings dragging a gutted boar across a wooden bridge. This was before she was forced to become a human pack animal in the Carpathians, carrying the personal belongings of cruel officers. At night, they chained her to a tree. Sometimes they burned her calves with a machine-gun barrel for fun. Which was why she always wore knee socks. After three years, she'd come home to find her babies in tiny graves. They were, she would say, short-lived but wonderful gifts. She did not now begrudge God for taking them. A falling star is brief, but isn't one nonetheless glad to have seen it? Her grace made us hate Mrs. Poltoi all the more. What was eating a sixth of a potato every day compared to being chained to a tree? What was being crammed in with a bunch of your cousins compared to having your kids killed?

The summer I was ten, Raccoon and I, already borderline rejects due to our mutually unraveling households, were joined by Art Siminiak, who had recently made the mistake of inviting the Kletzes in for lemonade. There was no lemonade. Instead, there was Art's mom and a sailor from Great Lakes passed out naked across the paper-drive stacks on the Siminiaks' sun porch.

This new, three-way friendship consisted of slumping in gangways, playing gloveless catch with a Wiffle, trailing hopefully behind kids whose homes could be entered without fear of fiasco.

Over on Mozart lived Eddie the Vacant. Eddie was seventeen, huge, and simple. He could crush a walnut in his bare hand, but first you had to put it there and tell him to do it. Once he'd pinned a VACANT sign to his shirt and walked around the neighborhood that way, and the name had stuck. Eddie claimed to see birds. Different birds appeared on different days of the week. Also, there was a Halloween bird and a Christmas bird.

One day, as Eddie hobbled by, we asked what kind of birds he was seeing.

"Party birds," he said. "They got big streamers coming out they butts."

"You having a party?" said Art. "You having a homo party?"

"I gone have a birthday party," said Eddie, blinking shyly.

"Your dad know?" Raccoon said.

"No, he don't yet," said Eddie.

His plans for the party were private and illogical. We peppered him with questions, hoping to get him to further embarrass himself. The party would be held in his garage. As far as the junk car in there, he would push it out by hand. As far as the oil on the floor, he would soak it up using Handi Wipes. As far as music, he would play a trumpet.

"What are you going to play the trumpet with?" said Art. "Your asshole?"

"No, I not gone play it with that," Eddie said. "I just gone use my lips, okay?"

As far as girls, there would be girls; he knew many girls, from his job managing the Drake Hotel, he said. As far as food, there would be food, including pudding dumplings.

"You're the manager of the Drake Hotel," Raccoon said.

"Hey, I know how to get the money for pudding dumplings!" Eddie said.

Then he rang Poltoi's bell and asked for a contribution. She said for what. He said for him. She said to what end. He looked at her blankly and asked for a contribution. She asked him to leave the porch. He asked for a contribution. Somewhere, he'd got the idea that, when asking for a contribution, one angled to sit on the

4

couch. He started in, and she pushed him back with a thick forearm. Down the front steps he went, ringing the iron bannister with his massive head.

He got up and staggered away, a little blood on his scalp.

"Learn to leave people be!" Poltoi shouted after him.

Ten minutes later, Eddie Sr. stood on Poltoi's porch, a hulking effeminate tailor too cowed to use his bulk for anything but butting open the jamming door at his shop.

"Since when has it become the sport to knock unfortunates down stairs?" he asked.

"He was not listen," she said. "I tell him no. He try to come inside."

"With all respect," he said, "it is in my son's nature to perhaps be not so responsive."

"Someone so unresponse, keep him indoors," she said. "He is big as a man. And I am old lady."

"Never has Eddie presented a danger to anyone," Eddie Sr. said.

"I know my rights," she said. "Next time, I call police."

But, having been pushed down the stairs, Eddie the Vacant couldn't seem to stay away.

"Off this porch," Poltoi said through the screen when he showed up the next day, offering her an empty cold-cream jar for three dollars.

"We gone have so many snacks," he said. "And if I drink a alcohol drink, then watch out. Because I ain't allowed. I dance too fast."

He was trying the doorknob now, showing how fast he would dance if alcohol was served.

"Please, off this porch!" she shouted.

"Please, off this porch!" he shouted back, doubling at the waist in wacky laughter.

Poltoi called the cops. Normally, Lieutenant Brusci would have asked Eddie what bird was in effect that day and given him a ride home in his squad. But this was during the One City fiasco. To cut graft, cops were being yanked off their regular beats and replaced by cops from other parts of town. A couple of Armenians from South Shore showed up and dragged Eddie off the porch in a club lock so tight he claimed the birds he was seeing were beakless.

"I'll give you a beak, Frankenstein," said one of the Armenians, tightening the choke hold.

Eddie entered the squad with all the fluidity of a hat rack. Art and Raccoon and I ran over to Eddie Sr.'s tailor shop, above the Marquee, which had sunk to porn. When Eddie Sr. saw us, he stopped his Singer by kicking out the plug. From downstairs came a series of erotic moans.

Eddie Sr. rushed to the hospital with his Purple Heart and some photos of Eddie as a grinning, wet-chinned kid on a pony. He found Eddie handcuffed to a bed, with an IV drip and a smashed face. Apparently, he'd bitten one of the Armenians. Bail was set at three hundred. The tailor shop made zilch. Eddie Sr.'s fabrics were a lexicon of yesteryear. Dust coated a bright yellow sign that read ZIPPERS REPAIRED IN JIFFY.

"Jail for that kid, I admit, don't make total sense," the judge said. "Three months in the Anston. Best I can do."

The Anston Center for Youth was a red brick former forge now yarded in barbed wire. After their shifts, the guards held loud, hooting orgies kitty-corner at Zem's Lamplighter. Skinny immigrant women arrived at Zem's in station wagons and emerged hours later adjusting their stockings. From all over Chicago kids were sent to the Anston, kids who'd only ever been praised for the level of beatings they gave and received and their willingness to carve themselves up. One Anston kid had famously hired another kid to run over his foot. Another had killed his mother's lover with a can opener. A third had sliced open his own eyelid with a pop-top on a dare.

Eddie the Vacant disappeared into the Anston in January and came out in March.

To welcome him home, Eddie Sr. had the neighborhood kids over. Eddie the Vacant looked so bad even the Kletzes didn't joke about how bad he looked. His nose was off center and a scald mark ran from ear to chin. When you got too close, his hands shot up. When the cake was served, he dropped his plate, shouting, "Leave a guy alone!"

Our natural meanness now found a purpose. Led by the Kletzes, we cut through Poltoi's hose, bashed out her basement windows with ball-peens, pushed her little shopping cart over the edge of the quarry, and watched it end-over-end into the former Slag Ravine.

Then it was spring and the quarry got busy. When the noon blast went off, our windows rattled. The three o'clock blast was even bigger. Raccoon and Art and I made a fort from the cardboard shipping containers the Cline frames came in. One day, while pretending the three o'clock blast was atomic, we saw Eddie the Vacant bounding toward our fort through the weeds, like some lover in a commercial, only fatter and falling occasionally.

His trauma had made us kinder toward him.

"Eddie," Art said. "You tell your dad where you're at?"

"It no big problem," Eddie said. "I was gone leave my dad a note."

"But did you?" said Art.

"I'll leave him a note when I get back," said Eddie. "I gone come in with you now."

"No room," said Raccoon. "You're too huge."

7

"That a good one!" said Eddie, crowding in.

Down in the quarry were the sad cats, the slumping watchman's shack, the piles of reddish, discarded dynamite wrappings that occasionally rose erratically up the hillside like startled birds.

Along the quarryside trail came Mrs. Poltoi, dragging a new shopping cart.

"Look at that pig," said Raccoon. "Eddie, that's the pig that put you away."

"What did they do to you in there, Ed?" said Art. "Did they mess with you?"

"No, they didn't," said Eddie. "I just a say to them, 'Leave a guy alone!' I mean, sometime they did, okay? Sometimes that one guy say, 'Hey, Eddie, pull your thing! We gone watch you.'"

"Okay, okay," said Art.

At dusk, the three of us would go to Mrs. H.'s porch. She'd bring out cookies and urge forgiveness. It wasn't Poltoi's fault her heart was small, she told us. She, Mrs. H., had seen a great number of things, and seeing so many things had enlarged her heart. Once, she had seen Göring. Once, she had seen Einstein. Once, during the war, she had seen a whole city block, formerly thick with furriers, bombed black overnight. In the morning, charred bodies had crawled along the street, begging for mercy. One such body had grabbed her by the ankle, and she recognized it as Bergen, a friend of her father's.

"What did you do?" said Raccoon.

"Not important now," said Mrs. H., gulping back tears, looking off into the quarry.

Then disaster. Dad got a check for shoulder pads for all six district football teams and, trying to work things out with Mom, decided to take her on a cruise to Jamaica. Nobody in our neighborhood had ever been on a cruise. Nobody had even been to Wisconsin. The disaster was, I was staying with Poltoi. Ours was a liquor household, where you could ask a question over and over in utter sincerity and never get a straight answer. I asked and asked, "Why her?" And was told and told, "It will be an adventure."

I asked, "Why not Grammy?"

I was told, "Grammy don't feel well."

I asked, "Why not Hopanlitski?"

Dad did this like snort.

"Like that's gonna happen," said Mom.

"Why not, why not?" I kept asking.

"Because shut up," they kept answering.

Just after Easter, over I went, with my little green suitcase.

I was a night panicker and occasional bed-wetter. I'd wake drenched and panting. Had they told her? I doubted it. Then I knew they hadn't, from the look on her face the first night, when I peed myself and woke up screaming.

"What's this?" she said.

"Pee," I said, humiliated beyond any ability to lie.

"Ach, well," she said. "Who don't? This also used to be me. Pee pee pee. I used to dream of a fish who cursed me."

She changed the sheets gently, with no petulance—a new one on me. Often Ma, still half asleep, popped me with the wet sheet, saying when at last I had a wife, she herself could finally get some freaking sleep.

Then the bed was ready, and Poltoi made a sweeping gesture, like, Please.

I got in.

She stayed standing there.

"You know," she said. "I know they say things. About me, what I done to that boy. But I had a bad time in the past with a big stupid boy. You don't gotta know. But I did like I did that day for good reason. I was scared at him, due to something what happened for real to me."

9

She stood in the half-light, looking down at her feet.

"Do you get?" she said. "Do you? Can you get it, what I am saying?"

"I think so," I said.

"Tell to him," she said. "Tell to him sorry, explain about it, tell your friends also. If you please. You have a good brain. That is why I am saying to you."

Something in me rose to this. I'd never heard it before but I believed it: I had a good brain. I could be trusted to effect a change.

Next day was Saturday. She made soup. We played a game using three slivers of soap. We made placemats out of colored strips of paper, and she let me teach her my spelling words.

Around noon, the doorbell rang. At the door stood Mrs. H.

"Everything okay?" she said, poking her head in.

"Yes, fine," said Poltoi. "I did not eat him yet."

"Is everything really fine?" Mrs. H. said to me. "You can say."

"It's fine," I said.

"You can say," she said fiercely.

Then she gave Poltoi a look that seemed to say, Hurt him and you will deal with me.

"You silly woman," said Poltoi. "You are going now."

Mrs. H. went.

We resumed our spelling. It was tense in a quiet-house way. Things ticked. When Poltoi missed a word, she pinched her own hand, but not hard. It was like symbolic pinching. Once when she pinched, she looked at me looking at her, and we laughed.

Then we were quiet again.

"That lady?" she finally said. "She like to lie. Maybe you don't know. She say she is come from where I come from?"

"Yes," I said.

"She is lie," she said. "She act so sweet and everything but she

10

lie. She been born in Skokie. Live here all her life, in America. Why you think she talk so good?"

All week, Poltoi made sausage, noodles, potato pancakes; we ate like pigs. She had tea and cakes ready when I came home from school. At night, if necessary, she dried me off, moved me to her bed, changed the sheets, put me back, with never an unkind word.

"Will pass, will pass," she'd hum.

Mom and Dad came home tanned, with a sailor cap for me, and, in a burst of post-vacation honesty, confirmed it: Mrs. H. was a liar. A liar and a kook. Nothing she said was true. She'd been a cashier at Goldblatt's but had been caught stealing. When caught stealing, she'd claimed to be with the Main Office. When a guy from the Main Office came down, she'd claimed to be with the FBI. Then she'd produced a letter from Lady Bird Johnson, but in her own handwriting, with "Johnson" spelled "Jonsen."

I told the other kids what I knew, and in time they came to believe it, even the Kletzes.

And, once we believed it, we couldn't imagine we hadn't seen it all along.

Another spring came, once again birds nested in bushes on the sides of the quarry. A thrown rock excited a thrilling upward explosion. Thin rivers originated in our swampy backyards; and we sailed boats made of flattened shoeboxes, Twinkie wrappers, crimped tinfoil. Raccoon glued together three balsa-wood planes and placed on this boat a turd from her dog, Svengooli, and, as Svengooli's turd went over a little waterfall and disappeared into the quarry, we cheered.

Sisters of the Moon

JENNIFER EGAN

S ILAS HAS A BROKEN HEAD. IT HAPPENED SOMETIME LAST
night, outside The Limited on Geary and Powell. None of
us saw. Silas says the fight was over a woman, and that he
won it. "But you look like all bloody shit, my friend," Irish says,
laughing, rolling the words off his accent. Silas says we should've
seen the other guy.

He adjusts the bandage on his head and looks up at the palm
trees, which make a sound over Union Square like it's raining.
Silas has that strong kind of shape, like high school guys who you
know could pick you up and carry you like a bag. But his face is
old. He wears a worn-out army jacket, the pockets always fat
with something. Once, he pulled out a silver thimble and pushed
it into my hand, not saying one word. It can't be real silver, but
I've kept it.

I think Silas fought in Vietnam. Once he said, "It's 1974, and
I'm still alive," like he couldn't believe it.

"So where is he?" Irish asks, full of humor. "Where is this bloke with half his face gone?"

Angel and Liz start laughing, I don't know why. "Where's this woman you fought for?" is what I want to ask.

Silas shrugs, grinning. "Scared him away."

SAN FRANCISCO IS OURS, we've signed our name on it a hundred times: SISTERS OF THE MOON. On the shiny tiles inside the Stockton Tunnel, across those buildings like blocks of salt on the empty piers near the Embarcadero. Silver plus another color, usually blue or red. Angel and Liz do the actual painting. I'm the lookout. While they're spraying the paint cans, I get scared to death. To calm down, I'll say to myself, If the cops come, or if someone stops his car to yell at us, I'll just walk away from Angel and Liz, like I never saw them before in my life. Afterward, when the paint is wet and we bounce away on the balls of our feet, I get so ashamed, thinking, What if they knew? They'd probably ditch me, which would be worse than getting caught—even going to jail. I'd be all alone in the universe.

Most people walk through Union Square on their way someplace else. Secretaries, businessmen. The Park, we call it. But Silas and Irish and the rest are always here. They drift out, then come back. Union Square is their own private estate.

Watching over the square like God is the St. Francis Hotel, with five glass elevators sliding up and down its polished face. Stoned, Angel and Liz and I spend hours sitting on benches with our heads back, waiting for the elevators to all line up on top. Down, up, down—even at 5 A.M. they're moving. The St. Francis never sleeps.

Angel and Liz expect to be famous, and I believe it. Angel just turned fifteen. I'm only five months younger, and Liz is younger

13

than me. But I'm the baby of us. Smoking pot in Union Square, I still worry who will see.

WE'VE BEEN TALKING for a week about dropping acid. I keep stalling. Today we go ahead and buy it, from a boy with a runny nose and dark, anxious eyes. Across the street is I. Magnin, and I get a sick feeling that my stepmother is going to come out the revolving doors with packages under her arms. She's a buyer for the shoe department at Saks, and in the afternoon she likes to walk around and view the competition.

Angel leans against a palm tree, asking in her Southern voice if the acid is pure and how much we should take to get off and how long the high will last us. She's got her shirt tied up so her lean stomach shows. Angel came from Louisiana a year ago with her mother's jazz band. I adore her. She goes wherever she wants, and the world just forms itself around her.

"What are you looking at?" Liz asks me. She's got short, curly black hair and narrow blue eyes.

"Nothing."

"Yes, you are," she says. "All the time. Just watching everything."

"So?"

"So, when are you going to do something?" She says it like she's joking.

I get a twisting in my stomach. "I don't know," I say. I glance at Angel, but she's talking to the dealer. At least she didn't hear us.

Liz and I look at I. Magnin. Her mother could walk out of there as easily as mine, but Liz doesn't care. I get the feeling she's waiting for something like that to happen, a chance to show Angel how far she can go.

*   *   *

14

Sisters of the Moon

WE FIND IRISH BEGGING on Powell Street. "Can you spare any part of a million dollars?" he asks the world, spreading his arms wide. Irish has a big blond face and wavy hair and eyes that are almost purple—I mean it. One time, he says, he got a thousand-dollar bill—an Arab guy just handed it over. That was before we knew Irish.

"My lassies," he calls out, and we get the hug of those big arms, all three of us. He inhales from Angel's hair, which is dark brown and flips into wings on both sides of her face. She's still a virgin. In Angel this seems beautiful, like a precious glass bowl you can't believe didn't break yet. One time, in Union Square, this Australian guy took hold of her hair and pulled it back, back, so the tendons of her throat showed through the skin, and Angel was laughing at first and so was the guy, but then he leaned down and kissed her mouth and Irish knocked him away, shouting, "Hey, motherfucker, can't you see she's still a child?"

"What nice presents have you brought?" Irish asks now.

Angel opens the bag to show the acid. I check around for cops and catch Liz watching me, a look on her face like she wants to laugh.

"When shall we partake?" Irish asks, reaching out with his cap to a lady in a green raincoat, who shakes her head like he should know better, then drops in a quarter. Irish could have any kind of life, I think—he just picked this one.

"Not yet," Angel says. "Too light."

"Tonight," Liz says, knowing I won't be there.

Angel frowns. "What about Tally?"

I look down, startled and pleased to be remembered.

"Tomorrow?" Angel asks me.

I can't help pausing for a second, holding this feeling of

everyone waiting for my answer. Then someone singing "Gimme Shelter" distracts them. I wish I'd just said it.

"Tomorrow's fine."

THE SINGER TURNS OUT to be a guy named Fleece, who I don't know. I mean, I've seen him, he's part of the gang of Irish and Silas and them who hang out in the Park. Angel says these guys are in their thirties, but they look older than that and act younger, at least around us. There are women, too, with red eyes and heavy makeup, and mostly they act loud and happy, but when they get dressed up, there are usually holes in their stockings, or at least a run. They don't like us—Angel especially.

Angel hands me the acid bag to hold while she lights up a joint. Across the Park I see three cops walking—I can almost hear the squeak of their boots. I cover the bag with my hand. I see Silas on another bench. His bandage is already dirty.

"Tally's scared," Liz says. She's watching me, that expression in her eyes like the laughter behind them is about to come pushing out.

The others look at me, and my heart races. "I'm not."

In Angel's eyes I see a flash of cold. Scared people make her moody, like they remind her of something she wants to forget. "Scared of what?" she says.

"I'm not."

Across the square, Silas adjusts the bandage over his eyes. Where is this woman he fought for? I wonder. Why isn't she with him now?

"I don't know," Liz says. "What're you scared of, Tally?"

I look right at Liz. There's a glittery challenge in her eyes but also something else, like she's scared, too. She hates me, I think. We're friends, but she hates me.

16

Irish tokes from the joint in the loudest way, like it's a tube connecting him to the last bit of oxygen on earth. When he exhales, his face gets white. "What's she scared of?" he says, and laughs faintly. "The world's a bloody terrifying place."

AT HOME THAT NIGHT I can't eat. I'm too thin, like a little girl, even though I'm fourteen. Angel loves to eat, and I know that's how you get a figure, but my body feels too small. It can't hold anything extra.

"How was school?" my stepmother asks.

"Fine."

"Where have you been since then?"

"With Angel and those guys. Hanging around." No one seems to notice my Southern accent.

My father looks up. "Hanging around doing what?"

"Homework."

"They're in biology together," my stepmother explains.

Across the table the twins begin to whimper. As he leans over their baby heads, my father's face goes soft—I see it even through his beard. The twins are three years old, with bright red hair. Tomorrow I'll tie up my shirt, I think, like Angel did. So what if my stomach is white?

"I'm spending the night tomorrow," I say. "At Angel's."

He wipes applesauce from the babies' mouths. I can't tell if he means to refuse or is just distracted. "Tomorrow's Saturday," I tell him, just in case.

WE SPEND ALL DAY at Angel's, preparing. Her mom went to Mexico with the band she plays violin for, and won't be back for a month. Candles, powdered incense from the Mystic Eye, on

17

Broadway, a paint set, sheets of creamy paper, Pink Floyd records stacked by the stereo, and David Bowie, and Todd Rundgren, and "Help Me," of course—Joni Mitchell's new hit, which we worship.

Angel lives six blocks from Union Square in a big apartment south of Market Street, with barely any walls. A foil pyramid hangs from the ceiling over her bed. All day we keep checking the square for Irish, but he's disappeared.

At sundown we go ahead without him. Candles on the window-sills, the white rug vacuumed. We cut the pills with a knife, and each of us takes one-third of all three so we're sure to get the same dose. I'm terrified. It seems wrong that such a tiny thing could do so much. But I feel Liz watching me, waiting for one wrong move, and I swallow in silence.

Then we wait. Angel does yoga, arching her back, pressing her palms to the floor with her arms bent. I've never seen anyone so limber. The hair rushes from her head in a flood of black, like it could stain the rug. Liz's eyes don't move from her.

When the acid starts to work, we all lie together on her mother's huge four-poster bed, Angel in the middle. She holds one of our hands in each of hers. Angel has the kind of skin that tans in a minute, and beautiful, snaking veins. I feel the blood moving in her. We wave our hands above our faces and watch them leave trails. I feel Angel warm beside me and think how I'll never love anyone this much, how without her I would disappear.

THE CITY AT NIGHT is full of lights and water and hills like piles of sand. We struggle to climb them. Empty cable cars totter past. The sky is a sheet of black paper with tiny holes poked in it. The Chinatown sidewalks smell like salt and flesh. It's 3 A.M. Planes drift overhead like strange fish.

Sisters of the Moon

Market Street, a steamy puddle at every curb. We find our way down alleys, our crazy eyes making diamonds of the shattered glass that covers the streets and sidewalks. Nothing touches us. We float under the orange streetlamps. My father, the twins—everything but Angel and Liz and me just fades into nothing, the way the night used to disappear when my real mother tucked me into bed, years ago.

In the Broadway Tunnel I grab for the spray cans. "Let me," I cry, breathless. Angel and Liz are too stoned to care. We have green and silver. I hold one can in each fist, shake them up, and spray huge round letters, like jaws ready to swallow me. I breathe in the paint fumes and they taste like honey. Tiny dots of cool paint fall on my face and eyelashes and stay there. Traffic ricochets past, but I don't care tonight—I don't care. In the middle of painting I turn to Angel and Liz and cry, "This is it, this is it!" and they nod excitedly, like they already knew, and then I start to cry. We hug in the Broadway Tunnel. "This is it," I sob, clinging to Angel and Liz, their warm shoulders. I hear them crying, too, and think, It will be like this always. From now on, nothing can divide us.

It seems like hours before I notice the paint cans still in my hands and finish the job. SISTERS OF THE MOON.

It blazes.

WE MAKE OUR WAY to Union Square. Lo and behold, there is Irish, holding court with a couple of winos and a girl named Pamela, who I've heard is a prostitute. Irish looks different tonight—he's got big, swashbuckling sleeves that flap like sails in the wind. He's grand. As we walk toward him, blinking in the liquidy light, an amazement at his greatness overwhelms us. He is a great man, Irish. We're lucky to know him.

Irish scoops Angel into his arms. "My beloved," he says. "I've been waiting all night for you." And he kisses her full on the lips—a deep, long kiss that Angel seems at first to resist. Then she relaxes, like always. I feel a small, sharp pain, like a splinter of glass in my heart. But I'm not surprised. It was always going to happen, I think. We were always waiting.

Angel and Irish draw apart and look at each other. Liz hovers near them. Pamela gets up and walks away, into the shadows. I sit on the bench with the winos and stare up at the St. Francis Hotel.

"You're high," Irish says to Angel. "So very high."

"What about you? Your pupils are gone," she says.

Irish laughs. He laughs and laughs, opening up his mouth like the world could fit in it. Irish might live on the streets, but his teeth are white. "I'll see you in Heaven," he says.

On the St. Francis Hotel the glass elevators float. Two reach the top, and two more rise slowly to join them. They hang there, all four, and I hold my breath as the fifth approaches and will the others not to move until it gets there. I keep perfectly still, pushing the last one up with my eyes until it reaches the top, and there they are, in a perfect line, all five.

I turn to show Angel and Liz, but they're gone. I see them walking away with Irish, Angel in the middle, Liz clutching at her arm like the night could pull them apart. It's Liz who looks back at me. Our eyes meet, and I feel like she's talking out loud, I understand so perfectly. If I move fast, now, I can keep her from winning. But the thought makes me tired. I don't move. Liz turns away. I think I see a bounding in her steps, but I stay where I am.

They turn to ghosts in the darkness and vanish. My teeth start to chatter. It's over. Angel is gone, I think, and I start to cry. She just walked away.

Then I hear a rushing noise. It's a sound like time passing, years racing past, so all of a sudden I'm much older, a grown-up woman looking back to when she was a girl in Union Square. And I realize that even if Angel never thinks of me again, at some point I'll get up and take the bus home.

The winos have drifted off. By my Mickey Mouse watch it's 5 A.M. I notice someone crossing the square—it's Silas, the dirty bandage still around his head. I yell out to him.

He comes over slowly, like it hurts to walk. He sits down next to me. For a long time we just sit, not talking. Finally I ask, "Was it really over a woman?"

Silas shakes his head. "Just a fight," he says. "Just another stupid fight."

I straighten my legs so that my sneakers meet in front of me. They're smudged but still white. "I'm hungry," I say.

"Me, too," Silas says. "But everything's closed." Then he says, "I'm leaving town."

"To where?"

"South Carolina. My brother's store. Called him up today."

"How come?"

"Had enough," he says. "Just finally had enough."

I know there's something I should say, but I don't know what. "Is he nice," I ask, "your brother?"

Silas grins. I see the young part of him then, the kind of mischief boys have. "He's the meanest bastard I know."

"What about Irish?" I ask. "Won't you miss Irish and those guys?"

"Irish is a dead man."

I stare at Silas.

"Believe it," he says. "In twenty years no one will remember him."

Twenty years. In twenty years I'd be thirty-four years old, my stepmother's age. It would be 1994. And suddenly I think, Silas is right—Irish is dead. And Angel, too, and maybe even Liz. Right

21

jennifer egan

now is their perfect, only time. It will sweep them away. But Silas was always outside it.

I put my hand in my pocket and find the thimble. I pull it out. "You gave me this," I tell him.

Silas looks at the thimble like he's never seen it. Then he says, "That's real silver."

Maybe he wants it back to sell, for his trip to South Carolina. I leave the thimble in my hand so that if Silas wants it he can just take it. But he doesn't. We both look at the thimble. "Thanks," I say.

We lean back on the bench. My high is wearing off. I have a feeling in my chest like feathers, like a bird waking up and brushing against my ribs. The elevators rise and fall, like signals.

"Always watching," Silas says, looking at me. "Those big eyes, always moving."

I nod, ashamed. "But I never do anything," I say. And all of a sudden I know, I know why Angel left me.

Silas frowns. "Sure you do. You watch," he says, "which is what'll save you."

I shrug. But the longer we sit, the more I realize he's right—what I do is watch. I'm like Silas, I think. In twenty years I'll still be alive.

On one side the sky is getting light, like a lid is being lifted up. I watch it, trying to see the day coming, but I can't. All of a sudden the sky is just bright.

"I wonder what people will look like in 1994," I say.

Silas considers. "Twenty years? Probably look like us again."

"Like you and me?" I'm disappointed.

"Oh yeah," Silas says with a wry grin. "Wishing they'd been here the first time."

I look at the blue bandanna tied around his wrist, his torn-up jeans and army jacket with a Grateful Dead skull on one pocket.

22

When I'm thirty-four, tonight will be a million years ago, I think—the St. Francis Hotel and the rainy palm tree sounds, Silas with the bandage on his head—and this makes me see how everything now is precious, how someday I'll know I was lucky to be here.

"I'll remember Irish," I say loudly. "I'll remember everyone. In twenty years."

Silas looks at me curiously. Then he touches my face, tracing my left cheekbone almost to my ear. His finger is warm and rough, and I have the thought that to Silas my skin must feel soft. He studies the paint on the tip of his finger, and smiles. He shows me. "Silver," he says.

Class Trip

VICTOR D. LaVALLE

HOOKERS, WILLY SAID. YOU KNOW THEM. YOU LOVE them.

He was trying to get us interested. What do you think? He was talking to three tenth-grade boys. Fifteen years old. Among all four we didn't have half a brain. Willy, bullet-shaped head and all, was good at convincing and he wasn't even working hard.

—We are hopping on that train, he continued, heading out to Manhattan and everyone here is getting his dick sucked. No arguments.

—Who's going to put up a fight? I asked. We were each calculating how best to get some money, which parent often left a purse or wallet unguarded.

Carter asked, —How much we'll need? He stood his tall ass up in front of me. When he stretched his arms over his head Carter could run his fingers around the lip of the visible universe.

Our building was budding with age groups, men and boys. Soon someone had beer; eventually it made the rounds from the eighteen-and-ups to us and after we'd taken our pulls from the tall brown bottles there were the boys we'd once been, ten or eleven, anticipating a first taste. We could all afford such open drinking until eight or nine at night because our adults were dying at jobs. Willy never left shit to settle, so before we went off he grabbed Carter, James and me, said, —This Friday. Get like thirty dollars.

Carter and I walked, no destination, just anywhere away from home. He was chattering about where he'd get his loot, not his mother or father, but that older brother who left his cash in his old shell-toed Adidas up on a shelf in his closet. Then he asked, —So what's that woman of yours going to say about you checking out these hos?

I had forgotten about her. —Guess I won't tell, I said.

He laughed, —Man, you know you can't keep no secrets when you get drunk.

—I've never been drunk around Trisha.

Carter nodded. —Well then, maybe. He began telling me something else, he was almost whispering so it seemed like a secret. I was distracted but absently swore I heard my girl's name. I wasn't listening. It was evening in Flushing, Queens, and the buildings got glowing in that setting-sun red.

FRIDAY, MAN, the whole day was full of explosive energy. During precalc a girl beside me dropped her book and in my head it sounded like a squad of soldiers battering through the door. When I saw any of the other guys we nodded conspiratorially. My girl made it easier on my conscience when she bowed out of school after third period. She clutched her belly and told me she was going home early, cramps were tearing up her insides. She had a big bag, full, and when I asked she reminded me of the trip she was taking to see her aunt, who lived in Massachusetts, some town near Boston. She'd be gone for days.

Then, in the evening, we rode the 7 out toward Manhattan. It was strange traveling with them; since about thirteen I had been coming out to wander alone. Most times I'd get off at Times Square where my ass would trip around for blocks trying to find something to kill me or make me laugh.

On the subway James scratched his balls, looked at an old asleep man, tortured in his wrinkled suit. He asked us, —What if I just punch that kid in the face? He pointed to the man. But we weren't really like that. None of us. Talk shit, that was our game. Run fast, that was our game.

—Don't start nothing, Willy said.

James sucked his teeth; the way his eyes were shaking in their sockets he seemed amped enough to hit this guy, but Willy talked him down until James sat back, sprawled out like he couldn't on his mother's couch. A year before, James got into it with an off-duty cop who was quick to show his badge and gun to James and me. The pistol was under his coat, outside his shirt, hanging on the rim of his jeans, the snubbed nose looking like a challenge. —So you're a cop, James had said. So what?

The cop was black, so I was especially scared.

—You should watch your mouth son, the cop said, though he wasn't very old himself.

James laughed that way he does, showing all his teeth; an expression that says, And?

Black Cop pressed the yellow strip to ring for his stop. In the back stairwell he said to me, —Your friend's going to get you into trouble someday.

I wasn't speaking; I nodded but my neck was soft with liquor, so I only managed a weak wobble of my head. He had made the mistake most people did, thought that because I was the quiet kid I was the one who should be saved.

AT TIMES SQUARE we discussed getting off, enjoying the flickering pleasures of video booths, but Willy was sure of his mission. He said, —Y'all will thank me when you have a mouth all on your knob.

We got off at Twenty-eighth Street, walked so quickly to the West Side Highway you'd have thought we were on wheels. A few blocks up, the Intrepid Museum was docked. I had been there three years before, with my mother and baby sister; I rode in the cockpit of a flight simulator imagining I could join the Air Force and float somewhere above the planet. James found sour balls in his jacket and sucked one.

—You keep making noises like that and some dude's going to think you're advertising, Carter said. We laughed, but then he pointed and silenced us all. There, forty feet away, was a hooker dressed all in tight silver. You can't underestimate what this meant to us; imagine Plymouth Rock.

—You suck dick? James asked. She didn't need to look up to know she should ignore us.

—Break out, she said, going through her tiny purse. She looked down the street, lit a cigarette, saw we had not left, said again, Break out.

Carter tried to make it clear. —My boy asked if you suck dick.

She whipped her red hair, real or fake, backward, elegantly. I frowned. Silver said, —You tell your boy I don't fuck with little kids. The way she switched her weight from foot one to foot two made us forget any indignation and check out her lovely hips.

—I'm saying, James charmed. I got the loot and you got the mouth, right?

Silver lost her temper, cursed at us, screamed a man's name. Then there he was, behind a rotten chain-link fence, amid these half-built homes of scavenged wood and sheets of plastic, all big shoulders and blond hair, like some *übermensch*, a fucking super-Nazi in an off-white overcoat.

Carter stayed behind to unload some more words at her; the rest of us were on the move. The expression on that guy, clearing the fence, crossing the street, was like he loved hurting people. Finally Carter appeared, stretching those long legs as he caught up to us. I looked over my shoulder, and the guy was still coming. My legs went faster. Soon I was whipping his Aryan ass like I was Jesse Owens.

THE FIRST TIME I held my girl's hand I was shaking so deep I couldn't control it. She looked at me. —You're shaking.

It was a strange second and I didn't say shit. This was six months before the night out with James, Willy and Carter.

Trisha said, —I think it's sweet.

We were outside school, by the library. She and I had walked out, to the October cool, because I wouldn't hold her hand in front of a crowd. —Are you that nervous? she asked.

Her hand wrapped around mine. I thought I should kiss her, touch her face, find that spot that works—opening her mouth, closing her eyes. I said, —Yeah, a little.

—Why? She was older than me. Sixteen.

—Just am.

We sat on the cold steps. She smiled. She had braces; they were shimmering and comely, there in her mouth. I had cuts across the backs of my hands. Trisha rubbed them with an open palm.

—How did these happen?

—I don't know.

—No, seriously, you can tell me these things.

I really didn't remember what had scarred them. She laughed; usually I got that reaction, laughter, from her only on the phone, where I could loosen up; in person I was always overcome by my goddamn emotions. When the cold air hit us harder, I thought of her, asked if she wanted to go in.

Trisha nodded. —It is cold. But we can stay.

I was quiet so long I forgot we were supposed to say anything.

Trisha stared to her right, to the wall where I had played handball at nine or ten. I was very tired all the time. It didn't seem strange that I was fifteen and already feeling ancient.

She had been attached when I met her. Dating someone older, a freshman in some upstate college. He still sent her things, like bus tickets. This guy promised that if she went to him he'd give her the thing she liked most: perfume. Nice stuff I couldn't afford; all she had to do was visit. Working in my favor was distance, with its power to break bonds.

—You're quiet, I said.

She squeezed my palm. —Your hand's stopped shaking.

—You want to go to a movie? I asked quickly. We weren't dating yet, that day, just the early affection.

Her laugh came out slow so, at first, I thought she was considering it. I let go of her, asked, —What's funny?

—You should have heard yourself, she said. She squeezed her nose between two short, thin fingers, talked all nasal, You want to go to a movie?

—I sounded like that?

She touched the back of my head. —You should get a fade.

—You think so?

29

—I think you'd look so good with one. And, sitting like that, it was on her to lean in for the kiss. I was surprised, uncomfortable.

Then Trisha stood; I still sat, touched her feet. —They're so small.

She said, —My feet are perfect. Even the toes are nice.

I stood, laughed, liked that she was arrogant about the stupidest things.

WHEN THE FOUR of us stopped running, Carter was the first to catch his breath, said, —Man, we could have fucked that dude up.

I punched him in the chest when I could stand straight. James and Willy heaved a minute more. We had no speed left, but we were safe. Not for the first time in our lives we were lucky.

Until a year ago none of these fellas had been my boy, but here we were looking out for one another. I went through friends quickly. That was the best thing about guys—trust comes quick and no one cries when it's over.

We walked to Twenty-seventh, where the hookers were a populace. This was their beauty; almost nothing worn, skin. We stood at a corner to watch these women move. The worst-looking one was more gorgeous than the rest of the world.

Here in the land of ass a-plenty, we were being ignored. Four black kids on foot spelled little cash and lots of hassles. These workers had no time for games. Station wagons sped through with single passengers acting alternately calm and surprised, as though they'd found this block by accident. Husbands, fiancés and boyfriends. Newer cars bursting with twenty-year-olds eased down the street, their systems pumping heavy.

—These girls are not going to take care of us, said Willy, the pragmatist. The rest of us dreamed ideally, waved twenties at the high heels thumping past.

A woman with her glorious brown chest mostly exposed saw us, said, —Go down to Twenty-fifth.

—What's there? Willy asked.

—Crackheads. She kept walking, moving in that extra-hips way that paid her bills. The backs of her thighs were right there, platformed and performing. Exposed. It is not an exaggeration to say I would have married her that night.

We made that move. Stopped at a car, the guy inside getting a blow job. His friends were waiting, herded around a telephone, laughing. The top of a woman's head worked furiously, faster than I'd have imagined possible. I craned my neck to try and see more.

—That's Nicky! one of his friends screamed. The car window was down and Nicky inside smiled back. We rejoiced with them, but only a little, any longer and a fight might break out. They were muscle guys in zebra-print pants, leather coats; their skin looked so tough I doubted anything short of a shotgun would pierce their shells.

On Twenty-fifth the market crashed, both customers and workers. Women here wore jeans and T-shirts like someone's fucked-up neighbor out for a stroll. This block looked like our school's auditorium had belched out its worst; there were slight variations on us, in groups, canvassing the street. Truly ugly men rode through in cars that rattled and died while waiting at a red light, crackheads hopped into their cars two at a time. Some rubbed close on all us boys. We tried to act calm.

James was tired and bored. A woman appeared from a shadowed doorway, he asked her, almost absently, —How much for you to suck my dick?

—Fifteen.

All of us but Willy bolted upright, so sure we were going to leave Manhattan unfulfilled. Willy stayed shrewd. —Yeah right. He'll give you five and so will the rest of us.

She brightened, scanned the crew. —All of you?

Willy nodded; she agreed. That was the benefit of going to a crackhead, you could haggle.

FINALLY IT WAS my turn. Carter and Willy leaned against a building while James, just done, rubbed his stomach. Trucks were parked on this block. Police cars seemed to have become extinct. Occasionally you heard their sirens bleating a few blocks up, but they seemed to have left everything on this block for dead. Charlene ushered me down the alley she'd made into her workplace. She was about my height and twice as old. We were well hidden but she took me farther, behind a green Dumpster, lid shut.

—You know why I wanted you last, right?

I smiled. Her scalp was hidden under a blue scarf with white dots, the haphazard folds making them look as random as the salt spread out on the sidewalk after it has snowed. She kicked away the cardboard she'd laid out when taking care of my friends. I wasn't thinking of Trisha.

—I wanted the good stuff from you, she said. She brought herself close; I was not going to fuck her, no way. Get my dick sucked and move on. Then came her punches, two of them: one in the face that didn't hurt, but the second got me in the throat and I went down. On my hands and knees, this little crackhead had taken me out. The concrete was cold and one palm rested on an empty bag of chips. She was in my pockets, but found nothing. Then she gave me the real one, something popping against my head like a fucking brick. It was a gun.

—Get up, she said. Stand. It was the shittiest piece you'll ever see; a rusting .22, one inch above a zip gun. She was in control. Now give me that money.

No games, I got it for her. She counted out all thirty dollars, slowly, in front of me, like she was trying to rub it in. You could say I was scared, but it was delayed, didn't go off in my stomach until the four of us were catching the train an hour later and I couldn't ease my token into the slot; Carter took it from my palsied hand and pushed me through.

—You robbed them all? I asked.

—Nope. Just you.

—Why me?

She put the money away, scratched at her pussy from outside her jeans. My head was bleeding. I saw that she was peeing her pants before I smelled it; the stain spread in her crotch and soon the thin yellow slacks were loosing droplets that fell to the ground between her and me. She answered my question. —I don't like your face, she said. You just don't look good.

THE WHOLE NEXT WEEK in school I was hoping for my girl's return, but Trisha was out for five days. I'd call her at home. One of her older sisters would only take a message, firmly say she'd call me, but the next night I dialed the number. I felt guilty, spent hours considering how much better life would be if I'd stayed out of the alley, if I'd been a better man.

Finally Trisha appeared. We went out to dinner. She sat at the table warm in her jacket and a turtleneck. She held my hand when we walked, but swatted me off when I tried to kiss her neck. This diner was good: the seats squeaked when you slid into a booth and a small cup of coleslaw came with every meal. — Tonight, she said, I'm paying.

—I won't argue with that.

She laughed. —You never have a problem with spending my money.

—I was going to buy you something, I told her.

She sipped her water. We were quiet until a waiter came trolling for orders.

She asked, —Where is it?

—I didn't have enough, I admitted.

—Yeah, I know you. You spent that money on nonsense.

I smiled. —You got that right, beautiful.

—So what was it?

A group came into the diner and in the wonderful anonymity of the American family, I thought they'd just left. —Look. I pointed. Trisha peeped them, but wasn't into laughing at stability. I was going to get you this bear.

—A teddy bear?

The food arrived. —Don't say it like that, I protested. It was a nice one. Had a smoking jacket and a pipe. He looked like me. Don't you think he would be cute?

She ate. Dinner done, she paid the bill. We got up and out. Flushing at night was like Flushing during the day, just darker. Together we walked to her building.

—Anyone ever ask why you're dating a younger man?

—Maybe.

She wore a new good smell applied to her skin, but I ignored it, busy instead rubbing my nose, my chin, my neck, learning my face's true dimensions.

—And what did you tell him?

She shrugged. —What should I have said?

We walked fast. Soon her building stood before us. It wasn't so big but tonight it seemed majestic. Trisha's two older sisters were outside. —Hey Anthony, Gloria said, looking to the others.

The secrets this bunch held among them were enough to destroy one thousand ex-boyfriends. Trisha smiled, waited.

—What? I asked.

—You aren't going to thank me for paying?

—You're right. Thank you so much. The food was delicious.

—I know. She touched my side.

—Am I ugly? I asked her.

—You? She put her face against my neck. She tried to tickle me but neither of us was laughing. On the street, traffic was still a thriving business; the sky was purple and lost.

Note to Sixth-Grade Self

JULIE ORRINGER

ON WEDNESDAYS WEAR A SKIRT. A SKIRT IS BETTER FOR dancing. After school, remember not to take the bus. Go to McDonald's instead. Order the fries. Don't even bother trying to sit with Patricia and Cara. Instead, try to sit with Sasha and Toni Sue. If they won't let you, try to sit with Andrea Shaw. And if Andrea Shaw gets up and throws away the rest of her fries rather than sit with you, sit alone and do not look at anyone. Particularly not the boys. If you do not look at them, they may not notice you sitting alone. And if they don't notice you sitting alone, there is still a chance that one of them will ask you to dance.

At three-thirty stand outside with the others and take the number seven bus uptown. Get off when they all get off. Be sure to do this. Do not stare out the window and lose yourself. You will end up riding out to the edge of town past the rusted gas-storage tanks, and you will never find the right bus home. Pay attention. Do not let the strap of your training bra slip out the armhole of your short-sleeved shirt. Do not leave your bag on the bus. As you cross the street, take a look at the public high school. The kids there will be eating long sticks of Roman candy and leaning on the chain-link fence. Do they look as if they care who dances with whom, or what steps you'll learn this week? News flash: They do not. Try to understand that there's a world larger than the one you inhabit. If you understand that, you will be far ahead of Patricia and Cara.

For now, though, you live in this world, so go ahead and follow the others across the street to Miggie's Academy of Dance. There is a low fence outside. Do not climb on it in your skirt. Huddle near the door with the other girls. See if anyone will let you listen. Do not call attention to yourself. Listen as Patricia, with her fascinating stutter, describes what she and Cara bought at the mall. Notice how the other girls lean forward as she works through her troublesome consonants: *G-G-Guess Jeans and an Esp-p-prit sweater.* They will talk about the TV shows they watch, who killed whom, who is sleeping with whom; they will compare starlets' hairstyles. None of this talk is of any importance. For God's sake, don't bother watching those TV shows. Keep reading your books.

At four o'clock, go inside with the others. Line up against the wall with the girls. Watch how the boys line up against their wall, popular ones in the middle, awkward ones at the sides. Watch how the girls jockey to stand across from the boys they like. Watch Brittney Wells fumble with the zipper of her nylon LeSportsac. Don't let her get next to you with that thing. Try to stand across from someone good. Do not let yourself get pushed all the way out to the sides, across from Zachary Booth or Ben Dusseldorf. Watch how Patricia and Cara stand, their hips shot to one side, their arms crossed over their chests. Try shooting your hip a little to one side. Rest your weight on one foot. Draw a circle on the wooden floor with one toe. Do not bite your fingernails. Do not give a loud sniff. Think of the word *nonchalant*. Imagine the eleventh-graders, the way they look when they smoke on the bus. Let your eyes close halfway.

When Miss Miggie comes out, do not look at her enormous breasts. Breasts like those will never grow on your scarecrow body. Do not waste your time wanting them. Instead, watch how she moves in her low-cut green dress: chin high, back straight, hips asway. Listen to the way she talks: Fawx Trawt, Chaw-chaw, Wawtz. Love how she talks, but do not pick it up. When you move north in three years, you cannot afford to say *y'all*. Listen as Miss Miggie describes what y'all will learn that day. Watch how her hand traces the dance steps in the air. Now that the boys are occupied, staring at her breasts, you can look openly at Eric Cassio. Admire his hair and eyes, but quickly. Like all boys he will feel you looking.

The first dance will always be a cha-cha. On the record they will sing in Spanish, a woman trilling in the background. It will start a thrill in your chest that will make you want to move. Watch Miss Miggie demonstrate the steps. Practice the steps in your little rectangle of floor. Watch how Patricia and Cara do the steps, their eyes steady in front of them, their arms poised as if they were already holding their partners. Now concentrate on dancing. Avoid Sasha and Toni Sue with their clumsy soccer-field legs. Ignore Brittney and that purse. When Miss Miggie looks at you, concentrate hard. Remember practicing with your father. Do not throw in an extra dance step that you are not supposed to know yet. Do not swish your skirt on purpose. Do not look at the boys.

Long before it is time to pick partners, you will feel the tightness in your stomach. Do not let it break your concentration. You have too many things to learn. Remember, if you want to have the most gold stars at the end of the eight weeks, you are going to have to work hard. Imagine dancing in a spotlight at the end-of-class ball, with the best boy dancer from all the seven private schools. On the Achievement Record, next to your name, there are already five stars. Patricia and Cara also have five stars. Everyone else has two or three. Think of the stars in their plastic box. You can almost taste the adhesive on their backs. Two more stars can be yours today, if you do not let yourself get nervous.

When it is time for the boys to pick, do not bite your hangnails. Do not pull at your skirt. Watch how Patricia and Cara lean together and whisper and laugh, as if they don't care whether or not they get picked. Watch how Miss Miggie brings her arms together, like a parting of the Red Sea in reverse, to start the picking. The boys will push off with their shoulder blades and make their way across the floor. Do not make eye contact! If you make eye contact you will drown. Do not, whatever you do, look at Eric Cassio. You do not care which one of those other girls he picks. You know it will not be you.

When the picking is over, hold your chin up and wait for Miss Miggie to notice you standing alone. She will take Zachary Booth by the shoulder and steer him over to you. When he is standing in front of you, look down at his white knee socks. Stand silent as he asks, with his lisp, if he can have thith danth. Ignore the snorts and whispers of your classmates. Do not think about Zachary Booth's hand warts. Let him take your right hand and put his left hand stiffly at your waist. Be glad you are dancing with a boy at all, and not with Brittney Wells, as you did last week.

When Miss Miggie starts the music, raise your chin and look Zachary Booth in the eye. Make sure he knows that even though he is the boy, you will be the one to lead. As much as he hates to dance with you, he will be grateful for that. It will be up to you alone to make sure you don't both look like fools. Squeeze his hand when it is time to start. Whisper the steps under your breath. When he falters, keep right on going. Let him fall back in step with you. Out of the corner of your eye, watch Miss Miggie drifting through the room as she claps the rhythm, her red mouth forming the words *one two*. When she looks your way, remember your father's advice: head high, shoulders back. Smile at Zachary Booth. Ignore the grimace he makes in return. If you dance well you may be picked to demonstrate.

And you know which boy will be picked. You know who is picked to demonstrate nearly every time, who Miss Miggie always *wants* to pick, even when she has to pick one of the others just to mix things up. Eric Cassio is not just great in *your* opinion. Already the world understands how excellent he is. The music swells toward its final cha-cha-cha and Miss Miggie's eyes scan the room. Her red lips come together like a bow. She raises her rack of breasts proudly and lifts her finger to point. The finger flies through the air toward Eric Cassio, and Miss Miggie calls his name. He scowls and looks down, pretending to be embarrassed, but there is a smile at the corner of his mouth. Patricia bites a fingernail. Understand that she is nervous. This gives you power. Do not flinch when Zachary Booth pinches your arm; do not let the burning in your eyes become tears. He does not concern you. The only thing that concerns you is who Miss Miggie will point to next. It could be anyone. It could be you. Her finger flies through the air. Is it you? Oh, God, it is.

Do not look at Patricia and Cara as they extend their tongues at you. Ignore Zachary Booth's explicit hand gesture. Forget you weigh sixty-nine pounds; stop wanting breasts so badly. So what if you wear glasses? So what if your skirt is not Calvin Klein? For this one moment you have no hangnails, no bony knees, and there is a secret between you and Eric Cassio. When the others clear the floor, look him square in the eye and share that secret. The secret is, you know he likes to dance. It goes back to the day when you were punished together for being tardy, when you had to transplant all the hybrid peas from the small white plastic pots to the big terra-cotta ones. Your hands touched, down in the bag of potting soil. When you got cold he gave you his green sweater. Later, as you were cleaning up—the water was running, no one could hear him—he told you he *liked* to dance. Remember these things. The fact that he ignored you at lunch that day, at recess, and every day afterward—even the fact that he is now Patricia's boyfriend—does not matter. He *likes* to dance. Look into his eyes, and he will remember he told you.

Let his arm come around you, tanned and slim. Take his hand; it is free of warts. The dance requires that you maintain eye contact with him almost constantly. Do not be afraid to meet his blue eyes. Smile. Remember what your father has taught you: Cuban motion. It is in the hips. A white boat rocking on waves. The half-hour demonstration with your mother, her hair up-swept, was not for nothing. Here you are. Miss Miggie lowers the arm onto the record, and the maracas shake into action.

When you dance with Eric Cassio, communicate through your hands. A press here, a sharp squeeze there, and you'll know what he wants you to do, and he'll know what you want him to do. As you change directions, catch Patricia's eye for one moment. Give your hips the Cuban motion. Make her watch. When you twirl, twirl sharp. Listen to Miss Miggie clapping in rhythm. Let all the misery fall out of your chest. Smile at Eric. He will smile back, just with the corner of his mouth. He is remembering transplanting the peas. He does not smile at Patricia that way; that is a smile for you.

Do the special pretzel thing with your arms, that thing Miss

41

Miggie has only shown you once; pull it off without a hitch. End with your back arched and your leg outstretched. Listen to the silence that comes over the room like fog. Remember the way they look at you. No one will applaud. Five seconds later, they will hate you more than ever.

THE NEXT DAY, watch out. You will pay for that moment with Eric. Wear pants, for God's sake. Take no chances. In gym you will play field hockey; remember that this is not one of your better games. You are on the red team, Patricia and Cara are on the blue. You are left wing forward. When you get the ball, pass it as quickly as you can. What will happen is inevitable, but it will be worse if you make them mad. It will happen at the end of the game, when you are tired and ready for gym to be over. As you race down the side of the field toward the ball, halfback Cara's stick will come out and trip you. You will fall and sprain your wrist. Your glasses will fly off and be broken in two at the nosepiece. You will cut your chin on a rock.

Lie still for a moment in the trampled clover. Try not to cry. The game will continue around you as if you do not exist. Only the gym teacher, leathery-skinned Miss Schiller, will notice that anything is wrong. She will pick you up by the arm and limp you over to the bench. Do not expect anyone to ask if you are okay. If they cared whether or not you were okay, this would never have happened. Let this be a lesson to you about them. When Patricia scores a goal they cluster around her, cheering, and click their sticks in the air.

At home, seek medical assistance. Do not let anything heal improperly. You will need that body later. As your mother binds your wrist in an Ace bandage, you will tell her you tripped on a rock. She will look at you askance. Through instinct, she will begin to understand the magnitude of your problem. When she is finished bandaging you, she will let you go to your room and be alone with your books. Read the final chapters of *A Little Princess*. Make an epic picture of a scene from a girls' boarding school in London on three sheets of paper. Push your brother around the living room in a laundry basket. That night, in the bath, replay in your head the final moment of your dance with Eric Cassio. Ignore the fact that he would not look at you that day. Relish the sting of bathwater on your cuts. Tell yourself that the moment with Eric was worth it. Twenty years later, you will still think so.

THAT WEEKEND something will happen that will seem like a miracle: Patricia will call you on the phone. She will tell you Cara's sorry for tripping you in gym. Look down at your purple swollen wrist, touch the taped-together bridge of your glasses. Say it's no big deal. Patricia will ask what you are doing that afternoon. You will whisper, "Nothing." She will ask you to meet her and Cara at Uptown Square.

—We're going shopping for d-d-dresses for the Miggie's B-ball, she'll say. Wanna come?

Now, think. *Think.* Do you really believe Cara could be sorry, that suddenly she and Patricia could crave your company? And even if they did, would you want these girls as friends? Try to remember who you're dealing with here. Try to tell Patricia you will not go shopping.

Of course, you will not refuse. You will arrange a time and place to meet. Then you will spend half an hour picking out an outfit, red Chinese-print pants and a black shirt, matching shoes and earrings. You will ask your mother to drive you to the mall, and she will consent, surprise and relief plain on her face. She will even give you her credit card.

When you arrive at the entrance to Uptown Square, with its marble arches and potted palms, you will pretend to see Patricia and Cara inside. You will kiss your mother and watch her drive away. Then you will stand beside the potted palms and wait for Patricia and Cara. You will take off your broken glasses and put them in your pocket, and adjust the hem of your shirt. You will wait there for ten minutes, fifteen, twenty. When you run inside to use the bathroom you will hurry your way through, afraid that you're keeping them waiting, but when you go outside again they will still not be there.

You will wonder whether Patricia meant *next* week. You will bite your nails down to the quick, then continue biting.

Stop this. They are not coming.

Go inside. Wander toward the fountain with the alabaster naked ladies. Sit down at the fountain's edge and look at the wavering copper and silver circles beneath the water. Don't waste time thinking about drowning yourself. Don't bother imagining your funeral, with your classmates in black clothes on a treeless stretch of lawn. If you die you will not be there to see it, and your classmates probably won't be either.

Instead, take a nickel from your pocket and make your own wish: Patricia and Cara strung upside-down from the tree in the schoolyard, naked for all the world to see. Kiss your nickel and toss it in. Feel better. Dry your eyes. Here you are in Uptown Square with your mother's credit card. Go to Maison Blanche, past the children's department, straight to Preteens. Tell the glossy-haired woman what kind of dress you want: something short, with a swirly skirt. Look through all the dresses she brings you; reject the ones with lace and flounces. On your own, look through all the others on the rack. You will almost give up. Then, at the very back, you will find your dress. It is midnight-blue with a velvet spaghetti-strap bodice and a satin skirt. Tell yourself it is the color of Eric Cassio's eyes. Try it on. Watch it fit. Imagine yourself, for a moment, as a teenager, an eleventh-grader, the girls you see in the upper school bathroom brushing their hair upside down and flipping it back. Flip your hair back. Twirl in front of the mirror. The dress costs fifty-eight dollars, with tax. Pay with your mother's credit card. The woman will wrap it in white tissue and seal it with a gold sticker, then slide it into a white store bag. By the time your mother comes to pick you up, you'll have almost forgotten about Patricia and Cara. When she asks you how your afternoon went, lie.

SCHOOL THIS NEXT WEEK will be hell. Everyone will know about Patricia and Cara's trick on you, how you went to the mall and waited. Now you will have to pay a price. People will come up to you all day and ask you to their birthday parties and family picnics and country clubs. Do not dignify them with a response, particularly not crying. This will be extremely difficult, of course. Try to understand what's going on: You got to dance with Eric Cassio, and he refused to act as if you made him sick. This is a threat to the social order.

By Tuesday afternoon, things will become unbearable. It is a dull week—preparations for a spring pageant, the history of the Louisiana Purchase, sentence diagramming in Language Arts—and people have nothing better to talk about. After lunch, on the playground, they gather around you as you try to swing. They needle you with questions: How many hours did you wait? Did you cry? Did you make believe you had a pretend friend? Did you have to call your mommy?

Get out of the swing. Be careful. You are angry. Words do not come easily around your classmates, particularly not at times like these. But you cannot let them continue to think that they have made you miserable. Tell them you went to Maison Blanche and bought a blue velvet dress.

—Liar! You can't afford a dress from Maison Blanche.

—I did.

—No, you d-didn't. I think you bought a d-d-d—

—A *diaper,* Cara finishes.

—It's a blue velvet dress. With spaghetti straps.

—They don't even h-h-h-have a dress like that there. You n-never went in there, you liar. You were too b-busy crying. *Waah-aah!* No one likes me! You bought a d-d-d-d-dirty baby diaper. You're wearing it right now! Ew, ew.

Ew, ew, ew. They run away from you, holding their noses, and tell their friends you had to wear a diaper because you kept stinking up your pants. Back in the classroom, before the teacher gets back, they push their desks into a tight little knot on the other side of the room. Finally you understand the vocabulary word *ostracize.* Look away from them. Stare at the blackboard. Swallow. Out of the corner of your eye, glance at Eric Cassio. He will be watching you, not laughing with the others. Patricia will lean over and whisper in his ear, and he will answer her. But he will not—not once—laugh at your expense.

When the teacher comes in and asks what on earth is going on, everyone will start moving the desks back without a word. Soon you will all get lost in the angles and word shelves of a sentence diagram. After that, Math. Then the bus ride home. Now you can spend all evening sulking in the alcove of your bedroom. When your parents come to tell you it's time for dinner, you will tell them you have a headache. You will cry and ask for orange children's aspirin. Half an hour later your little brother will come to you with a plate of food, and he will sit there, serious-eyed, as you eat it.

Later that night you will hear your parents in their bedroom, talking about sending you to a different school. Your father is the champion of this idea. When your mother argues that things might be getting better for you, you will secretly take her side. You tell yourself that leaving the school would mean giving up, letting the others win. You will not have that. You will not go to the schools your father suggests: Newman, your rival, or Lakeside, a religious day school. You will get angry at him for mentioning it. Doesn't he believe you can prove yourself to them, get friends, even become popular?

You blind, proud, stupid, poor dunce.

NEXT DAY, you will take the dress to school. Why, for God's sake? Why? Won't they see it at the Miggie's Ball anyway? But you insist on proving to them that it's real, despite the obvious danger. You will carry it in the Maison Blanche bag to show you really bought it there. When it's time for morning recess, you will casually take the bag out of your locker as if you have to move it to put some books away. Patricia and Cara will stop at your locker on their way out. You will pretend not to see them. Notice, however, that Eric Cassio is standing in the doorway waiting for them.

—Look, she b-brought a bag of baby d-d-d-d—

—You're stinking up the whole place, Cara says.

You pick up the bag so that the tissue inside crinkles, then steal a glance inside and smile to yourself.

—Is that your Kmart dress for the Miggie's Ball?

—Can I b-borrow it? Patricia takes the bag from you and holds it open. You feel a flash of fear, seeing it in her hands. Look at Eric Cassio. He is staring at his shoes. Patricia takes out the tissue-wrapped dress and tears the gold sticker you have kept carefully intact. As she shakes it out and holds it against herself, she and Cara laugh.

—Look at me. I'm Cinderella. I'm Cher.

Tell her to give it back.

—Oh, sure. C-come and g-get it. Patricia lofts the dress over your head in a blur of blue; Cara catches it.

—Don't you want it, stinky baby? Cara shakes it in your face, then throws it over your head again to Patricia.

Patricia holds the dress over your head. She is three inches taller than you. You jump and catch the hem in one hand and hold on tight. When Patricia pulls, you pull too. Finally she gives a sharp yank. There is a terrible sound, the sound of satin shearing, detaching itself from velvet. Patricia stumbles back with half your dress in her hands. Her mouth hangs open in a perfect O. Outside, kids shriek and laugh at recess. A kickball smacks against the classroom wall.

Cara will be the first to recover. She will take the half-dress from Patricia and shrug. Oh, well, she says. It was just an ugly dress.

—Yeah, Patricia says, her voice flat and dry. And a stupid b-brand.

Cara will throw the piece of dress at you. Let it fall at your feet. Suppress the wail of rage inside your rib cage. Do not look at Eric Cassio. Do not move or speak. Wait for them to leave. When the classroom door closes behind them, sit on the floor and stuff the rags of your dress back into the paper bag. Stare at the floor tile, black grains swirling into white. See if you can make it through the next five minutes. The next ten. Eventually, you'll hear the class coming back from recess. Get to your feet and dust off your legs. Sit down at your desk and hold the bag in your lap.

You will remember a story you heard on the news, about a brother and sister in Burma who got caught in a flood. As they watched from a rooftop, the flood stripped their house of its walls, drowned their parents against a bamboo fence, and washed their goats and chickens down the road. Their house is gone. Their family is gone. But they hold on to a piece of wood and kick toward dry land. Think how they must have felt that night, kicking into the flood, the houses all around them in splinters, people and animals dead.

ON SATURDAY, wear something good: a pair of white shorts and a red halter and sandals. Put your hair in a barrette. Try not to think about the dress in its bag at the bottom of your closet. That does not concern you. Go downstairs and get something to eat. You will not erase yourself by forgoing meals. After breakfast, when your mother asks if you'd like to make cookies, say yes. Look how much this pleases her. You have not felt like doing anything in weeks. Take out the measuring cups and bowls and all the ingredients. Mix the dough. Allow your brother to add the chocolate chips.

Put the cookies in the oven. Check them at three minutes, and at five. Your brother claps his hands and asks again and again if they are ready yet. When they are ready, open the oven door. A wash of sugary heat will hit your face. Pull on the mitts and take out the cookie sheet. Just then, the doorbell will ring.

Listen as your mother gets the door. You will hear her talking to someone outside, low. Then she'll come into the kitchen.

—There's a boy here for you, she says, twisting her hands in her apron. He wants to ride bikes.

—Who?

—I don't know. He's blond.

Do not drop the tray of cookies on the kitchen tile. Do not allow your head to float away from your body. The familiar tightness will gather in your throat. At first you will think it is another joke, that when you go to the door he will not be there.

But then there he is, in the doorway of the kitchen. It is the first time in years someone else your age has stood inside your house. And this is Eric Cassio, in his blue-striped oxford shirt and khaki shorts, his hair wild from the wind. Watch him stare at your brother, who's gotten a handful of cookie dough. Try talking. Offer him some cookies and milk. Your mother will take your brother, silently, out into the yard, and in a few moments you will hear him shrieking as he leaps through the sprinkler.

Now eat a cookie and drink milk with Eric Cassio. Do not let crumbs cling to your red halter. Wipe the line of milk from your upper lip. Watch Eric eat one cookie, then another. When he's finished he will take a rumpled white package from his backpack and push it across the table. You will be extremely skeptical. You will look at the package as if it were a bomb.

—I told my mom what happened at school, he says. She got you this.

Turn the package over. It is a clothing bag. When you open it you will find a dress inside, a different one, dark red with a jewel neckline and two small rosettes at the hip.

—I know it's not the same as the other one, he says.

Look at him, hard, to make sure this is not a joke. His eyes are steady and clear. Stand up and hold the dress up against you. You can see it is just the right size. Bite your lip. Look at Eric Cassio, speechless. Try to smile instead; he will understand.

—Patricia won the Miggie's thing, he says. She told me last night.

For a moment, you will feel bludgeoned. You thought it would be you. You and Eric Cassio. It was supposed to make all the difference. Patricia couldn't possibly have more stars than you. Then remember there's another important thing to ask him.

—Who's the boy?

He looks down into his lap, and you understand that the boy

50

is him. When he raises his eyes, his expression tells you that despite the dress, despite the hybrid peas, things are not going to change at school or at Miss Miggie's. He will not take walks with you at recess or sit next to you at McDonald's. You can see he is apologizing for this, and you can choose to accept or not.

Get to your feet and pull yourself up straight; raise your chin as your mother has shown you to do. Adjust the straps of your sandals, and make sure your halter is tied tight. Then ride bikes with Eric Cassio until dark.

Lost in the Funhouse

JOHN BARTH

FOR WHOM IS THE FUNHOUSE FUN? PERHAPS FOR LOVERS. For Ambrose it is *a place of fear and confusion.* He has come to the seashore with his family for the holiday, *the occasion of their visit is Independence Day, the most important secular holiday of the United States of America.* A single straight underline is the manuscript mark for italic type, *which in turn* is the printed equivalent to oral emphasis of words and phrases as well as the customary type for titles of complete works, not to mention. Italics are also employed, in fiction stories especially, for "outside," intrusive, or artificial voices, such as radio announcements, the texts of telegrams and newspaper articles, et cetera. They should be used *sparingly.* If passages originally in roman type are italicized by someone repeating them, it's customary to acknowledge the fact. *Italics mine.*

Ambrose was "at that awkward age." His voice came out high-pitched as a child's if he let himself get carried away; to be on the safe side, therefore, he moved and spoke with *deliberate calm* and *adult gravity*. Talking soberly of unimportant or irrelevant matters and listening consciously to the sound of your own voice are useful habits for maintaining control in this difficult interval. *En route* to Ocean City he sat in the back seat of the family car with his brother Peter, age fifteen, and Magda G____, age fourteen, a pretty girl an exquisite young lady, who lived not far from them on B____ Street in the town of D____, Maryland. Initials, blanks, or both were often substituted for proper names in nineteenth-century fiction to enhance the illusion of reality. It is as if the author felt it necessary to delete the names for reasons of tact or legal liability. Interestingly, as with other aspects of realism, it is an *illusion* that is being enhanced, by purely artificial means. Is it likely, does it violate the principle of verisimilitude, that a thirteen-year-old boy could make such a sophisticated observation? A girl of fourteen is *the psychological coeval* of a boy of fifteen or sixteen; a thirteen-year-old boy, therefore, even one precocious in some other respects, might be three years *her emotional junior.*

Thrice a year—on Memorial, Independence, and Labor Days—the family visits Ocean City for the afternoon and evening. When Ambrose and Peter's father was their age, the excursion was made by train, as mentioned in the novel *The 42nd Parallel* by John Dos Passos. Many families from the same neighborhood used to travel together, with dependent relatives and often with Negro servants; schoolfuls of children swarmed through the railway cars; everyone shared everyone else's Maryland fried chicken, Virginia ham, deviled eggs, potato salad, beaten biscuits, iced tea. Nowadays (that is, in 19__, the year of our story) the journey is made by automobile—more comfortably and quickly though without the extra fun though without the *camaraderie* of a general excursion. It's all part of the deterioration of American life, their father declares; Uncle Karl supposes that when the boys take *their* families to Ocean City for the holidays they'll fly in Autogiros. Their mother, sitting in the middle of the front seat like Magda in the second, only with her arms on the seat-back behind the men's shoulders, wouldn't want the good old days back again, the steaming trains and stuffy long dresses; on the other hand she can do without Autogiros, too, if she has to become a grandmother to fly in them.

Description of physical appearance and mannerisms is one of several standard methods of characterization used by writers of fiction. It is also important to "keep the senses operating"; when a detail from one of the five senses, say visual, is "crossed" with a detail from another, say auditory, the reader's imagination is oriented to the scene, perhaps unconsciously. This procedure may be compared to the way surveyors and navigators determine their positions by two or more compass bearings, a process known as triangulation. The brown hair on Ambrose's mother's forearms gleamed in the sun like. Though right-handed, she took her left arm from the seat-back to press the dashboard cigar lighter for Uncle Karl. When the glass bead in its handle glowed red, the lighter was ready for use. The smell of Uncle Karl's cigar smoke reminded one of. The fragrance of the ocean came strong to the picnic ground where they always stopped for lunch, two miles inland from Ocean City. Having to pause for a full hour almost within sound of the breakers was difficult for Peter and Ambrose when they were younger; even at their present age it was not easy to keep their anticipation, *stimulated by the briny spume,* from turning into short temper. The Irish author James Joyce, in his unusual novel entitled *Ulysses,* now available in this country, uses the adjectives *snot-green* and *scrotum-tightening* to describe the sea. Visual, auditory, tactile, olfactory, gustatory. Peter and Ambrose's father, while steering their black 1936 LaSalle sedan with one hand, could with the other remove the first cigarette from a white pack of Lucky Strikes and, more remarkably, light it with a match forefingered from its book and thumbed against the flint paper without being detached. The matchbook cover merely advertised U.S. War Bonds and Stamps. A fine metaphor, simile, or other figure of speech, in addition to its obvious "first-order" relevance to the thing it describes, will be seen upon reflection to have a second order of significance: it may be drawn from the *milieu* of the action, for example, or be particularly appropriate to the sensibility of the narrator, even hinting to the reader things of which the narrator is unaware; or it may cast further and subtler lights upon the thing it describes, sometimes ironically qualifying the more evident sense of the comparison.

To say that Ambrose's and Peter's mother was *pretty* is to accomplish nothing; the reader may acknowledge the proposition, but his imagination is not engaged. Besides, Magda was also pretty, yet in an altogether different way. Although she lived on B____ Street she had very good manners and did better than average in school. Her figure was very well developed for her age. Her right hand lay casually on the plush upholstery of the seat, very near Ambrose's left leg, on which his own hand rested. The space between their legs, between her right and his left leg, was out of the line of sight of anyone sitting on the other side of Magda, as well as anyone glancing into the rearview mirror. Uncle Karl's face resembled Peter's—rather, vice versa. Both had dark hair and eyes, short husky statures, deep voices. Magda's left hand was probably in a similar position on her left side. The boy's father is difficult to describe; no particular feature of his appearance or manner stood out. He wore glasses and was principal of a T____ County grade school. Uncle Karl was a masonry contractor.

Although Peter must have known as well as Ambrose that the latter, because of his position in the car, would be the first to see the electrical towers of the power plant at V____, the halfway point of their trip, he leaned forward and slightly toward the center of the car and pretended to be looking for them through the flat pinewoods and tuckahoe creeks along the highway. For as long as the boys could remember, "looking for the Towers" had been a feature of the first half of their excursions to Ocean City, "looking for the standpipe" of the second. Though the game was childish, their mother preserved the tradition of rewarding the first to see the Towers with a candy bar or piece of fruit. She insisted now that Magda play the game; the prize, she said, was "something hard to get nowadays." Ambrose decided not to join in; he sat far back in his seat. Magda, like Peter, leaned forward. Two sets of straps were discernible through the shoulders of her sun dress; the inside right one, a brassiere-strap, was fastened or shortened with a small safety pin. The right armpit of her dress, presumably the left as well, was damp with perspiration. The simple strategy for being first to espy the Towers, which Ambrose had understood by the age of four, was to sit on the right-hand side of the car. Whoever sat there, however, had also to put up with the worst of the sun, and so Ambrose, without mentioning the matter, chose sometimes the one and sometimes the other. Not impossibly Peter had never caught on to the trick, or thought that his brother hadn't simply because Ambrose on occasion preferred shade to a Baby Ruth or tangerine.

The shade-sun situation didn't apply to the front seat, owing to the windshield; if anything the driver got more sun, since the person on the passenger side not only was shaded below by the door and dashboard but might swing down his sunvisor all the way too.

"Is that them?" Magda asked. Ambrose's mother teased the boys for letting Magda win, insinuating that "somebody [had] a girlfriend." Peter and Ambrose's father reached a long thin arm across their mother to butt his cigarette in the dashboard ashtray, under the lighter. The prize this time for seeing the Towers first was a banana. Their mother bestowed it after chiding their father for wasting a half-smoked cigarette when everything was so scarce. Magda, to take the prize, moved her hand from so near Ambrose's that he could have touched it as though accidentally. She offered to share the prize, things like that were so hard to find; but everyone insisted it was hers alone. Ambrose's mother sang an iambic trimeter couplet from a popular song, femininely rhymed:

> "What's good is in the Army;
> What's left will never harm me."

Uncle Karl tapped his cigar ash out the ventilator window; some particles were sucked by the slipstream back into the car through the rear window on the passenger side. Magda demonstrated her ability to hold a banana in one hand and peel it with her teeth. She still sat forward; Ambrose pushed his glasses back onto the bridge of his nose with his left hand, which he then negligently let fall to the seat cushion immediately behind her. He even permitted the single hair, gold, on the second joint of his thumb to brush the fabric of her skirt. Should she have sat back at that instant, his hand would have been caught under her.

Plush upholstery prickles uncomfortably through gabardine slacks in the July sun. The function of the *beginning* of a story is to introduce the principal characters, establish their initial relationships, set the scene for the main action, expose the background of the situation if necessary, plant motifs and foreshadowings where appropriate, and initiate the first complication or whatever of the "rising action." Actually, if one imagines a story called "The Funhouse," or "Lost in the Funhouse," the details of the drive to

Ocean City don't seem especially relevant. The *beginning* should recount the events between Ambrose's first sight of the funhouse early in the afternoon and his entering it with Magda and Peter in the evening. The *middle* would narrate all relevant events from the time he goes in to the time he loses his way; middles have the double and contradictory function of delaying the climax while at the same time preparing the reader for it and fetching him to it. Then the *ending* would tell what Ambrose does while he's lost, how he finally finds his way out, and what everybody makes of the experience. So far there's been no real dialogue, very little sensory detail, and nothing in the way of a *theme*. And a long time has gone by already without anything happening; it makes a person wonder. We haven't even reached Ocean City yet: we will never get out of the funhouse.

The more closely an author identifies with the narrator, literally or metaphorically, the less advisable it is, as a rule, to use the first-person narrative viewpoint. Once three years previously the young people *aforementioned* played Niggers and Masters in the backyard; when it was Ambrose's turn to be Master and theirs to be Niggers Peter had to go serve his evening papers; Ambrose was afraid to punish Magda alone, but she led him to the whitewashed Torture Chamber between the woodshed and the privy in the Slaves Quarters; there she knelt sweating among bamboo rakes and dusty Mason jars, pleadingly embraced his knees, and while bees droned in the lattice as if on an ordinary summer afternoon, purchased clemency at a surprising price set by herself. Doubtless she remembered nothing of this event; Ambrose on the other hand seemed unable to forget the least detail of his life. He even recalled how, standing beside himself with awed impersonality in the reeky heat, he'd stared the while at an empty cigar box in which Uncle Karl kept stone-cutting chisels: beneath the words *El Producto*, a laureled, loose-toga'd lady regarded the sea from a marble bench; beside her, forgotten or not yet turned to, was a five-stringed lyre. Her chin reposed on the back of her right hand; her left depended negligently from the bench-arm. The lower half of scene and lady was peeled away; the words EXAMINED BY _____ were inked there into the wood. Nowadays cigar boxes are made of pasteboard. Ambrose wondered what Magda would have done, Ambrose wondered what Magda would do when she sat back on his hand as he resolved she should. Be angry. Make a teasing joke of it. Give no sign at all. For a long time she leaned forward, playing cow-poker with Peter against Uncle Karl and Mother and watching for the first sign of Ocean City. At nearly the same instant, picnic ground and Ocean City standpipe hove into view; an Amoco filling station on their side of the road cost Mother and Uncle Karl fifty cows and the game; Magda bounced back, clapping her right hand on Mother's right arm; Ambrose moved clear "in the nick of time."

At this rate our hero, at this rate our protagonist will remain in the funhouse forever. Narrative ordinarily consists of alternating dramatization and summarization. One symptom of nervous tension, paradoxically, is repeated and violent yawning; neither Peter nor Magda nor Uncle Karl nor Mother reacted in this manner. Although they were no longer small children, Peter and Ambrose were each given a dollar to spend on boardwalk amusements in addition to what money of their own they'd brought along. Magda too, though she protested she had ample spending money. The boys' mother made a little scene out of distributing the bills; she pretended that her sons and Magda were small children and cautioned them not to spend the sum too quickly or in one place. Magda promised with a merry laugh and, having both hands free, took the bill with her left. Peter laughed also and pledged in a falsetto to be a good boy. His imitation of a child was not clever. The boys' father was tall and thin, balding, fair-complexioned. Assertions of that sort are not effective; the reader may acknowledge the proposition, but. We should be much farther along than we are; something has gone wrong; not much of this preliminary rambling seems relevant. Yet everyone begins in the same place; how is it that most go along without difficulty but a few lose their way?

"Stay out from under the boardwalk," Uncle Karl growled from the side of his mouth. The boys' mother pushed his shoulder *in mock annoyance*. They were all standing before Fat May the Laughing Lady who advertised the funhouse. Larger than life, Fat May mechanically shook, rocked on her heels, slapped her thighs while recorded laughter—uproarious, female—came amplified from a hidden loudspeaker. It chuckled, wheezed, wept; tried in vain to catch its breath; tittered, groaned, exploded raucous and anew. You couldn't hear it without laughing yourself, no matter how you felt. Father came back from talking to a Coast-Guardsman on duty and reported that the surf was spoiled with crude oil from tankers recently torpedoed offshore. Lumps of it, difficult to remove, made tarry tidelines on the beach and stuck on swimmers. Many bathed in the surf nevertheless and came out speckled; others paid to use a municipal pool and only sun-bathed on the beach. We would do the latter. We would do the latter. We would do the latter.

Under the boardwalk, matchbook covers, grainy other things. What is the story's theme? Ambrose is ill. He perspires in the dark passages; candied apples-on-a-stick, delicious-looking, disappointing to eat. Funhouses need men's and ladies' room at intervals. Others perhaps have also vomited in corners and corridors; may even have had bowel movements liable to be stepped in in the dark. The word *fuck* suggests suction and/or and/or flatulence. Mother and Father; grandmothers and grandfathers on both sides; great-grandmothers and great-grandfathers on four sides, et cetera. Count a generation as thirty years: in approximately the year when Lord Baltimore was granted charter to the province of Maryland by Charles I, five hundred twelve women—English, Welsh, Bavarian, Swiss—of every class and character, received into themselves the penises the intromittent organs of five hundred twelve men, ditto, in every circumstance and posture, to conceive the five hundred twelve ancestors of the two hundred fifty-six ancestors of the et cetera et cetera et cetera et cetera et cetera et cetera et cetera et cetera of the author, of the narrator, of this story, *Lost in the Funhouse*. In alleyways, ditches, canopy beds, pinewoods, bridal suites, ship's cabins, coach-and-fours, coaches-and-four, sultry toolsheds; on the cold sand under boardwalks, littered with *El Producto* cigar butts, treasured with Lucky Strike cigarette stubs, Coca-Cola caps, gritty turds, cardboard lollipop sticks, matchbook covers warning that A Slip of the Lip Can Sink a Ship. The shluppish whisper, continuous as seawash round the globe, tidelike falls and rises with the circuit of dawn and dusk.

Magda's teeth. She *was* left-handed. Perspiration. They've gone all the way, through, Magda and Peter, they've been waiting for hours with Mother and Uncle Karl while Father searches for his lost son; they draw french-fried potatoes from a paper cup and shake their heads. They've named the children they'll one day have and bring to Ocean City on holidays. Can spermatozoa properly be thought of as male animalcules when there are no female spermatozoa? They grope through hot, dark windings, past Love's Tunnel's fearsome obstacles. Some perhaps lose their way.

Peter suggested then and there that they do the funhouse; he had been through it before, so had Magda, Ambrose hadn't and suggested, his voice cracking on account of Fat May's laughter, that they swim first. All were chuckling, couldn't help it; Ambrose's father, Ambrose's and Peter's father came up grinning like a lunatic with two boxes of syrup-coated popcorn, one for Mother, one for Magda; the men were to help themselves. Ambrose walked on Magda's right; being by nature left-handed, she carried the box in her left hand. Up front the situation was reversed.

"What are you limping for?" Magda inquired of Ambrose. He supposed in a husky tone that his foot had gone to sleep in the car. Her teeth flashed. "Pins and needles?" It was the honeysuckle on the lattice of the former privy that drew the bees. Imagine being stung there. How long is this going to take?

The adults decided to forgo the pool; but Uncle Karl insisted they change into swimsuits and do the beach. "He wants to watch the pretty girls," Peter teased, and ducked behind Magda from Uncle Karl's pretended wrath. "You've got all the pretty girls you need right here," Magda declared, and Mother said: "Now that's the gospel truth." Magda scolded Peter, who reached over her shoulder to sneak some popcorn. "Your brother and father aren't getting any." Uncle Karl wondered if they were going to have fireworks that night, what with the shortages. It wasn't the shortages, Mr. M____ replied; Ocean City had fireworks from pre-war. But it was too risky on account of the enemy submarines, some people thought.

"Don't seem like Fourth of July without fireworks," said Uncle Karl. The inverted tag in dialogue writing is still considered permissible with proper names or epithets, but sounds old-fashioned with personal pronouns. "We'll have 'em again soon enough," predicted the boys' father. Their mother declared she could do without fireworks: they reminded her too much of the real thing. Their father said all the more reason to shoot off a few now and again. Uncle Karl asked *rhetorically* who needed reminding, just look at people's hair and skin.

"The oil, yes," said Mrs. M____.

Ambrose had a pain in his stomach and so didn't swim but enjoyed watching the others. He and his father burned red easily. Magda's figure was exceedingly well developed for her age. She too declined to swim, and got mad, and became angry when Peter attempted to drag her into the pool. She always swam, he insisted; what did she mean not swim? Why did a person come to Ocean City?

"Maybe I want to lay here with Ambrose," Magda teased.

Nobody likes a pedant.

"Aha," said Mother. Peter grabbed Magda by one ankle and ordered Ambrose to grab the other. She squealed and rolled over on the beach blanket. Ambrose pretended to help hold her back. Her tan was darker than even Mother's and Peter's. "Help out, Uncle Karl!" Peter cried. Uncle Karl went to seize the other ankle. Inside the top of her swimsuit, however, you could see the line where the sunburn ended and, when she hunched her shoulders and squealed again, one nipple's auburn edge. Mother made them behave themselves. "*You* should certainly know," she said to Uncle Karl. Archly. "That when a lady says she doesn't feel like swimming, a gentleman doesn't ask questions." Uncle Karl said excuse *him;* Mother winked at Magda; Ambrose blushed; stupid Peter kept saying "Phooey on *feel like!*" and tugging at Magda's ankle; then even he got the point, and cannonballed with a holler into the pool.

"I swear," Magda said, in mock *in feigned* exasperation.

The diving would make a suitable literary symbol. To go off the high board you had to wait in a line along the poolside and up the ladder. Fellows tickled girls and goosed one another and shouted to the ones at the top to hurry up, or razzed them for bellyfloppers. Once on the springboard some took a great while posing or clowning or deciding on a dive or getting up their nerve; others ran right off. Especially among the younger fellows

the idea was to strike the funniest pose or do the craziest stunt as
you fell, a thing that got harder to do as you kept on and kept on.
But whether you hollered *Geronimo!* or *Sieg heil!,* held your nose
or "rode a bicycle," pretended to be shot or did a perfect jacknife
or changed your mind halfway down and ended up with nothing,
it was over in two seconds, after all that wait. Spring, pose,
splash. Spring, neat-o, splash. Spring, aw fooey, splash.

The grown-ups had gone on; Ambrose wanted to converse
with Magda; she was remarkably well developed for her age; it
was said that that came from rubbing with a turkish towel, and
there were other theories. Ambrose could think of nothing to say
except how good a diver Peter was, who was showing off for her
benefit. You could pretty well tell by looking at their bathing suits
and arm muscles how far along the different fellows were. Ambrose was glad he hadn't gone in swimming, the cold water
shrank you up so. Magda pretended to be uninterested in the diving; she probably weighed as much as he did. If you knew your
way around in the funhouse like your own bedroom, you could
wait until a girl came along and then slip away without ever getting caught, even if her boyfriend was right with her. She'd think
he did it! It would be better to be the boyfriend, and act outraged,
and tear the funhouse apart.

Not act; *be.*

"He's a master diver," Ambrose said. In feigned admiration.
"You really have to slave away at it to get that good." What would
it matter anyhow if he asked her right out whether she remembered, even teased her with it as Peter would have?

There's no point in going farther; this isn't getting anybody
anywhere; they haven't even come to the funhouse yet. Ambrose
is off the track, in some new or old part of the place that's not
supposed to be used; he strayed into it by some one-in-a-million
chance, like the time the roller-coaster car left the tracks in the

nineteen-teens against all the laws of physics and sailed over the boardwalk in the dark. And they can't locate him because they don't know where to look. Even the designer and operator have forgotten this other part, that winds around on itself like a whelk shell. That winds around the right part like the snakes on Mercury's caduceus. Some people, perhaps, don't "hit their stride" until their twenties, when the growing-up business is over and women appreciate other things besides wisecracks and teasing and strutting. Peter didn't have one-tenth the imagination *he* had, not one-tenth. Peter did this naming-their-children thing as a joke, making up names like Aloysius and Murgatroyd, but Ambrose knew *exactly* how it would feel to be married and have children of your own, and be a loving husband and father, and go comfortably to work in the mornings and to bed with your wife at night, and wake up with her there. With a breeze coming through the sash and birds and mockingbirds singing in the Chinese-cigar trees. His eyes watered, there aren't enough ways to say that. He would be quite famous in his line of work. Whether Magda was his wife or not, one evening when he was wise-lined and gray at the temples he'd smile gravely, at a fashionable dinner party, and remind her of his youthful passion. The time they went with his family to Ocean City; the *erotic fantasies* he used to have about her. How long ago it seemed, and childish! Yet tender, too, *n'est-ce pas?* Would she have imagined that the world-famous whatever remembered how many strings were on the lyre on the bench beside the girl on the label of the cigar box he'd stared at in the toolshed at age ten while she, age eleven. Even then he had felt *wise beyond his years;* he'd stroked her hair and said in his deepest voice and correctest English, as to a dear child: "I shall never forget this moment."

But though he had breathed heavily, groaned as if ecstatic, what he'd really felt throughout was an odd detachment, as though someone else were Master. Strive as he might to be transported, he heard his mind take notes upon the scene: *This is what they call* passion. *I am experiencing it.* Many of the digger machines were out of order in the penny arcades and could not be repaired or replaced for the duration. Moreover the prizes, made now in USA, were less interesting than formerly, pasteboard items for the most part, and some of the machines wouldn't work on white pennies. The gypsy fortune-teller machine might have provided a foreshadowing of the climax of this story if Ambrose had operated it. It was even dilapidateder than most: the silver coating was worn off the brown metal handles, the glass windows around the dummy were cracked and taped, her kerchiefs and silks long-faded. If a man lived by himself, he could take a department-store mannequin with flexible joints and modify her in certain ways. *However:* by the time he was that old he'd have a real woman. There was a machine that stamped your name around a white-metal coin with a star in the middle: *A___*. His son would be the second, and when the lad reached thirteen or so he would put a strong arm around his shoulder and tell him calmly: "It is perfectly normal. We have all been through it. It will not last forever." Nobody knew how to be what they were right. He'd smoke a pipe, teach his son how to fish and softcrab, assure him he needn't worry about himself. Magda would certainly give, Magda would certainly yield a great deal of milk, although guilty of occasional solecisms. It don't taste so bad. Suppose the lights came on now!

The day wore on. You think you're yourself, but there are other persons in you. Ambrose gets hard when Ambrose doesn't want to, *and obversely.* Ambrose watches them disagree; Ambrose watches him watch. In the funhouse mirror-room you can't see yourself go on forever, because no matter how you stand, your head gets in the way. Even if you had a glass periscope, the image of your eye would cover up the thing you really wanted to see. The police will come; there'll be a story in the papers. That must be where it happened. Unless he can find a surprise exit, an unofficial backdoor or escape hatch opening on an alley, say, and then stroll up to the family in front of the funhouse and ask where everbody's been; *he's* been out of the place for ages. That's just where it happened, in that last lighted room: Peter and Magda found the right exit; he found one that you weren't supposed to find and strayed off into the works somewhere. In a perfect funhouse you'd be able to go only one way, like the divers off the high-board; getting lost would be impossible; the doors and halls would work like minnow traps or the valves in veins.

On account of German U-boats, Ocean City was "browned out": streetlights were shaded on the seaward side; shopwindows and boardwalk amusement places were kept dim, not to silhouette tankers and Liberty-ships for torpedoing. In a short story about Ocean City, Maryland, during World War II, the author could make use of the image of sailors on leave in the penny arcades and shooting galleries, sighting through the crosshairs of toy machine guns at swastika'd subs, while out in the black Atlantic a U-boat skipper squints through his periscope at real ships outlined by the glow of penny arcades. After dinner the family strolled back to the amusement end of the boardwalk. The boys' father had burnt red as always and was masked with Noxzema, a minstrel in reverse. The grown-ups stood at the end of the boardwalk where the Hurricane of '33 had cut an inlet from the ocean to Assawoman Bay.

"Pronounced with a long *o*," Uncle Karl reminded Magda with a wink. His shirt sleeves were rolled up; Mother punched his brown biceps with the arrowed heart on it and said his mind was naughty. Fat May's laugh came suddenly from the funhouse, as if she'd just got the joke; the family laughed too at the coincidence.

Ambrose went under the boardwalk to search for out-of-town
matchbook covers with the aid of his pocket flashlight; he looked
out from the edge of the North American continent and wondered how far their laughter carried over the water. Spies in rubber rafts; survivors in lifeboats. If the joke had been beyond his
understanding, he could have said: *"The laughter was over his
head."* And let the reader see the serious wordplay on second
reading.

He turned the flashlight on and then off at once even before
the woman whooped. He sprang away, heart athud, dropping the
light. What had the man grunted? Perspiration drenched and
chilled him by the time he scrambled up to the family. "See anything?" his father asked. His voice wouldn't come; he shrugged
and violently brushed sand from his pants legs.

"Let's ride the old flying horses!" Magda cried. I'll never be an
author. It's been forever already, everybody's gone home, Ocean
City's deserted, the ghost-crabs are tickling across the beach and
down the littered cold streets. And the empty halls of clapboard
hotels and abandoned funhouses. A tidal wave; an enemy air
raid; a monster-crab swelling like an island from the sea. *The in-
habitants fled in terror.* Magda clung to his trouser leg; he alone
knew the maze's secret. "He gave his life that we might live," said
Uncle Karl with a scowl of pain, as he. The fellow's hands had
been tattooed; the woman's legs, the woman's fat white legs had.
An astonishing coincidence. He yearned to tell Peter. He wanted to
throw up for excitement. They hadn't even chased him. He
wished he were dead.

One possible ending would be to have Ambrose come across
another lost person in the dark. They'd match their wits together
against the funhouse, struggle like Ulysses past obstacle after obstacle, help and encourage each other. Or a girl. By the time they
found the exit they'd be closest friends, sweethearts if it were a

girl; they'd know each other's inmost souls, he bound together *by the cement of shared adventure;* then they'd emerge into the light and it would turn out that his friend was a Negro. A blind girl. President Roosevelt's son. Ambrose's former archenemy.

Shortly after the mirror room he'd groped along a musty corridor, his heart already misgiving him at the absence of phosphorescent arrows and other signs. He'd found a crack of light—not a door, it turned out, but a seam between the plyboard wall panels—and squinting up to it, espied a small old man, *in appearance not unlike* the photographs at home of Ambrose's late grandfather, nodding upon a stool beneath a bare, speckled bulb. A crude panel of toggle- and knife-switches hung beside the open fuse box near his head; elsewhere in the little room were wooden levers and ropes belayed to boat cleats. At the time, Ambrose wasn't lost enough to rap or call; later he couldn't find that crack. Now it seemed to him that he'd possibly dozed off for a few minutes somewhere along the way; certainly he was exhausted from the afternoon's sunshine and the evening's problems; he couldn't be sure he hadn't dreamed part or all of the sight. Had an old black wall fan droned like bees and shimmied two flypaper streamers? Had the funhouse operator—gentle, somewhat sad and tired-appearing, in expression not unlike the photographs at home of Ambrose's late Uncle Konrad—murmured in his sleep? Is there really such a person as Ambrose, or is he a figment of the author's imagination? Was it Assawoman Bay or Sinepuxent? Are there other errors of fact in this fiction? Was there another sound besides the little slap slap of thigh on ham, like water sucking at the chine-boards of a skiff?

When you're lost, the smartest thing to do is stay put till you're found, hollering if necessary. But to holler guarantees humiliation as well as rescue; keeping silent permits some saving of face—you can act surprised at the fuss when your rescuers find you and swear you weren't lost, if they do. What's more you might find your own way yet, *however belatedly*.

"Don't tell me your foot's still asleep!" Magda exclaimed as the three young people walked from the inlet to the area set aside for ferris wheels, carrousels, and other carnival rides, they having decided in favor of the vast and ancient merry-go-round instead of the funhouse. What a sentence, everything was wrong from the outset. People don't know what to make of him, he doesn't know what to make of himself, he's only thirteen, *athletically and socially inept*, not astonishingly bright, but there are antennae; he has . . . some sort of receivers in his head; things speak to him, he understands more than he should, the world winks at him through its objects, grabs grinning at his coat. Everybody else is in on some secret he doesn't know; they've forgotten to tell him. Through simple *procrastination* his mother put off his baptism until this year. Everyone else had it done as a baby; he'd assumed the same of himself, as had his mother, so she claimed, until it was time for him to join Grace Methodist-Protestant and the oversight came out. He was mortified, but pitched sleepless through his private catechizing, intimidated by the ancient mysteries, a thirteen-year-old would never say that, resolved to experience conversion like St. Augustine. When the water touched his brow and Adam's sin left him, he contrived by a strain like defecation to bring tears into his eyes—but felt nothing. There was some simple, radical difference about him; he hoped it was genius, feared it was madness, devoted himself to amiability and inconspicuousness. Alone on the seawall near his house he was seized by the terrifying transports he'd thought to find in toolshed, in Communion-cup. The grass was alive! The town, the river, himself, were not imaginary; time roared in his ears like wind; the world was *going on!* This part ought to be dramatized. The Irish author James Joyce once wrote. Ambrose M____ is going to scream.

There is no *texture of rendered sensory detail*, for one thing. The faded distorting mirrors beside Fat May; the impossibility of choosing a mount when one had but a single ride on the great carrousel; the *vertigo attendant on his recognition* that Ocean City was worn out, the place of fathers and grandfathers, straw-boatered men and parasoled ladies survived by their amusements. Money spent, the three paused at Peter's insistence beside Fat May to watch the girls get their skirts blown up. The object wás to tease Magda, who said: "I swear, Peter M____, you've got a one-track mind! Amby and me aren't *interested* in such things." In the tumbling-barrel, too, just inside the Devil's-mouth entrance to the funhouse, the girls were upended and their boyfriends and others could see up their dresses if they cared to. Which was the whole point, Ambrose realized. Of the entire funhouse! If you looked around, you noticed that almost all the people on the boardwalk were paired off into couples except the small children; in a way, that was the whole point of Ocean City! If you had X-ray eyes and could see everything going on at that instant under the boardwalk and in all the hotel rooms and cars and alleyways, you'd realize that all that normally *showed*, like restaurants and dance halls and clothing and test-your-strength machines, was merely preparation and intermission. Fat May screamed.

Because he watched the goings-on from the corner of his eye, it was Ambrose who spied the half-dollar on the boardwalk near the tumbling-barrel. Losers weepers. The first time he'd heard some people moving through a corridor not far away, just after he'd lost sight of the crack of light, he'd decided not to call to them, for fear they'd guess he was scared and poke fun; it sounded like roughnecks; he'd hoped they'd come by and he could follow in the dark without their knowing. Another time he'd heard just one person, unless he imagined it, bumping along as if on the other side of the plywood; perhaps Peter coming back for him, or Father, or Magda lost too. Or the owner and operator of the funhouse. He'd called out once, as though merrily: "Anybody know where the heck we are?" But the query was too stiff, his voice cracked, when the sounds stopped he was terrified: maybe it was a queer who waited for fellows to get lost, or a longhaired filthy monster that lived in some cranny of the funhouse. He stood rigid for hours it seemed like, scarcely respiring. His future was shockingly clear, in outline. He tried holding his breath to the point of unconsciousness. There ought to be a button you could push to end your life absolutely without pain; disappear in a flick, like turning out a light. He would push it instantly! He despised Uncle Karl. But he despised his father too, for not being what he was supposed to be. Perhaps his father hated *his* father, and so on, and his son would hate him, and so on. Instantly!

Naturally he didn't have nerve enough to ask Magda to go through the funhouse with him. With incredible nerve and to everyone's surprise he invited Magda, quietly and politely, to go through the funhouse with him. "I warn you, I've never been through it before," he added, *laughing easily;* "but I reckon we can manage somehow. The important thing to remember, after all, is that it's meant to be a *fun*house; that is, a place of amusement. If people really got lost or injured or too badly frightened in it, the owner'd go out of business. There'd even be lawsuits. No character in a work of fiction can make a speech this long without interruption or acknowledgment from the other characters."

Mother teased Uncle Karl: "Three's a crowd, I always heard." But actually Ambrose was relieved that Peter now had a quarter too. Nothing was what it looked like. Every instant, under the surface of the Atlantic Ocean, millions of living animals devoured one another. Pilots were falling in flames over Europe; women were being forcibly raped in the South Pacific. His father should have taken him aside and said: "There is a simple secret to getting through the funhouse, as simple as being first to see the Towers. Here it is. Peter does not know it; neither does your Uncle Karl. You and I are different. Not surprisingly, you've often wished you weren't. Don't think I haven't noticed how unhappy your childhood has been! But you'll understand, when I tell you, why it had to be kept secret until now. And you won't regret not being like your brother and your uncle. *On the contrary!*" If you knew all the stories behind all the people on the boardwalk, you'd see that *nothing* was what it looked like. Husbands and wives often hated each other; parents didn't necessarily love their children; et cetera. A child took things for granted because he had nothing to compare his life to and everybody acted as if things were as they should be. Therefore each saw himself as the hero of the story, when the truth might turn out to be that he's the villain, or the coward. And there wasn't one thing you could do about it!

Hunchbacks, fat ladies, fools—that no one chose what he was was unbearable. In the movies he'd meet a beautiful young girl in the funhouse; they'd have hairs-breadth escapes from real dangers; he'd do and say the right things; she also; in the end they'd be lovers; their dialogue lines would match up; he'd be perfectly at ease; she'd not only like him well enough, she'd think he was *marvelous*; she'd lie awake thinking about *him*, instead of vice versa—the way *his* face looked in different light and how he stood and exactly what he'd said—and yet that would be only one small episode in his wonderful life, among many many others. Not a *turning point* at all. What had happened in the toolshed was nothing. He hated, he loathed his parents! One reason for not writing a lost-in-the-funhouse story is that either everybody's felt what Ambrose feels, in which case it goes without saying, or else no normal person feels such things, in which case Ambrose is a freak. "Is anything more tiresome, in fiction, than the problems of sensitive adolescents?" And it's all too long and rambling, as if the author. For all a person knows the first time through, the end could be just around any corner; perhaps, *not impossibly* it's been within reach any number of times. On the other hand he may be scarcely past the start, with everything yet to get through, an intolerable idea.

Fill in: His father's raised eyebrows when he announced his decision to do the funhouse with Magda. Ambrose understands now, but didn't then, that his father was wondering whether he knew what the funhouse was *for*—specially since he didn't object, as he should have, when Peter decided to come along too. The ticket-woman, witchlike, mortifying him when inadvertently he gave her his name-coin instead of the half-dollar, then unkindly calling Magda's attention to the birthmark on his temple: "Watch our for him, girlie, he's a marked man!" She wasn't even cruel, he understood, only vulgar and insensitive. Somewhere in the world there was a young woman with such splendid understanding that she'd see him entire, like a poem or story, and find his words so valuable after all that when he confessed his apprehensions she would explain why they were in fact the very things that made him precious to her . . . and to Western Civilization! There was no such girl, the simple truth being. Violent yawns as they approached the mouth. Whispered advice from an old-timer on a bench near the barrel: "Go crabwise and ye'll get an eyeful without upsetting!" Composure vanished at the first pitch: Peter hollered joyously, Magda tumbled, shrieked, clutched her skirt; Ambrose scrambled crabwise, tight-lipped with terror, was soon out, watched his dropped name-coin slide among the couples. Shamefaced he saw that to get through expeditiously was not the point; Peter feigned assistance in order to trip Magda up, shouted "I see Christmas!" when her legs went flying. The old man, his latest betrayer, cackled approval. A dim hall then of black-thread cobwebs and recorded gibber: he took Magda's elbow to steady her against revolving discs set in the slanted floor to throw your feet out from under, and explained to her in a calm, deep voice his theory that each phase of the funhouse was triggered either automatically, by a series of photoelectric devices, or else manually by operators stationed at peepholes. But he lost his voice thrice as the discs unbalanced him; Magda was anyhow squealing; but at one point she clutched him about the waist to keep from falling, and her right cheek pressed for a moment against his belt-buckle. Heroically he drew her up, it was his chance to clutch her close as if for support and say: "I love you." He even put an arm lightly about the small of her back before a sailor-and-girl pitched into them from behind, sorely treading his left big toe and knocking Magda asprawl with them. The sailor's girl was a string-haired hussy with a loud laugh and light blue drawers; Ambrose realized that he wouldn't have said "I love you" anyhow, and was smitten with self-contempt. How much better it would be to be that common sailor! A wiry little Seaman 3rd, the fellow squeezed a girl to each side and stumbled hilarious into the mirror room, closer to Magda in thirty seconds than Ambrose had got in thirteen years. She giggled at something the fellow said to Peter; she drew her hair from her eyes with a movement so womanly it struck Ambrose's heart; Peter's smacking her backside then seemed particularly coarse. But Magda made a pleased indignant face and cried, "All right for *you*, mister!" and pursued Peter into the maze without a backward glance. The sailor followed after, leisurely, drawing his girl against his hip; Ambrose understood not only that they were all so relieved to be rid of his burdensome company that they didn't even notice his absence, but that he himself shared their relief. Stepping from the treacherous passage at last into the mirror-maze, he saw once again, more clearly than ever, how readily he deceived himself into supposing he was a person. He even foresaw, wincing at his dreadful self-knowledge,

75

that he would repeat the deception, at ever-rarer intervals, all his wretched life, so fearful were the alternatives. Fame, madness, suicide; perhaps all three. It's not believable that so young a boy could articulate that reflection, and in fiction the merely true must always yield to the plausible. Moreover, the symbolism is in places heavy-footed. Yet Ambrose M____ understood, as few adults do, that the famous loneliness of the great was no popular myth but a general truth—furthermore, that it was as much cause as effect.

All the preceding except the last few sentences is exposition that should've been done earlier or interspersed with the present action instead of lumped together. No reader would put up with so much with such *prolixity*. It's interesting that Ambrose's father, though presumably an intelligent man (as indicated by his role as grade-school principal), neither encouraged nor discouraged his sons at all in any way—as if he either didn't care about them or cared all right but didn't know how to act. If this fact should contribute to one of them's becoming a celebrated but wretchedly unhappy scientist, was it a good thing or not? He too might someday face the question; it would be useful to know whether it had tortured his father for years, for example, or never once crossed his mind.

In the maze two important things happened. First, our hero found a name-coin someone else had lost or discarded: *AMBROSE*, suggestive of the famous lightship and of his late grandfather's favorite dessert, which his mother used to prepare on special occasions out of coconut, oranges, grapes, and what else. Second, as he wondered at the endless replication of his image in the mirrors, second, as he *lost himself in the reflection* that the necessity for an observer makes perfect observation impossible, better make him eighteen at least, yet that would render other things unlikely, he heard Peter and Magda chuckling somewhere together in the maze. "Here!" "No, here!" they shouted to each other; Peter said, "Where's Amby?" Magda murmured. "Amb?" Peter called. In a pleased, friendly voice. He didn't reply. The truth was, his brother was a *happy-go-lucky youngster* who'd've been better off with a regular brother of his own, but who seldom complained of his lot and was generally cordial. Ambrose's throat ached; there aren't enough different ways to say that. He stood quietly while the two young people giggled and thumped through the glittering maze, hurrah'd their discovery of its exit, cried out in joyful alarm at what next beset them. Then he set his mouth and followed after, as he supposed, took a wrong turn, strayed into the pass *wherein he lingers yet.*

The action of conventional dramatic narrative may be represented by a diagram called Freitag's Triangle:

or more accurately by a variant of that diagram:

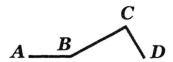

in which *AB* represents the exposition, *B* the introduction of conflict, *BC* the "rising action," complication, or development of the conflict, *C* the climax, or turn of the action, *CD* the dénouement, or resolution of the conflict. While there is no reason to regard this pattern as an absolute necessity, like many other conventions it became conventional because great numbers of people over many years learned by trial and error that it was effective; one ought not to forsake it, therefore, unless one wishes to forsake as well the effect of drama or has clear cause to feel that deliberate violation of the "normal" pattern can better can better effect that effect. This can't go on much longer; it can go on forever. He died telling stories to himself in the dark; years later, when that vast unsuspected area of the funhouse came to light, the first expedition found his skeleton in one of its labyrinthine corridors and mistook it for part of the entertainment. He died of starvation telling himself stories in the dark; but unbeknownst unbeknownst to him, an assistant operator of the funhouse, happening to overhear him, crouched just behind the plyboard partition and wrote down his every word. The operator's daughter, an exquisite young woman with a figure unusually well developed for her age, crouched just behind the partition and transcribed his every word. Though she had never laid eyes on him, she recognized that here was one of Western Culture's truly great imaginations, the eloquence of whose suffering would be an inspiration to unnumbered. And her heart was torn between her love for the misfortunate young man (yes, she loved him, though she had never laid though she knew him only—but how well!—through his words, and the deep, calm voice in which he spoke them) between her love et cetera and her womanly intuition that only in suffering and isolation could he give voice et cetera. Lone dark dying. Quietly she kissed the rough plyboard, and a tear fell upon the page. Where she had written in shorthand *Where she had written in shorthand* Where she had written in shorthand *Where she* et cetera. A long time ago we should have passed the apex of Freitag's Triangle and made brief work of the *dénouement;* the plot doesn't rise by meaningful steps but winds upon itself, digresses, retreats, hesitates, sighs, collapses, expires. The climax of the story must be its protagonist's discovery of a way to get through the funhouse. But he has found none, may have ceased to search.

What relevance does the war have to the story? Should there be fireworks outside or not?

Ambrose wandered, languished, dozed. Now and then he fell into his habit of rehearsing to himself the unadventurous story of his life, narrated from the third-person point of view, from his earliest memory parenthesis of maple leaves stirring in the summer breath of tidewater Maryland end of parenthesis to the present moment. Its principal events, on this telling, would appear to have been *A, B, C,* and *D.*

He imagined himself years hence, successful, married, at ease in the world, the trials of his adolescence far behind him. He has come to the seashore with his family for the holiday: how Ocean City has changed! But at one seldom at one ill-frequented end of the boardwalk a few derelict amusements survive from times gone by: the great carrousel from the turn of the century, with its monstrous griffins and mechanical concert band; the roller coaster rumored since 1916 to have been condemned; the mechanical shooting gallery in which only the image of our enemies changed. His own son laughs with Fat May and wants to know what a funhouse is; Ambrose hugs the sturdy lad close and smiles around his pipestem at his wife.

The family's going home. Mother sits between Father and Uncle Karl, who teases him good-naturedly who chuckles over the fact that the comrade with whom he'd fought his way shoulder to shoulder through the funhouse had turned out to be a blind Negro girl—to their mutual discomfort, as they'd opened their souls. But such are the walls of custom, which even. Whose arm is where? How must it feel. He dreams of a funhouse vaster by far than any yet constructed; but by then they may be out of fashion, like steamboats and excursion trains. Already quaint and seedy: the draperied ladies on the frieze of the carrousel are his father's father's mooncheeked dreams; if he thinks of it more he will vomit his apple-on-a-stick.

He wonders: will he become a regular person? Something has gone wrong; his vaccination didn't take; at the Boy-Scout initiation campfire he only pretended to be deeply moved, as he pretends to this hour that it is not so bad after all in the funhouse, and that he has a little limp. How long will it last? He envisions a truly astonishing funhouse, incredibly complex yet utterly controlled from a great central switchboard like the console of a pipe organ. Nobody had enough imagination. He could design such a place himself, wiring and all, and he's only thirteen years old. He would be its operator: panel lights would show what was up in every cranny of its cunning of its multifarious vastness; a switch-flick would ease this fellow's way, complicate that's, to balance things out; if anyone seemed lost or frightened, all the operator had to do was.

He wishes he had never entered the funhouse. But he has. Then he wishes he were dead. But he's not. Therefore he will construct funhouses for others and be their secret operator—though he would rather be among the lovers for whom funhouses are designed.

At the Café Lovely

RATTAWUT LAPCHAROENSAP

EVERY SO OFTEN I DREAM OF MY BROTHER'S FACE ON FIRE, his brown eyes—eyes very much like my own—staring at me through a terrible mask of flames. I wake to the scent of burning flesh, his fiery face looming before me as an afterimage, and in that darkness I am eleven again. I have not yet learned to trespass. I have not yet learned to grieve. Nor have I learned to pity us—my brother, my mother, and me—and Anek and I are in Bangkok sitting on the roof of our mother's house smoking cigarettes, watching people drifting by on their bicycles while the neighbors release their mangy dogs for the night to roam the city's streets.

It was a Saturday. Saturdays meant the city didn't burn the dump behind our house. We could breathe freely again. We wouldn't have to shut all the windows to keep out the stench, sleep in suffocating heat. Downstairs, we could hear Ma cooking in the outdoor kitchen, the clang of pots and pans, the warm smell of rice curling up toward us.

81

"Hey, kid," Anek said, stubbing his cigarette on the corrugated tin roof. "What's for dinner?" I sniffed the air. I had a keen sense of smell in those days. *Like a dog*, Anek told his friends once. *My little brother can smell your ma taking a crap on the other side of town.*

"Rice."

"Sure."

"Green beans. Fried egg."

"No meat?"

"No. I don't smell any meat."

"Oi." Anek threw a leaf over the edge of the roof. It hovered for a second before dropping swiftly to the street. "I'm tired of this. I'm tired of green beans."

Our father had been dead for four months. The insurance money from the factory was running out. There had been a malfunctioning crane and a crate the size of our house full of little wooden toys waiting to be sent to the children of America. Not a very large crate when I think about the size of the house, but big enough to kill a man when it fell on him from a height of ten meters. At the funeral, I was surprised by how little sadness I'd felt, as if it wasn't our father laid out before the mourners at all—wasn't him lying there in that rubberwood box, wasn't his body popping and crackling in the temple furnace like kindling—but a striking replica of our father in a state of rest. Pa had taken us to the wax museum once, and I remember thinking that he had somehow commissioned the museum to make a beautiful replica of himself and would be appearing any minute now at his own funeral.

After the cremation, we went with Ma to scatter the ashes at Pak Nam. We rode a small six-seater boat out to where the brown river emptied into the green sea. We leaned over the side—all three of us tipping the tiny tin urn together—while Ma tried to mutter a prayer through her tears.

Anek lit another cigarette.

"Are you going out tonight?" I asked.

"Yeah."

"Can I come with?"

"I don't think so."

"But you said last time—"

"Stop whining. I know what I said last time. I said I might. I said maybe. I made no promises, kid. I told you no lies. Last I checked, 'maybe' didn't mean 'yes.'"

A MONTH BEFORE, for my birthday, Anek had taken me to the new American fast-food place at Sogo Mall. I was happy that day. I had dreamed all week of hamburgers and french fries and a nice cold soda and the air-conditioning of the place. During the ride to the mall, my arms wrapped around my brother's waist, the motorcycle sputtering under us, I imagined sitting at one of those shiny plastic tables across from my brother. We'd be pals. After all, it was my birthday—he had to grant me that. We would look like those university students I had seen through the floor-to-ceiling windows, the ones who laughed and sipped at their sodas. Afterward, we would walk into the summer sun with soft-serve sundaes, my brother's arm around my shoulder.

The place was packed, full of students and families clamoring for a taste of American fast food. All around us, people hungrily devoured their meals. I could smell beef cooking on the grill, hear peanut oil bubbling in the deep-fryers. I stared at the illuminated menu above the counter.

"What should I get, Anek?"

"Don't worry, kid. I know just what you'd like."

We waited in line, ordered at the counter, took our tray to an empty booth. Anek said he wasn't hungry, but I knew he had only enough money to order for me: a small burger and some fries. I decided not to ask him about it. I wasn't going to piss him off, what with it being my birthday and what with people being so touchy about money ever since Pa died. As we walked to the booth, I told Anek we could share the meal, I probably wouldn't be able to finish it all myself anyway.

Even though he had been telling me all month about how delicious and great the place was, my brother looked a little uncomfortable. He kept glancing around nervously. It occurred to me then that it was probably his first time there as well. We had on our best clothes that day—Anek in his blue jeans and white polo shirt, me in my khakis and red button-down—but even then I knew our clothes couldn't compare with the other kids' clothes. Their clothes had been bought in the mall; ours had been bought at the weekend bazaar and were cheap imitations of what they wore.

Anek stared across the table at me. He smiled. He tousled my hair. "Happy birthday, kid. Eat up."

"Thanks, Anek."

I unwrapped the burger. I peeked under the bun at the gray meat, the limp green pickles, the swirl of yellow mustard and red ketchup drenching the bun. Anek stared out the window at the road in front of the mall. For some reason, I suddenly felt like I should eat as quickly as possible so we could get the hell out of there. I didn't feel so excited anymore. And I noticed that the place smelled strange—a scent I'd never encountered before—a bit rancid, like palaa fish left too long in the sun. Later, I would find out it was cheese.

I took a few apprehensive bites at the bun. I bit into the brittle meat. I chewed and I chewed and I chewed and I finally swallowed, the thick mass inching slowly down my throat. I took another bite. Then I felt my stomach shoot up to my throat like one of those bottle rockets Anek and I used to set off in front of Apae's convenience store just to piss him off. I remember thinking, Oh fuck, oh fuck, please no, but before I could take a deep breath to settle things, it all came rushing out of me. I threw up all over that shiny American linoleum floor.

A hush fell over the place, followed by a smattering of giggles.

"Oh, you fucking pussy," Anek hissed.

"I'm sorry, Anek."

"You goddamn, motherfucking, monkey-cock-sucking piece of low-class pussy."

I wiped my lips with my forearm. Anek pulled me to my feet, led me out through the glass double doors, his hand on my collar. I tried to say sorry again, but before I could mouth the words my heart felt like it might explode and—just as we cleared the doors—I sent a stream of gray-green vomit splashing against the hot concrete.

"Oh. My. Fucking. Lord. Why?" Anek moaned, lifting his face to the sky. "Oh why, Lord? Why hast thou forsaken me?" Anek and I had been watching a lot of Christian movies on TV lately.

When we came to a traffic stop an hour later, I was leaning against my brother's back, still feeling ill, thick traffic smoke whipping around us. Anek turned to me and said: "That's the first and last time, kid. I can't believe you. All that money for a bunch of puke. No more fucking hamburgers for you."

WE FINISHED watching the sun set over the neighborhood, a panoply of red and orange and purple and blue. Anek told me that Bangkok sunsets were the most beautiful sunsets in the world. "It's the pollution," he said. "Brings out the colors in the sky." Then after Anek and I smoked the last of the cigarettes, we climbed down from the roof.

At dinner, as usual, we barely said a word to each other. Ma had been saying less and less ever since that crate of toys killed our father. She was all headshakes and nods, headshakes and nods. We picked at our green beans, slathered fish sauce on our rice.

"Thanks for the meal, Ma."

Ma nodded.

"Yeah, Ma, this is delicious."

She nodded again.

Besides the silence, Ma's cooking was also getting worse, but we couldn't bring ourselves to say anything about it. What's more, she had perfected the art of moving silently through the house. She seemed an apparition in those days. She'd retreated into herself. She no longer watched over us. She simply watched. I'd be doodling in my book at the kitchen table and all of a sudden Ma would just be sitting there, peering at me with her chin in one hand. Or Anek and I would be horsing around in the outdoor kitchen after dinner, throwing buckets of dirty dishwater on each other, and we'd look over our shoulders to find Ma standing against the crumbling concrete siding of the house. Anek told me she caught him masturbating in the bathroom once. He didn't even realize she had opened the door until he heard it shut, a loud slam so he could know that she'd seen him. Anek didn't masturbate for weeks after that and neither did I.

One night I caught Ma staring at the bedroom mirror with an astonished look on her face, as if she no longer recognized her own sallow reflection. It seemed Pa's death had made our mother a curious spectator of her own life, though when I think of her now I wonder if she was simply waiting for us to notice her grief. But we were just children, Anek and I, and when children learn to acknowledge the gravity of their loved ones' sorrows they're no longer children.

"That woman needs help," Anek said after we washed the dishes that evening.

"She's just sad, Anek."

"Listen, kid, I'm sad too, okay? Do you see me walking around like a mute, though? Do you see me sneaking around the house like I'm some fucking ninja?"

I dropped it. I didn't feel like talking about the state of things that night, not with Anek. I knew he would get angry if we talked about Pa, if we talked about his death, if we talked about what it was doing to Ma. I never knew what to do with my brother's anger in those days. I simply and desperately needed his love.

I THINK ANEK felt bad about the hamburger incident because he started giving me lessons on the motorcycle, an old 350cc Honda our father had ridden to the factory every morning. After Pa died, Ma wanted to sell the bike, but Anek convinced her not to. He told her the bike wasn't worth much. He claimed it needed too many repairs. But I knew that aside from some superficial damage—chipped paint, an ugly crack in the rear mudguard, rusted-through places in the exhaust pipe—the bike was in fine working condition. Anek wanted the bike for himself. He'd been complaining all year about being the only one among his friends without a bike. We'd spent countless hours at the mall showroom, my brother wandering among the gleaming new bikes while I trailed behind him absentmindedly. And though I thought then that my brother had lied to my mother out of selfishness, I know now that Pa did not leave us much. That Honda was Anek's inheritance.

He'd kick-start it for me—I didn't have the strength to do it myself—and I'd hop on in front and ride slowly through the neighborhood with Anek behind me.

"I'll kill you, you little shit. I'll kill you if you break my bike," he'd yell when I approached a turn too fast or when I had trouble steadying the handlebars after coming out of one. "I'm gonna nail you to a fucking cross like Jesus-fucking-Christ."

My feet barely reached the gear pedal, but I'd learned, within a week, to shift into second by sliding off the seat. I'd accelerate out of first, snap the clutch, slide off the seat just so, then pop the gear into place. We'd putter by the city dump at twenty, twenty-five kilos an hour and some of the dek khaya, the garbage children whose families lived in shanties on the dump, would race alongside us, urging me to go faster, asking Anek if they could ride too.

I began to understand the way Anek had eyed those showroom bikes. I began to get a taste for speed.

"That's as fast as I'm letting you go," Anek once said when we got home. "Second gear's good enough for now."

"But I can do it, Anek. I can do it."

"Get taller, kid. Get stronger."

"C'mon, Anek. Please. Second is so slow. It's stupid."

"I'll tell you what's stupid, little brother. What's stupid is you're eleven years old. What's stupid is you go into turns like a drunkard. What's stupid is you can't even reach the gear pedal. Grow, kid. Give me twenty more centimeters. Then maybe we'll talk about letting you do third. Maybe."

"WHY CAN'T I come?"

"Because you can't, that's why."

"But you said last week—"

"I already told you, vomit-boy. I know what I said last week. I said maybe. Which part of that didn't you understand? I didn't say, 'Oh yes! Of course, buddy! I love you so much! You're my super pal! I'd love to take you out next Saturday!' now did I?"

"Just this once, Anek. I promise I won't bother you."

"I don't think so."

"Please?"

"'Please' nothing, little brother. Sit at home and watch a soap with Ma or something."

"But why, Anek? Why can't I go with you?"

"Because I'm going where grown men go, that's why. Because last I checked, last time I saw you naked, you were far from being grown."

"I promise I won't bother you, Anek. I'll just sit in a corner or something. Really. I promise. I'll stay out of your way. Just don't leave me here with Ma tonight."

WHEN WE WERE YOUNG, our mother would put on her perfume every evening before Pa came home. She would smell like jasmine, fresh-picked off a tree. Pa, he would smell of the cologne he dabbed on after he got out of the shower. Although I would never smell the ocean until we went out to Pak Nam to scatter his ashes, I knew that my father smelled like the sea. I just knew it. Anek and I would sit between them, watching some soap opera on TV, and I would inhale their scents, the scents of my parents, and imagine millions of tiny white flowers floating on the surface of a wide and green and bottomless ocean.

But those scents are lost to me now, and I've often wondered if, in my belated sorrow, with all my tardy regrets, I've imagined them all these years.

ANEK FINALLY GAVE IN and took me. We rode out to Minburi District along the new speedway, the engine squealing beneath us. We were going so fast that my face felt stretched impossibly tight.

I wanted to tell Anek to slow down but I remembered that I had promised to stay out of his way.

We were wearing our best clothes again that night, the same old outfits: Anek in his blue jeans and white polo shirt, me in my khakis and red button-down. When we walked out of the house Ma glanced up from the TV with a look that said *What are you all dressed up for?* and Anek told her he was taking me out to the new ice-skating rink, he heard it was all the rage. I even said, "Imagine that, Ma. Ice-skating in Bangkok," but she just nodded, her lips a straight thin line, and went back to watching television.

"'Imagine that, Ma' . . . ," Anek teased when we walked out.

"Eat shit, Anek."

"Whoa there. Be careful, little one. Don't make me change my mind."

When we arrived at the place, it was not what I had imagined at all. I expected mirror balls and multicolored lights and loud American music and hundreds of people dancing inside—like places I'd seen in the district west of our neighborhood, places all the farangs frequented at night. It didn't look like that. It was only a shophouse, like the thousands of tiny two-story shophouses all over the city—short and common, square and concrete, in need of a new paint job. A pink neon sign blinked in the tinted window. CAFÉ LOVELY, it said in English. I could hear the soft, muffled sounds of upcountry music reaching across the street.

"This is it?"

"I can take you home," Anek said. "That's not a problem."

The place smelled of mothballs. There was an old jukebox in the corner. A couple of girls in miniskirts and tank tops and heavy makeup danced and swayed with two balding, middle-aged local men. The men looked awkward with those girls in their arms, feet moving out of time, their large hands gripping the girls' slender waists. In a dark corner, more girls were seated at a table, laughing. They sounded like a flock of excited birds. I'd never seen so many girls in my life.

Three of Anek's friends were already at a table.

"What's with the baby-sitting?" one of them asked, grinning.

"Sorry," Anek said sheepishly as we sat down. "Couldn't bear to leave him home with my crazy ma."

"You hungry, kid?" said another. "Want a hamburger?"

"No thanks."

"Hey," Anek said. "Leave him alone. Let's just pretend he's not here."

The song ended. I saw a girl go up a set of stairs at the back, leading one of the men by the hand. I didn't even have to ask. I wondered if Anek, too, would be going up those stairs at the end of the night. And although I had been disappointed at first by the café's shoddy facade, I found myself excited now by its possibilities.

Anek must've seen me staring because he slapped me hard across the back of the head. "Ow," I cried, rubbing my head with a palm. "That fucking hurt."

"Keep your eyes to yourself, little man."

"That's right," one of his friends intoned, the one who'd asked if I wanted a hamburger. "Be careful what you wish for, boy. The AIDS might eat your dick."

"Not before it eats your mom's, though," I replied, and they all laughed, even my brother, Anek, who said, "Awesome," and smiled at me for the first time all evening.

ANEK HAD COME home one night when I was nine and told me that Pa had taken him out for his fifteenth birthday. The city dump was burning; there was a light red glow in the sky from the pyre. Even though our windows were shut, I could still smell the putrid scent of tires and plastic and garbage burning, the sour odor seeping through our windows. I was sleeping in my underwear, two fans turned on high, both fixed in my direction. Anek walked into the room, stripped down to his underwear, and thrust out his hand.

"Bet you can't tell me what this smell is."

I sniffed his fingers. It smelled like awsuan: oysters simmered in egg yolk. But somehow I knew it wasn't food.

"What is it?"

Anek chuckled.

"What is it, Anek?"

"That, my dear brother, is the smell of"—he put his hand up to his face, sniffed it hungrily—"heaven."

I blinked at him.

"A woman, kid. You know what that is? Pa took me to a sophaeni tonight. And let me tell you, little one, when he takes you for your fifteenth birthday, you'll never be the same again. This scent"—he raised his hand to his face again—"it'll change your fucking life."

ANEK AND HIS FRIENDS had already poured themselves a few drinks while I sat there sipping my cola—half listening to their banter, half watching the girls across the room—when one of Anek's friends stood up and said: "It's getting to that time of night, guys."

I didn't know what the hell was going on, I just thought he was a funny drunk, but then Anek got up and told the bartender we were going outside for a breath of fresh air. One of the girls came up to us, put a hand on Anek's shoulder, and said, "Leaving so soon?" but Anek told her not to worry, to be patient, he'd be back to give her what she wanted soon. The girl winked at me and said, "Who's the handsome little boy?" and I smiled back, but Anek had to be an asshole, so he said, "Oh, that's my virgin brother," which annoyed me because no girl had ever winked at me before and I thought she was beautiful.

I followed Anek and his friends out of the Café Lovely and into a small alley off the shophouse row. Anek didn't want to leave me by myself. He said it didn't look good—leaving a little boy alone in a place like that—but I could tell that he didn't want me to come, either. As we cut into the dark alley, I had a feeling that a breath of fresh air was the last thing we were going to get.

When we stopped, one of Anek's friends pulled out a small container of paint thinner from a plastic bag. "All right," he said, prying at the lid with a small pocketknife. The lid flew open with a loud pop and rolled down the dark alley, swirling to a stop by a Dumpster. I saw the quick shadows of roaches scattering in its wake. That's what the alley smelled like—roaches: dank and humid like the back room where Ma put away our father's belongings. Anek's friend poured half the can into the plastic bag, the liquid thick and translucent, the bag sagging from the weight, while the others flicked their cigarettes into the sewer ditch along the side of the alley. The thinner gave off a sharp, strong odor, punched little pinpricks in my nostrils, and reminded me of days when Pa and Anek used to fumigate the house. Anek's friend pulled out another plastic bag from his back pocket and put the first bag with the thinner inside of it.

"Okay." He held out the double bag with one hand, offering it to his friends, the way I'd seen butchers at the market holding dead chickens by the neck. I could hear the jukebox starting up again in the café, another old upcountry tune echoing softly down the alley. "Who's first?"

For a second, they all stood with their hands in their pockets.

Then Anek reached out and took the bag with a quick, impatient gesture.

"Let's just get this over with," he said. "I tell you guys, though, one hit and I'm done. I don't like having my little brother around this shit."

I realized then what they were doing. I knew what huffers were, but I'd always imagined little kids and strung-out homeless guys in the Klong Toey slum with their heads buried in pots of rubber cement. I suddenly became very afraid—I wanted to grab the bag out of my brother's hands—even as I longed to watch Anek do it, wanted, in fact, to do it myself, to show Anek and his friends my indifference.

Anek brought the mouth of the bag to his chin. He took a big, deep breath, pulled his entire body back like it was a sling-shot, then blew into the bag, inflating it like a balloon, the loose ends covering half his face, and it made a sound like a quick wind blowing through a sail. The bag grew larger and larger and I was afraid that it might burst, that the thinner would go flying everywhere. Anek looked at me the whole time he blew, his eyes growing wider and wider. He kept blowing and blowing and blowing, and I knew that my brother was blowing for a long time because one of the guys said, "Fucking inhale already, Anek," but he kept on blowing and blowing and all that time he kept looking at me with those eyes about to pop out of his head. I don't know what he was trying to tell me then, looking at me like that, but I remember noticing for the first time that he had our mother's eyes. He finally inhaled, sucked his breath back into his chest, the plastic balloon collapsing in on itself, and then my brother was blinking hard, teetering, like a boxer stunned by a swift and surprising blow, and I knew that whatever it was he had smelled, whatever scent he had just inhaled, it was knocking him off his feet. He handed the bag to one of the other guys and said, "C'mon kid,

94

let's get out of here," and I followed my brother out of the dark alley, back into the dimly lit street.

YEARS LATER, I'd be in a different alley with friends of my own, and one of the guys, high off a can of spray paint, would absent-mindedly light a cigarette after taking a hit and his face would burst into a sheet of blue flames. He ran around the alley wild with panic, running into the sides of the buildings, stumbling and falling and getting back to his feet again, hands flying violently around his burning face as if trying to beat back a swarm of attacking insects. He never made a sound, just ran around that alley with his face on fire in silent terror, the flames catching in his hair and his clothes, looking like some giant ignited match in the shape of a man. For a second, we couldn't quite comprehend what was happening—some of us laughed, most of us were just stunned—before I managed to chase the boy down, tackle him to the ground, and beat out the flames from his face with my T-shirt. His eyes were wild with terror and we just stared at each other for a moment before he started to weep hysterically, his body shaking under mine, the terrible scent of burnt flesh and singed hair filling the alley. His lashes and eyebrows had been burned cleanly off his face. His eyelids were raw, pink. His face began to swell immediately, large white welts blooming here and there. And he just kept on crying beneath me, calling for his mother and father, blubbering incoherently in the high, desperate voice of a child.

BACK AT THE CAFÉ, I could tell that the thinner was setting in. Anek kept tilting back in his seat, dilating his eyes. He took a long swig of his rye, poured himself another. I knew we wouldn't be going home for a while. The same girl who had winked at me earlier walked across the room and sat down at our table. She put her arm around my shoulder. I felt my body tense. She smelled like menthol, like the prickly heat powder Anek and I sprinkled on ourselves to keep cool at night.

"Hi, handsome."

"Hi."

I sipped at the last of my cola. Across the room, I noticed the girls looking our way, giggling among themselves.

"That's my brother," Anek drawled.

"I know, Anek."

"He's a little high," I said, laughing.

"Looks like it."

"Yeah." Anek smiled, slow and lazy. "Just a little."

"Where are the rest?" she asked me.

"Outside."

"What about you, handsome? Are you high?"

"No."

"Ever been?"

"Yeah. Of course. Plenty of times."

She laughed, threw her head far back. Menthol. I felt my heart pounding in my chest. I wanted to smear her carmine lips with my hands. I reached across the table for Anek's Krong Thips and lit one.

"You're adorable," she said, pinching one of my cheeks. I felt myself blush. "But you shouldn't be smoking those things at your age."

"I know," I said, smiling at her, taking a drag. "Cigarettes are bad."

"C'mon," Anek said, getting up abruptly, swaying a little bit. He reached out and grabbed her hand from my shoulder. "C'mon." He nodded toward the staircase. "Let's go."

She stood up, her hand dangling in my brother's, while I sat between them.

"What about the kid?" she asked, looking down at me.

"Oh, he'll be fine."

"Maybe not tonight, Anek. We shouldn't leave the kid by himself."

"Hey barf-boy," Anek said. "You gonna be okay?"

I looked up at my brother. He still had the girl's hand in his own. I took a long drag of my cigarette.

"Yeah. I'll be fine, Anek. I'm not a kid anymore."

Anek smiled as if he found me amusing. I wanted to wipe the smile off his face. I felt angry. I didn't want to be abandoned. Anek must've sensed this because there suddenly seemed something sad about my brother's smile. He dropped the girl's hand. He reached out and tapped me lightly on the head.

"Okay, kid. You don't have to be so tough all the time," he said finally. He took a deep breath, his voice a little steadier, his eyes a little wider. "Tell you what. I'm just gonna go put some music in the jukebox. Then Nong and I are gonna dance. Then we're gonna go upstairs for a while. Just a short while. We won't be long. I promise. Then, if you want, we'll go home, okay?" But I just took another drag of my cigarette, watched the girls in the corner, tried not to meet my brother's eyes.

She led him out to the dance floor. They stood by the jukebox and he slipped a few coins into the machine, steadying himself with one hand. A record came on, the sound of high Isan flutes and xylophones and a hand drum striking up the first few bars. Anek clumsily took one of the girl's hands, hooked an arm around her waist, and they started moving to the music. They stood close, their chins on each other's shoulders, though perhaps a little too close for the girl, because she leaned away from my brother a few times. But then again, maybe it was because my brother was high, drunk, and they kept losing their balance. They didn't look like dancers at all after a while; they looked like they were just holding each other up, falling into and out of each other's body.

I hadn't recognized the tune at first—I thought it was just another generic upcountry ballad—but then a woman's falsetto came soaring over the instruments and I remembered that it was an old record of Ma's, something she and Pa used to listen to in the early afternoon, hours before the endlessly growing mass of garbage burned behind our house. Those days curry and fish in tamarind sauce would be cooking on the stove, the aroma wafting into the house, and I swear that right then, listening to that music, I could smell it on the tip of my nose.

Oh beloved, so sad was my departure . . .

I looked at Anek and the girl. She couldn't have been more than sixteen years old—younger than my brother—but it seemed clear to me now that she was the one holding him up, directing his course, leading him. I wondered how many men she had held up tonight, how many more she would hold in the thousands of nights before her. I wondered whether she was already finding the force of their weight unbearable. I wondered whether I would be adding my weight to that mass one day. She held him close now and he, he pulled away, fell out of sync, though they continued to move across the floor as slowly and languorously as the music in the café.

. . . I am tired, I am broken, I am lost . . .

When the song ended, they pulled away from each other. Anek took the girl by the hand and led her toward the staircase.

As they began to mount the stairs, the girl said something to my brother and they both stopped to look back at me. My brother smiled weakly then, raised a hand in my direction. I looked away, pretended not to see the gesture, stirring the ash in the tray with my cigarette. When I looked back they were gone.

The place fell silent. A balding, middle-aged man walked down the stairs. He made for the door, his steps quick and certain, as if he couldn't wait to leave. When he passed by my table, I caught a whiff of him, and his scent lingered on my nostrils for a while. He smelled like okra.

I stood up. I don't know why I walked toward that staircase. Perhaps it was childish curiosity. Or perhaps I wanted to see, once and for all, what secrets, what sins, what comforts those stairs led one to. Or perhaps I wanted to retrieve Anek before he did whatever it was I thought he might do.

I had imagined darkness and was surprised, when I arrived at the top of the stairs, to find a brightly lit hallway flanked on both sides by closed doors. The corridor smelled sweet, sickly, as if it had been perfumed to cover up some stench. The bare walls gleamed under the buzzing fluorescent fixtures. I heard another song start up downstairs, laughter again from the table of girls. I walked slowly down the hallway; the noises downstairs faded to a murmur. I felt like I had surfaced into another world and left those distant, muffled sounds beneath me, underwater. As I crept along, careful to be silent, I began to hear a chorus of ghostly, guttural groans coming from behind the doors. I heard a man whimper; I heard another cry out incoherently. After a while, those rooms seemed—with their grunting and moaning—like torture chambers in which faceless men suffered untold cruelties. I wondered if my brother was making any of these noises. I thought of the video Anek had borrowed from one of his friends, the women in them cooing and squealing perversely, and how strange it was now that none of the women could be heard. Instead, I could hear only the men, growling away as if in some terrible, solitary animal pain. I imagined the men writhing against the women, and I wondered how these women—those girls sitting downstairs—could possibly endure in such silence.

Just as I turned the corner, a hand grabbed me by the collar, choking me. I was certain, for a moment, that I would now be dragged into one of the rooms and made to join that chorus of howling men.

"Little boy," a voice hissed in my ear. "Where do you think you're going?"

It was the bartender from downstairs. He looked down at me, brow furrowed, beads of spittle glistening at the corners of his lips. I smelled whiskey on his breath, felt his large, chapped hands on my neck as he pulled me toward him and lifted me off the concrete floor.

"You're in the wrong place," he whispered into my ear, while I struggled against his grip. "I should kill you for being up here. I should snap your head right off your fucking neck."

I screamed for Anek then. I sent my brother's name echoing down that empty hallway. I screamed his name over and over again as the bartender lifted me up into his thick, ropy arms. The more I struggled against the bartender, the more dire my predicament seemed, and I cried out for my brother as I had never cried out before. The men seemed to stop their moaning then and, for a moment, I felt as if my cries were the only sound in the world. I saw a few doors open, a couple of women sticking out their heads to look at the commotion. The bartender walked backward with me, toward the staircase, as I kicked and struggled against his suffocating embrace.

Then I saw my brother hobbling in his underwear, his blue jeans shackling his feet.

"Hey!" Anek yelled, staggering, bending down to gather up his jeans. "Hey!" The man stopped, loosened his grip on my body. "Hey!" Anek yelled again, getting closer now. "That's my little brother, you cocksucker. Put him down."

The bartender still had me, his breath hot on my neck. As Anek struggled to pull up his jeans I glimpsed the purple, bulbous head of his penis peeking over the waistband of his underwear. The bartender must've seen this too; he began to chuckle obscenely.

"Get him out of here, Anek," he said. Anek nodded grimly. The bartender put me down, shoved me lightly toward my brother. "You know I can't have him up here," he said.

"You okay, kid?" Anek asked, breathless, ignoring the bartender, bending down to look me in the eyes. I saw the girl standing in the hallway behind Anek, a towel wrapped loosely around her small body. She waved at me, smiling, and then walked back into the room. The other women disappeared as well. I heard the bartender going downstairs, the steps creaking under his weight. Soon, Anek and I were the only people left in that hallway, and for some reason—despite my attempts to steel myself—I began to cry. I tried to apologize to my brother through the tears.

"Oh shit," my brother muttered, pulling me to his chest. "C'mon, kid," he said. "Let's just go home."

WE WENT to the bathroom. I stood sniveling by a urinal while Anek leaned over a sink and dashed water on his face. When we came back out, his steps were no longer unsteady, though his voice still quavered slightly. Beads of water glistened on his face. He lit a cigarette at the door and waved to the bartender and the girls in the corner. I couldn't look at them now.

We stepped into the street. His friends were still in the alley, laughing and stumbling, flinging pieces of garbage from the Dumpster at each other. We stood at the mouth of the alley and Anek said, "See you later, boys," and one of them yelled back, "Wait, Anek! Wait! I have an idea! Let's put your kid brother in the dump!" But Anek just put an arm around my shoulder and said, "Maybe next time."

We crossed the street. Anek kick-started the motorcycle. It sputtered and wheezed and coughed before settling into a soft, persistent purr. I started to climb onto the back, but Anek said, "What the hell are you doing? Can't you see I'm in no shape to take us home?"

"You can't be serious, Anek."

"Serious as our pa is dead, kid."

I stood there for a moment, dumbfounded. I climbed onto the front seat.

"I swear to God, though, you make so much as a dent on my bike and I'll—"

But I had already cocked the accelerator and we were on our way. Slowly, of course. I slipped off the seat a little so I could reach the pedal, snapped the clutch with my left hand, and popped the bike into second gear. We sputtered for a while like that along the streets of Minburi, crawling at fifteen kilos, until I made a sharp right onto the bridge that would take us out to the new speedway.

YEARS LATER, I would ask Anek if he remembered this night. He would say that I made it up. He never would've taken me to the Café Lovely at such a young age, he'd say, never would've let me drive that bike home. He denies it now because he doesn't want to feel responsible for the way things turned out, for the way we abandoned our mother to that hot and empty house, for the thoughtless, desperate things I would learn to do. Later that same year, my mother would wake me up in the middle of the night. She would be crying. She would ask me to sleep again in her bed. And, for the first time, I would refuse her. I would deny Ma the comfort of my body.

After Anek moved to an apartment across the river in Thonburi, I gathered my father's belongings from the back room and pawned them while Ma was at work. I used the money to buy myself a motorcycle. When I got home, my mother was waiting for me. She came at me with a thousand impotent fists, and when she was finished, spent and exhausted, her small body quivering in my arms, she asked me to leave her house. I did. And I did not return to that house again until it was too late, until Anek called to say our mother was ill, that she wanted us by her side to accompany her through her final hours.

THAT NIGHT, as we rode back from the Café Lovely, I felt my brother's arms around my waist, his head slumped on my shoulder. I remember thinking then about how I'd never felt the weight of my brother's head before. His hot, measured breaths warmed my neck. I could still smell the thinner's faint, sour scent wafting from his face. I suddenly became afraid that Anek had fallen asleep and would tumble off the bike at any moment.

"Are you awake, Anek?"

"Yeah, I'm awake."

"Good."

"Do me a favor. Eyes on the road."

"I'm glad you're awake, Anek."

"Third."

"What's that?"

"I said third."

"You sure?"

"It's a onetime offer, little man."

I slipped off the seat, accelerated a little, twisted the clutch, and tapped the gear pedal as we hit the speedway. I was so excited we might as well have broken the sound barrier, but the engine jolted us forward just enough that my grip weakened and we went swerving along the empty speedway, weaving wildly back and forth at thirty kilometers an hour.

"Easy now. Easy. There, there, you have it. Just take a deep breath now. Holy shit, I almost had to break your ass back there. You almost had us kissing the pavement."

I could feel the palms of my hands slick against the throttle. Even at thirty kilos, the wind blew hot against our faces.

"Accelerate," Anek said.

"No fucking way."

"I said accelerate. This is a speedway, you know, not a slow-way. I'd like to get home before dawn."

"You're out of your mind, Anek. That's the thinner talking."

"Listen, if you won't do it, I'll do it myself," he said, reaching over me for the throttle.

"Fine," I said, brushing his hand away. "I'll do it. Just give me a second."

We slowly gathered speed along the empty highway—thirty-five, forty, forty-five—and after a while, the concrete moving swiftly and steadily below our feet, I was beginning to feel a little more comfortable. Anek put his arms around my waist again, his chin still on my shoulder.

"Good," he whispered into my ear. "Good, good. You've got it. You're fucking doing it. You're really coasting now, boy. Welcome to the third gear, my little man.

"Now," he said. "Try fourth."

I didn't argue this time. I just twisted the accelerator some more, popped the bike into fourth, sliding smoothly off the seat then quickly back on. This time, to my surprise, our course didn't even waver. It was an easy transition. We were cruising comfortably now at sixty, sixty-five, seventy, seventy-five, faster and faster and faster still, the engine singing a high note beneath us as we flew along that straight and empty speedway. We didn't say a word to each other the rest of the way. And nothing seemed lovelier to me than that hot wind howling in my ears, the night blurring around us, the smell of the engine furiously burning gasoline.

A Poetics for Bullies

STANLEY ELKIN

I 'M PUSH THE BULLY, AND WHAT I HATE ARE NEW KIDS AND sissies, dumb kids and smart, rich kids, poor kids, kids who wear glasses, talk funny, show off, patrol boys and wise guys and kids who pass pencils and water the plants—and cripples, *especially* cripples. I love nobody loved.

One time I was pushing this red-haired kid (I'm a pusher, no hitter, no belter; an aggressor of marginal violence, I hate *real* force) and his mother stuck her head out the window and shouted something I've never forgotten. *"Push,"* she yelled. *"You, Push. You pick on him because you wish you had his red hair!"* It's true; I *did* wish I had his red hair. I wish I were tall, or fat, or thin. I wish I had different eyes, different hands, a mother in the supermarket. I wish I were a man, a small boy, a girl in the choir. I'm a coveter, a Boston Blackie of the heart, casing the world. Endlessly I covet and case. (Do you know what makes me cry? The Declaration of Independence. "All men are created equal." That's beautiful.)

If you're a bully like me, you use your head. Toughness isn't enough. You beat them up, they report you. Then where are you? I'm not even particularly strong. (I used to be strong. I used to do exercise, work out, but strength implicates you, and often isn't an advantage anyway—read the judo ads. Besides, your big bullies aren't bullies at all—they're *athletes*. With them, beating guys up is a sport.) But what I lose in size and strength I make up in courage. I'm very brave. That's a lie about bullies being cowards underneath. If you're a coward, get out of the business.

I'm best at torment.

A kid has a toy bow, toy arrows. "Let Push look," I tell him.

He's suspicious, he knows me. "Go way, Push," he says, this mama-warned Push doubter.

"Come on," I say, "come on."

"No, Push. I can't. My mother said I can't."

I raise my arms, I spread them. I'm a bird—slow, powerful, easy, free. I move my head offering profile like something beaked. I'm the Thunderbird. "In the school where I go I have a teacher who teaches me magic," I say. "Arnold Salamancy, give Push your arrows. Give him one, he gives back two. Push is the God of the Neighborhood."

"Go way, Push," the kid says, uncertain.

"Right," Push says, himself again. "Right. I'll disappear. First the fingers." My fingers ball to fists. "My forearms next." They jackknife into my upper arms. "The arms." Quick as bird-blink they snap behind my back, fit between the shoulder blades like a small knapsack. (I am double-jointed, protean.) "My head," I say.

"No, Push," the kid says, terrified. I shudder and everything comes back, falls into place from the stem of self like a shaken puppet.

"The arrow, the arrow. Two where was one." He hands me an arrow.

"Trouble, trouble, double rubble!" I snap it and give back the pieces.

Well, sure. There *is* no magic. If there were I would learn it. I would find out the words, the slow turns and strange passes, drain the bloods and get the herbs, do the fires like a vestal. I would look for the main chants. *Then* I'd change things. *Push* would!

But there's only casuistical trick. Sleight-of-mouth, the bully's poetics.

You know the formulas:

"Did you ever see a match burn twice?" you ask. Strike. Extinguish. Jab his flesh with the hot stub.

"Play 'Gestapo'?"

"How do you play?"

"What's your name?"

"It's Morton."

I slap him. "You're lying."

"Adam and Eve and Pinch Me Hard went down to the lake for a swim. Adam and Eve fell in. Who was left?"

"Pinch Me Hard."

I do.

Physical puns, conundrums. Push the punisher, the conundrummer!

But there has to be more than tricks in a bag of tricks.

I don't know what it is. Sometimes I think *I'm* the only new kid. In a room, the school, the playground, the neighborhood, I get the feeling I've just moved in, no one knows me. You know what I like? To stand in crowds. To wait with them at the airport to meet a plane. Someone asks what time it is. I'm the first to answer. Or at the ball park when the vendor comes. He passes the hot dog down the long row. I want *my* hands on it, too. On the dollar going up, the change coming down.

I am ingenious, I am patient.

A kid is going downtown on the elevated train. He's got his little suit on, his shoes are shined, he wears a cap. This is a kid going to the travel bureaus, the foreign tourist offices to get brochures, maps, pictures of the mountains for a unit at his school—a kid looking for extra credit. I follow him. He comes out of the Italian Tourist Information Center. His arms are full. I move from my place at the window. I follow him for two blocks and bump into him as he steps from a curb. It's a *collision*—The pamphlets fall from his arms. Pretending confusion, I walk on his paper Florence. I grind my heel in his Riviera. I climb Vesuvius and sack his Rome and dance on the Isle of Capri.

The Industrial Museum is a good place to find children. I cut somebody's five- or six-year-old kid brother out of the herd of eleven- and twelve-year-olds he's come with. "*Quick,*" I say. I pull him along the corridors, up the stairs, through the halls, down to a mezzanine landing. Breathless, I pause for a minute. "I've got some gum. Do you want a stick?" He nods; I stick him. I rush him into an auditorium and abandon him. He'll be lost for hours.

I sidle up to a kid at the movies. "You smacked my brother," I tell him. "After the show—I'll be outside."

I break up games. I hold the ball above my head. "You want it? Take it."

I go into barber shops. There's a kid waiting. "I'm next," I tell him, "understand?"

One day Eugene Kraft rang my bell. Eugene is afraid of me, so he helps me. He's fifteen and there's something wrong with his saliva glands and he drools. His chin is always chapped. I tell him he has to drink a lot because he loses so much water.

"Push? Push," he says. He's wiping his chin with his tissues. "Push, there's this kid—"

"Better get a glass of water, Eugene."

109

"No, Push, no fooling, there's this new kid—he just moved in. You've got to see this kid."

"Eugene, get some water, please. You're drying up. I've never seen you so bad. There are deserts in you, Eugene."

"All right, Push, but then you've got to see—"

"Swallow, Eugene. You better swallow."

He gulps hard.

"Push, this is a kid and a half. Wait, you'll see."

"I'm very concerned about you, Eugene. You're dying of thirst, Eugene. Come into the kitchen with me."

I push him through the door. He's very excited. I've never seen him so excited. He talks at me over his shoulder, his mouth flooding, his teeth like the little stone pebbles at the bottom of a fishbowl. "He's got this sport coat, with a patch over the heart. Like a king, Push. No kidding."

"Be careful of the carpet, Eugene."

I turn on the taps in the sink. I mix in hot water. "Use your tissues, Eugene. Wipe your chin."

He wipes himself and puts the Kleenex in his pocket. All of Eugene's pockets bulge. He looks, with his bulging pockets, like a clumsy smuggler.

"Wipe, Eugene. Swallow, you're drowning."

"He's got this funny accent—you could die." Excited, he tamps at his mouth like a diner, a tubercular.

"Drink some water, Eugene."

"No, Push. I'm not thirsty—really."

"Don't be foolish, kid. That's because your mouth's so wet. Inside where it counts you're drying up. It stands to reason. Drink some water."

"He has this crazy haircut."

"*Drink*," I command. I shake him. "*Drink!*"

"Push, I've got no glass. Give me a glass at least."

110

"I can't do that, Eugene. You've got a terrible sickness. How could I let you use our drinking glasses? Lean under the tap and open your mouth."

He knows he'll have to do it, that I won't listen to him until he does. He bends into the sink.

"Push, it's *hot*," he complains. The water splashes into his nose, it gets on his glasses and for a moment his eyes are magnified, enormous. He pulls away and scrapes his forehead on the faucet.

"Eugene, you touched it. Watch out, please. You're too close to the tap. Lean your head deeper into the sink."

"It's *hot*, Push."

"Warm water evaporates better. With your affliction you've got to evaporate fluids before they get into your glands."

He feeds again from the tap.

"Do you think that's enough?" I ask after a while.

"I do, Push, I really do," he says. He is breathless.

"Eugene," I say seriously, "I think you'd better get yourself a canteen."

"A canteen, Push?"

"That's right. Then you'll always have water when you need it. Get one of those Boy Scout models. The two-quart kind with a canvas strap."

"But you hate the Boy Scouts, Push."

"They make very good canteens, Eugene. *And wear it!* I never want to see you without it. Buy it today."

"All right, Push."

"Promise!"

"All right, Push."

"Say it out."

He made the formal promise that I like to hear.

"Well, then," I said, "let's go see this new kid of yours."

He took me to the schoolyard. "Wait," he said, "you'll see." He skipped ahead.

"Eugene," I said, calling him back. "Let's understand something. No matter what this new kid is like, nothing changes as far as you and I are concerned."

"Aw, Push," he said.

"Nothing, Eugene. I mean it. You don't get out from under me."

"Sure, Push, I know that."

There were some kids in the far corner of the yard, sitting on the ground, leaning up against the wire fence. Bats and gloves and balls lay scattered around them. (It was where they told dirty jokes. Sometimes I'd come by during the little kids' recess and tell them all about what their daddies do to their mommies.)

"There. See? Do you see him?" Eugene, despite himself, seemed hoarse.

"Be quiet," I said, checking him, freezing as a hunter might. I stared.

He was a *prince*, I tell you.

He was tall, tall, even sitting down. His long legs comfortable in expensive wool, the trousers of a boy who had been on ships, jets; who owned a horse, perhaps; who knew Latin—what *didn't* he know?—somebody made up, like a kid in a play with a beautiful mother and a handsome father; who took his breakfast from a sideboard, and picked, even at fourteen and fifteen and sixteen, his mail from a silver plate. He would have hobbies—stamps, stars, things lovely dead. He wore a sport coat, brown as wood, thick as heavy bark. The buttons were leather buds. His shoes seemed carved from horses' saddles, gunstocks. His clothes had once grown in nature. *What it must feel like inside those clothes,* I thought.

I looked at his face, his clear skin, and guessed at the bones, white as beached wood. His eyes had skies in them. His yellow hair swirled on his head like a crayoned sun.

"Look, look at him," Eugene said. "The sissy. Get him, Push."

He was talking to them and I moved closer to hear his voice. It was clear, beautiful, but faintly foreign—like herb-seasoned meat.

When he saw me he paused, smiling. He waved. The others didn't look at me.

"Hello there," he called. "Come over if you'd like. I've been telling the boys about tigers."

"Tigers," I said.

"Give him the 'match burn twice,' Push," Eugene whispered.

"Tigers, is it?" I said. "What do you know about tigers?" My voice was high.

"The 'match burn twice,' Push."

"Not so much as a Master *Tugjah*. I was telling the boys. In India there are men of high caste—*Tugjahs*, they're called. I was apprenticed to one once in the Southern Plains and might perhaps have earned my mastership, but the Red Chinese attacked the northern frontier and . . . well, let's just say I had to leave. At any rate, these *Tugjahs* are as intimate with the tiger as you are with dogs. I don't mean they keep them as pets. The relationship goes deeper. Your dog is a service animal, as is your elephant."

"Did you ever see a match burn twice?" I asked suddenly.

"Why no, can you do that? Is it a special match you use?"

"No," Eugene said, "it's an ordinary match. He uses an ordinary match."

"Can you do it with one of mine, do you think?"

He took a matchbook from his pocket and handed it to me. The cover was exactly the material of his jacket, and in the center was a patch with a coat-of-arms identical to the one he wore over his heart.

I held the matchbook for a moment and then gave it back to him. "I don't feel like it," I said.

"Then some other time, perhaps," he said.

Eugene whispered to me. "His accent, Push, his funny *accent*."

"Some other time, perhaps," I said. I am a good mimic. I can duplicate a particular kid's lisp, his stutter, a thickness in his throat. There were two or three here whom I had brought close to tears by holding up my mirror to their voices. I can parody their limps, their waddles, their girlish runs, their clumsy jumps. I can throw as they throw, catch as they catch. I looked around. "Some other time, perhaps," I said again. No one would look at me.

"I'm *so* sorry," the new one said, "we don't know each other's names. You are?"

"I'm so sorry," I said. "You are?"

He seemed puzzled. Then he looked sad, disappointed. No one said anything.

"It don't sound the same," Eugene whispered.

It was true. I sounded nothing like him. I could imitate only defects, only flaws.

A kid giggled.

"Shh," the prince said. He put one finger to his lips.

"Look at that," Eugene said under his breath. "He's a sissy."

He had begun to talk to them again. I squatted, a few feet away. I ran gravel through my loose fists, one bowl in an hourglass feeding another.

He spoke of jungles, of deserts. He told of ancient trade routes traveled by strange beasts. He described lost cities and a lake deeper than the deepest level of the sea. There was a story about a boy who had been captured by bandits. A woman in the story—it wasn't clear whether she was the boy's mother—had

114

been tortured. His eyes clouded for a moment when he came to this part and he had to pause before continuing. Then he told how the boy escaped—it was cleverly done—and found help, mountain tribesmen riding elephants. The elephants charged the cave in which the mo—the *woman*—was still a prisoner. It might have collapsed and killed her, but one old bull rushed in and, shielding her with his body, took the weight of the crashing rocks. Your elephant is a service animal.

I let a piece of gravel rest on my thumb and flicked it in a high arc above his head. Some of the others who had seen me stared, but the boy kept on talking. Gradually I reduced the range, allowing the chunks of gravel to come closer to his head.

"You see?" Eugene said quietly. "He's afraid. He pretends not to notice."

The arcs continued to diminish. The gravel went faster, straighter. No one was listening to him now, but he kept talking.

"—of magic," he said, "what occidentals call 'a witch doctor.' There are spices that induce these effects. The *Bogdovii* was actually able to stimulate the growth of rocks with the powder. The Dutch traders were ready to go to war for the formula. Well, you can see what it could mean for the Low Countries. Without accessible quarries they've never been able to construct a permanent system of dikes. But with the *Bogdovii's* powder"—he reached out and casually caught the speeding chip as if it had been a ping-pong ball—"they could turn a grain of sand into a pebble, use the pebbles to grow stones, the stones to grow rocks. This little piece of gravel, for example, could be changed into a mountain." He dipped his thumb into his palm as I had and balanced the gravel on his nail. He flicked it; it rose from his nail like a missile and climbed an impossible arc. It disappeared. "The *Bogdovii* never revealed how it was done."

I stood up. Eugene tried to follow me.

"Listen," he said, "you'll get him."

"Swallow," I told him. "Swallow, you pig!"

I HAVE LIVED my life in pursuit of the vulnerable: Push the chink seeker, wheeler dealer in the flawed cement of the personality, a collapse maker. But what isn't vulnerable, *who* isn't? There is that which is unspeakable, so I speak it, that which is unthinkable, which I think. Me and the devil, we do God's dirty work, after all.

I went home after I left him. I turned once at the gate, and the boys were around him still. The useless Eugene had moved closer. *He* made room for him against the fence.

I ran into Frank the fat boy. He made a move to cross the street, but I had seen him and he went through a clumsy retractive motion. I could tell he thought I would get him for that, but I moved by, indifferent to a grossness in which I had once delighted. As I passed he seemed puzzled, a little hurt, a little—this was astonishing—guilty. *Sure* guilty. Why *not* guilty? The forgiven tire of their exemption. Nothing could ever be forgiven, and I forgave nothing. I held them to the mark. Who else cared about the fatties, about the dummies and slobs and clowns, about the gimps and squares and oafs and fools, the kids with a mouthful of mush, all those shut-ins of the mind and heart, all those losers? Frank the fat boy knew, and passed me shyly. His wide, fat body, stiffened, forced jokishly martial when he saw me, had already become flaccid as he moved by, had already made one more forgiven surrender. Who cared?

The streets were full of failure. Let them. Let them be. There was a paragon, a paragon loose. What could he be doing here, why had he come, what did he want? It was impossible that this hero from India and everywhere had made his home here; that he

116

lived, as Frank the fat boy did, as Eugene did, as *I* did, in an apartment; that he shared our lives.

In the afternoon I looked for Eugene. He was in the park, in a tree. There was a book in his lap. He leaned against the thick trunk.

"Eugene," I called up to him.

"Push, they're closed. It's Sunday, Push. The stores are closed. I looked for the canteen. The stores are closed."

"Where is he?"

"Who, Push? What do you want, Push?"

"*Him.* Your pal. The prince. Where? Tell me, Eugene, or I'll shake you out of that tree. I'll burn you down. I swear it. Where is he?"

"No, Push. I was wrong about that guy. He's nice. He's really nice. Push, he told me about a doctor who could help me. Leave him alone, Push."

"Where, Eugene? *Where?* I count to three."

Eugene shrugged and came down the tree.

I found the name Eugene gave me—funny, foreign—over the bell in the outer hall. The buzzer sounded and I pushed open the door. I stood inside and looked up the carpeted stairs, the angled banisters.

"What is it?" She sounded old, worried.

"The new kid," I called, "the new kid."

"It's for you," I heard her say.

"Yes?" His voice, the one I couldn't mimic. I mounted the first stair. I leaned back against the wall and looked up through the high, boxy banister poles. It was like standing inside a pipe organ.

"Yes?"

From where I stood at the bottom of the stairs I could see only a boot. He was wearing boots.

"Yes? What is it, please?"

"You," I roared. "Glass of fashion, mold of form, it's me! It's Push the bully!"

I heard his soft, rapid footsteps coming down the stairs—a springy, spongy urgency. He jingled, the bastard. He had coins—I could see them: rough, golden, imperfectly round; raised, massively gowned goddesses, their heads fingered smooth, their arms gone—and keys to strange boxes, thick doors. I saw his boots. I backed away.

"I brought you down," I said.

"Be quiet, please. There's a woman who's ill. A boy who must study. There's a man with bad bones. An old man needs sleep."

"He'll get it," I said.

"We'll go outside," he said.

"No. Do you live here? What do you do? Will you be in our school? Were you telling the truth?"

"Shh. Please. You're very excited."

"Tell me your name," I said. It could be my campaign, I thought. His *name.* Scratched in new sidewalk, chalked onto walls, written on papers dropped in the street. To leave it behind like so many clues, to give him a fame, to take it away, to slash and cross out, to erase and to smear—my kid's witchcraft. "Tell me your name."

"It's John," he said softly.

"What?"

"It's John."

"John what? Come on now. I'm Push the bully."

"John Williams," he said.

"John Williams? John Williams? Only that? Only John Williams?"

He smiled.

"Who's that on the bell? The name on the box?"

118

"She needs me," he said.

"Cut it out."

"I help her," he said.

"You stop that."

"There's a man that's in pain. A woman who's old. A husband that's worried. A wife that despairs."

"You're the bully," I said. "Your John Williams is a service animal," I yelled in the hall.

He turned and began to climb the stairs. His calves bloomed in their leather sheathing.

"*Lover,*" I whispered to him.

He turned to me at the landing. He shook his head sadly.

"We'll see," I said.

"We'll see what we'll see," he said.

That night I painted his name on the side of the gymnasium in enormous letters. In the morning it was still there, but it wasn't what I meant. There was nothing incantatory in the huge letters, no scream, no curse. I had never traveled with a gang, there had been no togetherness in my tearing, but this thing on the wall seemed the act of vandals, the low production of ruffians. When you looked at it you were surprised they had gotten the spelling right.

Astonishingly, it was allowed to remain. And each day there was something more celebrational in the giant name, something of increased hospitality, lavish welcome. John Williams might have been a football hero, or someone back from the kidnapers. Finally I had to take it off myself.

Something had changed.

Eugene was not wearing his canteen. Boys didn't break off their conversations when I came up to them. One afternoon a girl winked at me. (Push has never picked on girls. *Their* submissiveness is part of their nature. They are ornamental. Don't get me wrong, please. There is a way in which they function as part of the landscape, like flowers at a funeral. They have a strange cheerfulness. They are the organizers of pep rallies and dances. They put out the Year Book. They are *born* Gray Ladies. I can't bully them.)

John Williams was in the school, but except for brief glimpses in the hall I never saw him. Teachers would repeat the things he had said in their other classes. They read from his papers. In the gym the coach described plays he had made, set shots he had taken. Everyone talked about him, and girls made a reference to him a sort of love signal. If it was suggested that he had smiled at one of them, the girl referred to would blush or, what was worse, look aloofly mysterious. (*Then* I could have punished her, *then* I could.) Gradually his name began to appear on all their notebooks, in the margins of their texts. (It annoyed me to remember what *I* had done on the wall.) The big canvas books, with their careful, elaborate J's and W's, took on the appearance of ancient, illuminated fables. It was the unconscious embroidery of love, hope's bright doodle. Even the administration was aware of him. In Assembly the principal announced that John Williams had broken all existing records in the school's charity drives. She had never seen good citizenship like his before, she said.

It's one thing to live with a bully, another to live with a hero.

Everyone's hatred I understand, no one's love; everyone's grievance, no one's content.

I saw Mimmer. Mimmer should have graduated years ago. I saw Mimmer the dummy.

"Mimmer," I said, "you're in his class."

"He's very smart."

"Yes, but is it fair? You work harder. I've seen you study. You spend hours. Nothing comes. He was born knowing. You could have used just a little of what he's got so much of. It's not fair."

120

"He's very clever. It's wonderful," Mimmer says.

Slud is crippled. He wears a shoe with a built-up heel to balance himself.

"Ah, Slud," I say, "I've seen him run."

"He has beaten the horses in the park. It's very beautiful," Slud says.

"He's handsome, isn't he, Clob?" Clob looks contagious, radioactive. He has severe acne. He is ugly *under* his acne.

"He gets the girls," Clob says.

He gets *everything*, I think. But I'm alone in my envy, awash in my lust. It's as if I were a prophet to the deaf. Schnooks, schnooks, I want to scream, dopes and settlers. What good does his smile do you, of what use is his good heart?

The other day I did something stupid. I went to the cafeteria and shoved a boy out of the way and took his place in the line. It was foolish, but their fear is almost all gone and I felt I had to show the flag. The boy only grinned and let me pass. Then someone called my name. It was *him*. I turned to face him. "Push," he said, "you forgot your silver." He handed it to a girl in front of him and she gave it to the boy in front of her and it came to me down the long line.

I plot, I scheme. Snares, I think; tricks and traps. I remember the old days when there were ways to snap fingers, crush toes, ways to pull noses, twist heads and punch arms—the old-timey Flinch Law I used to impose, the gone bully magic of deceit. But nothing works against him, I think. How does he know so much? He is bully-prepared, that one, not to be trusted.

IT IS WORSE and worse.

In the cafeteria he eats with Frank. "You don't want those potatoes," he tells him. "Not the ice cream, Frank. One sandwich, remember. You lost three pounds last week." The fat boy smiles his fat love at him. John Williams puts his arm around him. He seems to squeeze him thin.

He's helping Mimmer to study. He goes over his lessons and teaches him tricks, short cuts. "I want you up there with me on the Honor Roll, Mimmer."

I see him with Slud the cripple. They go to the gym. I watch from the balcony. "Let's develop those arms, my friend." They work out with weights. Slud's muscles grow, they bloom from his bones.

I lean over the rail. I shout down, "He can bend iron bars. Can he pedal a bike? Can he walk on rough ground? Can he climb a hill? Can he wait on a line? Can he dance with a girl? Can he go up a ladder or jump from a chair?"

Beneath me the rapt Slud sits on a bench and raises a weight. He holds it at arm's length, level with his chest. He moves it high, higher. It rises above his shoulders, his throat, his head. He bends back his neck to see what he's done. If the weight should fall now it would crush his throat. I stare down into his smile.

I see Eugene in the halls. I stop him. "Eugene, what's he done for you?" I ask. He smiles—he never did this—and I see his mouth's flood. "High tide," I say with satisfaction.

Williams has introduced Clob to a girl. They have double-dated.

A WEEK AGO John Williams came to my house to see me! I wouldn't let him in.

"Please open the door, Push. I'd like to chat with you. Will you open the door? Push? I think we ought to talk. I think I can help you to be happier."

I was furious. I didn't know what to say to him. "I don't

want to be happier. Go way." It was what little kids used to say to me.

"*Please* let me help you."

"*Please* let me—" I begin to echo. "Please let me alone."

"We ought to be friends, Push."

"No deals." I am choking, I am close to tears. What can I do? *What?* I want to kill him.

I double-lock the door and retreat to my room. He is still out there. I have tried to live my life so that I could keep always the lamb from my door.

He has gone too far this time; and I think sadly, I will have to fight him, I will have to fight him. Push pushed. I think sadly of the pain. Push pushed. I will have to fight him. Not to preserve honor but its opposite. Each time I see him I will have to fight him. And then I think—*of course!* And *I* smile. He has done *me* a favor. I know it at once. If he fights me he fails. He fails if he fights me. *Push pushed pushes!* It's physics! Natural law! I know he'll beat me, but I won't prepare, I won't train, I won't use the tricks I know. It's strength against strength, and my strength is as the strength of ten because my jaw is glass! *He doesn't know everything, not everything he doesn't.* And I think, I could go out now, he's still there, I could hit him in the hall, but I think, No, I want them to see, I want *them* to see!

The next day I am very excited. I look for Williams. He's not in the halls. I miss him in the cafeteria. Afterward I look for him in the schoolyard where I first saw him. (He has them organized now. He teaches them games of Tibet, games of Japan; he gets them to play lost sports of the dead.) He does not disappoint me. He is there in the yard, a circle around him, a ring of the loyal.

I join the ring. I shove in between two kids I have known. They try to change places; they murmur and fret.

Williams sees me and waves. His smile could grow flowers.

"Boys," he says, "boys, make room for Push. Join hands, boys."
They welcome me to the circle. One takes my hand, then another.
I give to each calmly.

I wait. *He doesn't know everything.*

"Boys," he begins, "today we're going to learn a game that the
knights of the lords and kings of old France used to play in another century. Now you may not realize it, boys, because today
when we think of a knight we think, too, of his fine charger, but
the fact is that a horse was a rare animal—not a domestic European animal at all, but Asian. In western Europe, for example,
there was no such thing as a work horse until the eighth century.
Your horse was just too expensive to be put to heavy labor in the
fields. (This explains, incidentally, the prevalence of famine in
western Europe, whereas famine is unrecorded in Asia until the
ninth century, when Euro-Asian horse trading was at its height.) It
wasn't only expensive to purchase a horse, it was expensive to
keep one. A cheap fodder wasn't developed in Europe until the
tenth century. Then, of course, when you consider the terrific risks
that the warrior horse of a knight naturally had to run, you begin
to appreciate how expensive it would have been for the lord—unless he was extremely rich—to provide all his knights with horses.
He'd want to make pretty certain that the knights who got them
knew how to handle a horse. (Only your knights errant—an elite,
crack corps—ever had horses. We don't realize that most knights
were *home* knights; *chevalier chez* they were called.)

"This game, then, was devised to let the lord, or king, see
which of his knights had the skill and strength in his hands to
control a horse. Without moving your feet, you must try to jerk
the one next to you off balance. Each man has two opponents, so
it's very difficult. If a man falls, or if his knee touches the ground,
he's out. The circle is diminished but must close up again immediately. Now, once for practice only—"

124

"Just a minute," I interrupt.

"Yes, Push?"

I leave the circle and walk forward and hit him as hard as I can in the face.

He stumbles backward. The boys groan. He recovers. He rubs his jaw and smiles. I think he is going to let me hit him again. I am prepared for this. He knows what I'm up to and will use his passivity. Either way I win, but I am determined he shall hit me. I am ready to kick him, but as my foot comes up he grabs my ankle and turns it forcefully. I spin in the air. He lets go and I fall heavily on my back. I am surprised at how easy it was, but am content if they understand. I get up and am walking away, but there is an arm on my shoulder. He pulls me around roughly. He hits me.

"*Sic semper tyrannus,*" he exults.

"Where's your other cheek?" I ask, falling backward.

"One cheek for tyrants," he shouts. He pounces on me and raises his fist and I cringe. His anger is terrific. I do not want to be hit again.

"You see? You see?" I scream at the kids, but I have lost the train of my former reasoning. I have in no way beaten him. I can't remember now what I had intended.

He lowers his fist and gets off my chest and they cheer. "Hurrah," they yell. "Hurrah, hurrah." The word seems funny to me.

He offers his hand when I try to rise. It is so difficult to know what to do. Oh God, it is so difficult to know which gesture is the right one. I don't even know this. He knows everything, and I don't even know this. I am a fool on the ground, one hand behind me pushing up, the other not yet extended but itching in the palm where the need is. It is better to give than receive, surely. It is best not to need at all.

Appalled, guessing what I miss, I rise alone.

"Friends?" he asks. He offers to shake.

"Take it, Push." It is Eugene's voice.

"Go ahead, Push." Slud limps forward.

"Push, hatred's so ugly," Clob says, his face shining.

"You'll feel better, Push," Frank, thinner, taller, urges softly.

"Push, don't be foolish," Mimmer says.

I shake my head. I may be wrong. I am probably wrong. All I know at last is what feels good. "Nothing doing," I growl. "No deals." I begin to talk, to spray my hatred at them. They are not an easy target even now. "Only your knights errant—your crack corps—ever have horses. Slud may dance and Clob may kiss but they'll never be good at it. *Push is no service animal.* No. *No.* Can you hear that, Williams? There isn't any magic, but your no is still stronger than your yes, and distrust is where I put my faith." I turn to the boys. "What have you settled for? Only your knights errant ever have horses. *What have you settled for?* Will Mimmer do sums in his head? How do you like your lousy hunger, thin boy? Slud, you can break me but you can't catch me. And Clob will never shave without pain, and ugly, let me tell you, is *still* in the eye of the beholder!"

John Williams mourns for me. He grieves his gamy grief. No one has everything—not even John Williams. He doesn't have *me.* He'll never have me, I think. If my life were only to deny him that, it would almost be enough. I could do his voice now if I wanted. His corruption began when he lost me. "You," I shout, rubbing it in, "*indulger,* dispense me no dispensations. Push the bully hates your heart!"

"Shut him up, somebody," Eugene cries. His saliva spills from his mouth when he speaks.

"Swallow! *Pig, swallow!*"

He rushes toward me.

Suddenly I raise my arms and he stops. I feel a power in me. I

126

A Poetics for Bullies

am Push, Push the bully, God of the Neighborhood, its incarnation of envy and jealousy and need. I vie, strive, emulate, compete, a contender in every event there is. I didn't make myself. I probably can't save myself, but maybe that's the only need I don't have. I taste my lack and that's how I win—by having nothing to lose. It's not good enough! I want and I want and I will die wanting, but first I will have something. This time I will have something. I say it aloud. "This time I will have something." I step toward them. The power makes me dizzy. It is enormous. They feel it. They back away. They crouch in the shadow of my outstretched wings. It isn't deceit this time but the real magic at last, the genuine thing: the cabala of my hate, of my irreconcilableness.

Logic is nothing. Desire is stronger.

I move toward Eugene. *"I will have something,"* I roar.

"Stand back," he shrieks, "I'll spit in your eye."

"I will have something. I will have terror. I will have drought. I bring the dearth. Famine's contagious. Also is thirst. Privation, privation, barrenness, void. I dry up your glands, I poison your well."

He is choking, gasping, chewing furiously. He opens his mouth. It is dry. His throat is parched. There is sand on his tongue.

They moan. They are terrified, but they move up to see. We are thrown together. Slud, Frank, Clob, Mimmer, the others, John Williams, myself. I will not be reconciled, or halve my hate. *It's* what I have, all I can keep. My bully's sour solace. It's enough, I'll make do.

I can't stand them near me. I move against them. I shove them away. I force them off. I press them, thrust them aside. *I push through.*

127

The Beauty
Treatment

STACEY RICHTER

S HE SMILED WHEN SHE SAW ME COMING, THE BITCH, SHE smiled and stuck her fingers in her mouth like she was plucking gum out of her dental work. Then, with a little pout, like a kiss, I saw a line of silver slide toward my face. I swear to God, I thought she'd pried off her braces. I thought she'd worked one of those bands free and was holding it up to show me how proud she was to have broken loose of what we referred to, in our charming teenage banter, as oral bondage. The next thing I know there's blood all over my J. Crew linen fitted blouse, in edelweiss—a very delicate, almost ecru shade of white, ruined now. There's blood all over the tops of my tits where they pushed out my J. Crew edelweiss linen shirt and a loose feeling around my mouth when I screamed. My first thought was Fuck, how embarrassing, then I ran into the girls' room and saw it: a red gash parted my cheek from my left temple to the corner of my lip. A steady stream of blood dripped off my jawline into the sink. One minute later, Cyndy Dashnaw found the razor blade on the concrete floor of the breezeway, right where the Bitch had dropped it.

Elizabeth Beecher and Kirsty Moseley run into the bathroom and go Oh my God, then drag me screaming hysterically, all three of us screaming hysterically, to Ms. B. Meanwhile, the Bitch slides into her Mercedes 450SL, lime green if you can believe that—the A-1 primo daddy-lac of all time—and drives off smoking Kools. I'm in the nurse's office screaming with Ms. B. calmly applying pressure and ordering Mr. Pierce, the principal, to get in gear and haul my ass to the emergency room. This is what you get from watching too much TV, I'm thinking, and believing your workaholic father when he tells you during one of his rare appearances that you're the Princess of the Universe to which none can compare. And then watching teenage girls from Detroit on *Montel,* for God's sake—the *inner city*—froth and brag about hiding razors under their tongues and cutting up some ho because she glanced sideways at the boyfriend: I mean, help me. This is the twentieth century. My father's a doctor. The Bitch's father is a developer who's covered half of Scottsdale with lifestyle condos. We consume the most expensive drugs, cosmetics, and coffee known to man. Tell me: what was she thinking?

I went to the emergency room where the nurse gave me a shot to stop the screaming and eventually my mother came down and the nurse had to give her a pill to stop her from screaming too. Once Mother had sufficiently calmed she paged Dr. Wohl, who'd done her tits, and had him run down and stitch me up with some special Indonesian silk that would make me look, he promised, like a slightly rakish movie star. Afterward, during the healing process, was when my mother really started broadcasting the wonders of Smith College and Mount Holyoke or, if worse came to worse, Mills. Women's colleges were so liberating, she said, waving her tennis elbow around to signify freedom. It was such a blessing, she said, to study without all that nasty competition and distraction from boys. That's when I knew I was in for it. If my mother, who wanted nothing more than for me to marry a Jewish doctor like she had—to duplicate her glorious life and live bored and frustrated in the suburbs and flirt with the other bald, wrinkled, fat, ugly doctors at the tennis club on Wednesday afternoons—if *this* mother was trying to usher me away from the prying eyes of young, male, pre-med students, I knew it was all over for me. I knew my looks were shot.

And another thing—as if I'd relish the thought of living with a bunch of chicks in hormonal flux after a prime example, the Bitch, my best friend, sliced a gill into my cheek for no apparent reason. Why did she do it? they kept asking. What happened between you? Ask her yourself, I replied. Ask the Bitch. But I knew she would never tell. How could she? It was bad enough that they took her down to the police station and put her in a cell without air-conditioning until her daddy showed up with *two* lawyers and escorted her out of there like she was Queen of the May Parade. It was bad enough that she got kicked out of Phoenix Country Day and had to go to Judson—*Judson*, where bad kids from California with parents who didn't want them were sent to board. At Judson, even the high school students had to wear uniforms.

Uniforms, ha ha, it served her right. After The Accident as my mother called it, or The Beauty Treatment, as my father referred to it, I was treated like that guy my verbal teacher at Princeton Review told us about, the prodigal son, but a female version. Did I shop? I shopped till I dropped. I had all the latest stuff from the stores *and* the catalogs. I had six pairs of Doc Martens, a set of sterling flatware (for my dowry), and a Chanel suit. We flew to New York to get the suit. All this accompanied by the message— through word and gesture of Arthur and Judi, doting parents— that no matter what I had, I could not have enough. Not only did

I deserve this, I deserved this and more. I had suffered, and every available style of Swatch would bring relief.

The Bitch, meanwhile, was slogging through her days in a tartan skirt and knee socks. She was locked in a world without jewelry, handbags, or accessories. White shirt, button-down collar—no patterns, no decorations, no excuses. They couldn't even wear a demure white-on-white check. We got the lowdown from the Judson Cactus Wrens at soccer matches—big, bitter girls who charged the ball with clenched teeth and didn't even talk among themselves at half-time. They told us about the uniform requirements with a weird, stiff pride, like they were army recruits. Talk about future sadistic Phys Ed instructors, those Wrens were hard. Every time we had a game against them, half the Country Day girls got convenience periods and skipped out on a nurse's pass.

Even when I really did have my period, I never got a pass. I wasn't afraid of anything anymore, as long as the Bitch wasn't on the Judson soccer team, which she wasn't. I mean, what could happen that would be worse than what I had already gone through? Getting kicked in the shin? A torn earlobe? Being snubbed by Bobby English? Give me a break. I'd seen pain and passed through it. I was a superhero. I was a goddamn Jewish Joan of Arc riding a convertible Volkswagen Rabbit in a lemon yellow Chanel suit. After a few months, so many people had asked me what was wrong with my face that it stopped bothering me and I began to have fun with it. I even managed to work in some of my vocabulary words.

"I was on the back of Johnny Depp's motorcycle. He tried to feel me up, like the callow youth he is, and we wiped out."

And, "I was wearing Lee press-on nails and had the most vehement itch."

Or my personal favorite, "My father did it by accident, whilst

131

beating me zealously," which got horrified looks, especially from medical personnel.

All in all, things weren't so bad. Everyone at school was being really nice, and I was getting extra time to make up my homework. This while the Bitch had to either go straight home from school or go directly to the shrink. Even her stupid, doting mother thought she was crazy for a day or two; I know because her mom and my mom are friends, though I must say the relationship is, oh, a bit *strained*. The Bitch must have put them off with a fake story because if she ever told the truth they'd put her in the nuthouse with her schizophrenic brother where she probably belongs. She must have told them that I had stolen her boyfriend or shafted her on a dope deal. She must have told them something that would have sounded plausible on *Oprah* or *Montel,* something gritty and real—the kind of thing they wanted. When the truth is the Bitch started hating me one day out of the clear blue after we'd been friends for six years, since we were ten years old, because I wanted to go into a store and buy the sheet music for "Brokenhearted," a song made famous by the singer Brandy.

The Bitch hated Brandy. The Bitch was going through what Mr. Nesbit, our school counselor, referred to as a *phase.* The Bitch, natural born white girl, with a special pair of Mormon panties in her dresser and her own frequent flyer miles on her own credit card, wanted to be a homegirl. She had her dishwater hair done up in scrawny braids and got paste-on acrylic nails with a charm on the ring finger that said "Nubian." She wore deep brown lipstick from the Soul Collection at Walgreen's. When her braids got frizzy, which didn't take long, she slicked them back with Afro Sheen.

I, on the other hand, did not wish to be a homegirl. I figured it was my lot to try to survive as a rich, white Jewish girl who could not do the splits and therefore would never be a cheerleader and it would be fruitless to reach for anything else. I had nothing against black people, though it's true I didn't know any. Was it my fault there weren't any black families clamoring to send their children to Phoenix Country Day? Was it my fault my parents trundled me off to a snooty private school? Hell no! I was a pawn, a child, and the worst sin I was guilty of, according to those tablets Moses obtained, was taking off my bra for Bobby English and ridiculing my loving parents whenever I got a chance. Thus, I had no longings to be a homegirl, and it pissed the Bitch off. She said I was spoiled. She said we should be tough. She said black chicks were the coolest and saw the world for what it really was—a jungle; a merciless, dog-eat-dog world.

Which struck me as strange, especially considering the Bitch had the sweetest dog in the world named, perhaps ironically, Blackie. Blackie was getting pretty old but still had some spunk. Right up to the day of the razor incident, the Bitch and I would take her out to the golf course in the evenings and let her bite streams of water shooting from the sprinklers. That dog was great. We both loved Blackie and urged her to go get the sprinklers, to really kill 'em; then she would lie down panting in the wet grass and act like she was never going to get up. The Bitch and I frequently discussed what we would do if tragedy struck and the dog died. Blackie was fourteen and had been the Bitch's companion almost her entire life. The void, the terrible void that would be left behind. We discussed filling it with taxidermy. She would have her stuffed, the Bitch said, in the sprinkler-biting posture, because that was when Blackie was the happiest, and we were the happiest sharing in her joy. She would put it on her credit card.

The loss of Blackie loomed all the more ominous, I suppose, since the Bitch's adoring father basically never came home from work and the Bitch's mother was preoccupied trying to get the schizophrenic brother either into or out of commitment. The brother was smoking a lot of pot and talking to little guys from Canada or Planet Centaur, it just depended. On occasions he'd be struck by the notion that the Bitch was the Bride of Pure Evil and one day he stuck a fork in her thigh. In return, she bit him, took off her shirt and showed him her tits, which mortified him so much he ran around the house for a while, then curled up in the corner. After that, if he was slipping, she'd wear a nursing bra at home so she could flash him when he got out of line.

All the while Blackie padded around after the Bitch, hoping for attention. She was a nuzzler, and even if the Bitch was busy doing something else she would insinuate her nose underneath one of her hands and just freeze there, pretending to be petted. It was touching. At night she would fall into a twitchy sleep beside the Bitch's bed. Every now and then she'd struggle to her feet and go stick her nose under the Bitch's arm or foot for a minute and hold it there. It was like she had to touch the Bitch every so often to make sure she was still okay. That dog was great. In fact, Blackie was probably the one creature she could count on, aside from me, and I could see why her decrepitude made the Bitch nervous.

Around the time Blackie was fading and her brother was going insane, the Bitch started acting even more homegirl and tough and was irked to high hell that I wouldn't get with the program. She was listening to all this gangsta rap in her Mercedes and never taking off her wraparound shades until the teacher made a specific and pointed request. I mean, even our favorite teacher, Mrs. DeMarzo, who talked like Katharine Hepburn, had to tell her to take them off. She had all these garments from the mall in extra large sizes which she referred to as "dope." Of course, do I have to mention the Bitch is not one iota interested in *actually* hanging with the homegirls? I mean, she's not driving down to the South Side and having her Alpine stereo gouged from her dashboard while she rounds up some sistahs to talk jive with, or whatever. She is hanging with me and the other fair students of Phoenix Country Day School as always, but she's acting like she's too cool for us, like she's doing us a favor.

She was annoying, but I never considered dumping her. With me, in private, she wasn't so bad. I mean, the Bitch lived right down the street and we'd been best friends since fourth grade, when being best friends really meant something. I'd only seen one miracle in my sixteen years of life and the Bitch had been its agent. The miracle wasn't much, but it was enough to make me believe that there was some kind of power floating around in the universe and that the Bitch had a little influence with it. I figured that if I stuck close to her, my life would periodically be visited by blessings and magic, like in fairy tales. What happened was this: we were eleven years old, sitting in my room on top of the rainbow Marimekko print comforter, beneath the Olympische Spiele München posters, talking animatedly and intimately about whatever. Suddenly, the Bitch gasped and pointed to the candy-colored Venetian glass chandelier my mother brought back on the trip to Europe she took without my father. A beat of time passed. And then the chandelier winked out.

Actually, the power had gone out in the whole neighborhood. If there'd been a sound or a pulse in the light, I hadn't noticed it, and when I asked the Bitch why she'd pointed at the chandelier, she said, "Because I knew something was going to happen." Oh my God, was I a bored little girl. Did I ever want to hitch my star to someone who knew something was going to happen.

So I overlooked her flaws, her erratic behavior, her insistence I smoke Kools and endure the strains of gangsta rappers calling me a bee-atch because at least around her, things were interest-

135

ing. I tried to make light of her attitude, figuring it would pass, but I wasn't sacrificing anything of myself, understand? I mean, I wanted that Brandy sheet music. I didn't care that I couldn't play the piano or any other musical instrument. That wasn't the point. I wanted "Brokenhearted" because it had this great picture of Brandy, a beautiful girl, on the cover and I thought it was cool. Me, *I* thought it was cool. Well, the Bitch was just not having any of this. For one thing, Brandy's black, which apparently is her territory and she's the big fucking expert. For another thing, she says Brandy is "an ugly little crossover wimp" and not a real homegirl and I'm an asshole if I like her. I mean, so what? So, I like Brandy. So shoot me. So pitch a fit, which she did, peeling out in her 450SL and leaving me in the parking lot of a C-mall. So slice my face with a fucking razor blade.

Which she did the next time I saw her and I haven't seen her since, except for that one time at her shrink's office. This was after my mother had gotten all high and mighty because I'd only scored 590 on the quantitative part of the SAT, since math was right after lunch and frequently, I attended stoned. Of course, Judi couldn't give a shit if I did math or not; she hires an accountant to balance her checkbook, but since my youthful beauty was trampled she'd reasoned that I should fall back on my next best asset—the mind. Oh those smart girls! Do men ever love those clever girls! She said it over and over, with a fake, bright smile, when she thought I wasn't paying close attention.

I wasn't half as worried about my sullied good looks as she was. Doctor Wohl said we could smooth out the lumps with dermabrasion, plus he wasn't entirely wrong about the rakish charm. I'd begun wearing black Anna Sui numbers and hanging out at The Coffee Plantation in Biltmore Fashion Square, where the neo-beatnik kids considered me sort of a god. I rarely spoke and they were under the impression I had a boyfriend in France. I'd also realized the scar sort of went with the curves of my face, it cupped my cheekbone—I mean, if you're going to have a major facial scar, this was the one to have. One girl with piercings all over her nose came up to me and asked where I had it done.

It wasn't like I looked normal, but I was learning to adjust. I was feeling okay about myself—I rented *The Big Heat*, where the heroine gets coffee flung in her face, and I was beginning to feel like being maimed was kind of romantic. I mean, I got noticed, and I looked just fine from the right side. Still, Judi was putting all bets on the intellect and had dragged Arthur into her camp. Together they forced me to take a Princeton Review class to get my test scores up. I hated it all except vocabulary: *Perfidy:* betrayal, the deliberate breaking of trust. *Refractory:* resisting treatment, unmanageable. My verbal was 780. 780—that's almost perfect! I couldn't believe they were making me. It had been years since they'd forced me to do anything. It was cutting into my spare time, and it wasn't only me who suffered: I knew the neo-beatniks would be lost without their tragic center. Finally I went on strike and refused to eat in the dining room. I just took a plate, retired to my room, locked the door, and put on my headphones. A couple days of this, I thought, and they'll go into serious parenting withdrawal.

The second day Mom caved and weaseled her way in. She said I could quit the class if I'd do something for her. She said she'd talked to the Bitch's mother, and she'd said her therapist had recommended I go to one of the Bitch's sessions. She "wasn't happy," Judi said; she was "having trouble adjusting." This was like one of those moments when my mother gets all doe-eyed and yearns to save the environment, but a second later, it's *snap!* time for a manicure. But she was dead serious, and I knew this was my chance to get out of that fucking class. Even so, I wouldn't have done it. I wasn't scared of anything then except the

Bitch. I thought I saw her a million times, in the mall or the cineplex; I saw her big, smiling head gliding through the crowd, and then a swish of silver. At the last minute it was never her—the big head always morphed into some alternate head—but whether I created it or not, I felt like I was being stalked. Then I had these dreams where the Bitch and I were just hanging out, dancing to Chaka Khan, just hanging out like before when everything was normal—and those really gave me the creeps. I did not want to see her. No Bitch for me.

But then I changed my mind. Young and foolish I am. Also, I loved the idea of going to see the Bitch's shrink. I pictured a distinguished man with gray at his temples gasping at the sight of my scar when I walked in the room. Then, he would look at me with infinite compassion. I would take a seat on the leather lounger. My outfit is DKNY. My shoes are Kenneth Cole. The Bitch would be sitting in a straight-backed chair, her hair in cornrows. The Doctor would shake his head reproachfully.

"I never dreamed the wound was so dramatic," he says.

The Bitch would blush. I notice her body racked by waves of contrition. In her arms is an album by Brandy. A CD would be more practical but I like the way an album fills up her arms.

"This is for you," she'd say. "I've learned that it's okay for us to like different things. I celebrate your appreciation of Brandy."

I thank her. The Doctor looks on approvingly. I can tell by his glance that he thinks I'm a brave and noble girl. A few minutes later I leave. The Bitch is weeping softly. I feel a light, crisp sense of forgiveness. The Doctor has offered me free therapy, if I should ever want to share my burdens.

Well I'm here to tell you, buddy, it wasn't like that at all. First, there's no lounger, and the doctor is a streaked blond chick about my mother's age. I arrive late and she shows me to the office where the Bitch is already sitting on a swivel chair.

She barely looks up when I enter the room. My dress is DKNY. The Bitch is dressed like white trash in jeans and a T-shirt of normal proportions. She looks like hell. I mean, *I* look better than she does. I was always prettier than she was but she used to seem intriguing. Before, if she was in a room, you felt her presence immediately. The girl knew how to occupy space. Something came out of her—a lot of pesky teen rage but at times, something nicer. She had that glow, at least to me; she had a sense of excitement and wonder. But in the office she seems dulled, and the truth is, right away I feel sorry for the Bitch.

The Shrink looks like she came straight out of a Smith alumnae magazine—Ann Taylor suit, minimal makeup, low-heeled leather shoes. The picture of emotional efficiency. Her office, too, is a symphony in earth tones. She checks me and the Bitch out, then says something like, "Katie's been grappling with the conflict that occurred between the two of you, and now she needs to know how you feel about it."

She does not blink twice at my scar. She does not look at me with infinite compassion. I realize whose turf I'm on. She's an employee, and the Bitch's father writes the paychecks.

"I feel okay," I say. I keep trying not to look at the Bitch, but she's unavoidable. After hallucinating her face a million times, it's unnerving how unfamiliar she seems. She's gained weight, but it seems like she's not really there. There's something inert and lumpen about her. No rage, no nail charms. Nothing extreme. She's just examining her shoes—for God's sake—clogs.

"Just okay? Because Katie and I have been discussing the impact of the cutting, and for her it's really been quite profound."

The Bitch does not say anything. The Bitch is not looking at me. The Bitch is sitting with her head down and her mouth closed like the first day she came to school with braces. Then I realize something. "She's not even looking at it," I say. "She won't even check out the scar!"

I look at the Shrink like she's some kind of referee. She, apparently, is having none of that, and sits quite calmly glancing at the Bitch and me as though we were a light piece of entertainment intended to gaily pass the time. This goes on for a while. The Bitch looks at her clogs and a brown spot on the carpet. I look at the Bitch for as long as I can, then start reading the spines of the Shrink's books. *Personality Disorders*—ha, that should come in handy. I can hear the Bitch breathing, which is odd, because in all the years we hung out together I never noticed her breathing. It's like she's alive in some weird, biological way—the way those pithed frogs were alive in science class. Alive but damaged.

Finally, the Bitch clears her throat. She raises her head until her eyes hit the scar. She starts to wince, then freezes. I can tell she's trying to control her expression, but all the color drains out of her face in a smooth, descending line, like she's been pumped full of pink fluid and someone has pulled the plug.

That was when I knew for sure that I looked like shit, absolutely and for certain. I'd been fooling myself, believing I looked dashing and rascally, but in the shock on my best friend's face I saw the truth. I was ruined.

The Bitch started to cry. I started to cry. The Shrink tried to glance calmly at us as if we were a light piece of entertainment but you could sense the strain. I pulled a Kool out of my bag and lit it. The Shrink finally cracked and shot me a dirty look but I was beyond caring. I realized, after all I'd been through, that I still smoked Kools, just like the Bitch always had, like she'd encouraged me to, and the thought of that made me cry even harder. Something switched then and I wasn't crying about my face anymore. I was crying because the Bitch was the Bitch, and the friend I'd had since I was a kid, the friend who knew for certain something was going to happen to us, something magical and vivid, was lost forever. She was lost to us both. The wonder had been extinguished.

Eventually I got ahold of myself and squashed the Kool out in a piece of damp Kleenex. The Bitch had slumped over in her swivel chair and I didn't even want to look at her. My thoughts: fuck, shit, etc. It was weird. I began to feel practically like she was my friend again, us having had a simultaneous cry. I did not want that. I wanted her to stay the Bitch.

"Oh God," she says, unprompted by the Shrink.

I notice her braces are off. She's not looking at me. It's too much for her.

"Fuck," she says, to a spot on the carpet, "I'm really sorry."

Okay: I'm a girl who's going to Smith College. I'm going to Smith and then I'm going to law school to become a criminal lawyer who champions the rights of the victimized and oppressed. I'm going to have two cars, a Volvo for transportation and a Jag for thrills. I'll cut a feline figure in my Agnès B. clothes and I'll have a drawerful of jewels. Maybe I'll even get married to some average-looking dork, but I will never be pretty and I will never be loved by the handsome men who roam this earth. My dear mother told me long ago that youth and beauty will get you everything. Well, mine's fucked up and now I'll never have Everything. No magic, no wonder, no fairy tales.

My plan was to walk out of there with a light, crisp sense of forgiveness, but help me. I sat in a sea of beige and looked at the Bitch in her clogs, fat, miserable, and afraid, and I knew: if I really forgave her, something vast and infinite would open up inside me, some place wide and blue, and I couldn't enter such a place. It would be like some kind of health spa—where you go in naked, without any things. God, would I ever be lost in a place like that.

So I said, Oh Katie, that's okay, babe! No problema! I forgive you! with a hint of fake innocence in my voice—a little dose of manufactured niceness. She turned white again and the Shrink started urging me to get in touch with my feelings but you know, I had my finger right on them.

Later, when I got home, I went into the bathroom and stared at myself in the mirror for a while. It was the same mirror Katie and I used to stare at in the pitch black while chanting "Bloody Mary, Bloody Mary" over and over until we hallucinated the beheaded head of Mary Queen of Scots emerging in reflection, dripping like a porterhouse steak. She fought her way up from the land of the dead to punish us for tempting the dark with the sight of her terrible wound. Mary with her disgusting necklace of blood—she was a perfidious one! I didn't look anything like her. In fact, I had a certain glow about me. I was so radiant I looked almost pretty. From the right side, I actually was pretty.

Spending the Night with the Poor

JIM SHEPARD

I WAS AT THE PLATTSBURGH DANCE STUDIO FOR LIKE THIRTY seconds before I realized it was a rip-off. I even went back outside like I'd dropped a mitten or something, but my mother was already gone. I could see her taillights two stoplights down. She was the only Isuzu in a pack of pickups with gun racks.

The facilities were terrible. It was in a warehouse. The wooden floor ran out at one point and whoever was on that side was supposed to dance on cement. I was like, No thank you, and wherever they wanted to arrange me, I made sure I ended up back on the good side.

The teacher was clearly unqualified. It was supposed to be a musical theater course, six weeks, and it turned out she hadn't been in anything. "She probably just owns the records," Crystal whispered while we stood there freezing. There was no heat. Ms. Adams—she stressed the "Ms."—gave us her Opening Day

speech. It had to do with getting to Broadway one step at a time.
I was embarrassed for her. When she finished, she looked disappointed that we didn't all cheer and carry her around the room on
our shoulders. We just stood there warming our hands in our
armpits.

She asked if there were questions. "Do we have any *heat?*" I
asked, and Crystal gave me an elbow and I gave her one back.
She loved it.

At the back of the room a *Threepenny Opera* poster was taped
to a sawhorse. Pathetic.

"Is that a *Cats* sweatshirt?" I asked Ms. Adams. The way she
said it was, you could see she didn't get it.

"You're terrible," Crystal said.

Crystal was the reason I stayed at all. Nobody asked, but I
told my mother that night that it was horrible, and told her why.
She said what she always said—Well, Give It a Little Time. I
didn't argue. Not because I thought it would get better, but because of Crystal, and because what else did I have to do? Sit
around staring at my brother?

Crystal was so poor. I knew most of the kids would be pretty
low class, but it was either this or voice lessons and I really
wanted to do this. Crystal was poor like in the movies. She carried her stuff in a plastic bag. She brought a little Tupperware
thing of Coke instead of buying them from the machine. She was
clueless about her hair; she had it up with a butterfly clip, like
Pebbles. She wore blue eye shadow. And she was pretty anyway.
She had a good smile and a mouth like Courtney Love's.

She *walked* to the school, every day. We met twice a week,
after regular school: Mondays and Fridays. It was like a mile and
a half. Her parents had one car and her dad needed it. She had
two pairs of socks total, one gray ragg, one pair of guy's sweat
socks with the stripes across the top. Her coat she got from a

place called the Women's Exchange. Her older brother was retarded.

"So's mine," I told her.

He isn't but he might as well be.

She said her father worked in an office. I didn't say anything.

That Friday we were helping each other stretch and she said, "So are you a little rich or way rich?" I told her my family wasn't exactly going bankrupt. It was a good way to put it. I told her what my dad did. I told her where we lived.

"Good for you," she said, like she meant it.

I told her I was going to keep ragging on her socks until she got new ones.

"Oh, *that's* funny," she said, meaning that they were ragg socks.

But that next Monday she had different ones, and we didn't say anything about it. When we were getting ready to go I told her I was going to help her.

"Oh, yeah?" she said, yawning. She yawned so wide her eyes teared up. "How?"

I told her I'd been thinking about it all Sunday night.

"That's really great," she said. You could see she thought I was going to give her a Mounds bar or something.

I told her that since I was a foot taller I had a lot of clothes I'd outgrown or I wasn't using. Nothing was totally cheesy or worn out. Like this forest-green top I completely loved but wouldn't fit me anymore. Or this wool skirt that was Catholic school-looking but okay.

"Please," she said, and we rolled our eyes and laughed.

There was more stuff, too. I named other things and even threw in some things I did want. I always do stuff like that and afterwards regret it.

We were standing around the lobby of the building. It was

145

cold from everyone coming and going, but at least it was out of the wind. I was wearing a man's wool overcoat I really loved and a fur-lined winter cap my mom called smart, but so what? When you got through all of that it was still just me.

We were just standing around waiting, looking at different things.

"Listen," she said. "Doesn't your mother want you to hang on to your stuff, or give it to a relative?"

"My mother doesn't care," I said. That wasn't really true. But I figured that later, when Crystal found out, she'd be even more grateful.

I didn't bring her anything on Friday, though. I had the stuff ready and I just left it in my room. While my mom drove me there, I thought, Why couldn't you just *bring* it?

"You are so stupid," I thought. I realized I'd said it out loud.

My mother turned to me. "What?" she said.

I was embarrassed. I was sitting there turning colors, probably.

"Why are you stupid?" she said.

"How do you know I wasn't talking about you?" I said.

She smiled. "The way you said it," she said.

I had no answer for that.

"Why are you stupid?" she asked again.

"Why do you think?" I finally said.

"Don't snap at me," she said. "All right? I don't need it."

When we got there I got out of the car and slammed the door. I saw her face when she drove off and I thought this was what always happened; I made everyone feel bad for no reason.

Crystal was waiting for me on the good end of the dance floor. She'd saved a space by spreading her stuff out. I was still mad. She saw how I looked, so she was all ears with Ms. Adams. She didn't say anything and neither did I.

We ended early because Ms. Adams had a dentist's appointment. She told us about the periodontal work she needed to have done like we wanted to hear. Then she left. I felt like I'd just gotten there. Everyone else called their rides. My mother, of course, was still out. She hadn't even gotten home yet. I left a message on the machine. My brother was probably right there and didn't bother to pick up.

Crystal said she'd wait with me. Which was nice of her, though all she had to look forward to was a walk home anyway. I told her we'd give her a ride when my mom came.

We talked about how much we hated the class. The ad said we would do Sondheim and stuff. So far we'd been working through the chorus of "Some Enchanted Evening." According to Ms. Bad Gums, that was so we could get to know our voices.

"I already know my voice," Crystal always said, like she didn't want to know it any better.

She shared some Hershey's Kisses, which looked pretty old. The foil was faded. She told me she liked my Danskin. I told her she had great calves. She said she worked out every night, watching TV. The conversation kind of hung there.

"Have you thought about doing something with your hair?" I asked.

"Have you thought about doing something with your mouth?" she said back, meaning I was a wiseass, which was what my mother and brother always said. "You bitch," I said, and she said, "It takes one to know one," which was true.

She showed me how to look back behind the vending machines where the money rolled and people couldn't get to it. We found fifty cents and got a Reese's. I had money but I hung on to it.

When my mother finally drove up it was totally dark. Two of the big lights were out in front of the building. She beeped the horn and we ran from the lobby to the car.

"Where were you?" I said, and she gave me one of her I'm-not-going-to-dignify-that-with-a-response looks.

"Who's this?" she said.

"Crystal," I said.

"*Crystal?*" my mother said. She let it go at that.

"Can you take me to my dad's office instead?" Crystal asked.

"Sure," I said.

She gave my mother directions. She made zero small talk. I couldn't see her face.

We dropped her off. The office was a factory that made brake linings. I waved through the window. My mother pulled back into traffic.

"It's not such a horrible name," I said. I was sulking.

"It's a pretty horrible name," my mother said. "But it's only a name."

The next day I got the pile of clothes back together. It ended up filling a lawn bag. My mom came upstairs and asked what I was doing.

I told her. She sat on the bed. She watched for a little while. She said things like, "You want to get rid of *that?*"

"Is your friend going to take this the right way?" she said. "Did you tell her you were going to do this?"

I told her yes. She smiled. This was another one of her daughter's stupid ideas.

"Well, don't go crazy," she finally said. She got up and went downstairs.

Immediately my brother wandered into my room. I'm supposed to have privacy but it's like a train station.

"Get out of here," I said. "I don't go in your room."

"What do you want from me?" he said. "Go in my room."

I didn't let him see what was in the bag.

He had my stuffed Snoopy from when I was little by the ears

148

and he was pounding its forehead on the headboard. "Whaddaya doing?" he said. "Giving your clothes to the less fortunate?"

"None of your business," I said. Then I said, "Like you'd ever do anything for anybody."

"Why don't you do a telethon?" he said.

I got a book off my shelf and read until he left.

I complained about him to my mother and she reminded me he was going through a tough time. He had seven things he went out for his first year in high school and didn't get into any.

On Monday I told Crystal about him. I said, "Maybe we're both losers," meaning him and me.

"I doubt it," she said.

I'd left the bags of clothes home again. "I was going to bring the clothes this time," I finally said when we were getting ready to go.

"I should give *you* something," Crystal said.

"Oh, you don't have to do that," I said. What was she going to give me? Something she whittled?

She asked if I wanted to stay over Friday night.

"Sure," I said.

"Give me your number," she said, and I gave her a number.

I have like three friends, and they never call. They had to be practically dragged to my birthday party.

It was okay with my mother. "I am going to have a drink," she said, when I asked her what she thought. I told her it was Crystal, the girl she met. "I assumed," she said.

Later we ran it by my father, up in his study. Somebody on his team had totally screwed up a deposition, so he had to make another whole trip to someplace like Iowa. He asked who Crystal was. He said it was fine with him. "Spending the night with the poor," he said, and he gave me a hug.

"Very nice," my mother said to herself as we came back downstairs.

That Friday I loaded the lawn bag into the trunk. My mother would pick us up after the lessons and take us to Crystal's, and then pick me up Saturday afternoon after some errands.

Crystal was nervous in class. She was fidgety afterwards, waiting for my mother. I was flattered.

My mother was right on time, which I told Crystal wouldn't happen in a million years. "How are you, Mrs. Gerwig?" she said when she got in the car.

"I'm fine, Crystal," my mom said. "How about you?"

Crystal said she was fine, too.

"It's nice of your parents to invite Lynn over," my mother told her once we pulled onto the highway.

"I so love the twilight this time of year, don't you?" Crystal said back. I almost lost it.

We got off at the Riverside exit. I didn't know anyone lived down there, poor or not. All you could see from the highway was oil tanks.

Crystal gave directions while my mom turtled along like the whole thing was a trap. I kept hoping the houses wouldn't get any worse.

"Mom, the gas pedal. On the right," I said.

My mother just drove.

We were all quiet.

"Right here," Crystal said.

I peeped out of my window. What was I scared of? There weren't going to be enough cable channels?

On the way there I'd told myself that there wouldn't be anything so terrible about the house. I was wrong. It was a long white trailer. It had a yellow stripe. There were empty plastic buckets around the front porch. Something rusty was half buried in the yard. My mother pulled up so even the car wasn't too close to the curb. Her face was fine.

When she got out of the car Crystal's dad came out of the house. He looked like any other dad. He had on a Nirvana T-shirt. While they said hello I got the keys from my mom's hand and opened the trunk. I pulled out the bag and lugged it to the front door.

Her dad's name was Tom.

"Where you goin' with that?" her dad said.

"Lynn's givin' me some clothes," Crystal said. "The ones that don't fit her anymore."

My mother was wincing. Like Crystal and her father were blind.

I was still at the front door of the trailer. I could see people inside.

"It's just a lot of weird stuff, Dad," Crystal said.

"Hey, I don't care," Crystal's dad said. "If it's all right with Lynn's mother here," he said.

"It's fine with me," my mother said. After a second she crossed the yard to give me a hug. She looked at me. "You behave yourself," she said. She got back in the car and drove off.

"So what're we havin' for dinner?" Crystal's dad said.

"We should have hot dogs," Crystal said.

We all went in the house.

Her mother and her retarded brother were in the living room with the shades down, watching TV. I thought it was weird that her mother hadn't come out.

"Nice to meet you," I told them.

They were both fat, but not hugely fat. The brother had black hair combed sideways and his eyes were half closed. I couldn't tell if that was part of the way he was retarded or if he was just sleepy. His mother had next to her the biggest ashtray on earth. It was wider than the lamp table it was on.

Crystal said I should get the bag from the porch. She told

them while I went to get it that I'd given her this huge bag of clothes. They were looking at me when I came back in.

"Merry Christmas!" I said, because I couldn't think of anything else. I put it on the rug in front of the TV.

The house smelled. There were dirty coffee cups on the windowsill. I had my hands flat against my thighs.

Her father poked in from the kitchen and said, "What's in the bag?" but then didn't wait to find out. He called he was starting dinner.

Her brother dug around in the bag. Her mother watched. I still didn't know his name. I was still standing by the front door. Crystal felt bad at the way things were going but I couldn't do anything to help her feel better.

"So what's in there?" she said, like everything was okay. It was horrible.

Her brother pulled out stuff I didn't even remember throwing in. Some things I could still wear, and a blue velvet dress.

"Oh," her mother said, when her brother held up the dress.

A *Penthouse* magazine was lying around in plain sight. The room was cold and everyone was bundled up. You could smell sweat. The kitchen was on one side and they had framed pictures of Crystal and her brother around the door leading to the other rooms. It was a longer trailer than it looked.

The kitchen was clean. We ate in there, watching the TV on the counter. I looked every so often at the floors and the ceiling, and Crystal caught me at it.

We had pound cake for dessert. Her father and brother got into a fight about how much her brother could have.

Afterwards we hung out in Crystal's room. It was across from her mom and dad's. Her brother was going to sleep on the sofa. I thanked her parents for the very nice dinner, even though I hadn't seen her mother do anything. They said we should get ready for bed soon.

That was fine with me. It was about 7:30.

Her half of the room was neat. She had a throw rug, and her bed was made, with some books arranged big to small on a bookshelf in the headboard. Her brother's side was filthy. You could see that she'd tried to pick up. There were loose Oreos in some slippers under the dresser.

"You can sleep on my bed," Crystal said.

A poster of a muscle car flapped out from the ceiling over her brother's bed, like a sail. I told her I could sleep over there, but she said no.

I was still standing in the middle of the room. I didn't want to be there, and she knew it.

"Do you want to see some of my books, or play a game?" she said. "I got Clue."

"Okay," I said.

She didn't move. She sat on her brother's bed. I sat on hers. I smelled soap.

"Should we go to bed?" I finally said. She shrugged, looking down at my feet.

We brushed our teeth and got into our nightgowns. Even the water tasted weird. I was glad I brought my own towel. We called goodnight down the hall and got into bed. Then she had to get up to turn off the light. She got into bed again. The parking garage across the street lit up the whole room.

"Are you having an okay time?" she said, from her brother's bed.

"Yeah," I said. She shifted around on her back. They were watching some kind of travelogue in the living room and we both lay there, listening to it. I think she felt so bad she couldn't even ask them to turn it down.

"My cousin Katie has so much money," she said.

"Did you hear me?" she said.

"What am I supposed to say?" I said.

She sighed. It was like a bubble filling the house, pressing on my ears. I hated it there.

"I don't know why I say some things," she said. She started to cry.

"Are you crying?" I said. "What are you crying for?"

It just made her cry to herself. I hadn't asked very nicely.

"Why are you crying?" I said.

"Oh," she said, like she was going to answer, but she didn't.

We both lay there. I made a disgusted noise. I breathed in her smell on the pillow. She was quiet after that. The travelogue went off. I wondered if her brother had to stay up until her parents went to bed.

It was so bright in the room I could read my watch. When it was 11:30 I said, "I should go."

"What do you want from me?" she said, exactly the way my brother does.

I got up and got dressed without turning on the light. "I should use the phone," I said. She was still on her back.

I went out into the hall. The house was dark. The phone was in the kitchen. My mother answered on the second ring. I kept my voice down. I was worried she was going to make me explain, but she didn't. She said, "Are you all right?" Then she said my father would come.

It would take about a half hour. I had to wait. I hung up and went back into the bedroom and shut the door. "My father's coming," I said.

"Fine," Crystal said. She was sitting up. "You want the light on?"

"No," I said.

154

We sat there. I thought about the way I'd thought of her the night before. The night before I'd thought she needed beauty in her life.

"Take your clothes with you when you go," she said.

"This is totally me. I'm just being weird," I said.

I was going to quit the classes the next day by phone. If she tried to call me she'd find out the number I'd given her was fake. Like we said when a total dork asked for our number: I gave him my faux number. And she'd think I couldn't deal with her being so poor. She wouldn't realize it was everything else I couldn't deal with. I knew I deserved exactly what I got, all the rest of my life. And when I was stuck with her in her bedroom I didn't want her to deserve any more, either. But before that, for a little while, I wanted good things for her; I wanted to make her life a little better. I wanted to make her think, That Lynn—that Lynn's a nice girl. And wasn't that worth something?

Alcatraz

ALICIA ERIAN

M Y MOTHER PROMISED TO TAKE ME SHOPPING AFTER
the car was fixed, so that was how I found myself sitting next to her at the mechanic's that morning, reading over her shoulder as she wrote a letter to my Aunt Mitzy
saying I was still fat. "Hey, you can't write that!" I said, pointing to
the sentence about me with an orange fingertip. We were sitting
in the small office beside the garage, where people popped in to
pay for gas or buy themselves a snack for the road. I had just
eaten two bags of Cheetos myself and was considering a third
when I saw my name in my mother's fine hand.

"Oh," my mother said, acting as if she hadn't just written it.
"You're right, Roz." She began crossing it out and her face turned
red. She was pretty embarrassed, which shocked me, since I figured she would turn the tables on me and say something like
"Well! You shouldn't have been reading a private letter over my
shoulder!" Even though I knew she would go home and finish it

later (rewriting the crossed-out part and telling Aunt Mitzy how touchy I had gotten about it), I felt kind of powerful. When we went clothes shopping that afternoon, I hardly noticed I was the only thirteen-year-old in the misses department flipping through the size sixteen rack.

We got home before dinner, so I put on my snow clothes and crossed Hermitage Road, where they were putting up a new development—one much nicer than ours. Several foundations had already been dug and were now half-filled with snow, while a forklift sat abandoned in an empty lot. There were cement blocks piled up all over the place, metal barrels filled with construction trash, and a short row of Porta Pottis. The door to one was open and inside I found a picture of a half-naked woman in a skimpy Santa Claus outfit taped to the wall. I took it down and put it in my pocket for Jennings, who was at his grandmother's for the weekend.

It was hard work running around in the snow. Each time I hopped down into one of the foundations, it took me forever to pull myself back out again. I saw this as a challenge—another way to burn more calories, which was why I was out there in the first place. When I got home and the scale said I had only lost a pound, I thought it should have been more.

Mom and I ate spaghetti with Ragú for dinner. We usually made that or Old El Paso tacos, or else we went to McDonald's. We had eaten more natural foods when Jonquil was still living with us since she liked to cook, but now that she was gone Mom said it was crazy to go to that kind of trouble for just two people. Mom said it was on Jonquil's head that I had gotten so damn fat, and she hoped my sister could live with that.

After dinner Mom left to spend the night with her beau, a retired army sergeant who felt that any of the four branches of the military would serve to set Jonquil straight. I had a job babysitting for the two Hermann boys. We made a deal that I would let them stay up as late as they wanted as long as they didn't tell on me for smoking their parents' cigarette butts. Once the boys had fallen asleep in front of the TV, I carried them upstairs, put them to bed, and called my sister.

My mother had kicked her out the year before for becoming unruly. Jonquil, who had been seventeen at the time, moved in with her boyfriend, Vic, and got pregnant. She and Vic made plans to marry but then Jonquil had a miscarriage and they called the wedding off. The family was relieved, which so infuriated Jonquil (since she had suffered such pain), that she put the wedding back on again. Her bridal gown was her senior prom dress, while Vic, who was reedy and slack-jawed, borrowed one of his father's suits. I cried like a fool at the ceremony because now I knew there was no chance in hell Jonquil was ever coming back to us. Aunt Mitzy and my mother told me not to worry—that Vic was an inbred and it wouldn't last—and for once I was glad about how nasty they got when they were together.

Jonquil knew everything about sex and she taught it to me. She said she didn't want me to end up marrying a screwball like Vic just to prove a point, like she had. She said this right in front of him, on the weekends when I went to stay with them in their apartment, and he just laughed like she was telling a joke. He kissed her, too, and I watched as both their mouths opened and their tongues came out, all rude and wet. I could watch them kiss for hours and, in fact, sometimes that was what ended up happening.

But Jonquil wasn't kidding, and what I knew that Vic didn't was that she was going to leave him as soon as she saved up enough money. He was pursuing an art degree at a community college, which Jonquil described as "double jeopardy." Meanwhile, she supported both of them on her receptionist's salary from Dr. Flay, the TV hypnotist. He didn't perform on TV but he ran a lot of ads describing how he could stop people from smoking, overeating, or a combination of the two. He was a blond, handsome man, and sometimes, my sister told me, spoke to his clients in a made-up foreign accent. As an employee, Jonquil was entitled to a 50 percent discount on his services, and since he liked her so much (feeling her natural thinness made him look like a success), he extended that privilege to her family and friends. I had saved up some babysitting money, so when I called Jonquil that night from the Hermanns' house, it was to ask her to make me an appointment.

"What for?" she said.

"Because," I said. "Mom wrote and told Aunt Mitzy I was fat."

Jonquil made a light blowing sound.

"Are you smoking again?" I asked her.

"Uh-huh."

"But I thought Dr. Flay cured you."

"He did," Jonquil said. "I just forgot to say the key word before I went to the grocery store and it screwed me up. I bought a pack."

"Oh."

"Anyway," Jonquil said, "when I was your age, Mom wrote and told Aunt Mitzy I was a tramp, so don't worry about it."

"Why?"

"Huh?"

"Why did she say you were a tramp?"

"Don't be such a dumb ass, Roz."

"Sorry," I said. I blew smoke from one of Mrs. Hermann's cigarette butts. I could tell it was hers from the purple lipstick on the filter tip.

"What's that noise?" Jonquil asked me.

"Nothing. I was just sighing."

Eventually she gave in and made me an appointment for that week. I sat in a dentist's chair while Dr. Flay indeed spoke softly in an accent that reminded me of Count Dracula. He dimmed the lights and projected a small red dot on the white wall in front of me, which I was to focus on intently. Meanwhile, Dr. Flay stood behind me, massaging my temples and telling me I was getting sleepy, even though I wasn't. I felt bad for him that he was doing such a terrible job, so I played along, making my eyelids bob up and down when he came around front to see how I was doing. "*Thaht's eet,*" he said. "*Thaht's eet.*"

With my eyes now closed, Dr. Flay spoke frankly to me about the state of my body, saying I had three rolls of fat on my stomach, and wouldn't it be nicer to have just one? He said I had a pretty face, like my sister's, but that a double chin on a seventh grader was nothing short of heinous. He noted that my thighs squashed together so tightly as to be prohibitive, which I didn't understand, and then asked me point-blank how I thought I would ever get a boyfriend. I wanted to bring up Jennings then, but I was supposed to be hypnotized and so kept my mouth shut. It alarmed me somewhat that Dr. Flay's voice was getting closer and closer, so I took a quick peek. He stood directly in front of me with his hand on his groin. I shut my eyes immediately but it was too late; he had seen me. He dropped his accent, gave me my key word (which would remind me of our session and instantly decrease my appetite), and snapped his fingers. I assumed this meant I could open my eyes, and I did. Dr. Flay wished me luck and gave me a bill for fifty dollars, to be paid in cash to my sister.

On the way home Jonquil and I stopped at a Wendy's drive-thru. I said *hiccup* and she said *lizard*, and we neither overate nor smoked. "Do you think I'll really get thin?" I asked her as we sat in the parking lot, eating our baked potatoes. Jonquil didn't want to eat in the dining room because it was nonsmoking and if her key word hadn't worked, she would have been screwed.

A section of her long brown hair dipped into her potato, and she tucked it behind her ear, sucking the nonfat sour cream from the ends. "It's hard to say," she said. "The data are inconclusive."

Jonquil dropped me off at the end of my driveway, then spun her tires on the ice for a couple of seconds, trying to peel out. When I got inside, my mother said my sister had no manners, coming and going like that without so much as a hello, and demanded I agree with her on this point. I did so reluctantly, after which she further demanded my key word. I lied and said it was *Sputnik*, which we had just learned about that day in social studies. She had taco meat for Old El Paso simmering on the stove and asked me suspiciously if I was hungry. I said no and she beamed. It was nice, being able to make her happy for once, so I didn't bother mentioning Wendy's.

I finished my homework quickly, then ran across the street to see Jennings, whose bedroom light was on. His mother, a handsome divorcee who wore high heels and a small brunette hairpiece at the crown of her head, answered the door. "Well," she said, "don't you have pink cheeks! The cold agrees with you, Roslyn." She told me Jennings was in his room and to go on up. I think she thought we couldn't possibly be making love since I was so overweight and Jennings was sort of handsome, but we were.

We had been making love since a few months before, when I had beaten Jennings at the spelling bee. I was the best speller in school, while Jennings was second best, and when I got ejected early for misspelling *quietus*, I could tell he thought he had the whole thing wrapped up. After losing, however, I went to the library to see what the word meant, and found the main pronunciation to be qui-*ee*-tus, not qui-*ay*-tus, as Mrs. Googan had said.

My face burned with injustice. Had she not been so obscure I would never have spelled it Q-U-I-A-T-U-S, and, furthermore, would still be in the running. I lugged the dictionary back to the classroom to plead my case.

Mrs. Googan was shocked and appalled. Frankly, so was I. Jennings had a lot of friends—mean friends, who were already deeply offended by my weight. It wasn't like spoiling Jennings's chance to win the bee was going to make them treat me any better. At the same time, I wasn't sure things could get all that much worse.

In the end, Mrs. Googan allowed me back into the competition and I won. After school that day, I went across the street to apologize to Jennings, for what it was worth. He lay on his bed, inconsolable. I waited for him to kick me out of his room or call me fat ass or something, but he didn't. I went over to his bed and put my arm around him, and was momentarily surprised at how easy it was to get close to a popular person. Of course, Jennings and I had grown up together, so even though he was more popular than I was at school, there was a different hierarchy in the neighborhood. All the kids I babysat for adored me, and even though they were several years younger, the sheer volume of them conferred upon me a vague status of local, albeit fat, hero. Jennings knew this. He could call me names and play mean tricks on me at school all he wanted, but in the neighborhood we were nearly equals.

I had spent the weekend preceding the spelling bee with Jonquil and Vic, studying the dictionary and learning what an orgasm was, and all the ways a woman could get one, if she was lucky. "Jennings," I said that day in his room, "would you like to make love?" He stopped sniffling so much and said yes. I might not have offered except I believed his secondary sex characteristics had come in over the summer, and Jonquil told me when this happened, boys weren't so little and slippery inside you anymore.

After we had done it, Jennings thanked me and said he'd like to do it again soon. Having experienced my first orgasm with the minimum of effort, I agreed. Mostly we did it after school, before his mother got home. Then it didn't matter how noisy we were, or how long it took, or how often we wanted to do it. Through all of this, Jennings started to become a different person. In school, he was crueler to me than ever before, or so it seemed. We staged scenes where he shoved me against lockers for being so fat, then caught me just before I hurt myself and banged his own fist against the metal, so it just sounded bad. He grabbed me in front of his friends and whispered threats in my ear, which were really words of love such as, *I can't wait to see you this afternoon.* When we were alone, he told me he wanted to be a stunt coordinator when he grew up, so this was all just practice for him. He assured me constantly that my main problem was not so much that I was fat, but that I smelled bad, which I appreciated, since at least I could do something about that.

Now, standing in his doorway after returning from Dr. Flay's office, I announced, "Jennings, I've been hypnotized." He was lying on his side in bed, looking at *Playboy.* He set the magazine aside and I could see he had an erection inside his pants. He patted the bed for me to sit down beside him, and I did. "I think I got ripped off," I said, even though I hadn't overeaten at Wendy's.

"Why?" Jennings asked. He rolled over on his back so that his erection pitched a tent inside his khakis. That was what he called it.

"Because," I said. Absently, I put a hand on his crotch. "I didn't feel weird or anything. I didn't feel dizzy."

"Did you black out?" Jennings asked me.

I shook my head. "No."

"What stinks?" he said.

I smelled under my arm. "Me."

"How about I give you a bath?" Jennings asked, turning to look at me. He laid a hand over mine, which was still on his crotch.

"With your mother downstairs?"

He shrugged. "She's leaving in a few minutes."

"Okay," I said. We waited until we heard the front door slam then went into the bathroom. It wasn't the first bath Jennings had given me. He liked to wash between my legs then get in with me and do it underwater. Sometimes we fell asleep in the tub afterward. My mother always said I smelled good when I came back from Jennings's, and I told her it was Ms. Jennings's air freshener.

Before I left that evening I gave Jennings the picture of the lady Santa from the Porta Potti. He told me it was beautiful and that she looked just like me.

JENNINGS HELPED ME study for the next round of the spelling bee, a citywide competition. For every ten words I got right, he touched me between my legs; for every ten words I got wrong, I sucked him off, which was no kind of punishment, really, since I enjoyed being intimate with Jennings.

In school he was getting tired of pretending he didn't like me, and sometimes, accidentally, he'd smile and wave when we passed each other in the hall. I wished he wouldn't do that since it only further infuriated his friends, who were still fuming over the way I had insinuated myself back into the spelling bee. They couldn't understand why Jennings wasn't angrier with me, and as far as I could tell, he had made them no explanations.

His friend Garrett was particularly mad. Garrett had the face of a desperate baby bird, framed by long yellow hair that he constantly shook out of his eyes instead of pushing back with his hands. His legs were bowed and he wore aviator glasses, just like my brother-in-law, Vic. It seemed unfair that I should be attacked for being fat when someone like Garrett was running around free, but that was the way it went.

Garrett sat behind me in music class and kicked me hard in the behind while we listened to Beethoven's Fifth, trying to decipher the cello parts. I kept waiting for Mrs. Krieg to hear the sound of my chair squawking across the floor, which it did every time Garrett's foot landed on my ass, but he was careful to kick me only when the music got loud. What could I do? He had two friends sitting on either side of him, laughing each time he made his move. My neck began to hurt more than my butt from the whiplash of being jerked around. I reached back to rub it and Garrett stabbed me in the finger with his pencil.

One afternoon when Jennings washed me, he said I had a yellow-and-blue bruise on my backside. I told him Garrett had done it, hoping he would offer to kill him, but he didn't say anything. Later, in his bedroom, he took out a porno magazine showing two people doing it doggy-style and suggested this might be more comfortable for me in my condition. It did ease the pressure on my back, but I still hoped for a little bit more. As we lay together afterward beneath his down quilt, I said, "Jennings, I'm beginning to fear for my safety."

"I can see that," he said sympathetically. We always lay sideways, facing each other and hugging. Jennings's breath smelled of peanut butter and rum.

"Don't you fear for my safety?"

He looked me straight in the eye and said, "Yes."

I touched his hair, which was curly and dark. "Jennings," I said, "are you my boyfriend?"

"Yes," he said again.

Even though he was still looking straight at me, I suspected this was a lie and began to cry. I would have cried if he'd told me the truth, too. People said all kinds of crazy things to make others believe their lives weren't as bad as they really were, and for the most part it seemed to work. Only Jonquil told the truth on a regular basis, and she was the saddest person I had ever known.

Jennings thought I was crying because of Garrett and so quickly offered to hypnotize him the following day in the boys' bathroom, using Dr. Flay's technique. I reminded him that despite my key word I was getting fatter by the minute, and suggested Jennings beat Garrett up instead—an idea he resisted. "*Larynx*," he whispered in my ear.

"L-A-R-Y-N-X," I answered back. "*Larynx.*"

He laughed and pushed a brand-new erection up against my stomach. "No," he said. "The key word to keep Garrett from kicking you will be *larynx*."

The next day I met Jennings in the girls' rest room before music class. He confirmed he had successfully hypnotized Garrett using a small penlight during social studies, while the rest of the class sat in the dark watching a film about nuclear war. We stood on top of a toilet seat in the mauve-colored stall, touching each other as we spoke, and Jennings made me promise to come over to his house right away after school.

In music class I turned around in my seat and said, "*Larynx!*" forcefully to Garrett, who looked back at me blankly. "Turn around, ugly," his friends said, and I did, but I took my time about it. Garrett really did look hypnotized. He looked as stupid and bland as I had imagined he might, once stripped of all his cruelty.

Mrs. Krieg put on Beethoven, and to be sure I was safe, I turned around and whispered, "*Larynx!*" once more. Garrett wasn't even looking at me; he was noting the timpani with a pencil on his sheet music. "Shh!" Mrs. Krieg hissed at me, and I understood then that her hearing was selective.

When I went to see Jennings after school, eager to ask him how he had really made Garrett stop kicking me, Garrett himself was there, sitting on Jennings's bed. The two of them were flipping through a *Playboy* and both had erections in their pants. "Roz," Jennings said, setting the magazine aside and standing up. His penis pointed at me like a finger on an Uncle Sam poster. "I was thinking you could have sex with Garrett today instead of me. Just for today," he added hurriedly. Garrett stood up then, too, his erection pointing down at the ground. He cleared his throat and put his hands in his pockets.

"Oh," I said, trying not to sound scared. "No thanks." I stayed and talked with them for a while about nuclear holocaust, which didn't diminish their erections in the least. We all agreed germ warfare was the wave of the future, then I went home and called Jonquil. She was still at work so she couldn't talk long, but she told me not to go over to Jennings's house again, and to deny anything anyone might say about me in school from this day forward, should it come to that.

Things were okay for a while then. I ignored Jonquil's advice and continued making love with Jennings most afternoons, pretending nothing had ever happened with Garrett. In music class I stopped saying *larynx,* but Garrett didn't kick me anyway. I wondered if it had something to do with germ warfare and our shared views on that subject. I might have asked him about it had I not gone on to lose the citywide spelling bee.

"I should never have let you back into the competition!" Mrs. Googan screeched when I called to tell her the news. "Think how poor Jennings must feel right now!" I went across the street to ask him and he said he didn't give a shit. But if I wanted to make it up to him, he said, he had just gotten a new

Polaroid for Christmas and needed someone to pose. I sat on his bed with my legs apart and wearing a Santa hat, like the lady from the Porta Potti. When I left I took the pictures with me, which Jennings said was no fair until I reminded him of how he had tried to sell me to Garrett. "You broke the bond of trust," I informed him, copying something Jonquil had said, and he nodded pitifully.

What neither Mrs. Googan nor I had anticipated was that my losing the semifinals would reignite Garrett's anger on behalf of Jennings. He began a campaign of kicking so strenuous that I developed a cyst on my tailbone and had to stay home from school for a week. At the end of the week, when the cyst was at its most inflamed, the doctor sliced it open and drained all the pus. He proceeded to examine me inside and out, though I had no other health complaints, after which he tersely informed my mother that my hymen was missing.

My mother demanded to know where it had gone and I quickly claimed I had been born without one. She searched my room anyway, almost as if she were looking for it, and found the Polaroid pictures of me instead. "*Sputnik* my ass!" she said, flipping through them. "You haven't lost any weight at all!" I wanted to tell her Jennings loved those pictures and that contrary to what she or Dr. Flay might think, I didn't anticipate any future problems finding men. But I didn't, of course. I watched out my bedroom window as she charged across the street to Jennings's house, pictures in hand, prepared to shock and dismay his mother.

It had been light out when my mother left to see Ms. Jennings, and it was dark when she returned. She had been crying, I could tell, and she no longer had the Polaroids. "Where are my pictures?" I demanded to know, and she looked at me like I was Jonquil.

"*Your* pictures? *Your* pictures?"

I didn't have an answer to that. While she was gone I had cooked up some Old El Paso, and now we sat down together to eat it. My mother had one taco and I went ahead and had three, since she didn't seem in the mood to count. For once she watched me eat with a kind of interest, as if she were thinking, How in the world can a thirteen-year-old eat so damn much? Somebody tell me, *please*.

I smiled at her while I was chewing and she turned stern again. "Well!" she announced suddenly. "*Your* pictures have been chopped up and placed inside Leslie Jennings's purse to be disposed of at her office, where that sorry son of hers can't retrieve them and piece them back together."

"Oh," I said. I wiped red, spicy grease from my fingers, which smelled of beef and corn.

"As for you," my mother continued, "there will be no more visits across the street."

I didn't say anything. I had no intention of going back there anyway. It was a little late, but I was planning to listen to Jonquil from now on, no matter how sad it made me.

"I'm telling you," my mother continued, "if I find out you've been over there, you'll be out on the street like your sister."

There was no point in disputing that, either, since if she did put me out, my sister would take me in and I'd be happier than ever.

I returned to school to find that Garrett had been expelled for attacking me, and that Mrs. Krieg had been replaced by Mr. Sconzo, who was fat like me and said if anyone bothered me to let him know so he could kick some booty. He listened to old American folk music instead of classical, and told us to try to enjoy the songs as a whole instead of picking out all the little bitty parts.

Jennings and I were civil in school. He asked if I would mind leaving my bedroom curtains open at night when I undressed, which I saw no harm in doing. I missed him terribly.

THREE YEARS LATER, as sophomores in high school, Garrett and I were in class together again. It was math, and he had changed considerably since the seventh grade, wearing round glasses and a short haircut reminiscent of John Lennon before he was killed. Beyond that, everything else about him seemed thicker and more controlled, as if he were now less inclined to commit violence, though if he got it into his head to do so, it would probably hurt a lot more.

I, too, was different. Having replaced my malfunctioning key word with an unsensible diet, compulsive exercise, and moderate vomiting, the pounds had finally begun to drop off. My mother was elated and to celebrate taught me how to shave my legs and apply makeup. The word around school was that I was now officially pretty and could finally be treated as such. I thought this would mean dates and parties, but really it just meant no one threw me into lockers anymore or called me names, which would be unseemly at our ages anyway. Ultimately the past haunted us all, and no one was prepared to nominate me for elective office or drop my name in the hat for homecoming queen. I became the leader of a group of smart quiet girls and closeted gay boys, all of us sexually frustrated.

When Garrett walked into class that day, however, I experienced an overwhelming sense of anticipation, as if his purpose in being there extended well beyond the realm of geometry. He took the empty seat behind me seemingly out of habit, and, evolved as he appeared, I could not help but find myself preparing to be assaulted. When the bell rang and this had not happened I ran to the rest room, weepy over his generous restraint and how, to my great shame, this made me love him.

Meanwhile, unbeknownst to either of us, Jennings and I had gotten puppies within a month of each other and were now meeting regularly in the street while our dogs relieved themselves on the neighbors' lawns. He complimented me on my new figure and I squeezed the biceps he was cultivating for crew. His grades had improved drastically since we had stopped making love, and his mother had seen fit to enroll him in a private high school across town. He said the girls there were nothing like me, and now that I had gotten thin he could see he was really missing out.

I told Jennings that Garrett was in my math class and he said he knew since the two of them had kept in touch after Garrett's expulsion. Apparently he had gone on to spend time in a juvenile home, where a therapist suggested it was his mother he hated and not me, and that my weight had simply provoked him into attacking me because his mother was fat, too.

"Is that true?" I asked Jennings as we walked down the street together one fall morning. The dewy air reminded me of lying in the tub with him after sex, when the mirrors were all fogged up and the whole place smelled like a greenhouse. It wasn't something I would do again, but the memory of it made me think I had made the right choice at the time.

"Absolutely," Jennings said, pulling the choke chain on his mutt, Robbie, while Edna, my miniature terrier, looked on in horror. "He feels just terrible about the mix-up."

"So that's it? He's cured?" I said.

Jennings nodded. "Probably even more so now that you've lost all this weight."

Edna sidled up to a Cutlass Supreme, sniffed the back tire, then peed beside it. When she was finished, Robbie peed on top of her pee. Jennings and I watched without saying a word. Bodily fluids were of little consequence to the likes of us. "Well, he's good in math," I said finally, offering what little evidence I had of Garrett's reform.

Jennings turned to me then and dangled the end of Robbie's leash in my face. "You are getting very sleepy," he warned.

"What?" I said.

"Your eyelids are getting very heavy," he continued. "Soon you will fall asleep."

"Stop it, Jennings," I said, walking ahead.

He gave up and fell in beside me. "Sorry, Roz. It's just that Garrett asked me if I would hypnotize you so you'd have sex with him in the girls' rest room."

"I see," I said, panicking slightly at the thought of being sold again.

"He says he won't hurt you if you say no, but if you just give him a chance he thinks he could make you feel really good." He put a hand in his pocket then to hide the erection he had gotten.

"I don't do that anymore," I said weakly.

"Why not?" Jennings asked, surprised. "I do."

I shifted my gaze from his crotch to his face. "With who?"

He shrugged. "Different girls."

"Well," I said, feeling suddenly morose, "hypnotism doesn't work anyway."

"Sure it does," he said. "Just look at you."

I looked at Edna instead, who was digging a small hole in Jennings's front yard, where we had ended up, while Robbie sniffed her butt. From her kitchen window, I could see Ms. Jennings peering out at us; I didn't have to look at my own house to know my mother was at her post as well. "Spell *hypnotism*," I said to Jennings for old times' sake, and he did so incorrectly, replacing the N with an M. We began to laugh, and in an instant his mother was at the front door, calling her son inside.

The next day in math class I felt a tug at the back of my hair. It was painless and affectionate and I dared not turn around.

"Yes?" Mr. Alvarez said a few minutes later, looking over my head at Garrett, who presumably had his hand up.

Garrett cleared his throat. "May I please go to the rest room?"

Mr. Alvarez nodded and Garrett got out of his seat to collect the wooden hall pass on the teacher's desk.

I waited as long as I could before asking permission to use the rest room as well.

"No," Mr. Alvarez said. "Wait until Garrett comes back."

"But I can't wait," I said. "I have to go *now.*"

This was a new liberty we girls had begun to take in high school, meaning we would not be responsible for bleeding all over the classroom floor should our teachers not take heed. I had gotten my first period a month after Jennings and I stopped making love, and though I didn't have it that very day, Mr. Alvarez nodded knowingly and filled out a paper pass.

In the rest room I waited for another girl to wash her hands and leave before checking all the stalls. Garrett was in the last one, standing on the toilet seat. "*Alcatraz,*" he said softly. His voice was deeper than it had once been, his erection more forthright. He would not swim around inside me like a fish.

I stepped inside the stall and locked the door behind me. I had always been too afraid to scrutinize him before—even that time in Jennings's when we exchanged ideas about the end of the world— and so now I couldn't help but take him in. It seemed a kind of miracle that we should be so close without harm passing between us.

"*Alcatraz,*" he mentioned again after a short while, to remind me of why I was there, but he needn't have. It would be years before I would stop feeling grateful for my safety, before I would notice the ache in my tailbone warning me of unworthy men or bad weather.

For now, my only concern were the bulging blue-green veins running along his muscular forearms. As I held my breath and reached out to touch one of them, it quivered, like Edna's twiggy back legs when she was cold. I gripped the arm and used it to steady myself as I stepped up onto the toilet, where I found his cheek to be prickly and the bottoms of his earlobes like feathers between my fingertips. The hair was still yellow, and when I put my face into it and inhaled, the answer was gardenia. I held both forearms now, though I could not remember when I had taken the second one, and they gripped me protectively in return. The lips were wet and frightened as they came toward me, while inside the mouth, the teeth made tentative, idle threats.

A REAL DOLL

A.M. HOMES

I'M DATING BARBIE. THREE AFTERNOONS A WEEK, WHILE MY sister is at dance class, I take Barbie away from Ken. I'm practicing for the future.

At first I sat in my sister's room watching Barbie, who lived with Ken, on a doily, on top of the dresser.

I was looking at her but not really looking. I was looking, and all of a sudden realized she was staring at me.

She was sitting next to Ken, his khaki-covered thigh absently rubbing her bare leg. He was rubbing her, but she was staring at me.

"Hi," she said.

"Hello," I said.

"I'm Barbie," she said, and Ken stopped rubbing her leg.

"I know."

"You're Jenny's brother."

I nodded. My head was bobbing up and down like a puppet on a weight.

"I really like your sister. She's sweet," Barbie said. "Such a good little girl. Especially lately, she makes herself so pretty, and she's started doing her nails."

I wonder if Barbie noticed that Miss Wonderful bit her nails and that when she smiled her front teeth were covered with little flecks of purple nail polish. I wondered if she knew Jennifer colored in the chipped chewed spots with purple Magic Marker, and then sometimes sucked on her fingers so that not only did she have purple flecks of polish on her teeth, but her tongue was the strangest shade of violet.

"So listen," I said. "Would you like to go out for a while? Grab some fresh air, maybe take a spin around the backyard?"

"Sure," she said.

I picked her up by her feet. It sounds unusual but I was too petrified to take her by the waist. I grabbed her by the ankles and carried her off like a Popsicle stick.

As soon as we were out back, sitting on the porch of what I used to call my fort, but which my sister and parents referred to as the playhouse, I started freaking, I was suddenly and incredibly aware that I was out with Barbie. I didn't know what to say.

"So, what kind of a Barbie are you?" I asked.

"Excuse me?"

"Well, from listening to Jennifer I know there's Day to Night Barbie, Magic Moves Barbie, Gift-Giving Barbie, Tropical Barbie, My First Barbie, and more."

"I'm Tropical," she said. "I'm Tropical, she said, the same way a person might say I'm Catholic or I'm Jewish. "I came with a one-piece bathing suit, a brush, and a ruffle you can wear so many ways," Barbie squeaked.

She actually squeaked. It turned out that squeaking was Barbie's birth defect. I pretended I didn't hear it.

We were quiet for a minute. A leaf larger than Barbie fell from the maple tree above us and I caught it just before it would have hit her. I half expected her to squeak, "You saved my life. I'm yours, forever." Instead she said, in a perfectly normal voice. "Wow, big leaf."

I looked at her. Barbie's eyes were sparkling blue like the ocean on a good day. I looked and in a moment noticed she had the whole world, the cosmos, drawn in makeup above and below her eyes. An entire galaxy, clouds, stars, a sun, the sea, painted onto her face. Yellow, blue, pink, and a million silver sparkles.

We sat looking at each other, looking and talking and then not talking and looking again. It was a stop-and-start thing with both of us constantly saying the wrong thing, saying anything, and then immediately regretting having said it.

It was obvious Barbie didn't trust me. I asked her if she wanted something to drink.

"Diet Coke," she said. And I wondered why I'd asked.

I went into the house, upstairs into my parents' bathroom, opened the medicine cabinet, and got a couple of Valiums. I immediately swallowed one. I figured if I could be calm and collected, she'd realize I wasn't going to hurt her. I broke another Valium into a million small pieces, dropped some slivers into Barbie's Diet Coke, and swished it around so it'd blend. I figured if we could be calm and collected together, she'd be able to trust me even sooner. I was falling in love in a way that had nothing to do with love.

"So, what's the deal with you and Ken?" I asked later after we'd loosened up, after she'd drunk two Diet Cokes, and I'd made another trip to the medicine cabinet.

She giggled. "Oh, we're just really good friends."

"What's the deal with him really, you can tell me, I mean, is he or isn't he?"

"Ish she or ishn' she," Barbie said, in a slow slurred way, like she was so intoxicated that if they made a Breathalyzer for Valium, she'd melt it.

I regretted having fixed her a third Coke. I mean if she OD'd and died, Jennifer would tell my mom and dad for sure.

"Is he a faggot or what?"

Barbie laughed and I almost slapped her. She looked me straight in the eye.

"He lusts after me," she said. "I come home at night and he's standing there, waiting. He doesn't wear underwear, you know. I mean, isn't that strange, Ken doesn't own any underwear. I heard Jennifer tell her friend that they don't even make any for him. Anyway, he's always there waiting, and I'm like, Ken, we're friends, okay, that's it. I mean, have you ever noticed, he has molded plastic hair. His head and his hair are all one piece. I can't go out with a guy like that. Besides, I don't think he'd be up for it if you know what I mean. Ken is not what you'd call well endowed. . . . All he's got is a little plastic bump, more of a hump, really, and what the hell are you supposed to do with that?"

She was telling me things I didn't think I should hear and all the same, I was leaning into her, like if I moved closer, she'd tell me more. I was taking every word and holding it for a minute, holding groups of words in my head like I didn't understand English. She went on and on, but I wasn't listening.

The sun sank behind the playhouse, Barbie shivered, excused herself, and ran around back to throw up. I asked her if she felt okay. She said she was fine, just a little tired, that maybe she was coming down with the flu or something. I gave her a piece of a piece of gum to chew and took her inside.

On the way back to Jennifer's room I did something Barbie almost didn't forgive me for. I did something which not only shattered the moment, but nearly wrecked the possibility of our having a future together.

In the hallway between the stairs and Jennifer's room, I popped Barbie's head into my mouth, like lion and tamer, God and Godzilla.

I popped her whole head into my mouth, and Barbie's hair separated into single strands like Christmas tinsel and caught in my throat nearly choking me. I could taste layer on layer of makeup, Revlon, Max Factor, and Maybelline. I closed my mouth around Barbie and could feel her breath in mine. I could hear her screams in my throat. Her teeth, white, Pearl Drops, Pepsodent, and the whole Osmond family, bit my tongue and the inside of my cheek like I might accidentally bite myself. I closed my mouth around her neck and held her suspended, her feet uselessly kicking the air in front of my face.

Before pulling her out, I pressed my teeth lightly into her neck, leaving marks Barbie described as scars of her assault, but which I imagined as a New Age necklace of love.

"I have never, ever in my life been treated with such utter disregard," she said as soon as I let her out.

She was lying. I knew Jennifer sometimes did things with Barbie. I didn't mention that once I'd seen Barbie hanging from Jennifer's ceiling fan, spinning around in great wide circles, like some imitation Superman.

"I'm sorry if I scared you."

"Scared me!" she squeaked.

She went on squeaking, a cross between the squeal when you let the air out of a balloon and a smoke alarm with weak batteries. While she was squeaking, the phrase *a head in the mouth is worth two in the bush* started running through my head. I knew it had come from somewhere, started as something else, but I couldn't get it right. *A head in the mouth is worth two in the bush,* again and again, like the punch line to some dirty joke.

"Scared me. Scared me. Scared me!" Barbie squeaked louder and louder until finally she had my attention again. "Have you ever been held captive in the dark cavern of someone's body?"

I shook my head. It sounded wonderful.

"Typical," she said. "So incredibly, typically male."

For a moment I was proud.

"Why do you have to do things you know you shouldn't, and worse, you do them with a light in your eye, like you're getting some weird pleasure that only another boy would understand. You're all the same," she said. "You're all Jack Nicholson."

I refused to put her back in Jennifer's room until she forgave me, until she understood that I'd done what I did with only the truest of feeling, no harm intended.

I heard Jennifer's feet clomping up the stairs. I was running out of time.

"You know I'm really interested in you," I said to Barbie.

"Me too," she said, and for a minute I wasn't sure if she meant she was interested in herself or me.

"We should do this again," I said. She nodded.

I leaned down to kiss Barbie. I could have brought her to my lips, but somehow it felt wrong. I leaned down to kiss her and the first thing I got was her nose in my mouth. I felt like a St. Bernard saying hello.

No matter how graceful I tried to be, I was forever licking her face. It wasn't a question of putting my tongue in her ear or down her throat, it was simply literally trying not to suffocate her. I kissed Barbie with my back to Ken and then turned around and put her on the doily right next to him. I was tempted to drop her down on Ken, to mash her into him, but I managed to restrain myself.

"That was fun," Barbie said. I heard Jennifer in the hall.

"Later," I said.

Jennifer came into the room and looked at me.

"What?" I said.

"It's my room," she said.

"There was a bee in it. I was killing it for you."

"A bee. I'm allergic to bees. Mom, Mom," she screamed. "There's a bee."

"Mom's not home. I killed it."

"But there might be another one."

"So call me and I'll kill it."

"But if it stings me, I might die." I shrugged and walked out. I could feel Barbie watching me leave.

I TOOK a Valium about twenty minutes before I picked her up the next Friday. By the time I went into Jennifer's room, everything was getting easier.

"Hey," I said when I got up to the dresser.

She was there on the doily with Ken, they were back to back, resting against each other, legs stretched out in front of them.

Ken didn't look at me. I didn't care.

"You ready to go?" I asked. Barbie nodded. "I thought you might be thirsty." I handed her the Diet Coke I'd made for her.

I'd figured Barbie could take a little less than an eighth of a Valium without getting totally senile. Basically, I had to give her Valium crumbs since there was no way to cut one that small.

She took the Coke and drank it right in front of Ken. I kept waiting for him to give me one of those I-know-what-you're-up-to-and-I-don't-like-it looks, the kind my father gives me when he walks into my room without knocking and I automatically jump twenty feet in the air.

Ken acted like he didn't even know I was there. I hated him.

"I can't do a lot of walking this afternoon," Barbie said. I nodded. I figured no big deal since mostly I seemed to be carrying her around anyway.

"My feet are killing me," she said.

I was thinking about Ken.

"Don't you have other shoes?"

My family was very into shoes. No matter what seemed to be wrong, my father always suggested it could be cured by wearing a different pair of shoes. He believed that shoes, like tires, should be rotated.

"It's not the shoes," she said. "It's my toes."

"Did you drop something on them?" My Valium wasn't working. I was having trouble making small talk. I needed another one.

"Jennifer's been chewing on them."

"What?"

"She chews on my toes."

"You let her chew your footies?"

I couldn't make sense out of what she was saying. I was thinking about not being able to talk, needing another or maybe two more Valiums, yellow adult-strength Pez.

"Do you enjoy it?" I asked.

"She literally bites down on them, like I'm flank steak or something," Barbie said. "I wish she'd just bite them off and have it over with. This is taking forever. She's chewing and chewing, more like gnawing at me."

"I'll make her stop. I'll buy her some gum, some tobacco or something, a pencil to chew on."

"Please don't say anything. I wouldn't have told you except . . ." Barbie said.

"But she's hurting you."

"It's between Jennifer and me."

"Where's it going to stop?" I asked.

"At the arch, I hope. There's a bone there, and once she realizes she's bitten the soft part off, she'll stop."

"How will you walk?"

"I have very long feet."

I sat on the edge of my sister's bed, my head in my hands. My sister was biting Barbie's feet off and Barbie didn't seem to care. She didn't hold it against her and in a way I liked her for that. I liked the fact she understood how we all have little secret habits that seem normal enough to us, but which we know better than to mention out loud. I started imagining things I might be able to get away with.

"Get me out of here," Barbie said. I slipped Barbie's shoes off. Sure enough, someone had been gnawing at her. On her left foot the toes were dangling and on the right, half had been completely taken off. There were tooth marks up to her ankles. "Let's not dwell on this," Barbie said.

I picked Barbie up. Ken fell over backwards and Barbie made me straighten him up before we left. "Just because you know he only has a bump doesn't give you permission to treat him badly," Barbie whispered.

I fixed Ken and carried Barbie down the hall to my room. I held Barbie above me, tilted my head back, and lowered her feet into my mouth. I felt like a young sword swallower practicing for my debut. I lowered Barbie's feet and legs into my mouth and then began sucking on them. They smelled like Jennifer and dirt and plastic. I sucked on her stubs and she told me it felt nice.

"You're better than a hot soak," Barbie said. I left her resting on my pillow and went downstairs to get us each a drink.

We were lying on my bed, curled into and out of each other. Barbie was on a pillow next to me and I was on my side facing her. She was talking about men, and as she talked I tried to be everything she said. She was saying she didn't like men who were afraid of themselves. I tried to be brave, to look courageous and secure. I held my head a certain way and it seemed to work. She said she didn't like men who were afraid of femininity, and I got confused.

"Guys always have to prove how boy they really are," Barbie said.

I thought of Jennifer trying to be a girl, wearing dresses, doing her nails, putting makeup on, wearing a bra even though she wouldn't need one for about fifty years.

"You make fun of Ken because he lets himself be everything he is. He doesn't hide anything."

"He doesn't have anything to hide," I said. "He has tan molded plastic hair, and a bump for a dick."

"I never should have told you about the bump."

I lay back on the bed. Barbie rolled over, off the pillow, and rested on my chest. Her body stretched from my nipple to my belly button. Her hands pressed against me, tickling me.

"Barbie," I said.

"Umm Humm."

"How do you feel about me?"

She didn't say anything for a minute. "Don't worry about it," she said, and slipped her hand into my shirt through the space between the buttons.

Her fingers were like the ends of the toothpicks performing some subtle ancient torture, a dance of boy death across my chest. Barbie crawled all over me like an insect who'd run into one too many cans of Raid.

Underneath my clothes, under my skin, I was going crazy. First off, I'd been kidnapped by my underwear with no way to manually adjust without attracting unnecessary attention.

A Real Doll

With Barbie caught in my shirt I slowly rolled over, like in some space shuttle docking maneuver. I rolled onto my stomach, trapping her under me. As slowly and unobtrusively as possible, I ground myself against the bed, at first hoping it would fix things and then again and again, caught by a pleasure/pain principle.

"Is this a water bed?" Barbie asked.

My hand was on her breasts, only it wasn't really my hand, but more like my index finger. I touched Barbie and she made a little gasp, a squeak in reverse. She squeaked backwards, then stopped, and I was struck there with my hand on her, thinking about how I was forever crossing a line between the haves and the have-nots, between good guys and bad, between men and animals, and there was absolutely nothing I could do to stop myself.

Barbie was sitting on my crotch, her legs flipped back behind her in a position that wasn't human.

At a certain point I had to free myself. If my dick was blue, it was only because it had suffocated. I did the honors and Richard popped out like an escape from maximum security.

"I've never seen anything so big," Barbie said. It was the sentence I dreamed of, but given the people Barbie normally hung out with, namely the bump boy himself, it didn't come as a big surprise.

She stood at the base of my dick, her bare feet buried in my pubic hair. I was almost as tall as she was. Okay, not almost as tall, but clearly we could be related. She and Richard even had the same vaguely surprised look on their faces.

She was on me and I couldn't help wanting to get inside her. I turned Barbie over and was on top of her, not caring if I killed her. Her hands pressed so hard into my stomach that it felt like she was performing an appendectomy.

I was on top, trying to get between her legs, almost breaking her in half. But there was nothing there, nothing to fuck except a small thin line that was supposed to be her ass crack.

I rubbed the thin line, the back of her legs, and the space between her legs. I turned Barbie's back to me so I could do it without having to look at her face.

Very quickly, I came. I came all over Barbie, all over her and a little bit in her hair. I came on Barbie and it was the most horrifying experience I ever had. It didn't stay on her. It doesn't stick to plastic. I was finished. I was holding a come-covered Barbie in my hand like I didn't know where she came from.

Barbie said, "Don't stop," or maybe I just think she said that because I read it somewhere. I don't know anymore. I couldn't listen to her. I couldn't even look at her. I wiped myself off with a sock, pulled my clothes on, and then took Barbie into the bathroom.

AT DINNER I noticed Jennifer chewing her cuticles between bites of tuna-noodle casserole. I asked her if she was teething. She coughed and then started choking to death on either a little piece of fingernail, a crushed potato chip from the casserole, or maybe even a little bit of Barbie footie that'd stuck in her teeth. My mother asked if she was okay.

"I swallowed something sharp," she said between coughs that were clearly influenced by the acting class she'd taken over the summer.

"Do you have a problem?" I asked her.

"Leave your sister alone," my mother said.

"If there are any questions to ask, we'll do the asking," my father said.

"Is everything all right?" my mother asked Jennifer. She nodded. "I think you could use some new jeans," my mother said. "You don't seem to have many play clothes anymore."

"Not to change the subject," I said, trying to think of a way to stop Jennifer from eating Barbie alive.

"I don't wear pants," Jennifer said. "Boys wear pants."

"Your grandma wears pants," my father said.

"She's not a girl."

My father chuckled. He actually fucking chuckled. He's the only person I ever met who could actually fucking chuckle.

"Don't tell her that," he said, chuckling.

"It's not funny," I said.

"Grandma's are pull-ons anyway," Jennifer said. "They don't have a fly. You have to have a penis to have a fly."

"Jennifer," my mother said. "That's enough of that."

I decided to buy Barbie a present. I was at that strange point where I would have done anything for her. I took two buses and walked more than a mile to get to Toys "R" Us.

Barbie row was aisle 14C. I was a wreck. I imagined a million Barbies and having to have them all. I pictured fucking one, discarding it, immediately grabbing a fresh one, doing it, and then throwing it into a growing pile in the corner of my room. An unending chore. I saw myself becoming a slave to Barbie. I wondered how many Tropical Barbies were made each year. I felt faint.

There were rows and rows of Kens, Barbies, and Skippers. Funtime Barbie, Jewel Secrets Ken, Barbie Rocker with "Hot Rockin' Fun and Real Dancin' Action." I noticed Magic Moves Barbie, and found myself looking at her carefully, flirtatiously, wondering if her legs were spreadable. "Push the switch and she moves," her box said. She winked at me while I was reading.

The only Tropical I saw was a black Tropical Ken. From just looking at him you wouldn't have known he was black. I mean, he wasn't black like anyone would be black. Black Tropical Ken was the color of a raisin, a raisin all spread out and unwrinkled.

He had a short Afro that looked like a wig had been dropped down and fixed on his head, a protective helmet. I wondered if black Ken was really white Ken sprayed over with a thick coating of ironed raisin plastic.

I spread eight black Kens out in a line across the front of the row. Through the plastic window of his box he told me he was hoping to go to dental school. All eight black Kens talked at once. Luckily, they all said the same thing at the same time. They said he really liked teeth. Black Ken smiled. He had the same white Pearl Drops, Pepsodent, Osmond family teeth that Barbie and white Ken had. I thought the entire Mattel family must take really good care of themselves. I figured they might be the only people left in America who actually brushed after every meal and then again before going to sleep.

I didn't know what to get Barbie. Black Ken said I should go for clothing, maybe a fur coat. I wanted something really special. I imagined a wonderful present that would draw us somehow closer. There was a tropical pool and patio set, but I decided it might make her homesick. There was a complete winter holiday, with an A-frame house, fireplace, snowmobile, and sled. I imagined her inviting Ken away for a weekend without me. The six o'clock news set was nice, but because of her squeak, Barbie's future as an anchorwoman seemed limited. A workout center, a sofa bed and coffee table, a bubbling spa, a bedroom play set. I settled on the grand piano. It was $13.00. I'd always made it a point to never spend more than ten dollars on anyone. This time I figured, what the hell, you don't buy a grand piano every day.

"Wrap it up, would ya," I said at the checkout desk.

FROM MY BEDROOM window I could see Jennifer in the backyard, wearing her tutu and leaping all over the place. It was dangerous as hell to sneak in and get Barbie, but I couldn't keep a grand piano in my closet without telling someone.

"You must really like me," Barbie said when she finally had the piano unwrapped.

I nodded. She was wearing a ski suit and skis. It was the end of August and eighty degrees out. Immediately, she sat down and played "Chopsticks."

I looked out at Jennifer. She was running down the length of the deck, jumping onto the railing and then leaping off, posing like one of those red flying horses you see on old Mobil gas signs. I watched her do it once and then the second time, her foot caught on the railing, and she went over the edge the hard way. A minute later she came around the edge of the house, limping, her tutu dented and dirty, pink tights ripped at both knees. I grabbed Barbie from the piano bench and raced her into Jennifer's room.

"I was just getting warmed up," she said. "I can play better than that, really."

I could hear Jennifer crying as she walked up the stairs.

"Jennifer's coming," I said. I put her down on the dresser and realized Ken was missing.

"Where's Ken?" I asked quickly.

"Out with Jennifer," Barbie said.

I met Jennifer at her door. "Are you okay?" I asked. She cried harder. "I saw you fall."

"Why didn't you stop me?" she said.

"From falling?

She nodded and showed me her knees.

"Once you start to fall no one can stop you." I noticed Ken was tucked into the waistband of her tutu.

"They catch you," Jennifer said.

I started to tell her it was dangerous to go leaping around

with a Ken stuck in your waistband, but you don't tell someone who's already crying that they did something bad.

I walked her into the bathroom, and took out the hydrogen peroxide. I was a first aid expert. I was the kind of guy who walked around, waiting for someone to have a heart attack just so I could practice my CPR technique.

"Sit down," I said.

Jennifer sat down on the toilet without putting the lid down. Ken was stabbing her all over the place and instead of pulling him out, she squirmed around trying to get comfortable like she didn't know what else to do. I took him out for her. She watched as though I was performing surgery or something.

"He's mine," she said.

"Take off your tights," I said.

"No," she said.

"They're ruined," I said. "Take them off."

Jennifer took off her ballet slippers and peeled off her tights. She was wearing my old Underoos with superheroes on them, Spiderman and Superman and Batman all poking out from under a dirty dented tutu. I decided not to say anything, but it looked funny as hell to see a flat crotch in boys' underwear. I had the feeling they didn't bother making underwear for Ken because they knew it looked too weird on him.

I poured peroxide onto her bloody knees. Jennifer screamed into my ear. She bent down and examined herself, poking her purple fingers into the torn skin; her tutu bunched up and rubbed against her face, scraping it. I worked on her knees, removing little pebbles and pieces of grass from the area.

She started crying again.

"You're okay," I said. "You're not dying." She didn't care. "Do you want anything?" I asked, trying to be nice.

"Barbie," she said.

It was the first time I'd handled Barbie in public. I picked her up like she was a complete stranger and handed her to Jennifer, who grabbed her by the hair. I started to tell her to ease up, but couldn't. Barbie looked at me and I shrugged. I went downstairs and made Jennifer one of my special Diet Cokes.

"Drink this," I said, handing it to her. She took four giant gulps and immediately I felt guilty about having used a whole Valium.

"Why don't you give a little to your Barbie," I said. "I'm sure she's thirsty too."

Barbie winked at me and I could have killed her, first off for doing it in front of Jennifer, and second because she didn't know what the hell she was winking about.

I went into my room and put the piano away. I figured as long as I kept it in the original box I'd be safe. If anyone found it, I'd say it was a present for Jennifer.

WEDNESDAY Ken and Barbie had their heads switched. I went to get Barbie, and there on top of the dresser were Barbie and Ken, sort of. Barbie's head was on Ken's body and Ken's head was on Barbie. At first I thought it was just me.

"Hi," Barbie's head said.

I couldn't respond. She was on Ken's body and I was looking at Ken in a whole new way.

I picked up the Barbie head/Ken and immediately Barbie's head rolled off. It rolled across the dresser, across the white doily past Jennifer's collection of miniature ceramic cats, and *boom* it fell to the floor. I saw Barbie's head rolling and about to fall, and then falling, but there was nothing I could do to stop it. I was frozen, paralyzed with Ken's headless body in my left hand.

Barbie's head was on the floor, her hair spread out underneath it like angel wings in the snow, and I expected to see blood, a wide rich pool of blood, or at least a little bit coming out of her ear, her nose, or her mouth. I looked at her head on the floor and saw nothing but Barbie with eyes like the cosmos looking up at me. I thought she was dead.

"Christ, that hurt," she said. "And I already had a headache from these earrings."

There were little red dot/ball earrings jutting out of Barbie's ears.

"They go right through my head, you know. I guess it takes getting used to," Barbie said.

I noticed my mother's pin cushion on the dresser next to the other Barbie/Ken, the Barbie body, Ken head. The pin cushion was filled with hundreds of pins, pins with flat silver ends and pins with red, yellow, and blue dot ball ends.

"You have pins in your head," I said to the Barbie head on the floor.

"Is that supposed to be a compliment?"

I was starting to hate her. I was being perfectly clear and she didn't understand me.

I looked at Ken. He was in my left hand, my fist wrapped around his waist. I looked at him and realized my thumb was on his bump. My thumb was pressed against Ken's crotch and as soon as I noticed I got an automatic hard-on, the kind you don't know you're getting, it's just there. I started rubbing Ken's bump and watching my thumb like it was a large-screen projection of a porno movie.

"What are you doing?" Barbie's head said. "Get me up. Help me." I was rubbing Ken's bump/hump with my finger inside his bathing suit. I was standing in the middle of my sister's room, with my pants pulled down.

"Aren't you going to help me?" Barbie kept asking. "Aren't you going to help me?"

In the second before I came, I held Ken's head hole in front of me. I held Ken upside down above my dick and came inside of Ken like I never could in Barbie.

I came into Ken's body and as soon as I was done I wanted to do it again. I wanted to fill Ken and put his head back on, like a perfume bottle. I wanted Ken to be the vessel for my secret supply. I came in Ken and then I remembered he wasn't mine. He didn't belong to me. I took him into the bathroom and soaked him in warm water and Ivory liquid. I brushed his insides with Jennifer's toothbrush and left him alone in a cold-water rinse.

"Aren't you going to help me, aren't you?" Barbie kept asking.

I started thinking she'd been brain damaged by the accident. I picked her head up from the floor.

"What took you so long?" she asked.

"I had to take care of Ken."

"Is he okay?"

"He'll be fine. He's soaking in the bathroom." I held Barbie's head in my hand.

"What are you going to do?"

"What do you mean?" I said.

Did my little incident, my moment with Ken, mean that right then and there some decision about my future life as queerbait had to be made?

"This afternoon. Where are we going? What are we doing? I miss you when I don't see you," Barbie said.

"You see me every day," I said.

"I don't really see you. I sit on top of the dresser and if you pass by, I see you. Take me to your room."

"I have to bring Ken's body back."

I went into the bathroom, rinsed out Ken, blew him dry with

my mother's blow dryer, then played with him again. It was a boy thing, we were boys together. I thought sometime I might play ball with him, I might take him out instead of Barbie.

"Everything takes you so long," Barbie said when I got back into the room.

I put Ken back up on the dresser, picked up Barbie's body, knocked Ken's head off, and smashed Barbie's head back down on her own damn neck.

"I don't want to fight with you," Barbie said as I carried her into my room. "We don't have enough time together to fight. Fuck me," she said.

I didn't feel like it. I was thinking about fucking Ken and Ken being a boy. I was thinking about Barbie and Barbie being a girl. I was thinking about Jennifer, switching Barbie and Ken's heads, chewing Barbie's feet off, hanging Barbie from the ceiling fan, and who knows what else.

"Fuck me," Barbie said again.

I ripped Barbie's clothing off. Between Barbie's legs Jennifer had drawn pubic hair in reverse. She drawn it upside down so it looked like a fountain spewing up and out in great wide arcs. I spit directly onto Barbie and with my thumb and first finger rubbed the ink lines, erasing them. Barbie moaned.

"Why do you let her do this to you?"

"Jennifer owns me," Barbie moaned.

Jennifer owns me, she said, so easily and with pleasure. I was totally jealous. Jennifer owned Barbie and it made me crazy. Obviously it was one of those relationships that could only exist between women. Jennifer could own her because it didn't matter that Jennifer owned her. Jennifer didn't want Barbie, she had her.

"You're perfect," I said.

"I'm getting fat," Barbie said.

Barbie was crawling all over me, and I wondered if Jennifer

knew she was a nymphomaniac. I wondered if Jennifer knew what a nymphomaniac was.

"You don't belong with little girls," I said.

Barbie ignored me.

There were scratches on Barbie's chest and stomach. She didn't say anything about them and so at first I pretended not to notice. As I was touching her, I could feel they were deep, like slices. The edges were rough; my finger caught on them and I couldn't help but wonder.

"Jennifer?" I said massaging the cuts with my tongue, as though my tongue, like sandpaper, would erase them. Barbie nodded.

In fact, I thought of using sandpaper, but didn't know how I could explain it to Barbie: *you have to lie still and let me rub it really hard with this stuff that's like terry cloth dipped in cement.* I thought she might even like it if I made it into an S&M kind of thing and handcuffed her first.

I ran my tongue back and forth over the slivers, back and forth over the words "copyright 1966 Mattel Inc., Malaysia" tattooed on her back. Tonguing the tattoo drove Barbie crazy. She said it had something to do with scar tissue being extremely sensitive.

Barbie pushed herself hard against me, I could feel her slices rubbing my skin. I was thinking that Jennifer might kill Barbie. Without meaning to she might just go over the line and I wondered if Barbie would know what was happening or if she'd try to stop her.

We fucked, that's what I called it, fucking. In the beginning Barbie said she hated the word, which made me like it even more. She hated it because it was so strong and hard, and she said we weren't fucking, we were making love. I told her she had to be kidding.

"Fuck me," she said that afternoon and I knew the end was coming soon. "Fuck me," she said. I didn't like the sound of the word.

FRIDAY when I went into Jennifer's room, there was something in the air. The place smelled like a science lab, a fire, a failed experiment.

Barbie was wearing a strapless yellow evening dress. Her hair was wrapped into a high bun, more like a wedding cake than something Betty Crocker would whip up. There seemed to be layers and layers of angel's hair spinning in a circle above her head. She had yellow pins through her ears and gold fuck-me shoes that matched the belt around her waist. For a second I thought of the belt and imagined tying her up, but more than restraining her arms or legs, I thought of wrapping the belt around her face, tying it across her mouth.

I looked at Barbie and saw something dark and thick like a scar rising up and over the edge of her dress. I grabbed her and pulled the front of the dress down.

"Hey, big boy," Barbie said. "Don't I even get a hello?"

Barbie's breasts had been sawed at with a knife. There were a hundred marks from a blade that might have had five rows of teeth like shark jaws. And as if that wasn't enough, she'd been dissolved by fire, blue and yellow flames had been pressed against her and held there until she melted and eventually became the fire that burned herself. All of it had been somehow stirred with the head of a pencil, the point of a pen, and left to cool. Molten Barbie flesh had been left to harden, black and pink plastic swirled together, in the crater Jennifer had dug out of her breasts.

I examined her in detail like a scientist, a pathologist, a fucking medical examiner. I studied the burns, the gouged-out area, as if by looking closely I'd find something, an explanation, a way out.

A disgusting taste came up into my mouth, like I'd been sucking on batteries. It came up, then sank back down into my stomach, leaving my mouth puckered with the bitter metallic flavor of sour saliva. I coughed and spit onto my shirt sleeve, then rolled the sleeve over to cover the wet spot.

With my index finger I touched the edge of the burn as lightly as I could. The round rim of her scar broke off under my finger. I almost dropped her.

"It's just a reduction," Barbie said. "Jennifer and I are even now."

Barbie was smiling. She had the same expression on her face as when I first saw her and fell in love. She had the same expression she always had and I couldn't stand it. She was smiling, and she was burned. She was smiling and she was ruined. I pulled her dress back up, above the scar line. I put her down carefully on the doily on top of the dresser and started to walk away.

"Hey," Barbie said, "aren't we going to play?"

Brilliant Mistake

ROBERT BOSWELL

T HE RHYTHM OF THE SCHWINN WAS THE RHYTHM OF MY
life, a soulful gliding pulse like Smokey Robinson in
"Ooh Baby Baby"—that glottal skip, falsetto slide. The
temperature had topped out at one hundred nine, faded to one-
oh-four by dusk, would not drop into double figures all night
long, heat rising from the asphalt, rising from the vacant desert
lots, rippling up into the breathing air, smelling of tar, exhaust,
exhaustion. Standing on the pedals, I rode a ribbon through the
stalled traffic on Fourth Avenue, rolling up and down the concrete gutters, chugging to Smokey playing in my head, a song I
didn't hear so much as perform, pumping hard, then coasting,
the horizon going green on its way to black, shutting down for
the night, dimming like a bad bulb, while the Schwinn, purple
and chrome with a white banana seat, took me across the swelter-
ing town, my T-shirt growing dark with sweat, hair standing thick
with it, lips salty from it, on my way to see Karla Lowe, my girl-

friend, the summer before high school, a quarter of a century ago.

Karla had an oval swimming pool in her backyard, and her mouth, when shaping her last name, took the precise contour of her pool. "Lowe," I said aloud, tasting it like hard candy, leaning into a corner, my heart working its bump and throb, beating time with the Schwinn, with Smokey, with the bang and bang of being thirteen and being on my bike, Karla Lowe and her pool and her mouth like a pool waiting for me.

Her parents were out of town. I pictured the waters of her pool dark and turbulent, rainswept, as if a deep lake, a river jetty, a quarry some place where the powers of nature balanced out. Not that I was a stellar swimmer, not even a sound swimmer. I was a flail-and-thrash sort of swimmer—self-taught—a drowning sort of swimmer, but I could hold my breath a long time, longer than Lloyd Bridges, longer than Smokey embracing that "ooh" on the last note, and holding my breath, I would submerge, push off the rounded walls, traverse the pool beneath the surface, coasting, arms arching ahead, chest and hips in a slither, the water like air—a kind of flight.

From my house to Karla's, pumping hard: eighteen minutes, three erections. In the tall oleanders that concealed her yard, I hid my Schwinn, grime from the dirty leaves sticking to my slathered arms like dust to the screen of a lit TV. The music startled me, the fact of it, and the specific line, a black voice really doing it up:

"The purpose of the man is to love his woman."

Through a gap in the slats of the high cedar fence, I saw the shindig—big sister's party, seniors in high school shaking their hips by the pool, wearing bathing suits, making faces, twirling their arms like they'd seen on "American Bandstand," while others lounged in the water around the pool's dark lip, sipping drinks, smiling, rolling their high-school eyes. Boys in polo shirts and swimming shorts crowded the keg on the covered patio, gesturing with their paper cups. A couple standing near the fence began to moan, the boy kissing the girl the way I wanted to kiss Karla, his hands roaming from her bare back to the bottom of her bikini, a single finger rimming the wrinkled elastic band.

I entered the yard through the gate. Karla was leaning against a white wrought-iron patio post, her green one-piece lapping up her body, two high-school boys—juniors, maybe seniors—hovering about her, leering like old men, touching her naked arm. She saw me come in, raised her dark brows as a greeting, didn't snub me, not exactly, just let me know she preferred the older boys—for the night, anyway. Which struck me as *why not,* as *okay,* as *fair enough.*

I smiled, stared straight at her, smiled, and yanked off my shirt, stepped to the knobby rim of the oval pool, letting the round rise of the concrete press against my arches, then dove into the shallow water, disappeared beneath the surface, the night suddenly soundless, my arms aching ahead, chest and hips in a writhing glide, coasting, flying.

I came up in the deep end, still cutting through the water, angling toward the darkest corner of the pool, where two girls drank liquor and watched me slither near, ice tinkling in their glasses, shadows moving across their faces, watery light appearing beneath their eyes and vanishing.

"Who are you?" one asked me, her voice friendly, flirtatious, slightly slurred, slightly drunk.

I told her my name, coasting closer, just my name, my chin breaking the water, shadow and light riding my face, sliding up to them, bumping into them, my cheek suddenly against a girl's breast, my legs against their warm legs, my submerged body against their submerged bodies—a miscalculation, a boy just out of eighth grade staring at girls almost ready for college, an accident (sweet accident, brilliant mistake), which would have embarrassed me, but it made them laugh. They thought I'd done it on purpose.

"I know who you are," the girl said, the girl whose breast my cheek had brushed. "You go to East High," she said, her smile a piece of the moon, luminous and white, her wet hair pulled back, falling to her bare shoulders, the straps of her bathing suit loose and looping about her arms like exotic jewelry. "We go to Central," she said. "You're on the basketball team, aren't you?"

"I was on the basketball team," I said, which was true, but it was the junior-high team, the Woodard Termites, and I had been the tenth man on a ten-man team.

The other girl pulled herself from the pool, water cascading down her back and bottom, rippling the dark water. "I'll get us something more to drink," she said, looking at me, brows pitched. "Jack on the rocks okay?"

"Sure," I said, no idea what it meant. The space she emptied, I filled, as if her leaving created a current that sucked me over, a friendly tide. The girl's legs and mine rubbed together beneath the water, this girl I didn't know, maybe four years older than I, who might already have had sex, this girl, her legs against mine, her hair pulled back, her smile the moon. Then Smokey came over the stereo, "Ooh Baby Baby," the song I'd been hearing all day, my song, and I put my hand inside the top of her bathing suit.

Never had I done anything like it before, and I didn't know why I did it then, currents of air guiding my hand.

"Someone will see," she said but did nothing to remove it, smiling again, her hand gliding to my shoulder, touching the cut of my hair at the back of my neck.

Her breast was dimpled from the cool water, the nipple a pressure against the heart of my palm. I did not massage or squeeze her breast, but cupped it gently, as if to feel the rhythm of

201

her heart, or to help her pledge allegiance. Smokey's voice soared, and I felt her knee lift, parting my legs. My face did not touch hers, but there was no space between us, her breathing urgent against my cheek—warm, moist breaths.

Then the other girl returned with our drinks. Squatting, she sat on the pool's concrete rim before letting her legs slide into the water. I removed my hand, took the glass. Without drinking, without tasting a drop on my tongue, I dipped beneath the surface and pushed off the wall, coasting through the water, away from them, the ice in the glass floating up against my shoulder as it drifted away. I let the glass sink slowly to the pool's blue bottom.

I surfaced at the other end. Karla was with just one boy now, her back against the white post, the boy leaning over her, his hand touching the taut skin along her neck.

"I think I'm going to leave," I said and grabbed my shirt from the pool deck.

"See you," said she.

I rode the Schwinn, the warm night black now, still triple figures, but I was cooled by my wet body, pumping hard, water from my hair running down my cheeks, evaporating, the road loaded with headlights that grew near, that illuminated me, then let me go. Meanwhile, the party played on, and Karla was led inside to her own bedroom, her own bed, the green one-piece making a wet mark on the carpet, an oval like the pool itself, like Karla's mouth when speaking her name, the summer before high school, twenty-five years ago.

And still I think I left at the right time, still I think swimming underwater with the drink was a good exit, and the girl, a woman now, must remember our few minutes in the dark of the pool with the same appreciative mystery that I do.

It is the one perfect moment in my life.

Pretty Judy

KEVIN CANTY

JUDY'S WINDOW WAS NEAR THE TOP OF THE HOUSE, NEXT TO the supple tip of a tall, straight juniper tree, she'd lean out and call to the schoolchildren as they passed by, in the morning and again in the afternoon, especially the boys. A white house with green shutters in a lake of brilliant lawn, a tulip tree spreading over the grass and flowers and hedges, the pair of candle-shaped junipers guarding the chimney all the way up to the third story, all rambling, graceful, not too perfect. Her mother, Mrs. MacGregor, coached her at the beginning of every school year, so that by October Judy knew nearly everyone's name. October mornings, the rain splattering out of the leaves of the trees that lined the streets, their limbs meeting overhead, a tunnel of green turning gold, and Judy's high clear voice drifting down: Hi Jerry! Hi Mary! Hi Paul!

But school was out, this was June, another rainy month, but more optimistic. Paul was coming back alone from the high school courts, where he'd hit a yellow tennis ball against the backstop for forty-five minutes. He said to himself, I am solitary, I am not lonely. My mother is a pediatrician, my father is an architect, I am going to college. Still, it was sweet to hear the high, piping voice float down from her window: Hi Paul! Hi Paul!

Hi Judy!

Come say hi to me!

You couldn't tell what was wrong with Judy by looking at her face, except that she would forget sometimes to close her mouth, and easy questions would worry her. Everything she felt was on her face, now round as a cartoon sun, pleased, elbows on the sill, staring down at him. The neighborhood said she was nineteen, or even twenty-one, but really she was a kid, kid T-shirts, lollipop colors, big and pink, glossy blond hair cropped blunt at her neck. All day, in the summer emptiness, the familiar streets and sidewalks had felt strange to Paul; he was fifteen, growing out of his boy's body into something else; he had passed her house a thousand times and still knew nothing about her. What was it like in Judy's room?

In the driveway was a greasy spot where Judy's mother's station wagon was not.

Can I come in?

Come in, yes! Come say hi to me!

CURIOSITY wasn't all of it. He crept around to the kitchen door like a thief, though this was the proper door—in this neighborhood the front door was for company, the side or back for familiars. He prayed this was not the day for the cleaning woman. The neighborhood boys told rumors about Judy, and Paul did not want to be misunderstood, or understood at all; he wanted to be alone, weightless, he wanted this to be happening in his imagination. The halls of the MacGregors' house were mournful, serious, other people's dead peering down at him from smoky paintings. The stairs were light maple, like a bowling alley, but the banister was some dark wood, deep red, like dried, polished blood. He was still holding his tennis racket, a ticket of membership. Red carpets with dark patterns, baskets of dried grasses and leaves, neat and tidy, scented with wax and lemons. Their other children were away at college. Paul guessed wrong on the third floor, opened the wrong door—to the attic, bare wood and piles of old *New Yorkers* and clothes—and again he felt that his life and everything in it was just a sham, something put up quickly for the sake of a picture, the thickness of a photograph.

PAUL, SHE SAID, Pauletta Paulotta Paulola Pauleeleelu.

Standing plainly in the middle of the carpet, as if she wasn't sure what to do with her body, too big to hide.

How are you, Judy?

I was watching, she said. I always am.

Mournful deep green plaids on the cushions in the window seat, the rocking chair, the flounced bed; Paul had been expecting dolls, primary yellows. And she was big. She always surprised everyone at picnics or at the annual yard sale, Paul's height at least, and imposing. Not fat but big, with tiny feet—how could her feet support her? She was a familiar face, but apart from her face he knew nothing about her. He had never been alone with her before, nor in her room, and he did not know what he was doing there; he was nervous, waiting to leave, wanting to stay. He did not know where to stand. Windows open, a rainy trickle of air filtering through the trees. Paul looked down at the sidewalk, an empty place, waiting.

A car, Judy said. There's one. Make it go.

Go where?

I was playing with the cars, she said. I think that if I think, I can make them go faster or slow down or go the same, or maybe I don't. I don't know.

I'll make it go left, he said, and they both watched. The car went straight, tires swishing on the wet pavement. It had started to rain again. What was he supposed to say? Something. Beyond her familiar shape she was so unknown. A slight voltage of alarm.

That's nice, he said.

Judy looked at him, frowned. He was making her unhappy. Someday the perfect playmate, but it wouldn't be him. He could think of nothing that would make her better. They knelt together on the window-seat cushion, touching at the shoulder and the hip, a shared rainy sadness, neither of them was right. Gradually Paul became aware of her body, her warmth and weight. What would she allow him? A red Volvo passed under the window, a black sedan. His hand reached out, he watched it like a movie, and touched her bare forearm below the sleeve of her sweatshirt. Paul himself didn't touch her, only his hand.

Oh, Judy said.

PAUL FELT his heart start in his chest like a big rough motor, wondered what he had done. The sound of her voice, her little cry, was like nothing he had heard from a human voice, pure pleasure, he thought, she must have very sensitive skin. He touched her bare neck and saw her head wave blindly back and forth, eyes closed, like a dreamer seeing a beautiful city in the distance.

Oh, she said again, and Oh! as he touched her breast through the layers of fabric, sweatshirt and brassiere, remembering that the world could see them through her window, tugging her down to the carpeted floor, out of sight. She followed him obediently, it seemed to Paul that she was blind to anything but touch, drunk with it. He lifted her sweatshirt and then put his hand on the hard lace of her brassiere, no resistance, only her soft, lost voice, he rolled her onto her side, reached behind her and fumbled with the little hooks until by some miracle her bra came unsprung and her big soft breasts tumbled against him. Paul felt drunk himself, with excitement and with panic. He had fumbled in playrooms before, in cars and in the rough grass of the neighborhood parks, girls from the neighborhood who would negotiate a touch, or on some lucky Saturday allow his blind hand to wander in the darkness of their jeans, but this, this plain revelation, was new to him. She wouldn't stop him, wouldn't stop him from anything, her hunger for every new touch was so direct. He knew what he was risking, the air itself was lit with danger, knew that if either of them was going to stop this, it would not be her, but she was so close, so open to him.

Paul had one last lucid moment, sitting away to undo his belt, her sweatpants lying beside her and her shirt hiked around her shoulders, the defenseless bulk of Judy. "Oh," she said again and again, as if this moment's absence of his hands were more than she could bear; and Paul saw what he was doing, knew that it was wrong, he meant to apologize and to leave, yet there she was, he could not stop looking. He didn't, he remembered later, bother to fasten his belt again, but there wasn't any Judy anymore, only this: a pink mewling thing, cries that started back in her throat, as if he were hurting her, the last trace of language gone. Her little hands were callused, hard as a carpenter's. Later he would think of her in animal terms: she mewled like a kitten, bawled and bucked like a hungry calf, and still later—years after—he would decide that this was because there was so little human veneer to her; that sex and awareness were natural enemies, a battle every time between modesty, a sense of order and of embarrassment, and the little kindling flame of desire. But Judy's desire was pure, reservations, questions burnt away, an animal thing, he told himself, an animal thing, but he met her in it and matched her, lost in guilt, engulfed, unwilling to stop, to breathe. He couldn't seem to stop, he came as soon as he was inside her.

Don't stop, she said.

Paul's mouth had filled with sand, the whore, the horror. Pants around his knees, he slid shamefully from inside her and leaned against the window seat, a sickness quickly filling him that he would not be able to vomit out. Thoughts of escape.

Don't stop, she said again, turned her head toward Paul and briefly focused her eyes on him, then let them go blank again, turned her face to the wall, dropped her hand between her legs and quickly brought herself off again, cat-cries that the whole world could hear, listening from the window. Then said something he didn't catch.

What's that? he asked, dragging the words from somewhere inside.

Pretty Judy, she whispered to the wall.

Then he knew what she was asking for, and for a moment he thought that he would just leave, disappear. But some reserve of courage found him, and he reached out a reluctant hand and whispered, That's right. Pretty Judy.

Pretty Judy, she said.

He stroked the soft curve of her hip, her fascination hadn't left him, even in his shame. Pretty Judy, he said.

The slam of a car door jolted him upright, he went to the window and peered carefully through but it wasn't Mrs. MacGregor, not yet. The neighbors. But still.

She turned her face from the wall, like a dreamer, still half in sleep. You better go, she said. I don't want my mom to get mad.

PAUL HEARD THIS like a reprieve. He gathered his clothes back into order, looked back from the doorway, but she didn't seem to expect a kiss, still lying pink, inert, half-naked. And he didn't want to kiss her then. Had he at all? Yes, he remembered her busy, surprising tongue in his mouth. Demons of shame whipped him down the stairs, out into the clean, rain-washed streets and down the sidewalk, as if all this had happened in a sidewalk crack, an excursion out of time, a moment of imagination.

Hi Paul!

He tensed, heart in his throat, as if the trees and air had announced him guilty for all the neighborhood to hear. Looked up, saw her waving, back in her sweatshirt. Paul waved unsurely, turned his back on her, walked away, felt her eyes on his neck until he reached the cover of the sheltering trees. Walking away, betrayal. Closing his eyes, feeling her heavy breasts against him, he nearly tripped over one of the Morganfield kids rounding the driveway on a Big Wheel.

Hey, fuck you, the kid said.

Paul grinned. Fuck you, too, he said. A kid again for a moment, biggest kid on the block, he could get his way, but then he tripped over the word fuck, and remembered. He walked on toward his house and he knew, stood convicted: he was like her, they were equal. Not then, but in that green bedroom, two bodies, neither better than the other. This was the worst thing to know about himself: he was just like her, they were equal. He saw her busy hand between her legs, blank eyes, and thought of all the times in the shower or in his room.

This awful equality frightened him, worse than the guilt. He was just like her, and he tried to defend himself as he walked toward his house: her fault, but it wasn't, he knew it; only curiosity, but he knew the rumors before he went, he couldn't deny it. He could have stopped, anytime, he'd known. It seemed like somebody else, in memory, it had never happened.

It had never happened, as long as it was a secret, who would Judy talk to, who would Judy tell? He imagined her mouth rounding around the words I fucked Paul, and her mother's straight mouth and iron hair, a tidy, self-sacrificing fifty. Plaid skirts, church on Sunday. If she found out she would put him in jail, and that would be easy; better than this, this black, corrosive secret, cancer of the mind. But Judy would never tell, and Paul would never tell. He dragged his secret, like the body of a dead dog, up the back steps to his kitchen, where his mother, the pediatrician, was making tuna salad in the skylit brightness.

Hi sweetie, she said. Where's your tennis racket?

PAUL LIT like a man on a hot wire. He didn't have an answer for this, and his mother looked at him curiously, seeing right through his pants and his shorts to his wet, guilty dick. I loaned it to Colin, he finally said.

I thought he was in Denver.

Denmark, Paul said. He's coming home tomorrow.

Both of them took a moment to realize this made no sense. Paul added, I put it in his garage, as if this would make anything clear. He felt his hands grow until they were enormous bald red things, guilty secrets that would not be concealed, then realized he'd have to go on the offensive if he was going to escape.

He said, I don't know, I guess I'm having sort of a hard time.

His mother's handsome face darkened with concern. She was

a fan of emotional honesty, she thought it was healthy, a guarantee of a good childhood, her specialty. Although he would have to think of something to tell her later.

Paul said, Can we talk later? Right now I just want to think some things through. I'm basically OK. OK?

OK, his mother said, little furrows of concern rising at the inner edges of her eyebrows. She waved her chef's knife helplessly in the air as he retreated to his room, not one o'clock yet, watery afternoon light, the afternoon and the evening to be gotten through before there was any prospect of sleep, and sleep was all he wanted, the black invisibility. Paul wanted to become invisible to himself, he seemed like evidence. Thinking of his tennis racket, ticking like a terrorist's dream in Judy's room, thinking, I will be punished for this. The discovery, trial by disappointment, maybe worse.

Whatever, he thought. Anything he could touch would be easier than this. Anything outside himself. Jimi Hendrix stared down at him from the wall, psychedelic purple and green, a dirty mouth under a thin, sinister mustache. Paul took his purple Telecaster from its case in the closet, a better guitar than he should have had but money was not a problem in this house. He plugged it into a Tube Screamer and then into a headphone amp and turned the distortion up to ten and played his same stupid chords and clumsy leads. He was never better, never even good, but it passed the time, he could lose himself completely, a closed loop, fingers to guitar to amp to ears, no one else to hear him, like jacking off. Hendrix's eyes, eyes that could look at anything. The afternoon disappeared, a pencil line under an eraser. He played until his fingers hurt, and then till one of them bled a little.

Paul put his guitar away as the light was leaving the windows, no lamps yet, a gray, ghostly light, and from behind the pile of records at the back of his closet he took a tattered *Penthouse*, and opened it to a photograph of two girls faking sex with each other, ghostly girls in the half-light, secret skin in tight close-up, and Paul knew, looking at the picture, that he had thought of nothing else all afternoon: tongue in his mouth, animal voice in his ear, hard little carpenter's hands.

I will be good, he told himself, no idea what he meant.

THAT NIGHT he dreamt of her, woke up hard in the darkness of his room, a room that was newly strange, images of birds, of houses seen from a great height, persisting from some earlier part of his dream. A stranger to himself, an unsolvable problem, if train A leaves city X at five-thirty and travels north, he wandered the dark hallways toward the kitchen, hoping for ice cream. He'd barely eaten at dinner. Even his father had noticed. Summer school was out, his few friends had left town, nothing days. His mother sat with him after breakfast, inquired about drugs, he was scheduled to start a job in three weeks, did he need something to fill the time? Anomie, he said, bringing a smile to her face with the new word, the one thing he did right all day. The tennis racket ticked in a corner of Judy's room, without going off. Tuesday nothing Wednesday nothing Thursday nothing, but he prowled the streets, a thief of opportunity, telling himself that he was only going to get the racket back. His nights were populated with versions of Judy, *Penthouse* dolls, secret skin, not the child who called to him still, Hi Paul! when he walked by to see if Mrs. MacGregor's car was in the driveway—it always was—or the cleaning woman was there, but the tongue in his mouth, cries in his ear. He could not connect the two, could not believe that the afternoon had been anything but a dream, though now it was his everyday life that seemed like a dream, nothing weighed anything, nothing mattered, he found himself trying to read the clouds. It continued to rain, never hard, never letting up. Judy was growing inside him like a child, taking shape, stretching to be born, feeding on his blood. Even his father noticed.

He was only going to get the racket back. Friday morning he saw Mrs. MacGregor's car swish by under the arching trees, a flash of imitation wood grain, a chance. A man two streets over had built a speedboat in his basement, a beautiful shape of varnished, steam-bent maple, without thinking how he was going to get it out. This was twenty years before, the house had been sold twice, the boat was still there.

PAUL, SHE SAID, Pauletta Paulotta Paulola Pauleeleelu.

There in the corner was the tennis racket, and there she was. The air was turning fire-engine green, a whining in his ears like television, he wanted to lie down on the floor and cry like a baby boy.

She said, My mom is gone all day.

He lay down on the floor. Without affection, she came and lay beside him. The carpet was thick, soft and green, like a lawn, and as her clumsy fingers fumbled with his pants Paul wondered what the name for this was, fucking seemed too hard, making love seemed preposterous, maybe, as he lost the name for anything, maybe that was part of it, no name because it wasn't anything human. Paul gave up his thoughts, met Judy on the carpet as body to body, equals, he remembered, equals. As he gave himself over to her hard little hands, he realized that only the things around it were at all human: courtship and roses, satin, magazines, going steady, we only owned the box, the thing in the box belonged to someone else, before words; and words extinguished themselves in his brain, though his eye kept recording, memories like pictures, her face, which was like an empty house, the rain in the trees outside, the plaid bedspread. Better than anything, but he wondered, in the shocked quiet afterward, what he was letting himself in for. He didn't know anything.

She said, I want some ice cream, Paul. Get me some, please.

Left her lying on her side, her back to him, like an accident victim, heavy and inert. Nearly left, when he got to the kitchen, but remembered that his racket was still upstairs—the first joke, first hint that he was being played with. He thought of Judy and her cars, go left, now stop, and wondered who or what was watching him. Ice cream, two spoons, back along the morose hallways. What would it be like? A mommy, a daddy, a house. The ghostliness of these recent days came over him again, and he imagined that he would one day have all this, a house as big and fine as this one, a wife like Judy, only more intelligent, like looking down a deep hole into the future. A wife like Judy, what was so different? What was so wrong? But he knew as soon as he saw her, dressed again, big and drooping. They sat in the window seat and finished the ice cream, and when another kid walked by, Paul ducked out of sight and watched her lean out the window and wave, stretching her limbs eagerly like a plant bending toward the sun, and her smile and her sweet voice, Hi Larry! and the happiness that came and left her face so quickly, like breath on a mirror.

She seemed disappointed when her eyes turned into the room again and found him still there. Too much to think about. He pulled her down to the floor again.

THEN A WEEKEND at the beach with Mom and Dad, a relief in a way, he hoped things would become clearer, or go away. For the first time Paul was afraid of himself, what he was capable of. He thought of Judy in dirty particulars, every waking minute, he couldn't stop, he wanted air. He sat in the breakfast nook talking about the design of kites with his father, at the same time swearing to himself that he would never walk down her block, at the same time staring at his pornographic memories. He lay in the dunes alone, a hollow picket of sand rimmed with saw grass, out of the wind, feeling the warm, cleansing sun pour down on his skin, and the whole world seemed to turn into Judy: Judy in the softness of the sand, in the warmth of the sun, in the ebb and tickle of the wave's retreat, especially Judy in the way the sand retreated from under his feet in the outwash, left him standing uneven, unsure of even the ground.

He swore that he would never see her again, never closer than the sidewalk, but this was not the truth. He decided that the kindest thing to do would be to be friends, like regular people. He dreamt about putting his hand between her legs, and it was always her. In practical terms he watched a lot of television, played his guitar, took solitary walks. It seemed impossible for his parents to know nothing, he was wearing her on every inch of his skin, but they were too caught up in their own romance, getting to know each other again was how they put it. They seemed like children to Paul, willful, self-absorbed children.

He stole a chance to see her on Monday, she was glad to see him and he was so pleased to see her smile that he wondered if he were in love. More words for something that there weren't any words for, he was learning. No time for anything that day, though, he had to slip out over the roof to avoid the cleaning lady. A near miss, he was taking chances. He felt tainted but he knew he couldn't turn away from her. Friday was her day alone, he knew, her mother went to volunteer at the Anglican Senior Citizens' Day Care Center, her father worked, the cleaning lady disappeared back into the dark reaches of the invisible city. How would he live till Friday? He would not see her Friday, he made up his mind again and again. He was definite on this point.

*   *   *

Then the miracle: Mrs. MacGregor drove away at ten Wednesday morning, leaving Judy undefended in the house. Paul saw the station wagon from the window of his room, and knew as it turned the corner, went away, that it didn't matter what he thought, he was going. He stayed in his room for another half an hour, but it was futile, the only idea that presented itself was that it didn't matter, right or wrong, crazy or real, he was going. His will seemed to count for nothing at all. I will treat her with compassion, he declared to himself, like the human being that she is. This sounded like the Boy Scouts, even to his own ears: when he closed his eyes, trying to think, he saw her blank-eyed shiver at the touch of his fingertips. Sleepwalking, dreaming his hand in front of his face. He was wrong, he was born wrong, he was broken.

Judy, he said, is your mother gone?

She nodded.

All day?

All day, she said happily, just like a child, just like the child she really was. Mom said to get my lunch on the table.

I want to take you to the zoo, he said, surprising himself with a sudden rush of moral correctness. Go see the animals, the bears and the giraffes and the elephants. Do you want to?

No, I want to do it. I want you to do it.

We can do it later, don't you want to go?

She looked at him, the window, the carpeted floor. OK, she finally said, still reluctant. He was just starting to realize how much time she spent in a bad mood.

He asked, Are those the clothes you want to wear?

But she didn't know, too complicated a question, and so he let it drop, wondering if her mother dressed her still: a pink sweatshirt with a big yellow sun on it, blue sweatpants, Keds. Big sunny Judy. They could just stay, Paul knew it, the thought of all that tangible skin, the slippery, solid bulk of her beneath him, a thickness of cloth away from his empty hands, but he was going to be right today.

OUT THE BACK DOOR, then, through the alley as quickly as he could drag her along, the terror of discovery behind every fence. Even on the avenue, he kept his eyes fixed straight ahead, magic vision, if he couldn't see anyone then they couldn't see him, or sun-bright Judy either, waiting docile and obedient next to him in the bus shelter. He started to breathe again on the bus, the happy couple, Judy looking neat and nearly pretty on the seat beside him; and she was pretty to Paul, despite her size, he could touch her anywhere in memory and she seemed to him so much softer and enclosing than any normal girl could ever be. They rode across town without talking, watching the streets; and Paul felt that she could be anyone, that nothing was really so wrong, that they were different but other couples were different, too. The comfort of her nearness, her side pressed to his; but when they went through the poor part of town, deserted streets bright with advertising, a car on fire down one of the side streets surrounded by a village of flashing police cars, he remembered what a dangerous place the city was; a moment's worry, memory of things that hadn't happened yet.

The zoo was empty, the bears asleep, the giraffes staring thoughtfully as they ate, evaluating the flavor of every eucalyptus leaf. Paul felt the weight of how much he knew: elephant, sycamore, the distance to the stars, how to check the oil in his father's car, how to pay for things, her blank uncomprehending stare at the ticket booth, not even caring: beyond her. Yet her company was right for this place, she saw the strength of the tiger, ignored the path he had worn in the grass. The sadness of the rhinoceri, lying sideways in the mud like wrecked trucks, the manic intensity of the monkeys' stare and the bare patches on their skin where they had picked away each other's fur, all this eluded her; and she ran from cage to cage, laughing, delighted when anything moved. Her hair, glossy and fair as a blond child's, shined in the scattered sunlight, and her face in happiness was nearly pretty.

At first Paul liked her company, her cheerfulness, young and strong in the sun, delightful things to see, the promise of ice cream later. Gradually, though, he began to lose heart, there was too much she didn't see, and the other patrons stared at her when she talked in her overloud voice, Look Paul, look Paulie, elephants! He wanted to flip them all off, wanted to be transported, back to Judy's room. In his black heart he knew he had betrayed both of them. He wasn't interested in her, or she in him; what held them together was sex and nothing more. He was angry with her; she should have known.

SUDDENLY she whirled to face him, fear and anger on her face. No! she screamed. No, Paulie!

What?

I don't want to, Paulie!

People were staring, he looked around and saw a straggling band of badly retarded adults staring down into the empty otter pen, the pool where they weren't, their keepers explaining.

I don't want to!

What?

Go with them! I don't want to!

You don't have to.

I want to go! she said. I don't want to stay here!

OK, he said, all right. He put it together as he led her toward

218

the gate, she must have thought he meant to leave her here, or at least the fear. She stumbled, looking behind. The anger had passed from her face but the fear remained.

Ice cream, Paul said. You want some?

No! I want to go!

After we leave, he said. He had to calm her down somehow. Outside the gate she seemed less agitated, outside the bars, away from the cages. He led her past the duck pond, toward the derelict hot dog stand in faded red-and-white that stood across the pond from the entrance to the zoo. The morning sun was getting hot, Judy was tiring, so he had to drag her a little to get her to come along with him, but she brightened when she saw the boats, little paddleboats that seated two, which one pedaled like a bicycle.

Boats, Paulie! Judy shouted.

Don't you want some ice cream?

I want to go in the boats.

He knew then what a bad idea this trip had been. He was getting hot himself, and the prospect of paddling around this duck-fouled acre of water, exposed to the hot sun and fully visible to any passerby, did not please him. But there was no way around it. He paid the candy-striped boy behind the iron grille and took command of boat 17, an aqua plastic double bathtub, settled her into the sun-hot seat and pushed away. Again he saw the maimed and crippled ducks, their senseless fights, their shit fermenting on the concrete shore, while Judy, in the purity of her delight, saw only the sparkling sun on the water, the happy trees, the smiling clouds and the happy little boat. The sun embroidered on her sweatshirt, it felt like he was carrying a suitcase full of someone else's things. He began to feel a headache.

* * *

Three times around the little willow-draped island in the center of the pond, always in the same direction because Judy couldn't get the drift of paddling, they always went left. This tired him out, and he stopped, though he didn't want to. Judy looked to the left and to the right, and then she took his hand in her own hard little palm, led it to her bare forearm and sighed as she felt the soft pressure of his fingertips on her own sun-warm arm.

Oh, she said in drowsy delight.

For some reason this repelled him. We can't, he said, not here.

Just touch me.

Not here.

I want to go home, she said.

OK, Paul said, relieved. Let me put the boat away.

No, I want to go home.

We have to put the boat away.

Mom! she cried. I want my mom!

Abruptly she stood up, nearly tipping the little tub over, and looked around the shore, expecting to see her mother.

Mom! she cried out. Mom! Mom!

A silence spread along the dirty shores of the pond, and every stranger's face was turned toward them. He took her hand, tried to coax her down onto the seat again, but she shook free, and he could not move the boat with her standing up. Twice she nearly fell into the water, and then he gave up, closed his eyes and hoped for whatever there was to hope for, which was nothing, nothing he could think of. The sun was pleasant, though, and the sound of the water lapping against the fiberglass hull, little hollow drumming notes, like a marimba.

Mom! Judy yelled. Mom!

She was nearly crying, baffled, near the end of her rope. Heavy, flustered. He wondered what would happen next, wondered, if he never opened his eyes, if this could still be imaginary. Then heard the sound of an outboard motor start and stop and start again. He followed Judy's gaze: a tin Sears boat with three uniforms in it, the candy-striped kid from the ticket stand riding the motor, a park policeman sitting nervously in the middle, gripping the rim of the boat, and in the prow, standing, a zoo guard in his red uniform, one foot propped on the seat, smoking, looking like an admiral in the Italian navy, gold braid and a peculiar hat, and he was leaning forward, elbows on his raised knee, and staring at Judy and at Paul, and only then, at that moment, as he watched the zoo policeman take one last drag from his cigarette, then hurl the butt into the rushing, tea-colored water, did Paul realize how badly this was all going to end.

Thunderbird

MARK JUDE POIRIER

I T'S JULY, THE SUN'S HOT AND WHITE IN MY EYES, AND A DIRTY
kid named Peter rides up, thinking he can use the jumps we
built from old real-estate signs. We spent all of June clearing
trash and tangled barbwire from this dirt lot behind Taco Bell so
we could have a good place to ride our bikes. Jay even had to get
a tetanus shot when he cut his arm on an old mattress spring.
And Peter just shows up. I think, *Go away, go away,* but Jay and
Phil don't say anything.

Peter had crooked bangs like his mom cut his hair in their
kitchen, and his teeth and lips are stained purple from juice. He
has a crappy bike—a Huffy, from Gemco or Zody's. We have Di-
amondbacks from real bike shops. Jay even has hundred-dollar
Tough Wheels. I didn't go near Peter at school last year. He's the
type of kid who'd shove me into a urinal or wind a rubber band
and let it loose in my hair or start a rumor that my mom's a lesbian, all for no reason.

But Peter hits the jumps and soars way higher than any of us ever has. His front and back wheel hit the dirt at the same time. He looks over at us and smiles, knows we're watching him, knows he's good, better than us, even though he has a shitty bike and we have good ones.

"MY DAD was runner-up to be an astronaut," Peter says. The four of us share a plate of nachos covered in bright orange cheese, sitting at a faded plastic picnic table in the shade of a truck. Jay bought the nachos. He always does. His mother gives him five dollars a day because she feels guilty that his dad ran off like my dad did. Jay's dad ran off with their old neighbor, a lady named Deborah who Jay's mom says has a drug problem.

I know Peter's lying about his dad almost being an astronaut, but I don't care. I like his froggy voice. It makes my stomach feel nervous and my neck tingle in a good way.

"Bullshit," Phil says. "Your dad was a realtor, and he couldn't sell any houses, so now your family's poor."

I stare down at the stained cement, my dumb, too-skinny ankles, my new sneakers—blue slip-on Vans. When I finally look up, Peter's pedaling away toward Bear Canyon Road, his heavy bicycle rocking back and forth between his legs. Peter has hair on his legs already.

"It's true," Phil says. "They had to drain their pool because they couldn't afford the water bills." Phil snatches the last two chips and stuffs them in his mouth with a loud crackle.

"How do you know?" Jay asks.

"My mom," Phil says, still chewing.

Phil's mom dresses like a teenager in tank tops and really small running shorts to show off her tanned skin. She never wears a bra and I've seen her nipples twice: once when she was driving us to Skate Country and she twisted around to reach in the backseat for Phil's skates and the other time when she leaned over to pick up a penny on their kitchen floor. She looks at me like she knows all of my secrets, and whenever I go over to Phil's house—every time—she asks me, "What do you hear from your father these days, Craigy?" I have to tell her that I haven't heard from him in a long time, then she pretends to be on my side and says, "Men . . ." as she shakes her head, like she can't believe it. She does the same thing to Jay. Behind Phil's back, Jay and I talk about what a bitch she is. Jay's seen her nipples three times and says he saw her scratch her pussy with a spatula out by their pool. She didn't actually stick the spatula in her shorts or anything, but we joke that the hamburgers she grilled tasted like fish burgers that day. If Phil knew this, he'd kill us.

PETER LIES to us all summer. He says he spent two nights in the tunnels under Tucson Mall and caught an albino cockroach, says his uncle invented Pac-Man, says he was color-blind in fifth grade and now he isn't. Each time he lies, I brace myself for Phil's response, but Phil doesn't say anything, and I let Peter's voice go through me like a chill and ask him questions to make him talk more.

PETER AND I stay at the track longer than the others, jumping our bikes until the sky goes from orange to purple. My arms ache from jumping, but I'm getting better. Better than Phil and Jay, not as good as Peter.

We sit on the warm curb and eat thirty-nine-cent bean burritos, and Peter grabs my hand. Peter's hand is dry and rough and my retarded hand is sweaty. "Your life line is long," he says. He traces the line on my hand and it tickles into my wrist and up my arm. "My mom taught me this." He smiles right at me, the right side of his smile hooking higher than the left. "This line means you'll be rich."

All I can say is "Cool" and hope that he examines every line on both my hands and that my hands stop sweating so much.

"Your love line is short, but you'll be rich so who cares?"

"Not me."

"You can tell someone's fortune from their head, too," Peter says. "From their scalp. My mom said she'll teach me."

"You believe it?" I ask. Peter still holds my hand.

"No," Peter says, then he squeezes my fingers together, hard, until all the good feelings stop and I pull my hand away.

IT'S THE SECOND Monday since school started and everyone wants to talk to Peter because he was on the news. He found a dead homeless lady on our dirt track next to the third jump. He was on all the channels and on the front page of the *Arizona Daily Star.*

"Did you touch her?" Lacy Clark asks him at lunch. Lacy has big tits and she French-kisses us at parties. She always wears tight Izods and Jordache jeans. Her purse is grubby, made of pink parachute material.

"I poked her with a stick," Peter says. "Just to see if she was alive."

"I would have freaked out," Lacy says. Her hands are in her back pockets and her eyes are bugged. She looks at Peter like he's a star and sticks out her tits. "Is it true she was covered in beetles?"

Peter smiles at her like he's embarrassed and shy, but he's not. He's faking it. I can tell.

"There were some bugs on her," Peter says, "but not tons."

Peter got to meet Steve Fogleman, the reporter from Channel 7 who has a thick mustache and curly brown hair. Steve Fogleman called Peter's discovery of the dead lady "gruesome" and Peter "courageous." All Peter did was poke her with a stick and call 9-1-1 from the telephone booth at Taco Bell. I want to ask Peter if Steve Fogleman wears makeup, but I don't because he and Lacy are talking about Mademoiselle Rosenblatt, our French teacher and Lacy's and my homeroom teacher, and when I try to add something, Lacy looks at me like I'm annoying her, like I should go away, so I do.

IT TOOK LESS than a week and now Peter and Lacy are officially a couple. They sit together at lunch and write notes during social studies. They're so popular that girls besides Lacy have written *Peter + Lacy* on their notebooks. During homeroom each morning, I listen to Lacy brag about what she and Peter talked about on the phone the night before. The girls gather around her like what she has to tell them is important. "He was totally imitating Mr. Thone. I was cracking up! Then he started to imitate Mademoiselle Rosenblatt. It was so funny."

PETER'S HAIR is combed in a new way: a perfect part down the middle and lightly feathered on the sides—like Orioles pitcher Jim Palmer. All the girls love it, especially Lacy, who raved about it all morning in homeroom. I wanted my hair like that last year, but I have a cowlick and I can't get it to part in the middle no matter how much of my mother's hair gel I use, so I comb it to the side.

I'm glad my hair won't part in the middle like Peter's when Phil calls the style "disco fag hair" at lunch. I watch Lacy's face go slack as she glares at Phil. Peter looks at Phil through half-closed eyes, like he wants to fight.

"What?" Phil says. "It *is* disco fag hair."

"We all decided it looked really good," Kim Fenster says. "So you guys better shut up about it." Kim Fenster has a wide gap between her two front teeth and she only wears concert T-shirts. Her older sister who Phil's mom says is a druggie brings her to see every group that comes to the convention center downtown. Today's shirt is Pink Floyd's *The Wall*: a creepy cartoon of a monster-teacher looking over a pile of bricks. The only band I've ever seen is Styx, and my mom made us leave after like half an hour because my older brother started coughing from all the smoke. He's asthmatic.

"I didn't say anything," Jay says. "God."

"Me neither," I mumble. I kind of want to say how good his hair looks, how I want to have the same style.

"All three of you are jealous," Kim says. "Losers."

WE PLAY a game of two-on-one that we invented where the guy without a teammate can't be guarded outside the key. It's mainly a shooting game, lame and boring, and I can tell by how slow Jay and Phil move that they think it's lame, too, but no one else will play with us because of what Phil said about Peter's hair. It's hot on the dusty courts under the noon sun and our sneakers squeak on the cement with every move. If Phil weren't such a dick, we'd be inside, hanging out in the common room with everyone else.

THE NEXT DAY, Kim Fenster calls me Alpo Mouth during break, because Lacy told her I had bad breath when we kissed at Jay's party in July. Two other girls call me Alpo Mouth as I wait in lunch line.

Phil and Jay bark at me and tell me to sit at another table, that my breath's making them sick. I don't feel like pretending to like the stupid basketball game anyway, and it's over a hundred degrees again, so I hide in the library and flip through this week's and last week's *Sports Illustrated* for articles about Jim Palmer or the Orioles. There's nothing good, only some stats, so I read *Rolling Stone* instead. Someone drew tits and a dick on a photo of David Lee Roth. Someone draws tits and dicks on almost every magazine in here.

Phil and Jay find me in the library, and they start barking at me from behind the glass display of Kachina dolls, until Mrs. Rydell threatens to write them up. When they finally leave, Mrs. Rydell walks over to me.

"Do you know those boys' names?" she asks.

"No," I say.

She looks down at the magazine I'm reading and points to the picture of David Lee Roth. "Did you do that?" she asks, thinking I drew the dick and tits.

My throat bunches up and I feel like I might cry. "No," I say, and my voice cracks. "I swear I didn't." I know she doesn't believe me.

Instead of going to pre-algebra after lunch, I walk across the tennis courts in front of a PE class, leave school, and no one says anything. I hike along the Rillito riverbed to the mall, and I spend my last two dollars on Chicken McNuggets. As I head to the far end of the mall, I secretly drop one of my six McNuggets in the fountain in front of Sam Goody. I play the display video games at Sears. They have Asteroids for Atari set up, and because it's a school day, I don't have to wait in line to play. Even though it's not that fun and your ship only shoots in eight different angles, I play so much that my thumb is sore, then I leave and check on the McNugget in the fountain. It's now the size of a potato, all mushy and white, just like I knew it would be. I hang around the fountain for a while, pretend to be waiting for someone, watching, but no one notices the bloated McNugget, and I walk home, imagining a bratty little girl pointing at the McNugget and screaming, or the janitor who thinks it's some sort of jellyfish, calling a scientist to examine it. It will take them weeks to figure out what it is, and there will be articles about it in the paper. Steve Fogleman will report live from the Tucson Mall even though the McNugget will have been taken to a lab at a university weeks before.

A GUY ONCE WROTE in to "Ask Beth" and said he thought he was gay. He was only thirteen, and Beth wrote that boys can't really know if they're gay until they're at least fifteen, that a boy's sexuality isn't completely formed until that age. So I have three more years to do what I always do after school: page thirty-six, the Jim Palmer Jockey Underwear ad, Jim sitting on a stool in nothing but the tiniest blue underpants.

I stand at the sink with the magazine propped up on the tissue box. The fan's on and I run the water so no one can hear even if they're pressing their ear right up against the door. I can finish in under three minutes, including setup and cleanup. I've timed myself.

I wash as much down the drain as I can see, then I wipe out the marble sink with toilet paper and flush the toilet paper. I run the water some more so it doesn't look like I've wiped out the sink. I sniff the sink up close. If any water drops splashed on the Jockey ad or even on the next page, I sprinkle water drops on a bunch of other pages so the Jockey page doesn't stand out. I shove the magazine back in the middle of the stack on top of the toilet, and I'm done.

* * *

MR. THONE makes Peter and me partners for a science project where we have to germinate bean seeds on wet paper towel and keep track of the growth.

"You want to come over to my house, or do you want to do it at yours?" Peter asks me, like he doesn't care.

"Yours," I say too quickly.

"Don't call me Disco Fag at my house."

"I won't," I say. "Phil invented it."

"Bring your skateboard," he says, then we both shut up because Mr. Thone starts lecturing about plants again. Everyone pays attention in Mr. Thone's class because he failed eleven kids last year. They all had to go to summer school at Amphi High School, and one kid got stabbed in the arm by a nineteen-year-old from Nogales.

I SIT on the edge of the drained pool, my legs dangling over the cracked tiles. Peter pulls off 180s pretty high on the walls. He sticks his tongue out a little as he concentrates. I feel like a loser because it's my skateboard he's using, and I suck at it. I can't even go like a foot up the wall without bailing.

Just as I notice my legs are getting sunburned, Peter announces we should work on the project. As we walk toward a metal gate, he trips on a rotten cushion from a pool chair, hits the cement deck pretty hard, flat on his face. My skateboard flies back into the pool. I reach down and grab his arm to help him up, asking if he's all right, but he just looks at me like he wants to kill me and shakes my hand from his arm.

Peter stands by himself and lifts his shirt to check out the skinned part of his chest and stomach. He has a line of brown curly hair leading from his belly button into his shorts. I don't.

"Shit," he says, now looking at his bleeding elbow. "Sorry

about your board." He jumps into the low end to get it for me.

It's hotter in Peter's kitchen than it is outside, and it smells like vitamins. He grabs a handful of fake cheap-brand Froot Loops called Fruit Circles from an open box on the counter and doesn't offer me any. As we walk upstairs to his room, I ask, "Did you ever learn that head thing?"

"What?" he says, crunching the cereal.

"The scalp fortune-telling thing."

"No," he says. "I mean yes." He doesn't say he'll do it on me, and I don't ask.

There are tons of clothes on Peter's bed, his dresser is missing a drawer, and his window has a crack in it that someone tried to fix with masking tape. Two porno magazines in the middle of his floor are opened to close-up pictures of wet pink and purple pussies. Peter sees me looking down at them, and he grabs one. He flips it open to a picture of a black guy getting a blow job from a chubby blonde woman who has her hands bound behind her back with electrical tape. Her eyes are rolled white like she might throw up. The black man's dick is big and veiny and his balls hang low. The woman wants out of there, I can tell. Like, maybe she was kidnapped and forced to suck his dick. She looks like my mother's friend Linda, who used to babysit my brother and me until she moved to Flagstaff to get away from her ex-husband who was a stalker. I feel myself getting hard, and I feel bad, try to think of something horrible, like rotten food or a smashed jackrabbit on the side of the road, but it doesn't work. It never works.

"You think Samuel's dick is this big?" Peter asks me.

"I don't care," I say. Samuel is one of four black kids in our whole school. "That's gross."

"We can see at camp in April," Peter says, smiling like he's excited. "We all have to take showers together."

"I know." The whole seventh grade goes to Y Camp in Oracle for three nights. Last year, when they came back, they started to call Brad Diaz a donkey because his dick was so big. Lots of girls got felt up, two got fingered. I plan on eating tons of cereal and making myself barf the night before we're supposed to go. I'll make sure my mother and brother hear me so they know it's real and I'll pretend that I'm really disappointed that I can't go. I can't take showers with other guys. I know that.

Peter shoves some clothes aside and sits on his bed, continues to flip through the magazine. "I touched Lacy's pussy," he says. "She let me. She has tons of hair."

I pretend to be interested in a map of the Grand Canyon tacked up next to Peter's window. I walk over to the map so he can't see my boner. "When are we going to start the project? Do you still even have the beans?" I ask.

"One more thing," Peter says, then he jumps up from his bed and reaches under his dresser. He pulls out a dirty baseball hat with "Thunderbird" on the front in gold thread. "You know where I got this?"

"Where?" I ask.

"From the dead lady," he says. He puts it on his head, adjusts it. "Before I told anyone about her, I grabbed it and stuffed it in my backpack."

He tried to put it on my head, but I swat it away.

"You chicken?" he asks. He picks it up from the floor and steps really close to me like he might want to fight. He looks right into my eyes. His eyes are light brown, the color of butterscotch.

"She might have had lice," I say, smiling on purpose like I'm sort of joking, even though I'm not. "Or a disease." I imagine tons of bugs pouring out of her crusty eye sockets, some of them laying eggs in the hat. My boner still won't go away.

"Chicken," Peter says. "Craig is chicken, Craig is a chicken. . . ."

His face is so close to mine that I can feel his breath on my lips, see a few tiny hairs between his eyebrows. I smell the fruity cereal he ate, and I wish I had remembered to have a piece of gum. Our breaths mix in the tiny space between our mouths, and I can't move.

"I'm not" is the only thing I can say. My face is hot and my eyes close by themselves.

"All right," Peter finally says, and I open my eyes. "You don't have to wear it." He flings the hat across the room. "I don't know why you have to be such a baby, and I don't know why you had to close your eyes like that."

Peter puts both his hands on my head and presses on my scalp with his fingertips, tracing tiny circles. I smell the cereal again as he moves his hands down to my face, pushing my cowlick flat and stopping on my cheeks. "God," he says loudly, dropping his hands from my face. He's angry. "And don't tell Lacy or any of the other girls about the magazines."

I swallow, then say, "I won't."

PETER'S ON THE NEWS for a second time because the police found two more dead homeless women. Steve Fogleman interviews him again and Peter says, "I hope the police catch the person who killed them." Steve Fogleman squeezes Peter's shoulder and calls him "brave."

LACY'S WEARING the dead lady's Thunderbird cap on Monday. It matches her purple Izod like she planned her outfit. Under the lights of the hallway, the hat looks even dirtier—there are white lines of salt from the dead lady's sweat. Lacy and Peter walk by me and whisper to each other and laugh.

Before pre-algebra I tell Jay that Lacy's wearing the dead lady's hat. "Peter stole it," I add when Jay doesn't say anything.

"Duh," Jay says. "They were talking about it on the bus this morning." Jay sits at his desk. "They were talking about something else, too, homo," Jay says.

My stomach falls, like I'm jumping my bike or I'm suddenly starving. "What?"

"Peter said you wanted to look at Samuel's dick at Y Camp," Jay says loudly so everyone can hear. "In the showers."

"Peter said that, not me. I swear to God."

Wanda, a girl who wore the same yellow shirt nine days in a row and has tons of white zits on her forehead, looks over. "Are you gay?" she asks me. "Just admit it." She sometimes smells like concentrated urine and someone said they saw her mother in line for government cheese downtown. "Are you?"

"Peter also said you bet Samuel's dick was really long and you were afraid to wear the dead lady's hat," Jay says.

"I didn't want to get lice or anything," I say.

The bell rings and Mr. Dunn tells us to settle down and begins to take roll.

I write Jay a note: *I didn't say that about Samuel. I swear to God. And the hat is probably police evidence.*

He doesn't even unfold it, and it falls on the floor when the bell rings for next period. I haven't heard a word Mr. Dunn has said or watched him do any problems on the board in the last forty-five minutes. I don't even care that I'll probably flunk the quiz on Friday.

Kim Fenster and some of her friends bust up to me in the hall. Kim's wearing the Thunderbird hat now, and she stands in front of me with her hands on her hips like she wants to block my way. "You're a pervert," she says. "And you're prejudice and I'm telling Samuel you said you wanted to look at his dick." She has a big wad of pink gum in her mouth, packed into her cheek.

"I didn't say anything," I tell her. "I swear to God."

"Peter said you'd probably lie about it because he said you were all embarrassed after you said it." I've never seen Kim fight anyone—girls or boys—but I bet she'd win. Her concert T-shirt today is Alice Cooper's *Madhouse Rock*. It has a picture of Alice screaming and a splattered blood background. Alice's makeup drips off his face.

"Peter said his dad was runner-up to be an astronaut, which is a total lie," I say. I notice then that Kim has hairy arms. Almost like a man. Way hairier than mine.

"You're gay and you want to see Samuel's dick," she says.

"Peter said it, not me," I say. She has hairy ape arms. I wonder why no one has ever made fun of her for them. *Ape arms, ape arms. . . .*

"In case you haven't noticed, Peter has a girlfriend," she says. Some of her friends giggle. "Duh."

I leave school, cut through the faculty parking lot. No one sees me. I don't have any money, so I can't drop a McNugget in the fountain. I play the display video games at Sears again, but after a few minutes a lady whose Sears name tag says *Mrs. Wilson* asks me if I need any help, but I know she really just wants me to leave. I tell her that I don't need any help and she says, "It's only 1:20. Why aren't you in school?"

"I go to private school," I lie.

"Which one?"

"Salpointe Catholic."

"Salpointe's a high school," Mrs. Wilson says. Her glasses make her eyes look small.

"I know," I say. "I go there." I pretend to concentrate on the game more than I actually do, just so I don't have to look at her any longer. It's Space Invaders, the same patterns of missiles set after set. I could play for hours without losing a ship. I could play with my eyes closed.

"I don't believe you're in high school, and I don't believe that Salpointe has the day off."

"I'm a freshman," I say, thinking that I might start crying. I'm not even sure why. My throat bunches up, and I try to swallow it down.

"I can call security," she threatens. "You can't just hang out here all day. That's called loitering and it's illegal."

I drop the joystick and walk out, not looking back at her, the Sears Bitch. I could walk to the other end of the mall and play the display games at JCPenney's, but I don't. I hurry through, past two fat security guards, who don't even look at me. The mall is full of old ladies and men who wear windbreakers and ball caps and ugly walking shoes. They just walk around the mall all day, doing nothing. One couple wears matching purple outfits, which reminds me of the Thunderbird hat. I wonder if one of the old men I pass is the murderer. Any of them could be. I imagine that I solve the mystery, report the murderer. I'd be on the news a lot more than Peter. Steve Fogleman would interview me, call me a hero, and invite me over to his condo to hang out. We'd sit on his sofa and watch videos and eat burritos. Steve would kiss me and his mustache would tickle.

I rush out of the cool mall into a wall of heat, the white sun so bright I can't see for a minute, then I sort of jog across the parking lot toward the riverbed. It's too early to go home, so I sit on top of a knocked-over cement trash can behind Sunset Sports and read *Never Cry Wolf*.

After a minute, I notice a skinny man sitting in his truck about twenty feet away. He's chewing on a toothpick and he has his radio tuned to 13K-HIT, which is playing a stupid song by Toto that goes on forever. When I look up at him again, he nods and smiles, so I put the book in my backpack and start to walk away. Then he turns down his radio and loudly asks, "Do you like *Playboy*?"

I begin to run along the riverbed, thinking the guy was planning on abducting me. I'm not stupid. Even if he had asked if I liked *Playgirl,* I wouldn't have gone near his truck. I run faster, my mouth dry, my neck burning in the afternoon sun. Even if the guy had been handsome and not wearing his shirt and asked if I liked *Playgirl,* I wouldn't have gone near his truck. I decide the only way I would have walked over to his truck is if the guy was handsome, not wearing a shirt, offered *Playgirl,* and was someone I already knew, like if he was my mother's boyfriend, and he really liked me more than he liked my mother. Like, he was only dating my mother so he could be near me. We'd have to break it to my mother eventually, but we'd have a secret relationship for a few months. The guy would pick me up at school, and we'd go over to his giant house in the foothills, and we'd mess around. Every day. And I'd tell my mother I was on the soccer team and that's why I couldn't get home until later.

MY MOTHER keeps junk mail and new magazines in a big wicker basket by her bed. I kneel down and start flipping through the magazines, and I find one after only a minute: Jim Palmer sits on a gray cube. He wears tiny striped underpants. *The Jockey Fashion Statement is Bold,* it says. I know my mother and brother aren't home yet, but I hide the magazine under my shirt just in case they come home as I transport it to the bathroom downstairs. The magazine is cool against my stomach.

I prop the new magazine on the tissue box and unzip my shorts. I imagine I live with Jim Palmer, and he has real arcade games in his mansion that I can play for free. During baseball games I sit in the bull pen with Jim and the other Orioles. The other Orioles like me and ask me questions about what I'm learning at school. They tell me that Jim is pitching better now that he has me in his life. After Jim pitches another winning game, he takes me in his red Porsche for pizza. On the way home, he lets me drive and tells me to take it easy on the curves in the road. He insists we take a bath together every night in his giant Jacuzzi, and I show him how to press himself up against the water jet, like I sometimes do in the pool when I'm positive no one is around.

I'M SURE Kim Fenster has arranged a fight between me and Samuel, and I almost don't go to school. The school has called my mother, though, and told her I left early yesterday and ditched three classes. She doesn't even ask me why I did it, just tells me I'm grounded for three weeks—a week for each class I missed. I don't care about being grounded. Jay and Phil are dicks and there's no one else to hang out with. "You come right home after school," my mother tells me as I leave this morning, and I think, *Big whoop.*

On the bus, no one sits next to me and no one talks to me. They all know that Samuel's going to beat me up. Samuel will find me the moment I step off the bus, and he'll begin by punching me in the stomach. I'll fall onto the asphalt, and Jay and Phil will call me a fag and bark at me while Samuel kicks me in the head. I'll barely stand up, and Samuel will shove me, and I'll hit my head on the curb, and I'll die, and no one will say anything and Samuel will never even get in trouble.

I DON'T even see Samuel when I get to school, and when I walk into homeroom, Lacy's crying in the corner, huddled with a few other crying girls. I sit at a desk near no one and listen to find out what's going on. I hope that Peter dumped Lacy, told her he no longer liked her and that her friends were too mean to me and that I'm his best friend now. The two of us will ride BMX on the track or skateboard in the parking garages downtown every afternoon when my grounding is over. Until then, Peter will come over to my house and we'll play video games or swim and he'll tell my fortune from my palm or my head whenever I want.

Mademoiselle Rosenblatt walks into the room. She's sniffing and her eyes are red like she's been crying, too. She takes roll, reads the boring announcements, and then says, "I gather you've all heard the bad news about Kimberly Fenster. Our homeroom and Mr. Carlson's homeroom will meet in the auditorium during second period. A grief counselor from the school district will help us and answer any questions we might have."

Kim Fenster was hit by a car on Tanque Verde Road. She was riding her bike to her older sister's apartment less than a mile from her house. Before second period, I hear a few other things like they still hadn't found her arm, she had been going over there to get marijuana, her mom was drunk so she couldn't drive her, she had been decapitated by a truck's mirror. They're all probably lies. It all seems so fake. Just yesterday, she was being a bitch to me and now she's dead, one of her hairy ape arms possibly missing.

I think I wished her dead yesterday or this morning. I must have. I'm always wishing people dead. I know I wished Phil dead yesterday. I imagined him and his mom both dead, in a car accident. I've wished Jim Palmer's real-life wife dead, I'm sure. Or I wished she never even existed, which I think is worse.

Samuel's in Mr. Carlson's homeroom and he sits right behind me during grief counseling. He's wearing the Thunderbird cap today.

239

The grief counselor is a lady with short hair, big red glasses, and big red earrings. She wears sandals with pants. I don't really hear what she says because I'm trying to remember if I did wish Kim Fenster dead or not. Samuel leans over and whispers, "I'm going to kick your ass, faggot."

I sit there, the feeling in my stomach like Samuel already did kick my ass, and I look at the grief counselor's toenails, how they match her dumb glasses and earrings, my heart racing, my throat tightening, until I finally turn around to face Samuel, who has the hat on sideways now. "I didn't say that," I blurt sort of loudly, my voice cracking. "Peter said it and everyone knows he's a liar and—"

But before I can say anything else, I feel Mademoiselle Rosenblatt's fingernails digging into my arm. She tugs me out of my seat and pulls me into the hall, not even letting me grab my backpack. "What is wrong with you, Craig?" she yells. She's crying and her makeup runs down her face like Alice Cooper on Kim Fenster's T-shirt. "What is wrong with you?"

As she guides me to the office, through the empty halls, yelling at me the whole way, I can only think of Jim Palmer. He has never allowed a grand slam. He's won the Cy Young three times. If the Orioles make it to the World Series this year and Jim pitches a winning game, he'll be the only pitcher to win World Series games in three different decades. His perfect hair, long legs, shaggy chest. *The Jockey Fashion Statement is Bold.*

And sitting there in the principal's office on the wooden bench, waiting to be punished for disrupting the grief counseling, I can barely stay still. I can't help but smile, knowing that I have Jim Palmer for three more years, as often as I want, until I turn fifteen and have to let him go.

Lyndon

AMBER DERMONT

M Y FATHER DIED BECAUSE OUR HOUSE WAS INFESTED with ladybugs. Our French neighbors, the Herouxs, had imported a hearty species of the insect to combat aphids in their garden. The ladybugs bred and migrated. Hundreds upon hundreds were living in our curtains, our cabinets, the ventilation system. At first, we thought it was hilarious and fitting for us to be plagued by something so cute and benign. But these weren't nursery rhyme ladybugs. Not the adorable, shiny, red-and-black beetles. These ladybugs were orange. They had uneven brown splotches. When I squished their shells between my thumb and forefinger, they left a rust-colored stain on my skin and an acrid smell that wouldn't wash off. Dad used a vacuum hose to suck up the little arched creatures, but they quickly replaced themselves. The numbers never dwindled. Dad must have smoked a lot of pot before he climbed the ladder to our roof. My guess is that he wanted to cover the opening in the chimney. He'd suspected that the flue wasn't closed all the way. Our house was three stories high. When he fell, he landed on the Herouxs' cement patio, his skull fractured, his neck broken.

For months after his death, I kept finding the ladybugs everywhere. When I stripped my bed, I'd find them in the sheets. When I did laundry, I'd find their dead carapaces in the dryer. When I woke up in the morning, I'd find a pair scuffling along my freshly laundered pillowcases. Then just like that, they were gone.

LONG AFTER the last ladybug's departure, I pulled a pair of sunglasses from Mom's purse on the car seat, fogged the lenses with my breath, rubbed the plastic eyes against my chest, and said to her, "You missed the scenic overlook."

Mom swiped her sunglasses away from me. "There will be other stops, Elise," she said.

We were driving through the Texas Hill Country in an upgraded rental car, cruising a roadway called the Devil's Backbone. Our destination: LBJ. His ranch. His reconstructed birth site. The rental car guy had flashed a brilliant smile when he bumped us up from a white Taurus to a monster green SUV. Mom couldn't resist bullying the skinny clerk. "No one screws me on gas mileage. I'm not paying extra to fuel that obscenity. Knock ten dollars off the daily fee." As the car clerk hammered his keyboard and readjusted the price, Mom winked at me.

My mother the investment banker. Every morning, well before dawn, she would maneuver her own Ford Explorer across the George Washington Bridge into Manhattan, cell-phoning her underlings while cutting off other commuters. Mom called her first-year analysts "Meat" and bragged that she, in turn, was known as "The Lion." Mom always wore her long, straightened red hair loose and down her back. She'd sport short skirts and sleeveless dresses, showing off her sculpted calves and biceps. Mom specialized in M&As, corporate restructuring, and bankruptcy. She traveled a lot. Dad had brainstormed our presidential sightseeing tours as a way for him to keep me entertained while Mom flew off to Chicago and Denver, dismantling pharmaceutical corporations along the way.

"I really think we were supposed to stop at that overlook." We coasted past juniper trees, live oaks, limestone cliffs. As far as I could tell, the whole point of driving the Devil's Backbone was to stop at that particular overlook and view the span of gently sloping hills from the highest vantage point. "Dad would have turned back," I said.

Mom just kept driving. I passed time by reading snippets from the *Lonely Planet Guide to Texas* and rattling off the names of local towns: Wimberley, Comfort, and Boerne. I flipped down the sun visor, replaited my French braids in the vanity mirror. I'd worn my favorite outfit: red high-top sneakers, baggy khaki shorts, and a T-shirt I'd special-ordered at a mall in Teaneck. For twenty-eight dollars, a man from Weehawken had ironed black velvet letters onto the front of a tiny green jersey. The letters spelled out Victim. When my mother asked how I got off being so self-pitying, I told her it was the name of my favorite underground band.

The Devil's Backbone reminded me of the shingles sore tormenting my lower torso. The giant scab resembled a hard red shell. The family doctor had explained how sometimes the chicken pox virus would remain dormant in a nerve ending, waiting for the immune system to weaken before reemerging. He was concerned because he'd never seen shingles in anyone my age. Usually he treated it in older patients, or in cases occurring with cancer or AIDS. People closing in on death. I told Mom the shingles were proof I was special. The agony wasn't limited to the blisters on my back. My whole body felt inflamed, as if a rabid wolf were hunting rabid squirrels inside my chest. The doctor recommended ibuprofen for the pain. He gave me pamphlets describing stress-reducing breathing exercises. The first few nights Mom slipped me half a Vicodin and a nip of Benedictine brandy. As I tried to sleep, I heard her roaming from living room to bedroom to family room. I listened. My mother the widow did not weep, did not cry out for her dead husband.

A YEAR AFTER my father died, my mother's breasts began to grow. She developed a deep, embarrassing plunge of cleavage, a pendulous swinging bosom that attacked my own flat body each time she hugged me good night. Mom's belly had pouted. Ballooned. I could detect the domed button of her navel pressing out against the soft silk of her blouses. Her ankles swelled and I became suspicious. Mom was maybe six months into her pregnancy. I did the math. Dad had been pushing dead too long to be the father. I was about to enter my sophomore year at the Academy of Holy Angels. Before school started, I wanted the shingles on my back to disappear, I wanted to tour the reconstructed birthplace of Lyndon Baines Johnson, and I wanted my mother to admit to me that she was pregnant.

WITH DAD GONE, I'd insisted on upholding our family's tradition of visiting presidential landmarks. Dad and I had been doing them in chronological order. We'd seen the big ones: Mount Vernon, Monticello, The Hermitage, Sagamore Hill. Weeks before Dad broke his neck, we'd spent a lively afternoon in the gift shop of the John Fitzgerald Kennedy Library, rubbing our faces in the soft velour of JFK commemorative golf towels. The less popular the sites, the more obscure the leader of our country, the more Dad got excited: "Elise, can you imagine? John Tyler actually sat in this breakfast nook and ate soft-boiled eggs from those egg cups." In Columbia, Tennessee, I tore white azalea petals from James K. Polk's ancestral garden while Dad rambled on about the Mexican War, the "dark horse," and the "Fifty-four Forty or Fight." At the Albany Rural Cemetery, Dad and I knelt solemnly before the grave of Chester Alan Arthur. A giant marble angel with voluminous wings towered over us. We prayed to our favorite forgotten leader, the father of civil service reform. One year, we spent Christmas in Cape Cod at a beachside inn that had been a secret getaway for Grover Cleveland and his mistress. Mom couldn't make that trip, so Dad and I tramped by ourselves on the snow-covered sand dunes, plotting my own future run for the presidency. "You need a catchphrase. And a trademark hairdo so the cartoonists can immortalize you."

ALL DAY we'd been driving in various stages of silence and radio static. Mom asked whether I'd like to stop for sundaes. I considered patting her belly and making a joke about cravings for ice cream and pickles. I had expected Mom to nix my travel plans for us, but really, I just wanted her to be honest and say to me, "Elise, I can't fly. Not in my condition." Instead, when I said, "Johnson," Mom folded her arms against her burgeoning chest. She swung her hair over her shoulders, and said, "Texas in August? Why can't it be Hawaii? I'm certain Lyndon Johnson loved the hula."

The day before, we'd visited the Sixth Floor Museum in Dallas. Mom and I took the elevator up to the top of the Texas School Book Depository. We slowly worked our way through the permanent exhibit dedicated to the Kennedy assassination. Though a glass wall surrounded the actual Oswald window, Mom and I got close enough to size up the short distance between the building and the X on the street below. The X marked the spot where Kennedy was first hit. I'd always imagined Dealey Plaza as an enormous expanse of traffic and park, but here it was in front of me, tiny and green, more like a miniature replica made by a film crew. One SUV after another covered the X as the cars drove over the site in perpetual reenactment of Kennedy's last ride. This was the bona fide scene of the infamous crime. Mom whispered, "Even I could make that shot." She hugged me from behind and I felt the baby's heartbeat vibrate through her belly. In anticipation of our trip, I'd begun calling my secret sibling "Lyndon." I asked, "Is Lyndon kicking?" Mom ignored me. Weeks ago, when I'd asked her point blank if she was pregnant and quizzed her on what she intended to do with the baby, instead of answering the question she told me that her new goal in life was to get me away from "the fucking Holy Angels."

Dad was the Catholic. Mom's family had come over on the Mayflower. "Elise, a lot of Yankees brag about tracing their roots back. Always be conscious of your place in history. Most of the people on that ship were poor. Your relatives were the lucky ones with money." Before her parents divorced and squandered everything, my mother grew up rich in Manhattan. Her childhood bedroom had a view of the Sheep Meadow and the Central Park Reservoir. Both of Mom's doormen were named Fritz. When she turned six, her folks hired Richard Avedon to take the snapshots at her birthday party. At sixteen, she'd curtsied before Princess Grace at a charity fund-raiser for retired racehorses. I often felt as though Dad and I were descended from one class of people, while Mom hailed from another class entirely.

My father sold pies for a living. Nominally, he was the vice president of "The Pie Piper," his parents' international bakery corporation, but mostly what Dad chose to do was drive his pie truck around the Tri-State Area. Checking and restocking Safeways and Star Markets. Shelving lemon cream, Coconut Dream, and chocolate meringue pies. Dad had a jacket with TEAMSTER embroidered on the back. He liked to brag that he knew the fastest routes in and out of Manhattan, at any point during the day. He knew when best to take the Lincoln Tunnel.

Dad felt that my aristocratic heritage and working-class lineage would make me an ideal political candidate. He cast me as a liberal Democrat and cast himself as my campaign manager. Dad first ran me in third grade for homeroom line leader. I lost to Andorra Rose, whose mother, on election day, made two dozen chocolate cupcakes with pink rosebuds in the center. Dad viewed this loss as a tactical oversight. Our future campaigns always involved the Pie Piper donating dozens of pies and pastries to Holy Angels. In fifth grade, I was class treasurer. In seventh grade, I was student representative to the advisory council on redesigning our school uniforms. Dad imagined I would win the governership of New Jersey, and from there, if I could find the right Southern running mate, become the first woman president of the United States.

I was twelve the afternoon I caught Dad sprawled out on the Philadelphia Chippendale, one hand holding a silver lighter, the other hand cradling a short ceramic pipe. There'd been a bomb scare at Holy Angels and the nuns had begrudgingly sent us home early. Dad was wearing his boxer shorts and watching a rerun of *The Joker's Wild*. He flung a cashmere blanket over his lap, swung his legs off my mother's two-hundred-year-old sofa and said, "Honey, come meet James Buchanan." I sat beside my bare-chested father, his blond hair flattened on one side, and watched him twirl his pipe around. "Made this in college. Art class. The clay morphed in the kiln." He showed me the blunt end of the pipe. "Looks just like our bachelor president. His first lady was his niece. Handsome fellow." On the TV, Wink Martindale exclaimed, "Joker! Joker! Joker!" Dad smiled, "Don't worry. Your mom has seen me smoke."

My father confided to me that he'd had panic attacks as a kid. "I'd be paralyzed with fear. Knocked out with it. The only thing that helped was reading almanacs." Dad memorized historical facts, like the years each president served in office, and he'd repeat these dates in an effort to calm himself down. "Zachary Taylor 1849–50, Rutherford Birchard Hayes 1877–81, Franklin Pierce 1853–57." At fifteen, Dad discovered pot.

I loved sitting in the living room while Dad toked up. Marijuana haze drifted around me, settling on the folds of my wool pleated skirt. I'd lean my neck down against my Peter Pan collar and catch the wonderful stink of weed lingering against my blouse. I was a nervous kid. I often threw up before big tests. No one at Holy Angels invited me to their sleepovers anymore, on account of my loud, thrashing night terrors. Even my closest friend, Alana Clinton, often insisted I take a chill pill. I'd attempted hypnosis therapy to treat the warts on my hands, the muscle spasm in my left eye, the mysterious rashes that appeared across my stomach, my inner-ear imbalance, and my tooth-grinding problem. Only breathing in my father's pot smoke truly relaxed me. He never let me inhale directly from Buchanan, but he'd grant me a contact high. Afterward, the two of us would split one of my father's ancestral peach pies. This happened once or twice a week. Mom didn't know.

MOM AND I pulled off the Devil's Backbone and stopped for soft-serve at a place called The Frozen Armadillo. She got a chocolate and vanilla twist with a cherry-flavored dip, and I ordered a vanilla cone covered in something advertised as Twinkle-Kote. Outside in the August heat, the ice cream dripped down our arms. We decided to eat the cones in the air-conditioned rental car. I told Mom my theory about LBJ and the Kennedy assassination. I was convinced that Lyndon was the real culprit. Nothing that big could happen in Texas without Lyndon's approval.

"Motive is obvious," I said. "Who gains the most from Kennedy dying? LBJ gets to be president. Who's responsible for the investigation and subsequent cover-up? LBJ gets to appoint the Warren Commission. There's proof that LBJ actually knew Jack Ruby. All LBJ ever wanted was to be president. Not vice president. He was an old man. Time was running out." I told my mother that there had been talk of Kennedy dropping LBJ from the ticket in '64.

"How do you know so much?" she asked.

"It's Dad's fault," I said.

"You know, your father always wanted to be a high school history teacher."

"What stopped him?" I asked.

"Well, sweetie," Mom said, wiping ice cream off my nose, "convicted felons aren't allowed to teach children."

Mom balanced her own ice cream cone against the steering wheel and turned on the ignition. She headed out toward Johnson City. We drove past brown, sandy hills crowned by patches of cacti with round, thorned leaves.

"Take it back," I told her. "What you said. Take it back."

"You shouldn't idealize your father. You didn't know him as well as you'd like to think."

"From the looks of it," I pointed to Mom's belly, "Dad didn't know you at all." I was deciding between calling my mother a "bitch" and calling her a "fucking bitch" when she chucked the rest of her ice cream cone at the side of my face. The ice cream splattered against my hair and cheek. The wafer cone landed on the side of my leg. I picked it up and threw it back at her. I pulled the top of my own ice cream off of its cone and aimed for Mom's chest. She shrieked, swerving the car and throwing back at me whatever clumps of ice cream she could pull from her cleavage. We each lost sense of our target, hurling any ice cream slop we could get hold of. The rental car's green cloth upholstery and side windows clouded over in a sticky, cherry-flavored film. Chocolate ice cream melted in streams down Mom's chest. The black velvet letters on my Victim T-shirt soaked up my dessert. Mom drove and swore. She called me ungrateful and threatened to leave me right there on the spine of the Devil's Backbone. Mom didn't notice the bend in the road. She screamed in confusion as our rental car lurched through a very real white picket fence, careening down a hill and into an orchard. She pumped and locked the brakes just in time for us to hit a patch of peach trees.

The air bags did not work. No explosion of white pillow. In that brief instant, as I watched the seat belt jerk Mom back and hold her safely in place, I thought of how the pressure and force of the air bag would have crushed Mom's belly, crippling Lyndon, killing the start of him. Mom saved me from the windshield by holding her right arm out straight against my chest. "Holy fuck," she said.

Mom surveyed me. "Are you all right?" she asked. We got out of the car together, the two of us still dripping with ice cream. We marveled at the damage. A peach tree appeared to be growing out of the hood of our rental car. Mom picked up a pink-and-yellow fruit, brushing the fuzz against her lips before taking a bite. "You and your presidents," she said. "That's it. I'm through. And you can be damned sure I'm not taking you to Yorba Linda. There's no fucking way I'm visiting Nixon."

* * *

Lyndon

I INSISTED ON HIKING the remaining mile and a half to the LBJ Ranch. The car was not my problem. I was a kid and this was my summer vacation. I stayed a hundred yards in front of my mother. She played with her cell phone the entire time, dialing and redialing numbers. From her loud cursing, I could tell that there was no service, no way to call a tow truck or taxi. No way to complain to her mystery lover about me. I imagined my mother had many young lovers. For all I knew, she didn't know who Lyndon's father was. I didn't want to think about The Lion having sex. I wanted to remember the Saturday mornings when I'd wake up early, sneak into my parents' room, and burrow a narrow tunnel between their sleeping bodies. I'd trace the beauty marks on Mom's back, naming the largest ones. With the tips of my fingers, I'd smooth out the worry lines on my father's forehead. Their bed was an enormous life raft. I would imagine that the three of us were the last family left in the world. I loved my parents best when they were asleep and I was standing guard.

ON THE LBJ TOUR BUS, the man sitting closest to the door stood up to give my mother his seat. She smiled and said, "Not necessary." We'd taken turns washing up by ourselves in the ladies' room of the park's Visitor Center. While Mom pulled knots of peanut Twinkle-Kote from her hair, I watched a short film about the ranch, the birthplace, and the family cemetery. The birthplace wasn't really the birthplace. The original birthplace had been torn down. LBJ actually had a facsimile of the house rebuilt during his presidency. He decorated the house in period pieces, but none of the furnishings were original except for a rawhide cushioned chair. The film showed Lyndon in a cowboy hat and sports coat posing on the front porch of his make-believe home. Dad would have loved the film. He would have leaned over and repeated the story about LBJ and the goat fucker.

"Do you know about LBJ and the goat fucker?" I said to Mom. "When Johnson first ran for office, he told his campaign manager to spread a rumor that his opponent had sex with farm animals. When the manager pointed out that this wasn't true, Johnson said, 'So what. Force the bastard to admit, "I never fucked a goat." He'll be ruined—'"

"You curse like your father." Mom sighed.

The Reconstructed birthplace was the first stop on the tour. The park ranger/bus driver was a chatty, older woman named Cynthia. She bounced around the bus taking our tickets, sporty and spry in her light green ranger's uniform. A row of bench seats ran along each side of the bus facing a wide center aisle. Another row of seats ran along the back. There were nine other people on the bus: the polite man closest to the door, a pair of elderly, identical twin sisters who wore matching red windbreakers, a middle-aged German couple toting two large canvas backpacks, and a family of four. The mother and father of the family laughed as their young daughter hugged her baby brother and scooped him up onto her lap. The little blond boy had a crazy cowlick I wanted to flatten and fix. Mom and I sat in the very back row, several seats apart from each other.

As we drove past the banks of the Pedernales River, Cynthia described the lawn chair staff meetings Lyndon held at his ranch during Vietnam. She told us that Lady Bird had kindly donated all of the land and the ranch to the National Park Service, but chose to live part-time in the main ranch house. I could feel my shingles sore rubbing against my T-shirt, the pain ratcheting up inside of me. I was still angry at Mom. I held my breath to calm myself and ran through dates: "Andrew Johnson 1865–69, Benjamin Harrison 1889–93, Warren Gamaliel Harding 1921–23."

Mom leaned over and said, "Lady Bird is shrewd. Putting the ranch into a trust is an excellent way of avoiding taxes."

We drove past lazy orange-and-white Hereford cattle grazing by the river. An ibex shot out from behind a sycamore tree, and then another ibex followed, and another. The cows ignored the elegant brown-and-white horned antelopes. Cynthia said, "Lady Bird also runs an exotic animal safari on the ranch. As exotic animals are legal in Texas, hunters can pay the Johnson family to come and stalk rare creatures from the Dark Continent." My mother whispered, "Lady Bird's a genius."

I'D ALWAYS THOUGHT that Dad liked Mom because her mother's maiden name was Van Buren. One afternoon, my father told me how he and Mom began dating. "You have to be careful with this information," he said. "Your mother doesn't know the whole story." My parents met their freshman year in college. The same day Dad met Mom, he also met another woman, a sculpture major named Lisel. She had wavy black hair, a German accent, and an apartment off-campus. Dad liked both women and was stuck deciding whether to pursue Mom or Lisel. He decided to go after Lisel. He was dressed up and on his way to meet the German sculptress for their first serious date when he bumped into Mom. "She'd been playing rugby and she was totally covered in mud and sweat. She asked me if I wanted to take a shower with her. I went back to her dorm." Dad smiled. "And that's the moment when my life began." He said something else about Mom being a sexy lady, but I clutched my hands to my ears and blocked him out.

THE RECONSTRUCTED birthplace was white with green shutters. It was small. Just two bedrooms, a kitchen, and a breezeway. Cynthia showed us the bedroom where Johnson was birthed. A queen-size bed dominated the room. I noticed long, shiny black beetles crawling over the chenille bedspread. One of the beetles flew up and circled past me. Cynthia said, "His mother claimed that he had it wrong. She kept insisting that Lyndon was actually born in the smaller bedroom, but LBJ was adamant."

In the kitchen I saw the rawhide chair, the one authentic piece. I wanted to run my hand over the cow fur. Right by the kitchen table stood a baby's wooden high chair with LADY BIRD etched across the backrest. Cynthia said that the First Lady had been kind enough to donate her own Roycrafter high chair for the replica. Mom mouthed "Lady Bird" to herself and rested her hands on her belly. I pictured a plump, kicking baby fidgeting in the chair. "Mom, if you want," I said. "I could steal the high chair for you."

"What's a lady bird?" Mom asked Cynthia.

"A lady bird is what we in the South call ladybugs."

Mom looked at me. She shook her head. "Those little killers."

SOMETIMES WHEN I hung out with my Dad while he smoked Buchanan, I'd get paranoid. Even though I understood how girls got pregnant, I'd imagine one of my father's sperm magically escaping from his boxer shorts, swimming through his pants, landing on my leg and inching up my Holy Angels uniform. I imagined being pregnant with Dad's baby, but I couldn't imagine anything after that. In her grief Mom had fucked someone. Maybe The Lion had some Meat after all. She probably couldn't explain her own pain over losing Dad. At least not to me. I knew harboring a baby while I looked on could only make her feel alone. While he was alive, Mom was certain I loved Dad more than her. "The two of you have your own secret society," she'd say.

Lyndon

Now that he was dead, Mom was convinced I'd love the memory of him more than I'd ever love her. I wanted to tell her she was dead wrong, but I wasn't sure that she was.

THE JOHNSON FAMILY graveyard, nothing more than a small plot of land squared off by a stone wall, stood straight across from the birthplace. Mom and I walked hand in hand in the August heat to the cemetery. Cynthia and our bus mates were still loitering beside the house. Mom told me that Dad had been arrested before I was born. He'd been pulled over for speeding in his pie truck. The cop noticed a baggie of pot in the ashtray. A very big baggie of pot. Dad was arrested, tried, and found guilty of possession with intent to distribute. "Your grandfather could have made the whole thing go away, but instead, he let your father do six months in prison. Minimum security, a life lesson. I was pregnant with you the whole time he was locked up."

Mom tucked a wisp of loose hair behind my left ear. "I figured you should know about your father's past, you know, for your political career."

I wanted to tell her that I was sorry. As much as I loved my father, I was mystified as to why Mom, who worked ninety hours a week, would stay married to a man who was happiest when lying down on a couch, a man who couldn't keep his balance on the roof of his own house. A man who could never find his wallet or remember to tie his shoes. A man who panicked every time the phone rang. I would never understand how she had come to love him.

"I'm sorry about the rental car," I said.

"Insurance will cover it."

Mom and I looked out at the family gravestones. The tallest one was Lyndon's.

"Honey, your Dad was a wonderful, frustrating, lovely, ridiculous man."

WHEN WE reboarded the bus, our tour guide Cynthia smiled and informed us, "You're all very lucky. Lady Bird is in Bermuda this week. The Secret Service has okayed us for a drive-by of the ranch house."

Mom shouted down the length of the bus to Cynthia, "Can't we leave the bus and visit the inside of the house?"

"I'm afraid not, ma'am."

"But that's why we came here," the elderly twins said in unison.

"Sorry, ladies. Those are the rules." Cynthia turned the bus onto a red dirt road.

Without even the slightest look in my direction, Mom shouted, "My daughter has visited every presidential home in the country. We came all the way from New Jersey."

"Security risk." Cynthia said. "Plus, the ranch house is Lady Bird's primary residence. None of us would want a bunch of strangers trudging through our homes while we were out of town."

"It's fine, Mom." I said.

"Besides, you've seen the birthplace," Cynthia said.

"The reconstructed birthplace," Mom retorted. "Elise, you came here to see the house, and I'm going to make sure you see it." My pregnant mother pushed herself up from her seat on the moving bus, clutched her leather purse and waddled to the front. Cynthia continued to drive. Mom held onto a railing and leaned into the back of Cynthia's chair. Cynthia shook her head. And then she shook her head so violently that her mirrored sunglasses flung off her face and skittered to the floor of the bus. Mom kept right on talking. She reached into her purse and pulled out her wallet. Everyone on the bus heard Cynthia say, "Ma'am, I am a ranger for the National Park Service. I cannot be intimidated."

While my mother continued to buzz in her ear, Cynthia picked up the microphone on her CB and radioed headquarters. She spoke in a quick, clipped lingo that I did not understand. Then Mom swiped at the CB, grabbing at the spiral speaker cord. The entire bus and I witnessed their slap fight for control over the CB. Neither Mom nor Cynthia could hold onto the gadget, and the black cord snapped and struck against the dashboard console. Mom leaned in and appeared to snare Cynthia in a headlock. None of my fellow passengers moved. The polite man who had offered Mom his seat looked at me and said, "Can't you calm her down?" Then Mom let go of Cynthia and said in a hoarse voice, "You win." Cynthia announced that the bus would return to the Visitor Center, immediately. We would not be driving by the Johnson Ranch house today. The German couple spoke German, in quick, violent snatches. The little boy with the cowlick put his hands over his ears and screamed in three sharp blasts before his sister covered his mouth with the back of her hand. I felt my shingles pain run down my neck and arms, felt the ladybug shell on my back harden.

Mom strode down the length of the bus, past identical fierce glares from the twin sisters. She sat beside me. I shook my head and said, "This is not Manhattan. We're in the Republic of Texas. Pushy doesn't work here."

Mom said, "Don't worry, kid. I got it covered."

CYNTHIA SPED back to the Visitor Center. She tried to calm the agitated passengers by turning on the bus's stereo system and blasting Lyndon Johnson's favorite song, "Raindrops Keep Fallin' on My Head." I stared out the window at the terraced farmland and tried to remember why I ever cared about the presidents. I loved them because my father loved them. Since he'd died I'd been trying every day to reclaim his sense of history. All I'd managed to do was recreate his level of stress and discomfort. The red sore on my back proved to me that I was nothing more than the nervous daughter of a panicked man. That was my place in the passage of time, my inheritance. I could never be president. I was the would-be pothead child of a convicted felon and a whore. I tried to picture my father relaxed, stoned, resigned to his shortcomings. His eyes bloodshot, his smile goofy, a halo of ladybugs flying over his blond head: that was the father I loved.

When Cynthia parked the bus, she pointed to Mom and me and said, "You two stay seated. For the rest of you, I'm sorry but this is the last stop," Mom clutched my arm. As Cynthia ushered our fellow travelers off the bus, I imagined the Secret Service descending upon us. We were a family of felons. I figured the penalty for assaulting a park ranger included a prison sentence. Maybe now, with the threat of incarceration pending, Mom would admit her pregnancy. I was furious with her. She'd ruined our vacation, stained my Victim T-shirt, tarnished my father's reputation.

Through the bus window, Mom watched Cynthia confer with a fellow ranger in the Visitor Center. Mom said, "I told Ranger Cindy to wait ten minutes in case those Germans got curious."

THE JOHNSON RANCH house was smaller than I had imagined. The white paint on the outside of the house needed a touch-up. The large bow windows sagged in their rotting castings. Before Cynthia dropped us off she pointed out the security cameras and told us which ones were working. "I'll give you twenty minutes like we agreed. The house is locked, but you can view the grounds and Lyndon Baines Johnson's antique car collection."

A massive live oak stood on the front lawn. Lyndon, or some other hunter, had attached two plaques with enormous stuffed deers' heads directly to the tree's trunk. Mom petted a buck's antlers. I'm not sure what Mom promised or paid Cynthia for our private tour of the Johnson Ranch. Mom believed in cash, and always had at least a thousand dollars stashed on or near her person. She also believed in threats and bribes. With a phone call, Mom could place a lien on your ancestral home or buy you the ostrich farm you'd always dreamed of owning. Mom knew how to bargain. How to make a deal. She was fearless. She knew that she couldn't appreciate the presidents the way Dad and I had, but she could give me something Dad never could. Mom could provide access. She could make things happen. She had what it took to be president.

We walked into the open-air front of the airplane hanger that held Lyndon's cars: a red Ford Phaeton, a Fiat 500 Jolly Ghia, a vintage fire truck, and a little green wagon. The sun had tanned Mom's face. She looked beautiful, victorious. I put my arms around her, rubbed her tummy. "What is it?" I asked. She looked down at me and placed my hand flat on the crown of her belly. "It's a boy."

Inside the hangar, I recognized one of the automobiles, a small blue-and-white convertible. "This is one of those land-and-sea cars. An amphibious car. Johnson used to drive his friends around the ranch, take them down to the river, and scare everyone by plunging them into the water. The car turns into a boat."

Mom opened the driver's-side door. "Get in," she said.

We sat in the white-leather seats, proud of our hard-earned view of the Texas hills. Mom took out a linen handkerchief from her purse and handed it to me. "Your father told me this thing helped you guys relax."

I knew by the weight and size of the gift that it was Buchanan. I unwrapped the pipe. The bowl was still packed with a small amount of pot. I'd never smoked Buchanan before.

"Your father died too young to have a will," Mom said. "Just think of this as your inheritance."

"I don't suppose you have a lighter." Mom handed me a silver Zippo with Dad's initials. She watched me light the pipe. I coughed. The smoke burned my throat. I offered Mom Buchanan, but she shook her head no and pointed to her belly.

"When the baby's older," she said, "I want you to tell him about his dad. I want him to know where he came from."

His dad.

We sat together in this magic convertible, me smoking, Mom breathing in the air at my side. We needed a new getaway car. One that could take us back home and beyond. Up the Hudson and along the Garden State Parkway. I gazed down the hill to the Pedernales. Mom pointed out a zebra. I laughed. It was just a gray spotted pony. Everything was clear. I would skip Nixon. Dad would understand. Instead, I'd take my little brother to Omaha, Nebraska, then to Michigan. Gerald Ford, 1974–77, born Leslie Lynch King. He was renamed after his adopted father. Ford didn't know who his real father was until he was practically an adult. I'd tell my brother about Ford and all the men fate brought to power, the chief executives, all the fearless men in charge. He'd know that Andrew Jackson was thirteen when he fought the British in the Battle of Hanging Rock. I'd explain the difference between John Adams and John Quincy Adams. I'd give him reasons to like Ike, to be grateful for the Monroe Doctrine, to appreciate the irony of William Henry Harrison dying of pneumonia one month into his term after staying out in the cold to deliver his endless inauguration address.

Mom said, "Now smoke in moderation. Don't get caught. Don't let your grades slip. Promise me."

I could hear the walkie-talkie static and chatter coming from the Secret Service agents. We'd been caught. Mom would certainly be arrested. Cynthia would lose her job. I'd be left to raise Lyndon alone. Dad's pot was strong, but mellow. For the first time in our relationship Mom and I had a deal, an understanding. I began to hum "Hail to the Chief." As the agents approached in their dark, shiny suits, I promised Mom I would tell Lyndon, my running mate and my half brother, all the things I knew about my father, his father.

How We Avenged the Blums

NATHAN ENGLANDER

I F YOU HEAD OUT TO GREENHEATH, LONG ISLAND, TODAY,
you'll find that the schoolyard where Zvi Blum was attacked
is more or less as it was. The bell at the public school still
rings through the weekend, and the bushes behind the lot where
we played hockey still stand. The only difference is that the sharp
screws and jagged edges of the jungle gym are gone, the playground stripped of all adventure, sissified and padded and covered with a snow of shredded tires.

It was onto this lot that Zvi Blum, the littlest of the three
Blum boys, stepped. During the week we played in the parking
lot of our yeshiva, where slap shots sent gravel flying, but on
Shabbos afternoons we ventured onto the fine, uncracked asphalt
at the public school. The first to arrive for our game, Zvi wore his
helmet with the metal face protector snapped in place. He had on
his gloves and held a stick in his hand.

Zvi worked up a sweat playing a fantasy game while he

waited for the rest of us to arrive. After a fake around an imagined opponent, he found himself at a real and sudden halt. The boy we feared most stood before him. It was Greenheath's local Anti-Semite, with a row of friends beyond. The Anti-Semite had until then abided by a certain understanding. We stepped gingerly in his presence, looking beaten, which seemed to satisfy his need to beat us for real.

The Anti-Semite took hold of Zvi's face mask as if little Blum were a six-pack of beer.

Zvi looked past the bully and the jungle gym, through the chain-link fence and up Crocus Avenue, hoping we'd appear, a dozen or more boys, wearing helmets, wielding sticks. How nice if, like an army, we'd arrived.

The Anti-Semite let go of Zvi's mask.

"You Jewish?" he asked.

"I don't know," Zvi said.

"You don't know if you're Jewish?"

"No," Zvi said. He scratched at the asphalt with his stick.

The bully turned to his friends, taking a poll of suspicious glances.

"Your mother never told you?" the Anti-Semite asked.

Zvi shifted his weight and kept on with his scratching. "It never came up," he said.

Zvi remembered a distinct extended pause while the Anti-Semite considered. Zvi thought—he may have been wishing—that he saw the first of us coming down the road.

He was out cold when we got there, beaten unconscious with his helmet on, his stick and gloves missing. We were no experts at forensics, but we knew immediately that he'd been worsted. And because he was suspended by his underwear from one of the bolts on the swing set, we also knew that a wedgie had been administered along the way.

We thought he was dead.

We had no dimes even to make a telephone call, money being forbidden on the Sabbath. We did nothing for way too long. Then Beryl started crying, and Harry ran to the Vilmsteins, who debated, while they fetched the *mukzeh* keys, which of them should drive in an emergency.

SOME WHISPERED that our nemesis was half-Jewish. His house was nestled in the dead end behind our school. And the ire of the Anti-Semite and his family was said to have been awakened when, after he had attended kindergarten with us at our yeshiva for some months, and had been welcomed as a little son of Israel, the rabbis discovered that only his father was Jewish. The boy, deemed gentile, was ejected from the class and led home by his shamefaced mother. Rabbi Federbush latched the back gate behind them as the boy licked at the finger paint, nontoxic and still wet on his hands.

We all knew the story, and I wondered what it was like for that boy, growing up—growing large—on the other side of the fence. His mother sometimes looked our way as she came and went from the house. She didn't reveal anything that we were mature enough to read—only kept on, often with a hand pressed to the small of her back.

AFTER ZVI'S BEATING, the police were called.

My parents wouldn't have done it, and let that fact be known.

"What good will come?" my father said. Zvi's parents had already determined that their son had suffered nothing beyond bruising: his bones were unbroken and his brain unconcussed.

"Call the police on every anti-Semite," my mother said, "and they'll need a separate force." The Blums thought differently. Mrs. Blum's parents had been born in America. She had grown up in Connecticut and attended public school. She felt no distrust for the uniform, believed the authorities were there to protect her.

The police cruiser rolled slowly down the hill with the Blums in procession behind it. They marched, the parents and three sons, little Zvi with his gauze-wrapped head held high.

The police spoke to the Anti-Semite's mother, who propped the screen door open with a foot. After her son had been called to the door for questioning, Mrs. Blum and Zvi were waved up. They approached, but did not touch, the three brick steps.

It was word against word. An accusing mother and son, a pair disputing, and no witnesses to be had. The police didn't make an arrest, and the Blums did not press charges. The retribution exacted from the Anti-Semite that day came in the form of a motherly chiding.

The boy's mother looked at the police, at the Blums, and at the three steps between them. She took her boy by the collar and, pulling him down to a manageable height, slapped him across the face.

"Whether it's niggers or kids with horns," she said, "I don't want you beating on those that are small."

WE'D LONG IMAGINED that Greenheath was like any other town, except for its concentration of girls in ankle-length denim skirts and white-canvas Keds, and boys in sloppy oxford shirts, with their yarmulkes hanging down as if sewn to the side of their heads. There was the fathers' weekday ritual. When they disembarked from the cars of the Long Island Railroad in the evenings, hands reached into pockets and yarmulkes were slipped back in place. The beating reminded us that these differences were not so small.

Our parents were born and raised in Brooklyn. In Greenheath, they built us a Jewish Shangri-la, providing us with everything but the one crucial thing Brooklyn had offered. It wasn't
stickball or kick-the-can—acceptable losses, though nostalgia ran
high. No, it was a *quality* that we were missing, a toughness. As a
group of boys thirteen and fourteen, we grew healthy, we grew
polite, but our parents thought us soft.

Frightened as we were, we thought so too, which is why we
turned to Ace Cohen. He was the biggest Jew in town, and our
senior by half a dozen years. He was the toughest Jew we knew,
the only one who smoked pot, who had ever been arrested, and
who owned both a broken motorcycle and an arcade version of
Asteroids. He left the coin panel open and would play endlessly
on a single quarter, fishing it out when he was finished. In our admiration we never considered that at nineteen or twenty we
might want to move out of our parents' basements, or go to college. We thought only that he lived the good life—no cares, no
job, his own Asteroids, and a mini-fridge by his bed where he
kept his Ring Dings ice-cold.

"Not my beef, little Jewboys," is what he told us, when we
begged him to beat up the Anti-Semite on our behalf. "Violence
breeds violence," he said, slapping at buttons. "Older and wiser—
trust me when I tell you to let it go."

"We called the police," Zvi said. "We went to his house with
my parents and them."

"Unfortunate," Ace said, looking down at little Zvi. "Unfortunate, my buddy, for you.

"It's a delicate thing being Jewish," Ace said. "It's a condition
that aggravates the more mind you pay it. Let it go, I tell you. If
you insist on fighting, then at least fight him yourselves."

"It would be easier if you did," we told him.

"And I bet, big as your Anti-Semite is, that he, too, in direct proportion, also has bigger friends. Escalation," Ace said. "Escalation built in. You don't want this to get so bad that you really need me."

"But what if we did?" we said.

Ace didn't answer. Frustrated and defeated, we left him—Ace Cohen, blowing the outlines of asteroids apart.

THEY WERE ALL heroes to us, every single one of Russia's oppressed. We'd seen *Gulag* on cable television, and learned that for escapes across vast snowy tundras, two prisoners would invite a third to join, so that they could eat him along the way. We were moved by this as boys, and fantasized about sacrifice, wondering which of our classmates we'd devour.

Our parents were active in the fight for the refuseniks' freedom in the 1980s, and every Russian Jew was a refusenik whether he wanted to be or not. We children donated our reversible-vested three-piece suits to help clothe Jewish unfortunates of all nations. And when occasion demanded, we were taken from our classes and put on buses to march for the release of our Soviet brethren.

We got our own refusenik in Greenheath right after Zvi's assault. Boris was the janitor at a Royal Hills yeshiva. He was refilling the towel dispenser in the faculty lounge when he heard of our troubles. Boris was Russian and Jewish, and he'd served in Brezhnev's army and the Israeli one to boot. He made his sympathies known to the teachers from Greenheath, voicing his outrage over our plight. That very Friday a space was made in the Chevy Nova in which they carpooled while listening to *mishna* on tape.

Boris came to town for a Shabbos, and then another, and had he slept twenty-four hours a day and eaten while he slept, he still couldn't have managed to be hosted by a fraction of the families that wanted to house and feed him and then feed him more.

The parents were thrilled to have their own refusenik—a menial laborer yet, a young man who for a living pushed a broom. They hadn't been so excited since the mothers went on an AMIT tour of the Holy Land and saw Jews driving buses and a man wearing *tzitzit* delivering mail. Boris was Greenheath's own Sharansky, and our parents gave great weight to his dire take on our situation. His sometimes fractured English added its own gravity to the proceedings. "When hooligan gets angry," he would say, "when drinking too much, the Anti-Semite will charge."

The first, informal self-defense class was given the day Boris was at Larry Lipshitz's playing Intellivision Hockey and teaching Larry to smoke. It ended with Larry on the basement floor, the wind knocked out of him and a sort of wheeze coming from his throat. "How much?" he said to Boris. "How much what?" was Boris's answer. He displayed a rare tentativeness that Larry might have noticed if he hadn't been trying to breathe. "For the lesson," Larry said. And here was the wonder of America, the land of opportunity. In Russia if you punched someone in the stomach, you did it for free. A monthly rate was set, and Larry spread the word.

That was also the day that Barry Pearlman was descended upon by our nemesis as he left Vardit's Pizza and Falafel. His food was taken. The vegetarian egg rolls (a staple of all places kosher, no matter the cuisine) were bitten into. A large pizza and a tahini platter were spread over the street. Barry was beaten, and then, as soon as he was able, he raced back into the store. Vardit, the owner, wiped the sauce from little Pearlman. She remade his order in full, charging only the pizza to his account. The Pearlmans didn't want trouble. The police were not called.

BARRY PEARLMAN was the second to sign up. Then came the Kleins and cockeyed Shlomo, whose mother sent him because of the current climate, though really she wanted him to learn to defend himself from us.

Our rabbis at school needed to approve of the militant group we were forming. They remembered how Israel was founded with the aid of NILI and the Haganah and the undergrounds of yore. They didn't much approve of a Jewish state without a messiah, but they gave us permission to present our proposal to Rabbi Federbush, the founder of our community and the dean of our yeshiva.

His approval was granted, but only grudgingly. The old man is not to be blamed. Karate he knew nothing of; the closest sport he was familiar with was wrestling, and this from rabbinic lore— a Greco-Roman version. His main point of protest, therefore, was that we'd be wrestling the uncircumcised publicly and in the nude. When the proposal was rephrased, and he was told that we were being trained to battle the descendants of Amalek, who attacked the Israelites in the desert; that we were gearing up to face the modern-day spawn of Haman (cursed be his name); when told it was to fight the Anti-Semite, he nodded his head, understanding. "Cossacks," he said, and agreed.

IT WASN'T exactly a pure martial art but an amalgam of Israeli Krav Maga, Russian hand-to-hand combat, and Boris's own messy form of endless attack. He showed us how to fold a piece of paper so it could be used to take out an eye or open a throat, and he told us always to travel with a circuit tester clipped to our breast pocket like a pen. When possible, Boris advised us, have a new gun waiting at each destination. He claimed to have learned this during a stint in the Finger of God, searching out Nazis in Argentina and then—acting as a military tribunal of one—finding them guilty and putting a bullet between their eyes.

We were taught to punch and kick, to stomp and bite, while the mainstay of all suburban martial-arts classes—when you can avoid confrontation, you do it—was removed. Boris told us to hold our ground. "Worst cases," he said, "raise hand like in defeat, and kick for ball."

After a few weeks of lessons, we began to understand the power we had. Boris had paired Larry Lipshitz, that wisp of a boy, with Aaron, the middle Blum. They went at it in Larry's backyard, circling and jabbing with a paltry amount of rage. Boris stood off to the side, his arms resting on his paunch—a belly that on him was the picture of good health, as if it were the place from which all his strength emanated, a single muscle providing power to all the other parts.

Boris spat in the grass and stepped forward. "You are fighting," he said. "Fight." He put his foot to Aaron's behind and catapulted him into his opponent. "Friends later. Now win." Larry Lipshitz let out a yawp befitting a larger man and then, with speed and with grace, he landed the first solid roundhouse kick we'd seen delivered. It was no sparring partner's hit but a shoulder fake and all-his-might strike, the ball of Lipshitz's bare foot connecting with Aaron's kidney. Larry didn't offer a hand. He stepped back like a champion and raised his fists high. Aaron hobbled to the nearest tree and displayed for us the first fruits of our training. He dropped his pants, took aim, and, I tell you, it was nothing less than water to wine for us when Aaron Blum peed blood.

IT'S CURIOUS that the story most often used to inspire Jewish battle-readiness is that of Masada, an episode involving the last holdouts of an ascetic Israelite sect, who committed suicide in a mountain fortress. The battle was fought valiantly, though without the enemy present. Jews bravely doing harm to themselves.

270

The only Roman casualties died of frustration in their encampment below—eight months in the desert spent building a ramp to storm fortress walls for a slaughter, and the deed already done when they arrived.

When Israeli army recruits complete basic training they climb up that mountain and scream out into the echo, "A second time Masada won't fall." Boris made us do the same over the edge of Greenheath Pond, a body of water whose circulation had slowed, a thick green soup that sent back no sound.

MOSTLY THE HARASSMENT was aimed at the Blum boys and their house. I don't know if this was because of their proximity to the Anti-Semite's house, the call to the police, or the Anti-Semite's public slap in the face. I sometimes can't help thinking that the Blum boys were chosen as targets because they looked to the bully as they looked to me: enticingly victimlike and small. Over time an M-80 was used to blow up the Blum mailbox, and four tires were slashed on a sensible Blum car. A shaving-cream swastika was painted on their walkway, but it washed away in the rain before anyone could document that it had ever existed.

When we ran into the Anti-Semite, insults were inevitably hurled, and punches thrown. Larry took a thrashing without managing his now legendary kick. Shaken, he demanded his money's worth of Boris, and made very clear that he now feared for his life. Boris shrugged it off. "Not so easy," he assured him. "Shot and lived. Stabbed and lived. Not so easy to get dead."

My father witnessed the abuse. He came upon the three Blum boys crawling around and picking up pennies for the right to cross the street—the bully and his friends enforcing. My father scattered the boys, all but the three Blums, who stood there red in the face, hot pennies in their hands.

The most severe attack was the shotgun blast that shattered the Blums' bay window. We marked it as the start of dark days, though the shells were packed only with rock salt.

WE STEPPED UP our training and also our level of subterfuge. We memorized *katas* and combinations. We learned to march in lock-step; to run, leap, and roll in silence.

Lying on our backs in a row with feet raised, heads raised, and abdomens flexed, we listened to Boris lecture while he ran over us, stepping from stomach to stomach, as if crossing a river on stones. Peace, Boris insisted, was maintained through fear. "Do you know which countries have no anti-Semite?" he asked. We didn't have an answer. "The country with no Jew."

The struggle would not end on its own. The bully would not mature, see the error of his ways, or learn to love the other. He would hate until he was dead. He would fight until he was dead. And unless we killed him, or beat him until he thought we had killed him, we'd have no truce, no peace, no quiet. In case we didn't understand the limitations of even the best-case scenario, Boris explained it to us again. "The man hits. In future he will hit wife, hit son, hit dog. We want only that he won't hit Jew. Let him go hit someone else."

Despite all the bumps pushed back into foreheads and the braces freed from upper lips, I'm convinced our parents thought our training was worth the effort. Our mothers brought frozen steaks to press against black eyes and stood close as our fathers tilted our chins and hid smiles. "Quite a shiner," they would say, and they could hardly stand to give up staring when the steaks covered our wounds.

Along with the training injuries we had other setbacks. One was a tactical error when, post–shotgun blast, we went as a group to egg the Anti-Semite's house. Shlomo thought he heard a noise, and yelled "Anti-Semite!" in warning. We screamed back, dropped our eggs, and fled in response. This all took place more than a block away from the house. We hadn't even gotten our target in sight.

We weren't cohesive. We knew how to move as a group but not as a gang.

We needed practice.

After two thousand years of being chased, we didn't have any hunt in us.

WE SOUGHT HELP from Chung-Shik through Yitzy—an Israeli with an unfortunate heritage. Yitzy's parents had brought him to America with the last name Penis, which even among kind children doesn't play well. We teased Yitzy Penis ruthlessly, and as a result he formed a real friendship with his gentile neighbor Chung-Shik, the only Asian boy in town. Both showed up happily, Yitzy delighted at being asked to bring his pal along.

And so we proposed it, our plan.

"Can we practice on you?" we asked.

"Practice what?" Chung-Shik said amiably, Yitzy practically aglow at his side.

When no one else answered, Harry spoke.

"A reverse pogrom," he said.

"A what?"

"We just want to menace you," Harry said. "Chase you around a bit as a group. You know, because you're different. To get a feel for it."

Chung-Shik looked to his friend. You could see we were losing him, and Yitzy had already lost his smile.

That's when Zvi pleaded, almost a cry of desperation, "Come on, you're the only different kid we know."

Yitzy held Chung-Shik's stare, the Asian boy looking back, not scared as much as disappointed.

"Chase me instead," Yitzy said, sort of pantomiming that he could be Chung-Shik and Chung-Shik could be him, switch off the yarmulke and all.

We abandoned the idea right then. It wouldn't be the same.

OUR FAILED offensive got back to Boris—the reverse pogrom that wasn't, and the continuing rise in Blum-related trouble and chases-home-from-school. The rock salt still stung us all.

We met in the rec room of the shul. Boris had swiped a filmstrip and accompanying audiocassette from the yeshiva he worked at in Royal Hills. He advanced the strip in the projector, a single frame every time the tape went beep. We knew the film well. We knew when the image would shift from the pile of shoes to the pile of hair, from the pile of bodies to the pile of teeth to the pile of combs. The film was a sacred teaching tool brought out only on Yom Hashoah, the Holocaust memorial day.

Each year the most memorable part was the taped dramatization, the soundman's wooden blocks *clop-clopping*, the sound of those boots coming up the stairs. First they dragged off symbolic father and mother. And then, *clop, clop, clop*, those boots marched away.

The lights still dimmed, we would form two lines—one boys, one girls. We marched back to class this way singing "Ani Ma'amin" and holding in our heads the picture they'd painted for us: six million Jews marching into the gas chambers, two by two; a double line three million strong and singing in one voice, "I believe in the coming of the Messiah."

Boris did not split us into two quiet lines. He did not start us on a moving round of that song, or the equally rousing "We Are Leaving Mother Russia," with its coda, "When they come for us, we'll be gone." After the film, he turned the lights back on and said to us, yelled at us, "Like sheep to the slaughter. Six million Jews is twelve million fists." And then he segued from fists and Jewish fighting to the story of brave Trumpeldor, who, Boris claimed, lost an arm in the battle of Tel Hai and then continued fighting with the one.

Galvanized, we went straight to the Anti-Semite's house. Zvi Blum, beaten, bothered, dug a hunk of paving stone out of the walkway to avenge his family's bay window. He tossed that rock with all his might; limited athlete that he was, it hooked left and hit the wall of the house with a great bang. We fled. Still imperfect, still in retreat, we ran with euphoria, hooting and hollering, victorious.

A NEWFOUND energy emerged at the start of the next class, which was also the start of a new session. We lined up to pay Boris what was now a quarterly fee. He took three months' worth of cash in one hand, patted us each on the back with the other, and said, "Not yet leaders, but you've turned into men." Boris even said this to the Conservative boy, though it was Elliot's first lesson. He then addressed us regarding our successful mission. "Anti-Semite will come back harder," he said, declaring that only a strong offense would see this conflict to its end. Pyrotechnics were in order.

We ventured out to the turnpike that marked the border of our town. In the alley behind ShopRite, we worked on demolitions following recipes from Boris's training along with the instructions on some pages torn from an Abbie Hoffman book. We made smoke bombs that didn't smoke and firebombs that never burned. And though we suspected that the recipes themselves were faulty, Boris shook his head as if we'd never learn.

We struck with our bomb making, working feverishly, with Boris timing each attempt and at intervals yelling, "Too late, already dead." Then Elliot stood up with a concoction of his own, a bottle with a rag stuffed in the top, and announced, "This is how you build a bomb."

To prove it he lit the rag, arced back, and threw the bottle. We watched it soar, easily traceable by its fiery tail. We heard it hit and the sound of glass and then nothing. "So what," Aaron said. "That's not a bomb. By definition it has to go *boom!*" We went back to work until Boris said, "Lesson over," and a yellow light began to chip at the darkness in the sky, a warm yellow light and smoke. "Not a bomb," Elliot said, looking proud and terrified in equal measure. His bottle, we discovered, had hit the Te-Amo Cigar & Smoke Shop. It had ignited the garbage in the rear of the store. The drive-through window was engulfed in flames. "Simplest sometimes best," Boris said. And "Class dismissed." We started to panic, and he said, "Fire could be from anything." Right then, his pocket full of our money, and already in full possession of our hearts and heads, Boris walked off. He walked toward the burning store, so close to the flames that we covered our eyes. True to his teachings, Boris didn't turn and run. He didn't stop, either. We know for sure that he went back to Royal Hills and worked another day. All our parents ever said was "green card," and we heard that Boris continued west to Denver and built a new life.

MR. BLUM was still at the office. The three boys Blum were each manning a window and staring out into the dark. They had, on their own and in broad daylight, gone down the hill with toilet paper and shaving cream. They'd draped the trees and marked the sidewalks, unleashing on their target the suburban version of tar and feathers. Then they'd run up to the house and taken their posts, holding them through nightfall. When their mother pulled the car into the garage after her own long day at work, she saw only what the boys hadn't done. She made her way back down the driveway to the curb, where the garbage pails stood empty, one of them tipped by the wind. Basic responsibilities stand even in times of trouble. She had not borne three sons so that she'd have to drag garbage pails inside.

No one knows the quality of the Anti-Semite's night vision. The only claim that could be made in his defense is that until the lapse the Blum boys had been the sole draggers of the garbage pails on every other trash day in memory. In the Blum boys' defense—and they would forever feel they needed one—three watched windows leaves one side of the house unguarded. All that said, the sound of metal pails being dragged up a gravel driveway brought the Anti-Semite racing out of the dark—and masked his approach for Mrs. Blum.

Mrs. Blum, of course, had not been in our class. She had no notion of self-defense and was wholly unfamiliar with weaponry. When this brute materialized before her, his arm already in motion, she did not assume a defensive posture. She did not raise her fists or prepare to lunge. What she did was turn at the last instant to get a look at the tiny leather wand sticking out from his swinging hand. She had never seen a blackjack before. When the single blow met with the muscles of her back, it sent a shock through her system so great that she saw a thousand pinpricks in her eyes and felt her legs give way completely. Connecticut or no, Mrs. Blum was a Jew. "*Shanda!*" she said to the boy, who was already loping off.

Oh, those poor Blums. As we had found Zvi, Zvi discovered

his own mother—not hanging from a bolt but curled in the grass. Inside the house, an ice pack in place and refusing both hospital and house call, Mrs. Blum told her sons what she'd seen.

"*Shanda!*" she said again. "*Busha!*"

The boys agreed. A shame and an embarrassment.

When their mother lifted the receiver to call the police, Aaron pressed his finger down into the cradle of the phone. Mrs. Blum looked at her son and then replaced the receiver as Aaron slid his finger away. "Not this time," he said. And this time she didn't.

WHEN MY MOTHER told my father what had happened, he didn't want to believe it. "Nobody ever wants to believe what happens to the Jews," she said, "not even us." My father simply shook his head. "Since when," my mother said, "do anti-Semites have limits? They will cross all lines. Greenheath no better." Then she, too, took to shaking her head. I was sorry I'd told her, sorry to witness her telling him. We'd known our parents would respond with hands to mouth and *oy-vey-iz-mirs*, but none of us expected to see such obvious disillusionment with the world they'd built. I turned away.

Though we'd been abandoned, Boris's wisdom still held sway. We were going to see to it that the Anti-Semite never hit back again. "Anti-Semite school," Harry Blum called it, mustering a Boris-like tone. A boy who attacks a woman half his size, who had already attacked her son, would, if able, do the same thing again. We decided we would use Zvi as our siren—set him out in the middle of the lot at the public school, so the Anti-Semite might be drawn by the irresistible call of the vulnerable Jew. The rest of us would stay hidden in those bushes and then fall on our enemy as one. But looking from face to face, taking in skinny Lipshitz and fat Beryl, the three Blums full of anger and without any reach—we realized that we couldn't defeat the Anti-Semite, even as a group.

Boris was right. It was true what he'd said about us. We were ready, we were raring, and we were useless without a leader. We went off like that, leaderless, to Ace Cohen's house.

TEARS, mind you. We saw tears in Ace Cohen's eyes. He stopped playing his Asteroids and did not get back into bed. Little Mrs. Blum attacked—it was too much to bear. Such aggression, he agreed, needed to be avenged. "So you'll join us," we said, assuming the matter had been decided. But he wouldn't. He still didn't want any part of us. A singular matter, the blow to Mrs. Blum. And likewise a singular matter, he felt, was the act of revenge.

One punch is what is offered. "You've got me, my Heebie-Jeebies. But only for one swing." We pressed him for more. We begged of him leadership. He showed us his empty hands. "One punch," he said. "Take it or leave it."

CERTAIN THINGS went according to plan. When the Anti-Semite arrived, he showed up alone. That he passed on a Saturday, and in a mood to confront Zvi, we took as a sign of the righteousness of our scheme.

We had already been hiding in those bushes all morning. Sore and stiff, we were sure that the creaking of our joints would give us away, that the sound of our breathing, as all our hearts raced, would reveal the trap we'd laid.

And Zvi—what can be said about that brave Blum, out there alone on the asphalt between the jungle gym and the bushes, cooking under the hot sun? Zvi was poised in his three-piece suit, a red yarmulke like a bull's-eye on top of his head.

The Anti-Semite immediately began to badger Zvi. Zvi, empowered, enraged, and under the impression that we would immediately charge, spewed his own epithets back. The moment was glorious. Little Zvi in his suit, addressing—apparently—the brass belt buckle on that mountain of a bully, raised an accusing finger. "You shouldn't have," Zvi said. His words came out tough; they came out beautiful—so well that they reached us in the bushes, and clearly moved the Anti-Semite to the point of imminent violence.

The situation would have been perfect if not for one unfortunate complication: the small matter of Ace Cohen's resistance. Ace Cohen was unwilling to budge. We begged him to charge with us, to rescue Zvi. "Second thoughts," he said. "A fine line between retaliation and aggression. Sorry. I'll need to see some torment for myself." We implored him, but we didn't charge alone. We all stayed put until push came to shove, until the Anti-Semite started beating Zvi Blum in earnest, until Zvi—his clip-on tie separated from his neck—hit, with a thud, the ground.

Then we sprang out of the bushes, on Ace's heels. We had the Anti-Semite surrounded, and Zvi pulled free with relative ease.

Ace Cohen, three inches taller and fifty pounds heavier, faced the bully down.

"Keep away" is all Ace said. Then, without form or chi power, his feet in no particular stance, Ace swung his fist so wide and so slowly that we couldn't believe anyone might fail to get out of the way. But maybe the punch just looked slow, because the bully took it. He caught it right on the chin. He took it without rocking back—an exceptional feat even before we knew that his jaw was broken. He remained stock-still for a second or two. Not a bit of him moved except for that bottom jaw, which had unhinged like a snake's and made a solid quarter turn to the side. Then he dropped.

Ace pushed his way through the circle we'd formed. It closed right back up around the Anti-Semite, bloodied and now writhing before us.

As I watched him, I knew I'd always feel that to be broken was better than to break—my failing. I also knew that the deep rumble rolling through us was only nerves, a sensitivity to imagined repercussion, as if a sound were built in to revenge.

What we really shared in that instant was simple. Anyone who stood with us that day will tell you the same. With the Anti-Semite at our feet, confusion came over us all. We stood there looking at that crushed boy. And none of us knew when to run.

Good Monks

MALINDA McCOLLUM

A DELIRIOUS MOMENT. PICTURE THIS. PALE MAN SHOUT-
ing, "I am drunk on water and the bitterest love!" In the
near-empty diner his voice surprising as a first drop of
blood.

Severa eyed the man from her booth along the glass wall of
Andy's Eats. She was stretching a cup of coffee into the infinite,
sip by sip.

"Water!" the pale man shrieked. "Love!" His table was in the
center of the diner. On it, onion rings and a red malt, untouched.
Two streaky-haired kids seated at a long chrome counter spun on
their stools and waggled their boots at him. Severa recognized
them as sophomores from school. There were just chippers, occasional flyers, not too hardcore.

"Kool-Aid!" one of the kids yelled.

"Insanity!" said the other, cracking up.

A waitress tending to a candy display at the register sighed. Her eyes looked like cranberries. Her arms disappeared into a carton of Zagnuts.

"Water!" the pale man screamed again.

The waitress withdrew from the Zagnuts and started toward him.

Severa shouldered her heavy leather bag and walked to the man, arriving just before the waitress. Coming right up, mister.

"He's mine," she said, grabbing the man's arm. "I'll take him."

"Yours?" the waitress said.

"For now and maybe always." She worked her hand up the wide sleeve of the man's coat. He quieted in her hold.

"Why weren't you all at the same table?" the waitress asked. "Why were you letting him scream?"

"You have beautiful eyes," Severa told her.

"So you're going to pay for him? Since he's yours and all?"

Severa tugged on the man until he stood. "I can let him sit here and scream," she said, "or I can get him out of here."

"You can't pay for him?"

"Let's see if he can pay for me." She spoke loudly to the man. "Do you have money? Can you settle your debts?"

The man reached inside his jacket and came back with three perfectly folded bills.

"There. Now we're all square." She placed the money on the table. The waitress seemed uncertain, so Severa repeated, "You have beautiful eyes."

The waitress's face dimmed as she worked the question: Complimenting or making fun?

"If you weren't on duty," Severa cooed, "I'd ask you home. I have this peppermint lotion I could rub on your feet."

For some reason, that decided it. The lady's whole body went stiff.

"Bitch," the waitress said, "get out now."

OUTSIDE, beyond the nimbus of the diner's floodlight, the night was its darkest, hoarding all. Someone somewhere was playing bad chords on a guitar. Severa bit her lip. Doubt and worry, worry and doubt. In the diner she had made more waves than was good for her.

"I'm drunk on water," the man said, softer now, on the sidewalk. Under his coat his arm was fleshy and bare. Severa gave it a few squeezes.

"Goes down easy, don't it," she said. So all right: she needed money. Her boyfriend Doug had left her. Alone, she had nothing. A few weeks ago she'd spent most of their savings on a nose job. And now she needed to eat, didn't she? She did!

"You like my face?" she said to the man. "You see symmetry there?"

"Water," the man said dully, "oh, oh, water."

"What about bitter love?" she said. "Don't forget that."

The man stumbled forward a few steps, but she didn't let him go. There was a slat bench up against the diner wall, and she led him to it, to get a better view. A slight guy, gentle-looking, with smooth skin and single-lidded eyes.

"Where you from, man?" she asked. "Your face ain't like mine, for real."

"Laos," the pale man said. His voice oozed through the air like something liquid. "Bordered by five different countries on all sides."

"No way to the sea," she said. "I relate."

"Somvay," said the man.

"Lola," said Severa.

Somvay placed his hands in prayer position and nodded. She sat next to him. A thick wig, a bandanna stretched over her head like a mantilla, dark glasses, and lots of makeup, but still she nuzzled into Somvay's arm when a car drove past them, casting its white pitiless light. Better safe.

"So I heard they have prostitutes in Laos that jerk guys off with their feet." She lifted her feet and rubbed her kicks together. "Look, Daddy, no hands!"

Somvay stared at her. "Most sacred," he said finally, gesturing to her head. "Least sacred." He pointed to her feet. Then he slapped his cheeks lightly and drew a deep breath.

In her bag was a roll of duct tape and a thermos of beer with codeine stirred in. The idea came from Doug. He used to go ganking with his ex-girlfriend. The ex-girlfriend would dress tarty and lure a drunk weakling somewhere lonely. Then she'd drug him or Doug would hit him and they'd take everything he had. To Severa, it seemed heavy on effort as compared to reward, but Doug was convinced it was worth it, the chance of getting caught low. When the mark awoke, disoriented and embarrassed, he was unlikely to go to the police. And even if he did, his story would be fuzzy. Doug didn't want to go back to jail.

Somvay touched her arm. "What happened here?" he asked, lifting her bandaged wrist.

"I fell," she lied. She had punched through a window. "I was running after my dog and I tripped."

"Where did you get your dog?" He let her go.

"The shelter," she lied again.

"Good. Good for you. You saved it from death."

She studied him. "Buddhist?"

"Yes."

"Me too! I have some books. Later on, we should chant chant chant."

A hick girl in tight jeans swung past the bench then, massaging the neck of the boy walking with her.

"Fuck him!" Severa yelled. "I did!"

The girl turned quickly, like she might start something, but then she kept walking. That's right, chick.

"I'm drunk," Somvay announced.

"So why you drinking tonight?" Severa asked him.

"My girl," he started, "my flower, she won't let me go. In Laos, where I am from, I bicycled to her house every day, to help her learn to read. We sat upon the hill behind her house and she stared across the river at Thailand. I had to take her hand and place it on the page to bring her attention back."

"Here," Severa said and gave him the red thermos from her bag. "Some beer to cut that water's power."

He unscrewed the cup cap and poured himself a drink.

"One night my mother awakened me in the dark. I took my soccer ball, and a small bag of clothing, and followed my mother to the banks of the river. When I saw the barge there, I tried to run away, back to my flower. But a man grabbed me, and took my mother's hand, and we floated across the Mekong."

"Mekong," Severa said, trying it out.

"For many months after we lived in an earthen hut in a Thai camp. There was a well at the edge of camp, but it ran dry quickly. I would go with my mother, and I still remember the fear as we came to it, that this time we would be too late." Somvay paused. "And then the taste of water on my tongue, sweet as something sugar."

He sipped from the thermos cup.

"Here there is plenty of water and I still am not satisfied. I drink and drink and I am still thirsty. I have lost my way."

"I know how you feel," Severa said. She patted his leg. "My boyfriend and I just broke up."

Above, the moon peeked out of a neat envelope of clouds. Then the air was heavier and heavier until it started to rain down upon them.

"Oh no," Somvay said. "No, no." His shoulders sagged.

"Close your mouth," Severa commanded. "We don't want you any more drunk."

THE TAXI DRIVER was as tanned as a detasseler. Severa put Somvay in the rear of the cab and settled in the front seat. She figured the driver would look at her less there than if she sat in the back, with him working the rearview mirror.

"So I heard that fat prostitutes let johns get away with more," she told the cabbie. "The rule of the marketplace makes it like that."

"The rule of the marketplace is one hell of a bitch," the cabbie said slowly. "The rule of the marketplace kicks your ass good."

"The market is a bitter and suffering place," said Somvay from the back. "Take the marketplace away."

"Oh, don't mind him," Severa said. "He's a major Buddhist. He talks big. Me, I'm the kind of gal that appreciates works way more than faith." She drew close to the cabbie's ear. "What good things you done lately?"

"I've done a few."

"Please," she said, "tell me about your good things. At length."

"Well," the cabbie drawled, "well, there is a certain length I could tell you about."

"I'm drunk," said Somvay.

Severa passed back the thermos.

"So about that length," the cabbie said. His voice was easy, but she could hear the meanness underneath. All right.

"How long?" she asked.

"Until what?" Somvay leaned into the space between the front seats. "What are you saying?"

"I'd have to say I've never measured," the cabbie said. The moon had moved and now lit the bronze hollows of his face.

"What they say," Somvay broke in, voice thick, "is that pain is what it is you measure pleasure by."

"No, pumpkin," Severa corrected him, "pain is what it is you measure pain by."

"Both of y'all are wrong," the cabbie said. "Pleasure is what you measure pleasure by." And then his heavy fingers were up on her thigh.

Right on. "Stop the cab!" she yelled. The cabbie, unbothered, pulled to the curb. Severa threw open the door and called for Somvay to join her. He did, stepping gingerly out of the car. The rain was almost nothing now.

"You owe me ten bucks, girlie," the cabbie said.

Severa helped Somvay lower himself to the sidewalk, then marched around to the driver's side. Smiling her wicked smile, she bent to his open window. "I owe you shit. You're lucky I'm not reporting you. You'd never drive a cab again."

The cabbie grasped her head. His hands covered her whole ears. "Listen, honey," he said, pulling her in, fingering the bones of her skull, "I'm giving you this one for free. This little lesson. It's real easy picking up a bruise. It's real tough getting rid of it."

"Thanks, Working Man!" she said, jerking away. She danced to the sidewalk and threw a rock at the cab as it drove off.

The rock missed. She cursed. It was a bad sign.

* * *

SEVERA AND SOMVAY made their way through dense woods to a clearing all the kids called the Lost Planet. Not easy—first a slick weedy ravine, next train tracks, then a faint path to the Planet's rocky beach. A lime pit there foamed purple, Des Moines' own small terrible sea.

Severa removed her dark glasses and held fast to Somvay by the loops of his jeans. He stepped tentatively with not enough bend in his knees. When they arrived at the bank of the lime pit, she let go of him for a moment, to squeeze some dampness from her wig. Somvay tripped and ended up on all fours.

"Come on," she said impatiently, kneeling, "let's attempt to remain upright." His face was flushed, so she untied the bandanna from her hair and wiped his cheeks and ears. Sweat wet her fingers through the cloth. When she was little her dad had worked summer construction, and when he came home sweaty, he shook salt onto his palm and licked it off. He said it was to replace what he lost during the day. She loved seeing him do it. It seemed smart. One hot August she ran around the block in a wool sweater so she could come in and eat salt straight, like her dad. Instead she fainted and broke her head on the sidewalk and a neighbor had driven her to the hospital to get stitches.

"I am in trouble," Somvay said. "I am drunk and I have lost my way."

"Oh no," she said. "We're going to have some fun is all."

"I do not want to be here."

"Lie down." She gave him a little shove and he sat, heavily. "Lie back."

When he did, his shirt rode up, revealing his smooth belly, the aching cut of his hips. He really was beautiful, and for a second she considered changing plans, letting him take her home, cook her something spicy, wake her in the morning with a kiss as long and clear as a ringing bell. But instead she set her bag on the ground and straddled him, pushing his arms over his head.

"Here," she said, "here in America, we free ourselves by getting totally confined." She retrieved the roll of tape and taped his wrists together.

"Ah, a Baci ceremony," he said, and it was the happiest she'd seen him. "Make three knots: one for good health, one for prosperity, one for joy."

"Let me help you off with your shoes." Severa slid back and pulled his canvas kicks from his feet. No socks, so she applied the duct tape to his bare ankles. She was starting to sweat under her wig so she removed it and put it on the ground.

"You can kill me," Somvay said suddenly, "but not yet."

She stopped her preparations. "Not ever," she said, annoyed. "Who do you think I am?" She repositioned herself on his stomach, knees close to his body. He wore a delicate silver chain high on his throat, and when she touched it she felt his pulse against her thumb.

"Relax," she said. "Tell me more about Laos."

He obeyed. "When I was a boy I played ball around the wat with my friends. Beautiful trees there, and the temple's golden roof. My mother warned me to be very careful about kicking the ball, because if I were to lose control of it, and if it were to hit a monk, I would lose merit. We were careful, but we were boys and one day I kicked the ball with the top of my foot so it would fly over my friend Thong. It flew, but when it came down it hit a monk. In the head!"

Behind her, the terrible sea gurgled and breathed.

"I froze," he continued. "And the monk looked at me, eyes black, and then bowed and said, 'Thank you. For the opportunity to practice patience.'" Somvay brought his arms up an inch from the ground, and she felt him shift beneath her. "And now I say thank you. For this. For the reminder that I own nothing, not even my body."

"Cut it out," she said, truly nervous now.

"*Bo pen nyang,*" he said. "Never mind." He laughed, and it was like a red scarf in the air.

She kissed him on the mouth, just once, hard, and when she stopped his eyes were shut, his breath light. She reached under him for his wallet. Inside, a credit card—she could use that tonight at least—and thirty-five dollars cash. Behind the bills was a cracked photograph, and when she removed it she saw a young monk in orange robes, lacquer bowl in hand, standing beneath a well-leafed tree. Somvay, of course, same soft eyes and flat cheeks. She slid the photo and credit card into her jeans. She laid the wallet next to her wig. She rose and circled Somvay's still body. The lime pit taunted her, that terrible sea. For a second she imagined floating across it, away from her dirty little life, hitting Thailand, super-green, on the other shore.

But everything's working, she reassured herself. I'm alive. Isn't that the real truth?

Then she heard. The growl of an engine, a dark beat pumping through bad speakers. She grabbed her wig and bag and reached under Somvay's arms. He was out. Holding her breath she dragged him to a spread of brush, dirt funneling into where his jeans gaped from his waist. When she heard the vehicle pop over a log blocking the Planet's secret path, she dropped Somvay and moved away into other weeds.

A truck careened into the Planet. Two men in the cab. And then she saw Somvay's wallet near the bank of the pit. And his bound ankles, not quite in the weeds, shined on by the big moon.

* * *

SEVERA HUDDLED in the dirt. The men were First Class Cranksters, she could see right away, scabby and bone-thin. Just skinny little zipheads, she told herself. And hadn't her dad once showed her some killer judo moves? But then again the crank had probably made the men vicious and paranoid enough to pack heat.

Still: the wallet. The ex-monk in the woods. Severa closed her eyes and slowed her breath and tried to tap into the vibes of any good forces that might be lurking, able to help.

The men had left the truck's headlights on, which lit the clearing nice and bright. One of the them, a blue-skinned guy with long arms, hurriedly fired a camp stove and unloaded boxes of chemicals and a collection of small empty jars. The other, small and hairless, cut open a series of Vicks inhalers, removed the cottons, and mixed them with water in a glass meat-loaf dish.

"I bumped into this girl last night," she heard the bald man say, "this South-of-Grand girl, and she goes, 'Trade you the rings off my fingers for a gram.'"

The blue man sprayed starter fluid into a jar and shook it until there were clouds inside. "I'd have said, 'How 'bout you give me your fingers instead.'"

The bald man frowned.

"I'd bite off a finger and use it to get her wet!"

"Nice," the bald man said. He dumped a cupful of clear fluid into the meat-loaf dish and balanced it on the camp stove. A smell like nail-polish remover made Severa's eyes tear.

Something rustled the high grasses around her, something stronger than wind. When she looked, Somvay was squirming. She slid toward him, keeping an eye on the clearing. In their rush to cook up, the men had missed the wallet and the ankles both, but now Somvay was getting noisy. Kneeling behind him, she pulled his body—slowly, slowly—further into the weeds. His eyes blinked open. A sound burbled in his throat. Could he breathe? Watching the men, Severa held one finger to her lips and untaped his mouth.

"Water," Somvay said.

The blue man looked up.

"Quiet," Severa whispered fiercely. "None here."

"Who's there?" the blue man said. He started toward their hiding weeds, and Severa saw the gun in his pants. So she re-taped Somvay's mouth and stepped into the clearing. It was exactly like going on stage.

"Hey, you all seen a giant black guy out here?" she said. "I lost track of my boyfriend somewhere in these woods."

The men appraised her. She tried to look ugly and old.

"You're not law, right, dressed like that?" the blue man asked.

She made herself giggle stupidly. "No, no, these are date clothes. My boyfriend and I come down here on weekends and practice with his gun."

"Glad to hear it," the blue man said. "Because I've been in jail once and I'd kill somebody first before I went back."

"You mean you'd kill yourself before going back," the bald man corrected him.

"Is that what I said?" the blue man asked Severa, smiling. "Did my brother hear me right?"

She ignored the question. "You two are brothers?"

"We're brothers," the bald man said. "You can call him Luke and me Pat."

"But we're not like your brother," blue Luke said. "That's one crazy brother, leaving a little girl alone in the woods."

With men, Severa knew, the key is to not let them think they scare you. Don't give them anything. Just get away.

"Enjoy your crappy redneck heroin," she said. "I'm gone."

"Wait a minute," Luke said. "I don't want to chase you."

She stuck in her place.

"If you're lost, it's no good to run all over," he said.

"Really is better to stay still," advised Pat.

"All right," she said, voice light, "I can hang for a time." She found room for herself between a pile of Prestone cans and a box of Red Devil Lye.

Luke took a step toward her and sent the cans clattering with his foot. Then he settled into the empty space he'd made. His neck was dirty above the collar of his shirt. His pupils were big as dimes.

Severa stared back, trying to be cool. She had a plan. If he made a move, she'd yell, "Thank you, Lord, for sending him!" If he kept going she'd whisper, "Praise Jesus for every act you do." That might make him lose his nerve.

In the meantime, she yawned and twisted away from him, pretending to stretch. She cast a quick glance toward where Somvay was. Her stomach wobbled when she saw him sitting head above the grass line, arms untaped. He was going to free himself and leave her. Then where would she be?

Her spine cracked, and she twisted back to center. Pay attention, girl. That's everything now. Her best hope was that these guys fixed and left fast.

"Can I see your gun?" she asked Luke sweetly, to distract him.

He took the gun from his waistband and pointed it at her.

Not so scary. In fact, something about a gun in her face made her feel like she was exactly where she was supposed to be.

"Come on, man," said Pat. "That's uncool."

"You think?" Luke let the barrel hover eye level a few seconds more and then stood and replaced the gun in his pants. "Well, that's all right. Night's long. Besides, I got to go drain myself of poisons before I put new poison in."

"I have to piss too," said Pat.

"Why don't you first stay with her," Luke said. "We sure wouldn't want anybody to be alone." He loped toward the truck, slow and easy as a cop.

Severa watched to make sure he didn't veer toward Somvay. Then she turned back to Pat. He avoided her glance, scrambling up to gather the cans his brother had scattered. His ears were dull yellow and scarred.

"What's with them angry ears?" she said.

He stopped and used a can to poke one lightly. "Used to be a firefighter," he said. "These days they got helmets with protectors. Back then, your ears were all out."

"Poor you," she said, pretending sympathy.

"Better before," Pat said, "with your ears like antennas. Hot ears meant it was time to bail." He let the cans fall from his arms into a brown Hy-Vee bag. "Fellas today are so covered up they can't feel it. It's too late before they know trouble's there."

Severa eyeballed him sharply. Was this iced-up tweaker making metaphors? Was he, in fact, a bright guy?

Pat wasn't saying. He wasn't even paying attention to her anymore. He knelt by the camp stove, warming his hands and scanning the black sky. "I loved that job," he sighed. "I loved my chief like he was my own daddy. If that man pointed me to the Gates of Hell, I would have grabbed a hose and charged in."

"You know," she said, trying to play his sudden softness, "I think bald guys are the smartest and most soulful of all guys. It's like without hair to worry about they have more time to think deep."

Pat massaged the sweat on his face up to his scalp. She watched him try not to be pleased. "You're putting me on," he said finally. "But still. I ought to let you run right now. But what Luke would do . . ." He whistled. "Go along nice is all I can say. Don't make things harder than they got to be."

Her blood sped up, getting her dizzy. She took a deep breath and watched the dish on the fire steam. Over the summer she and Doug had tried to make raisins by drying grapes on a blanket in the sun. While they waited, Doug had her do bong hits. Pretty soon she was all over that blanket, popping hot fruit with her teeth.

"My turn," she heard Luke say. He squatted next to her, smelling like a sick cat. Pat got to his feet and jogged toward the truck.

Severa prepared to fight.

But Luke had other things in mind. He arranged his works on a rock, then took a packet of crystal from his pocket and fixed a shot. His muscles tensed. A rare red came to his cheeks.

"So," he asked when he finished shooting, "where do you think your brother is now?"

She was rethinking the whole boyfriend tale. Luke might like the idea of having to use force on her. Best plan was to get the brothers beating on each other, in the wild of their after-shot flash.

"I'm talking to you," Luke said. He leaned closer and toyed with the hem of her skirt. His finger bled from the nail bed. When it brushed against her, her quadriceps flexed against her will.

"Stop," she said. "I don't want your poison blood on me."

"I asked you a question." He moved the finger to her wrapped-up wrist. She already had a story made up about spraining it during karate lessons, but Luke didn't ask. He touched her neck, and she cleared her throat and spoke.

"You seen right through me, guy. You know I don't have a boyfriend. I'm just playing coy."

"Playing coy," Luke said softly. Then he grabbed her head and kissed her. It was like jumping into a pool of dead fish.

"Your mouth is trash!" she spit, pushing him away.

Luke grinned, eyes strobing. "Anyhow, I'm too speedy to fuck. At present."

She made herself chuckle. "Oh, who am I fooling. I saw something with you and me right away. The thing is your brother's coming on real strong."

"Yeah?" Luke knuckled his eyebrows and then gazed at her sadly. "That boy always wants what's mine. But I cut him slack again and again. You know how it goes. Next to water, blood's thick."

"Next to water, everything's thick," Severa said. "But then, like, you have this lime pit, for example. Compared to what's in there, blood's real thin. Plus there's more you should know." She leaned in, bolder. "Your brother said we ought to gank you and snatch the crank and run."

Luke's face darkened. "One night . . ." he started. "One night my brother died three times. Three! But I kept bringing him around. I sat him in a cold tub and kept him alive." He ground his teeth. "This is how I get paid back?"

"He said you barely had enough brains to keep your body breathing. He said it's like your head's full of meat."

Thank you, Crank, for how fast you turn a person upside-down mad! Luke began a scratching and grumbling spree, clawing at his cheeks and the inside of his arms. He kept at it until his brother returned and sat cross-legged, folding his hands nice in his lap.

"You talk to this girl?" Luke demanded right away.

"Sure I did," said Pat.

"You say anything I should know about?"

"I might have made a suggestion." Pat polished his head,

sheepishly, with his sleeve. "But forget her. Let's get to work."

Luke's chest heaved like some tacky romance starlet. His nostrils blew out like a bull in a ring. It worried Severa some. Had she pressed the guy too hard?

"Why don't you turn on the music in the truck first," Luke said, supersteely. "I'll get you fixed up."

Pat struggled to his feet. "All I do anymore is get up and walk," he complained.

As his brother left, Luke dumped a half-spoon of lye into a bottle, added water, and shook until the pellets dissolved. A dark path appeared in Severa's mind—why fix liquid lye?—but she tried not to take it. She stared past the pit to where the downtown flickered pink, like it was on fire. When she looked back, Luke was pressing his blue lips together as he drew the straight lye into a syringe.

A hard Spanish rap boiled out of the truck. Pat jittered back, shaking his fists like maracas. Luke handed him the dirty shot and a length of brown tube.

"Hey, don't," Severa started, but Luke clapped his hand over her mouth, hard enough to make her cavities ache.

"You can go next," Pat told her, tying off. He got ready and pressed the plunger down. "I feel bad," he said after the needle hit the vein. Then the plunger broke off in his fingers. He pulled the shot away. There was a mark where the needle had just pierced the skin. He stabbed at it with the broken syringe.

Luke let go of Severa and grabbed the shot and threw it into the lime pit.

"Don't waste it!" Pat groaned, white and woozy.

Luke wiped new tears from his eyes. "Oh Jesus," he said. "I did wrong."

Pat dragged himself closer and touched Luke's shoulder. "It's OK," he said. "Just hurry and fix me one more."

"My own only brother," Luke moaned. "How could I?"

Severa knew the right move now was to bolt, before Luke turned and said, "Look what you made me do." But when she rose to leave, he drew the gun.

"Take it," he ordered. "Shoot me in my brain. If he goes, I want to go too."

"Stop," objected Pat. He tried to stand, then went ghosty and sank to the ground.

Luke spoke only to her. "Shoot me in my brain before I shoot you."

Severa took the gun from him. Holding it made her hand so much bigger. She was so much bigger. Even raising the gun to her temple didn't shrink her. Even the barrel against her weak pulse.

"Not you!" Luke insisted. "Me!"

She'd always imagined a real peace would come just before kicking. Now she waited for it, toying with the trigger, but not firing. She waited for something, but nothing appeared. It surprised her. Was dying as black and white as anything? Until the very instant it happened, did you stay right here?

"Who's that?" Pat said suddenly, before falling into a full faint. Luke let loose with a sob and hunched over his brother in the sand.

Severa turned to see Somvay approaching on bare feet. Silver tape flapped at his ankles. His coat hung wrinkled and loose. The lipstick on his chin from when she'd kissed him now—of course—looked like blood. Still, he seemed calmer. She felt awful.

"I probably shouldn't have done all this," she said, lowering the cold gun.

Somvay's cheeks glowed. Did the moon make him look like that?

"Will you again?" he asked.

"No," she said. But then thought: How true is that? So she said, "At least not exactly in the same way."

Somvay nodded and reached for the gun. Wary, she swung it behind her.

"Are you still drunk?"

His arm was steady. "Please."

"Nononono," Luke crooned. Severa checked him from the corner of her eye. Pat was flat out, maybe asleep, maybe something deeper. Luke brushed a stripe of sand stuck to his brother's head. His kissed his brother's nose. Then he stopped and glared at her.

"You better shoot me fast," he said. "You better."

"Don't listen," she said, turning back to Somvay. "Talk to me. Tell me more about Laos."

"Please," he said, palm out. "I do not want to be here."

The gun stayed in the small of her back. "Are you a monk anymore?"

Behind her, she could hear Luke lurch to standing. "Who's a monk?"

"He is," Severa said, trying to change the air's flavor. "A monk," she repeated, like just speaking it could chill the scene.

"Not now," said Somvay.

Luke pushed past her and bellied up to Somvay. "If you're a monk, do something," he demanded. "Wake him up. Bring him back."

Somvay's voice was low and even. "You cannot return to a place unless you first leave it. First go away, then come back and learn more."

Luke stepped off, sort of shocked, like he'd just seen sun after a whole week of moon. "You're telling me," he began, "you're saying everybody's got to die before things get better?"

"The fuck he is," said Severa. "What kind of monk says that?"

Good Monks

Somvay sighed. "I am no monk," he said. "I am no more than a lonely man."

A wet, horrible sound interrupted them. They all looked at flat Pat. Pink bubbles gushed past his teeth to his chin.

"Guy?" Luke was pleading with Somvay now. "You got anything? Any power prayer words you can say?"

But Somvay was saving his last word. He relaxed his shoulders and let his head fall. Severa felt her arm jerk wildly in its socket, spinning her around as Luke stripped the gun from her. He pointed the gun at his face. Then he took dead aim at her.

"You got warned," Luke said, shaky. "Didn't you?"

Beside her, Somvay dropped to his knees. Severa shut her eyes and waited for the world to break. Just one more second and it breaks.

Run, Somvay whispered.

So she ran. Through mud and pale-barked trees. Then she heard three shots, each ringing the same truth to her: *It's not me. It's not me. It's not me.*

A Child's Book of
Sickness and Death

CHRIS ADRIAN

M Y ROOM, 616, IS ALWAYS WAITING FOR ME WHEN I
get back, unless it is the dead of winter, rotavirus sea-
son, when the floor is crowded with gray-faced tod-
dlers rocketing down the halls on fantails of liquid shit. They are
only transiently ill, and not distinguished. You earn something in
a lifetime of hospitalizations that the rotavirus babies, the RSV
wheezers, the accidental ingestions, the rare tonsillectomy, that
these sub-sub-sickees could never touch or have. The least of it is
the sign that the nurses have hung on my door, silver glitter on
yellow poster board: *Chez Cindy.*

My father settles me in before he leaves. He likes to turn
down the bed, to tear off the paper strap from across the toilet,
and to unpack my clothes and put them in the little dresser. "You
only brought halter tops and hot pants," he tells me.

"And pajamas," I say. "Halter tops make for good access. To
my veins." He says he'll bring me a robe when he comes back,

though he'll likely not be back. If you are the sort of child who only comes into the hospital once every ten years, then the whole world comes to visit, and your room is filled with flowers and chocolates and aluminum balloons. After the tenth or fifteenth admission the people and the flowers stop coming. Now I get flowers only if I'm septic, but my Uncle Ned makes a donation to the Short Gut Foundation of America every time I come in.

"Sorry I can't stay for the H and P," my father says. He would usually stay to answer all the questions the intern du jour will ask, but during this admission we are moving. The new house is only two miles from the old house, but it is bigger, and has views. I don't care much for views. This side of the hospital looks out over the park and beyond that to the Golden Gate. On the nights my father stays he'll sit for an hour watching the bridge lights blinking while I watch television. Now he opens the curtains and puts his face to the glass, taking a single deep look before turning away, kissing me goodbye, and walking out.

After he's gone, I change into a lime green top and bright white pants, then head down the hall. I like to peep into the other rooms as I walk. Most of the doors are open, but I see no one I know. There are some orthopedic-looking kids in traction; a couple wheezers smoking their albuterol bongs; a tall thin blonde girl sitting up very straight in bed and reading one of those fucking Narnia books. She has CF written all over her. She notices me looking and says hello. I walk on, past two big-headed syndromes and a nasty rash. Then I'm at the nurse's station, and the welcoming cry goes up, "Cindy! Cindy! Cindy!" Welcome back, they say, and where have you *been*, and Nancy, who always took care of me when I was little, makes a booby-squeezing motion at me and says, "My little baby is becoming a woman!"

"Hi everybody," I say.

See the cat? The cat has feline leukemic indecisiveness. He is losing his fur, and his cheeks are hurting him terribly, and he bleeds from out of his nose and his ears. His eyes are bad. He can hardly see you. He has put his face in his litter box because sometimes that makes his cheeks feel better, but now his paws are hurting and his bladder is getting nervous and there is the feeling at the tip of his tail that comes every day at noon. It's like someone's put it in their mouth and they're chewing and chewing.
Suffer, cat, suffer!

I AM A FORMER twenty-six-week miracle preemie. These days you have to be a twenty-four-weeker to be a miracle preemie, but when I was born you were still pretty much dead if you emerged at twenty-six weeks. I did well except for a belly infection that took about a foot of my gut—nothing a big person would miss but it was a lot to one-kilo me. So I've got difficult bowels. I don't absorb well, and get this hideous pain, and barf like mad, and need tube feeds, and beyond that sometimes have to go on the sauce, TPN—total parenteral nutrition, where they skip my wimpy little gut and feed me through my veins. And I've never gotten a pony despite asking for one every birthday for the last eight years.

I am waiting for my PICC—you must have central access to go back on the sauce—when a Child Life person comes rapping at my door. You can always tell when it's them because they knock so politely, and because they call out so politely, "May I come in?" I am watching the meditation channel (twenty-four hours a day of string ensembles and trippy footage of waving flowers or shaking leaves, except late, late at night, when between two and three a.m. they show a bright field of stars and play a howling theremin) when she simpers into the room. Her name is Margaret. When I was much younger I thought the Child Life people were great because they brought me toys and took me to the playroom to sniff Play-Doh, but time has sapped their glamour and their fun. Now they are mostly annoying, but I am never cruel to them, because I know that being mean to a Child Life specialist is like kicking a puppy.

"We are collaborating with the children," she says, "in a collaboration of color, and shapes, and words! A collaboration of poetry and prose!" I want to say, people like you wear me out, honey. If you don't go away soon I know my heart will stop beating from weariness, but I let her go on. When she asks if I will make a submission to their hospital literary magazine I say, "Sure!" I won't, though. I am working on my own project, a child's book of sickness and death, and cannot spare thoughts or words for Margaret.

Ava, the IV nurse, comes while Margaret is paraphrasing a submission—the story of a talking IV pump written by a seven-year-old with only half a brain—and bringing herself nearly to tears at the recollection of it.

"And if he can do that with half a brain," I say, "imagine what I could do with my whole one!"

"Sweetie, you can do anything you want," she says, so kind and so encouraging. She offers to stay while I get my PICC but it would be more comforting to have my three-hundred-pound Aunt Mary sit on my face during the procedure than to have this lady at my side, so I say no thank you, and she finally leaves. "I will return for your submission," she says. It sounds much darker than she means it.

The PICC is the smoothest sailing. I get my morphine and a little Versed, and I float through the fields of the meditation

305

channel while Ava threads the catheter into the crook of my arm. I am in the flowers but also riding the tip of the catheter, à la *Fantastic Voyage,* as it sneaks up into my heart. I don't like views, but I like looking down through the cataract of blood into the first chamber. The great valve opens. I fall through and land in daisies.

I am still happy-groggy from Ava's sedatives when I think I hear the cat, moaning and suffering, calling out my name. But it's the intern calling me. I wake in a darkening room with a tickle in my arm and look at Ava's handiwork before I look at him. A slim PICC disappears into me just below the antecubital fossa, and my whole lower arm is wrapped in a white mesh glove that looks almost like lace, and would have been cool back in 1983, when I was negative two.

"Sorry to wake you," he says. "Do you have a moment to talk?" He is a tired-looking fellow. At first I think he must be fifty, but when he steps closer to the bed I can see he's just an ill-preserved younger man. He is thin, with strange hair that is not so much wild as just wrong somehow, beady eyes and big ears, and a little beard, the sort you scrawl on a face, along with devil horns, for purposes of denigration.

"Well, I'm late for cotillion," I say. He blinks at me and rubs his throat.

"I'm Dr. Chandra," he says. I peer at his name tag: Sirius Chandra, MD.

"You don't look like a Chandra," I say, because he is as white as me.

"I'm adopted," he says simply.

"Me too," I say, lying. I sit up and pat the bed next to me, but he leans against the wall and takes out a notepad and pen from his pocket. He proceeds to flip the pen in the air with one hand, launching it off the tips of his fingers and catching it again with finger and thumb, but he never writes down a single thing that I say.

See the pony? She has dreadful hoof dismay. She gets a terrible pain every time she tries to walk, and yet she is very restless, and can hardly stand to sit still. Late at night her hooves whisper to her, asking, "Please, please, just make us into glue," or they strike at her as cruelly as anyone who ever hated her. She hardly knows how she feels about them anymore, her hooves, because they hurt her so much, yet they are still so very pretty—her best feature, everyone says—and biting them very hard is the only thing that makes her feel any better at all. There she is, walking over the hill, on her way to the horse fair, where she'll not get to ride on the Prairie Wind, or play in the Haunted Barn, or eat hot buttered morsels of cowboy from a stand, because wise carnival horses know better than to let in somebody with highly contagious dismay. She stands at the gate watching the fun, and she looks like she is dancing but she is not dancing.

Suffer, pony, suffer!

"WHAT DO YOU KNOW about Dr. Chandra?" I ask Nancy, who is curling my hair at the nursing station. She has tremendous sausage curls and a variety of distinctive eyewear that she doesn't really need. I am wearing her rhinestone-encrusted granny glasses and can see Ella Thims, another short-gut girl, in all her glorious, gruesome detail where she sits in her little red wagon by the clerk's desk. Ella had some trouble finishing up her nether parts, and so was born without an anus, or vagina, or a colon, or most of her small intestine, and her kidneys are shaped like spirals. She is only two, but she is on the sauce, also. I've known her all her life.

"He hasn't rotated here much. He's pretty quiet. And pretty nice. I've never had a problem with him."

"Have you ever thought someone was interesting? Someone you barely knew, just interesting, in a way?"

"Do you like him? You like him, don't you?"

"Just interesting. Like a homeless person with really great shoes. Or a dog without a collar appearing in the middle of a graveyard."

"Sweetie, you're not his type. I know that much about him." She puts her hand out, flexing it swiftly at the wrist. I look blankly at her, so she does it again, and sort of sashays in place for a moment.

"Oh."

"Welcome to San Francisco." She sighs. "Anyway, you can do better than that. He's funny-looking, and he needs to pull his pants up. Somebody should tell him that. His mother should tell him that."

"Write this down under 'chief complaint,' " I had told him. "I am *sick* of love." He'd flipped his pen and looked at the floor. When we came to the social history I said my birth mother was a nun who committed indiscretions with the parish deaf-mute. And I told him about my book—the cat and the bunny and the peacock and the pony, each delightful creature afflicted with a uniquely horrible disease.

"Do you think anyone would buy that?" he asked.

"There's a book that's just about shit," I said. "Why not one that's just about sickness and death? Everybody poops. Everybody suffers. Everybody dies." I even read the pony page for him, and showed him the picture.

"It sounds a little scary," he said, after a long moment of pen-tossing and silence. "And you've drawn the intestines on the outside of the body."

"Clowns are scary," I told him. "And everybody loves them. And hoof dismay isn't pretty. I'm just telling it how it is."

"There," Nancy says, "you are *curled!*" She says it like, you are *healed.* Ella Thims has a mirror on her playset. I look at my hair and press the big purple button under the mirror. The playset honks, and Ella claps her hands. "Good luck," Nancy adds, as I scoot off on my IV pole, because I've got a date tonight.

One of the bad things about not absorbing very well and being chronically malnourished your whole life long is that you turn out to be four and a half feet tall when your father is six-four, your mother is five-ten, and your sister is six feet even. But one of the good things about being four and a half feet tall is that you are light enough to ride your own IV pole, and this is a blessing when you are chained to the sauce.

When I was five I could only ride in a straight line, and only at the pokiest speeds. Over the years I mastered the trick of steering with my feet, of turning and stopping, of moderating my speed by dragging a foot, and of spinning in tight spirals or wide loops. I take only short trips during the day, but at night I cruise as far as the research building that's attached to, but not part of, the hospital. At three a.m. even the eggiest heads are at home asleep, and I can fly down the long halls with no one to see me or stop me except the occasional security guard, always too fat or too slow to catch me, even if they understand what I am.

My date is with a CFer named Wayne. He is the best-fed CF kid I have ever laid eyes on. Usually they are blond, and thin, and pale, and look like they might cough blood on you as soon as smile at you. Wayne is tan, with dark brown hair and blue eyes, and big, with a high wide chest, and arms I could not wrap my two hands around. He is pretty hairy for sixteen: I caught a glimpse of his big hairy belly as I scooted past his room. On my fourth pass (I slowed each time and looked back over my shoulder at him) he called me in. We played a karate video game. I kicked his ass, then I showed him the meditation channel.

He is here for a tune-up—every so often the cystic fibrosis kids will get more tired than usual, or cough more, or cough differently, or a routine test of their lung function will be precipitously sucky, and they will come in for two weeks of IV antibiotics and aggressive chest physiotherapy. He is halfway through his course of tobramycin, and bored to death. We go down to the cafeteria and I watch him eat three stale donuts. I have some water and a sip of his tea. I'm never hungry when I'm on the sauce, and I am absorbing so poorly now that if I ate a steak tonight the whole cow would come leaping from my ass in the morning.

I do a little history on him, not certain why I am asking the question, and less afraid as we talk that he'll catch on that I'm playing intern. He doesn't notice, and fesses up the particulars without protest or reservation as we review his systems.

"My snot is green," he says. "Green like that." He points to my green toenails. He tells me that he has twin cousins who also have CF, and when they are together at family gatherings he is required to wear a mask so as not to pass on his highly resistant mucoid strain of Pseudomonas. "That's why there's not camp for CF," he says. "Camps for diabetes, for HIV, for kidney failure, for liver failure, but no CF camps. Because we'd infect each other." He wiggles his eyebrows then, perhaps not intentionally. "Is there a camp for people like you?" he asks.

"Probably," I say, though I know that there is, and would have gone this past summer if I had not been banned the year before for organizing a game where we rolled a couple of syndromic kids down a hill into a soccer goal. Almost everybody loved it, and nobody got hurt.

Over Wayne's shoulder I see Dr. Chandra sit down two tables

away. At the same time that Wayne lifts his last donut to his mouth, Dr. Chandra lifts a slice of pizza to his, but where Wayne nibbles like an invalid at his food, Dr. Chandra stuffs. He just pushes and pushes the pizza into his mouth. In less than a minute he's finished it. Then he gets up and shuffles past us, sucking on a bottle of water, with bits of cheese in his beard. He doesn't even notice me.

When Wayne has finished his donut I take him upstairs, past the sixth floor to the seventh. "I've never been up here," he says.

"Heme-Onc," I say.

"Are we going to visit someone?"

"I know a place." It's a call room. A couple of years back an intern left his code cards in my room, and there was a list of useful door combinations in one of them. Combinations change slowly in hospitals. "The intern's never here," I tell him as I open the door. "Heme-One kids have a lot of problems at night."

Inside are a single bed, a telephone, and a poster of a kitten in distress coupled with an encouraging motto. I think of my dream cat, moaning and crying.

"I've never been in a call room before," Wayne says nervously.

"Relax," I say, pushing him toward the bed. There's barely room for both our IV poles, but after some doing we get arranged on the bed. He lies on his side at the head with his feet propped on the nightstand. I am curled up at the foot. There's dim light from a little lamp on the bed stand, enough to make out the curve of his big lips and to read the sign above the door to the hall: LASCIATE OGNE SPERANZA, VOI CHI'INTRATE.

"Can you read that?" he asks.

"It says, 'I believe that children are our future.'"

"That's pretty. I'd be nice if we had some candles." He scoots a little closer toward me. I stretch and yawn. "Are you sleepy?"

"No."

He's quiet for a moment. He looks down at the floor, across the thin, torn bedspread. My IV starts to beep. I reprogram it. "Air in the line," I say.

"Oh." I have shifted closer to him in the bed while fixing the IVs. "Do you want to do something?" he asks, staring into his lap. "Maybe," I say. I walk my hand around the bed, like a five-legged spider, in a circle, over my own arm, across my thighs, up my belly, up to the top of my head to leap off back onto the blanket. He watches, smiling less and less as it walks up the bed, up his leg, and down his pants.

> *See the zebra? She has atrocious pancreas oh! Her belly hurts her terribly—sometimes it's like frogs are crawling in her belly, and sometimes it's like snakes are biting her inside just below her belly button, and sometimes it's like centipedes dancing with cleats on every one of their little feet, and sometimes it's a pain she can't even describe, even though all she can do, on those days, is sit around and try to think of ways to describe the pain. She must rub her belly on very particular sorts of trees to make it feel better, though it never feels very much better. Big round scabs are growing on her tongue, and every time she sneezes another big piece of her mane falls out. Her stripes have begun to go all the wrong way, and sometimes her own poop follows her, crawling on the ground or floating in the air, and calls her cruel names.*
>
> *Suffer, zebra, suffer!*

ASLEEP in my own bed, I'm dreaming of the cat when I hear the team; the cat's moan frays and splits, and the tones unravel from each other and become their voices. I am fully awake with my eyes closed. He lifts a mangy paw, saying good-bye.

"Dr. Chandra," says a voice. I know it must belong to Dr. Fell, the GI attending. "Tell me the three classic findings on X-ray in necrotizing enterocolitis." They are rounding outside my room, six or seven of them, the whole GI team: Dr. Fell and my intern and the fellow and the nurse practitioners and the poor little med students. Soon they'll all come in and want to poke my belly. Dr. Fell will talk for five minutes about shit: mine, and other people's, and sometimes just the idea of shit, a Platonic ideal not extant on this earth. I know he dreams of gorgeous, perfect shit the way I dream of the cat.

Chandra speaks. He answers *free peritoneal air* and *pneumatosis* in a snap but then he is silent. I can see him perfectly with my eyes still closed: his hair all ahoo; his beady eyes staring intently at his shoes; his stethoscope twisted crooked around his neck, crushing his collar. His feet turn in, so his toes are almost touching. Upstairs with Wayne I thought of him.

Dr. Fell, too supreme a fussbudget to settle for two out of three, begins to castigate him: a doctor at your level of training should know these things; children's lives are in your two hands; you couldn't diagnose your way out of a wet paper bag; your ignorance is deadly, your ignorance can *kill*. I get out of bed, propelled by rage, angry at haughty Dr. Fell, and at hapless Dr. Chandra, and angry at myself for being this angry. Clutching my IV pole like a staff I kick open the door and scream, scaring every one of them: "Portal fucking air! Portal fucking air!" They are all silent, and some of them white-faced. I am panting, hanging now on my IV pole. I look over at Dr. Chandra. He is not panting, but his mouth has fallen open. Our eyes meet for three eternal seconds and then he looks away.

Later I take Ella Thims down to the playroom. The going is slow, because her sauce is running and my sauce is running, so it takes some coordination to push my pole and pull her wagon while keeping her own pole, which trails behind her wagon like a dinghy, from drifting too far left or right. She lies on her back with her legs in the air, grabbing and releasing her feet, and turning her head to say hello to everyone she sees. In the hall we pass nurses and med students and visitors and every species of doctor, attendings and fellows and residents and interns, but not my intern. Everyone smiles and waves at Ella, or stoops or squats to pet her or smile closer to her face. They nod at me, and don't look at all at my face. I look back at her, knowing her fate. "Enjoy it while you have it, honey," I say to her, because I know how quickly one exhausts one's cuteness in a place like this. Our cuteness has to work very hard here. It must extend itself to cover horrors—ostomies and scars and flipper-hands and harelips and agenesis of the eyeballs—and it rises to every miserable occasion of the sick body. Ella's strange puffy face is covered, her yellow eyes are covered, her bald spot is covered, her extra fingers are covered, her ostomies are covered, and the bitter, nose-tickling odor of urine that rises from her always is covered by the tremendous faculty of cuteness generated from some organ deep within her. Watching faces I can see how it's working for her, and how it's stopped working for me. Your organ fails, at some point—it fails for everybody, but for people like us it fails faster, having more to cover than just the natural ugliness of body and soul. One day you are more repulsive than attractive and the good will of strangers is lost forever.

It's a small loss. Still, I miss it sometimes, like now, walking down the hall and remembering riding down this same hall ten years ago on my Big Wheel. Strangers would stop me for speeding and cite me with a hug. I can remember their faces, earnest and open and unassuming, and I wonder now if I ever met someone like that where I could go with them, after such a blank beginning. Something in the way that Dr. Chandra looks at me has that. And the Child Life people look at you that way, too. But they have all been trained in graduate school not to notice the extra head, or the smell, or the missing nose, or to love these things, professionally.

In the playroom I turn Ella over to Margaret and go sit on the floor in a patch of sun near the door to the deck. The morning activity, for those of us old enough or coordinated enough to manage it, is the weaving of gods' eyes. At home I have a trunkful of gods' eyes and potholders and terra-cotta sculptures the size of your hand, such a collection of crafts that you might think I'd spent my whole life in camp. I wind and unwind the yarn, making and then unmaking, because I don't want to add anything new to the collection. I watch Ella playing at a water trough, dipping a little red bucket and pouring it over the paddles of a waterwheel. It's a new toy. There are always new toys, every time I come, and the room is kept pretty and inviting, repainted and re-carpeted in less time than some people wait to get a haircut, because some new wealthy person has taken an interest in it. The whole floor is like that, except where there are pockets of plain beige hospital nastiness here and there, places that have escaped the attentions of the rich. The nicest rooms are those that once were occupied by a privileged child with a fatal syndrome.

I pass almost a whole hour like this. Boredom can be a problem for anybody here, but I am never bored watching my gaunt yellow peers splashing in water or stacking blocks or singing along with Miss Margaret. Two wholesome Down's syndrome twins—Dolores and Delilah Cutty, who both have leukemia and are often in for chemo at the same time I am in for the sauce—are having a somersault race across the carpet. A boy named Arthur who has Crouzon's syndrome—the bones of his skull have fused together too early—is playing Chutes and Ladders with a girl afflicted with Panda syndrome. Every time he gets to make a move, he cackles wildly. It makes his eyes bulge out of his head. Sometimes they pop out—then you're supposed to catch them with a piece of sterile gauze and push them back in.

Margaret comes over, after three or four glances in my direction, noticing that my hands have been idle. Child Life specialists abhor idle hands, though there was one here a few years ago, named Eldora, who encouraged meditation and tried to teach us Yoga poses. She did not last long. Margaret crouches down—they are great crouchers, having learned that children like to be addressed at eye level—and, seeing my gods' eye half-finished and my yarn tangled and trailing, asks if I have any questions about the process.

In fact I do. How do your guts turn against you, and your insides become your enemy? How can Arthur have such a big head and not be a super-genius? How can he laugh so loud when tomorrow he'll go back to surgery again to have his face artfully broken by the clever hands of well-intentioned sadists? How can someone so unattractive, so unavailable, so shlumpy, so low-panted, so pitiable, keep rising up, a giant in my thoughts? All these questions and others run through my head, so it takes me a while to answer, but she is patient. Finally a question comes that seems safe to ask. "How do you make someone not gay?"

See the peacock? He has crispy lung surprise. He has got an aching in his chest, and every time he tries to say something nice to someone, he only coughs. His breath stinks so much it makes everyone run away, and he tries to run away from it himself, but of course no matter where he goes, he can still smell it. Sometimes he holds his breath, just to escape it, until he passes out, but he always wakes up, even when he would rather not, and there it is, like rotten chicken, or old, old crab, or hippopotamus butt.

He only feels ashamed now when he spreads out his feath-
ers, and the only thing that gives him any relief is licking a
moving tire—a very difficult thing to do.
    Suffer, peacock, suffer!

IT'S NOT SAFE to confide in people here. Even when they aren't
prying—and they do pry—it's better to be silent or to lie than to
confide. They'll ask when you had your first period, or your first
sex, if you are happy at home, what drugs you've done, if you
wish you were thinner and prettier, or that your hair was shiny.
And you may tell them about your terrible cramps, or your dis-
tressing habit of having compulsive sex with homeless men and
women in Golden Gate Park, or how you can't help but sniff a little bleach every morning when you wake up, or complain that
you are fat and your hair always looks as if it had just been rinsed
with drool. And they'll say, I'll help you with that bleach habit
that has debilitated you separately but equally from your physical
illness, that dreadful habit that's keeping you from becoming
more perfectly who you are. Or they may offer to teach you how
the homeless are to be shunned and not fellated, or promise to
wash your hair with the very shampoo of the gods. But they come
and go, these interns and residents and attendings, nurses and
Child Life specialists and social workers and itinerant tamale-
ladies—only you and the hospital and the illness are constant.
The interns change every month, and if you gave yourself to each
of them they'd use you up as surely as an entire high-school football team would use up their dreamiest cheerleading slut, and
you'd be left like her, compelled by your history to lie down
under the next moron to come along.

Accidental confidences, or accidentally fabricated secrets, are
no safer. Margaret misunderstands; she thinks I am fishing for
validation. She is a professional validator, with skills honed by a

thousand hours of role playing—she has been both the queru-
lous young lesbian and the supportive adult. "But there's no reason to change," she tells me. "You don't have to be ashamed of
who you are."

This is a lesson I learned long ago, from my mother, who
really was a lesbian, after she was a nun but before she was a wife.
"I did not give it up because it was inferior to anything," she told
me seriously, the same morning she found me in the arms of
Shelley Woo, my neighbor and one of the few girls I was ever able
to lure into a sleepover. We had not, like my mother assumed,
spent the night practicing tender, heated frottage. We were hugging as innocently as two stuffed animals. "But it's all *right*," she
kept saying against my protests. So I know not to argue with Margaret's assumption, either.

It makes me pensive, having become a perceived lesbian. I
wander the ward thinking, "Hello, nurse!" at every one of them I
see. I sit at the station, watching them come and go, spinning the
big lazy Susan of misfortune that holds all the charts. I can imagine sliding my hands under their stylish scrubs—not toothpaste-
green like Dr. Chandra's scrubs, but hot pink or canary yellow or
deep-sea blue, printed with daisies or sun faces or clouds or even
embroidered with dancing hula girls—and pressing my fingers in
the hollows of their ribs. I can imagine taking off Nancy's rhine-
stone granny-glasses with my teeth, or biting so gently on the
ridge of her collarbone. The charge nurse—a woman from the
Philippines named Jory—sees me opening and closing my mouth
silently, and asks if there is something wrong with my jaw. I shake
my head. There's nothing wrong. It's only that I am trying to open
wide enough for an imaginary mouthful of her soft brown boob.

If it's this easy for me to do, to imagine the new thing, then is
he somewhere wondering what it would feel like to press a cheek
against my scarred belly, or to gather my hair in his fists? When I

was little my pediatrician, Dr. Sawyer, used to look in my pants every year and say, "Just checking to make sure everything is *normal.*" I imagine an exam, and imagine him imagining it with me. He listens with his ear on my chest and back, and when it is time to look in my pants he stares long and long and says, "It's not just *normal,* it's *extraordinary!*"

A glowing radiance has just burst from between my legs, and is bathing him in converting rays of glory, when he comes hurrying out of the doctor's room across from the station. He drops his clipboard and apologizes to no one in particular, and glances at me as he straightens up. I want him to smile and look away, to duck his head in an aw-shucks gesture, but he just nods stiffly then walks away. I watch him pass around the corner, then give the lazy Susan a hard spin. If my own chart comes to rest before my eyes, it will mean that he loves me.

> *See the monkey? He has chronic kidney doom. His kidneys are always yearning toward things—other monkeys and trees and people and different varieties of fruit. He feels them stirring in him and pressing against his flank whenever he gets near to something that he likes. When he tells a girl monkey or a boy monkey that his kidneys want to hug them, they slap him or punch him or kick him in the eye. At night his kidneys ache wildly. He is always swollen and moist-looking. He smells like a toilet because he can only pee when he doesn't want to, and every night he asks himself, how many pair of crisp white slacks can one monkey ruin?*
> *Suffer, monkey, suffer!*

EVERY FOURTH NIGHT he is on call. He stays in the hospital from six in the morning until six the following evening, awake all night on account of various intern-sized crises. I see him walking in and out of rooms, or peering at the two-foot-long flow sheets that lean on giant clipboards on the walls by every door, or looking solemnly at the nurses as they castigate him for slights against their patients or their honor—an unsigned order, an incorrectly closed medication, the improper washing of his hands. I catch him in the corridor in what I think is a posture of despair, sunk down outside Wayne's door with his face in his knees, and I think that he has heard about me and Wayne, and it's broken his heart. But I have already dismissed Wayne days ago. We were like two IV poles passing in the night, I told him.

Dr. Chandra is sleeping, not despairing, not snoring but breathing loud through his mouth. I step a little closer to him, close enough to smell him—coffee and hair gel and something like pickles. A flow sheet lies discarded beside him, so from where I stand I can see how much Wayne has peed in the last twelve hours. I stoop next to him and consider sitting down and falling asleep myself, because I know it would constitute a sort of intimacy to mimic his posture and let my shoulder touch his shoulder, to close my eyes and maybe share a dream with him. But before I can sit Nancy comes creeping down the hall in her socks, a barf basin half full of warm water in her hands. A phalanx of nurses appears in the hall behind her, each of them holding a finger to her lips as Nancy kneels next to Dr. Chandra, puts the bucket on the floor, and takes his hand away from his leg so gently I think she is going to kiss it before she puts it in the water. I just stand there, afraid that he'll wake up as I'm walking away, and think I'm responsible for the joke. Nancy and the nurses all disappear around the corner to the station, so it's just me and him again in the hall. I drum my fingers against my head, trying to think of a way to get us both out of this, and realize it's just a step or two to the dietary cart. I take a straw and kneel down next to him. It's a lot of volume, and I imagine, as I drink, that it's flavored by his hand. When I throw it up later it seems like the best barf I've ever done, because it is for him, and as Nancy holds my hair back for me and asks me what possessed me to drink so much water at once I think at him, it was for you, baby, and feel both pathetic and exalted.

I follow him around for a couple call nights, not saving him again from any more mean-spirited jokes, but catching him scratching or picking when he thinks no one is looking, and wanting, like a fool, to be the hand that scratches or the finger that picks, because it would be so interesting and gratifying to touch him like that, or touch him in any way, and I wonder and wonder what I'm doing as I creep around with increasingly practiced nonchalance, looking bored while I sit across from him, listening to him cajole the radiologist on the phone at one in the morning, when I could be sleeping, or riding my pole, when he is strange-looking, and cannot like me, and talks funny, and is rumored to be an intern of small brains. But I see him stand in the hall for five minutes staring at an abandoned tricycle, and he puts his palm against a window and bows his head at the blinking lights on the bridge in a way that makes me want very much to know what he is thinking, and I see him, from a hiding place behind a bin full of dirty sheets, hopping up and down in a hall he thinks is empty save for him, and I am sure he is trying to fly away.

Hiding on his fourth call night in the dirty utility room while he putters with a flow sheet at the door to the room across the hall, I realize that it could be easier than this, and so when he's moved on, I go back to my room and watch the meditation channel for a little while, then practice a few moans, sounding at first too distressed, then not distressed enough, then finally getting it just right before I push the button for the nurse. Nancy is off tonight. It's Jory who comes, and finds me moaning and clutching at my belly. I get Tylenol and a touch of morphine, but am careful to moan only a little less, so Jory calls Dr. Chandra to come evaluate me.

It's romantic, in its way. The lights are low, and he puts his warm, freshly washed hands on my belly to push in every quadrant, a round of light palpation, a round of deep. He speaks very softly, asking me if it hurts more here, or here, or here. "I'm going to press in on your stomach and hold my hand there for a second, and I want you to tell me if it makes it feel better or worse when I let go." He listens to my belly, then takes me by the ankle, extending and flexing my hip.

"I don't know," I say, when he asks me if that made the pain better or worse. "Do it again."

See the bunny? She has high colonic ruin, a very fancy disease. Only bunnies from the very best families get it, but when she cries bloody tears and the terrible spiders come crawling out of her bottom, she would rather be poor, and not even her fancy robot bed can comfort her, or even distract her. When her electric pillow feeds her dreams of happy bunnies playing in the snow, she only feels jealous and sad, and she bites her tongue while she sleeps, and bleeds all night while the bed dabs at her lips with cotton balls on long steel fingers. In the morning a servant drives her to the Potty Club, where she sits with other wealthy bunny girls on a row of crystal toilets. They are supposed to be her friends, but she doesn't like them at all.

Suffer, bunny, suffer!

WHEN HE VISITS I straighten up, carefully hiding the books that Margaret brought me, biographies of Sappho and Billie Jean King and H.D. She entered quietly into my room, closed the door, and drew the blinds before producing them from out of her pants and repeating that my secret was safe with her, though there was no need for it to be secret, and nothing to be ashamed of, and she would support me as fully in proclaiming my homosexuality as she did in the hiding of it. She has already conceived of a banner to put over my bed, a rainbow hung with stars, on the day that I put away all shame and dark feelings. I hide the books because I know all would really be lost if he saw them and assumed the assumption. I do not want to be just his young lesbian friend. I lay out refreshments, spare cookies and juices and puddings from the meal trays that come, though I get all the food I can stand from the sauce.

I don't have many dates, on the outside. Rumors of my scarred belly or my gastrostomy tube drive most boys away before anything can develop, and the only boys that pay persistent attention to me are the creepy ones looking for a freak. I have better luck in here, with boys like Wayne, but those dates are still outside the usual progressions, the talking more and more until you are convinced they actually know you, and the touching more and more until you are pregnant and wondering if this guy ever even liked you. There is nothing normal about my midnight trysts with Dr. Chandra, but there's an order about them, and a progression. I summon him and he puts his hands on me, and he orders an intervention, and he comes back to see if it worked or didn't. For three nights he stands there, watching me for a few moments, leaning on one foot and then the other, before he asks me if I need anything else. All the things I need flash through my mind, but I say no, and he leaves, promising to come back and check on me later, but never doing it. Then on the fourth night, he does his little dance and asks, "What do you want to do when you grow up. I mean, when you're bigger. When you're out of school, and all that."

323

chris adrian

"Medicine," I say. "Pediatrics. What else?"

"Aren't you sick of it?" he asks. He is backing toward the door, but I have this feeling like he's stepping closer to the bed.

"Maybe. But I have to do it."

"You could do anything you want," he says, not sounding like he means it.

"What else could Tarzan become, except lord of the jungle?"

"He could have been a dancer, if he wanted. Or an ice-cream man. Whatever he wanted."

"Did you ever want to do anything else, besides this?"

"Never. Not ever."

"How about now?"

"Oh," he says. "Oh, no. I don't think so. No, I don't think so." He startles when his pager vibrates. He looks down at it. "I've got to go. Just tell Jory if the pain comes back again."

"Come over here for a second," I say. "I've got to tell you something."

"Later," he says.

"No, now. It'll just take a second." I expect him to leave, but he walks over and stands near the bed.

"What?"

"Would you like some juice?" I ask him, though what I really meant to do was to accuse him, ever so sweetly, of being the same as me, of knowing the same indescribable thing about this place and about the world. "Or a cookie?"

"No thanks," he says. As he passes though the door I call out for him to wait, and to come back. "What?" he says again, and I think I am just about to know how to say it when the code bell begins to chime. It sounds like an ice-cream truck, but it means someone on the floor is trying to die. He jumps in the air like he's been goosed, then takes a step one way in the hall, stops, starts the other way, then goes back, so it looks like he's

324

trying to decide whether to run toward the emergency or away from it.

I get up and follow him down the hall, just in time to see him run into Ella Thims's room. From the back of the crowd at the door I can see him standing at the head of the bed, looking depressed and indecisive, a bag mask held up in his hand. He asks someone to page the senior resident, then puts the mask over Ella's face. She's bleeding from her nose and mouth, and from her ostomy sites. The blood shoots around inside the mask when he squeezes the bag, and he can't seem to get a tight seal over Ella's chin. The mask keeps slipping while the nurses ask him what he wants to do.

"Well," he says. "Um. How about some oxygen?" Nancy finishes getting Ella hooked up to the monitor and points out that she's in a bad rhythm. "Let's get her some fluid," he says. Nancy asks if he wouldn't like to shock her, instead. "Well," he says. "Maybe!" Then I get pushed aside by the PICU team, called from the other side of the hospital by the chiming of the ice-cream bell. The attending asks Dr. Chandra what's going on, and he turns even redder, and says something I can't hear, because I am being pushed farther and farther from the door as more people squeeze past me to cluster around the bed, ring after ring of saviors and spectators. Pushed back to the nursing station, I am standing in front of Jory, who is sitting by the telephone reading a magazine.

"Hey, honey," she says, not looking at me. "Are you doing okay?"

See the cat? He has died. Feline leukemic indecisiveness is always terminal. Now he just lies there. You can pick him up. Go ahead. Bring him home and put him under your pillow and pray to your parents or your stuffed plush Jesus to bring him back, and say to him, "Come

325

back, come back." He will be smellier in the morning, but no more alive. Maybe he is in a better place, maybe his illness could not follow him where he went, or maybe everything is the same, the same pain in a different place. Maybe there is nothing all, where he is. I don't know, and neither do you.

Goodbye, cat, goodbye!

ELLA THIMS died in the PICU, killed, it was discovered, by too much potassium in her sauce. It put her heart in that bad rhythm they couldn't get her out of, though they worked over her till dawn. She'd been in it for at least a while before she was discovered, so it was already too late when they put her on the bypass machine. It made her dead alive—her blood was moving in her, but by midmorning of the next day she was rotting inside. Dr. Chandra, it was determined, was the chief architect of the fuck-up, assisted by a newly graduated nurse who meticulously verified the poisonous contents of the solution and delivered them without protest. Was there any deadlier combination, people asked each other all morning, than an idiot intern and a clueless nurse?

I spend the morning on my IV pole, riding the big circle around the ward. It's strange, to be out here in the daylight, and in the busy morning crowd—less busy today, and a little hushed because of the death. I go slower than usual, riding like my grandma would, stepping and pushing leisurely with my left foot, and stopping often to let a team go by. They pass like a family of ducks, the attending followed by the fellow, resident, and students, all in a row, with the lollygagging nutritionist bringing up the rear. Pulmonary, Renal, Neurosurgery, even the Hypoglycemia team are about in the halls, but I don't see the GI team anywhere.

The rest of the night I lay awake in bed, waiting for them to come round on me. I could see it already; everybody getting a turn to kick Dr. Chandra outside my door, or Dr. Fell standing casually with his foot on Dr. Chandra's neck as the team discussed my latest ins and outs. Or maybe he wouldn't even be there. Maybe they send you home early when you kill somebody. Or maybe he would just run and hide somewhere. Not sleeping, I still dreamed about him, huddled in a linen closet, sucking on the corner of a blanket, or sprawled on the bathroom floor, knocking his head softly against the toilet, or kneeling naked in the medication room, shooting up with Benadryl and morphine. I went to him in every place, and put my hands on him with great tenderness, never saying a thing, just nodding at him, like I knew how horrible everything was. A couple rumors float around in the late morning—he's jumped from the bridge; he's thrown himself under a trolley; Ella's parents, finally come to visit, have killed him; he's retired back home to Virginia in disgrace. I add and subtract details—he took off his clothes and folded them neatly on the sidewalk before he jumped; the trolley was full of German choir boys; Ella's father choked while her mother stabbed; his feet hang over the end of his childhood bed.

I don't stop even to get my meds—Nancy trots beside me and pushes them on the fly. Just after that, around one o'clock, I understand that I am following after something, and that I had better speed up if I am going to catch it. It seems to me, who should really know better, that all the late, new sadness of the past twenty-four hours ought to count for something, ought to do something, ought to change something, inside of me, or outside in the world. But I don't know what it is that might change, and I expect that nothing will change—children have died here before, and hapless idiots have come and gone, and always the next day the sick still come to languish and be poked, and they will lie in bed hoping, not for healing, a thing which the wise have all long given up on, but for something to make them feel better, just for a little while, and sometimes they get this thing, and often they don't. I think of my animals and hear them all, not just the cat but the whole bloated menagerie, crying and crying, *make it stop.*

Faster and faster and faster—not even a grieving short-gut girl can be forgiven for speed like this. People are thinking, *she loved that little girl* but I am thinking, *I will never see him again.* Still, I almost forget I am chasing something and not just flying along for the exhilaration it brings. Nurses and students and even the proudest attendings try to leap out of the way but only arrange themselves into a slalom course. It's my skill, not theirs, that keeps them from being struck. Nancy tries to stand in my way, to stop me, but she wimps away to the side before I get anywhere near her. Doctors and visiting parents and a few other kids, and finally a couple security guards, one almost fat enough to block the entire hall, try to arrest me, but they all fail, and I can hardly even hear what they are shouting. I am concentrating on the window. It's off the course of the circle, at the end of a hundred-foot hall that runs past the playroom and the PICU. It's a portrait frame of the near tower of the bridge, which looks very orange today against the bright blue sky. It is part of the answer when I understand that I am running the circle to rev up for a run down to the window that right now seems like the only way out of this place. The fat guard and Nancy and a parent have made themselves into a roadblock just beyond the turn into the hall. They are stretched like a Red-Rover line from one wall to the other, and two of them close their eyes, but don't break, as I come near them. I make the fastest turn of my life and head away down the hall.

It's Miss Margaret who stops me. She steps out of the playroom with a crate of blocks in her arms, sees me, looks down the hall toward the window, and shrieks "Motherfucker!" I withstand the uncharacteristic obscenity, though it makes me stumble, but the blocks she casts in my path form an obstacle I cannot pass. There are twenty of them or more. As I try to avoid them I am reading the letters, thinking they'll spell out the name of the thing I am chasing, but I am too slow to read any of them except the farthest one, an R, and the red Q that catches under my wheel. I fall off the pole as it goes flying forward, skidding toward the window after I come to a stop on my belly outside the PICU, my central line coming out in a pull as swift and clean as a tooth pulled out with a string and a door. The end of the catheter sails in an arc through the air, scattering drops of blood against the ceiling, and I think how neat it would look if my heart had come out, still attached to the tip, and what a distinct, once-in-a-lifetime noise it would have made when it hit the floor.

Junior

Elizabeth Stuckey-French

THE CITY POOL WAS FULL OF CHILDREN THAT DAY, BUT I don't think that's what bothered me. I was fourteen and happy to be out with my friends. It was sunny but cool for mid-July in Iowa. A breeze flipped up the edges of our beach towels as we lined them up on the crumbling cement, anchoring them with clogs, a bottle of coconut oil, and a transistor radio which seemed to play nothing but Sammy Davis, Jr., singing "The Candy Man." My friends flopped down on their backs and fell asleep, but I couldn't relax. I sat cross-legged in my faded bikini, a hand-me-down from my sister Daisy.

Daisy was lifeguarding, but she couldn't see me, didn't even know I was there. She looked like a stranger perched above the masses in her red tank suit and mirror sunglasses, her nose a triangle of zinc oxide. In one month, she was going away to college, leaving me to take care of our father. I couldn't let myself think about how dreary life would be without Daisy. I gazed out at the pool, which was circular, with the deep part and diving island in the center. A group of four or five children splashed around at the edge of the deep water, shrieking and dunking each other. A smaller girl in a green one-piece bathing suit dog-paddled near the splashers, barely keeping her chin above water. She wanted to play too, but the other children—friends? neighbors? sisters and brothers?—ignored her. Teenagers were doing cannonballs off the high dive, and their waves sloshed over her head. Nobody except me seemed to notice. The girl was paddling as hard as she could, getting nowhere.

I stood up and waded into the water, which reeked of chlorine, and began swimming the breaststroke toward the group of children, holding my head up as a snake does. The older kids moved off toward the slide, leaving the little girl behind. When she saw me, she opened her eyes wide and reached out. I didn't have a clue how to rescue someone. I took her hand and she clawed her way up my arm. She was on me like a monkey. Her legs swung up and wrapped around my neck, dunking me, choking me. I tried to stand, but I couldn't touch bottom. She kicked me, hard, in the jaw. I shoved her away but she held on to me. I'd had enough of this kind of treatment. My hand gripped her head like a rubber ball. I held her underwater and watched her thin body squirming in its green ruffled suit.

Someone finally screamed, and the lifeguards began blowing their whistles. Daisy dove from her chair in a red flash. Still I held the girl under. It's too late now, was the only thought I remember having. A man tackled me from behind, and Daisy jerked the girl from the water. The man gripped me tightly to his blubbery chest, as if I were trying to run away. Over on the cement Daisy knelt beside the girl and gave her mouth-to-mouth. After a few seconds Daisy stood up, holding the squalling girl, stroking her wet hair. The ruffles on the girl's suit were flipped up and plastered to her body. "Daisy," I called out. When Daisy looked over at me, her face slack with shock, I realized what I'd done.

Everything after that seemed nightmarish but inevitable. Daisy and I were taken up to the pool manager's office, dripping wet, to sit in plastic chairs and wait for the police. The detective who came wore a velour suit and looked familiar, like someone I might've seen at church. Daisy reported what had happened in a businesslike voice, while I stared at the tufts of hair on my big toes, wondering if I should shave them. The detective asked me if I had anything to add. "She tried to drown me first," I said.

"That's not how the witnesses tell it," he said.

I glanced over at Daisy. "Sorry," she said, ever the honest one. "I didn't see that part."

At my hearing, we sat on a bench in front of the juvenile judge—first the detective, then my father, hanging his head, then my sister Daisy, her arm around my father, and then me. My mother, who'd washed her hands of us, didn't show. Because of my previous record—shoplifting and truancy—the judge decided to send me to the Cary Home in Des Moines for one school year.

THE CARY Home for Girls was an elegant brick house tucked into a cul-de-sac on the edge of an upper-class neighborhood. From the outside, you'd never know it contained six teenage delinquents and their live-in counselors. We bad girls attended class in the large attic of the house, ate pizza burgers, did homework together, and watched reruns of "The Dick Van Dyke Show." It hardly felt like punishment.

At night, though, things fell apart. I had relentless dreams about Lisa Lazar, the little girl from the pool. She came to the Cary Home in her ruffled bathing suit and invited me outside to play. When she smiled, crooking her finger at me, I woke up terrified. I would stare at the buzzing streetlight outside my bedroom window and wonder what someone like me was doing at the Cary Home, someone who, until recently, had played by the rules, was fairly popular, had a semi-cute boyfriend, and tried her best to get decent grades.

In April, near the end of my stay at Cary Home, my father called to tell me that his sister, Marie-Therese, was coming to see me. "She wants to help out," he said. I'd never met my aunt before. She and my father exchanged Christmas cards and birthday phone calls, but that was about it. "Marie stays on the move. She's a wheeler-dealer," was my father's only explanation of why we never saw her. I wasn't sure what a wheeler-dealer was, but it sounded intriguing.

On the evening of her visit, I stepped into the living room and saw a fattish woman in baggy shorts and huaraches sprawled on the sofa, snoring. I recognized her dark curly hair and sharp features from an old photo I'd once found in my father's desk at the *Magruder Times*, of which he was the editor—a photo of my father and Marie-Therese as children, posing in chaps and cowboy boots in front of some mountains in New Mexico, where they grew up. I said, "Hello?"

She bounced up, wide awake. "I'm your aunt Merry," she said, shaking my hand. "M-E-R-R-Y, as in Christmas."

We sat down across from each other and she explained that she'd recently changed her name to Merry because she'd moved to Columbus, Ohio. "Midwesterners don't like anything Frenchy," she said.

"That's true," I said. I was disappointed that she'd changed her name and looked so ordinary and lived in Ohio. Out of the corner of my eye, I saw my roommate, the klepto, in the yard, peering in through the screen window. She was sneaking out to meet her boyfriend the arsonist. She bugged out her eyes and flicked her tongue. I ignored her. I asked Merry, "Why'd you decide to come see me?"

"Brother said family could visit," she said. "And I'm family, last I checked."

"Thanks," I said. My parents had never once been to see me at the home. My father was too ashamed, and my mother was too busy looking after her own father, Smitty, who owned the *Times*. Daisy, who'd postponed college for a year, drove over every Sunday and took me out to the movies or the Frozen Custard. We always got teary when we said good-bye. She would ruffle my hair and call me Squirt, willing me to be innocent again.

"Listen, sugar," said Merry, leaning forward with her elbows on her knees. "I called Brother last week 'cause I got the feeling something was wrong. He's worried sick. I offered to look after you, just for the summer. Transitional period. Before you go home."

So they didn't want me back. "I committed a crime," I said. "That's why I'm here."

"Nice place, too." Merry looked around at our cozy living room, furnished in Early American sofas and chairs that could swallow you whole.

"I don't want to be in the way," I said. "Don't you have a family in Ohio?" I knew she'd been married twice and had stepchildren.

"Oh, sure," she said. "But we won't be going to Ohio. We'll be staying out at the homeplace, in New Mexico."

My father once wrote a piece for the newspaper about what it was like to grow up on a ranch—haying, feeding livestock, planting and watering alfalfa—but he never talked to us about New Mexico. His parents had been to visit us a few times when I was little, but I barely remembered them. Now his father was dead and his mother was a sick old lady. "Why do we have to go out there?" I asked Merry.

She took my hand and squeezed it. One of her eyes was blue,

the other green. "I'm a psychic," she said. "You're going to be helping me with a job. Mom has offered us the use of her home."

"I tried to kill someone," I said. "A small child."

"I know, sugar," Merry said. "You did an extremely vicious thing." She stood up and slung her purse strap over her shoulder, as if that settled that.

I was relieved, if only for a moment, to think that it did.

AUNT MERRY and I left for New Mexico the last week of June. In Kansas she insisted that I drive her Lincoln Continental. I had my learner's permit, but I'd never driven on the interstate.

"Don't sweat it," Merry said. "The Queen Mary handles like a dream."

I sat up straight, my hands gripping the wheel as we rolled across Kansas at 70 miles per hour. Merry propped her bare feet up on the dashboard, knees tucked under her purple caftan. If I dropped down to 65, she would bark out, "What are you waiting for? A tow?" If I sped up to 75, she'd imitate a police siren.

But most of the time she talked about herself. "I wear different-colored contacts," she said. "Throws people off balance. They pop out sometimes, but I always find them. I have ESP. Had it since I was a kid. Once Brother lost his G-Man ring and I led him right to the spot, in the schoolyard, where it fell off his finger. Unfortunately, someone had stepped on it by then. When I was your age, Mom put me on the radio. My own psychic call-in show. I directed a woman right to where her baby wandered off to—the bottom of a well. Brother was so jealous."

I didn't want to reveal how eager I was to learn anything about my father. "Was he?" I said in a neutral tone.

"He was," Merry said. "He got stuck with all the chores. Didn't stand up for himself. Held it all in, till he couldn't take it anymore." She started humming "Rock of Ages" and stared out the window, letting me know she was finished with that subject.

We passed a muddy lot packed tight with cattle that seemed to go on for miles, bigger than anything I'd ever seen in Iowa. Finally I asked Merry, "Do you still have a radio show?"

"Oh no, but I still help people find things. They call me up from all over the U.S. and Canada. Missing dogs are my specialty." She studied her feet and wiggled her red-painted toes.

Merry was more childlike, and more self-confident, than any adult I'd ever known. She didn't seem to realize, or care, how weird she was. I said, "How do you find missing dogs?" Up ahead, in my lane, a station wagon was going much too slow.

"Pass him, pass him!" Merry yelled. We surged around the station wagon and veered back into our own lane. Merry went on in her ordinary voice, "Say, for example, some rich guy calls me from Indiana. He and his wife are missing their yellow Lab, Captain Crunch. Someone stole him right out of his pen. Man and his wife are distraught. Dog's a kid substitute. They've been offering a two-thousand-dollar reward, but no leads. I'm quiet for a while, and then I say, 'Your dog is safe. I see a late-model Ford, dark green, with two men in it. They drag Captain Crunch into their car. I see them driving to New Mexico. They're taking the dog to Los Alamos, for research purposes. But they stop at a convenience store in Española, and the Captain escapes.'

"'Thank God,' says the man. 'Where is he now?'

"'I can't tell exactly,' I say. 'Put an ad in the *Santa Fe New Mexican*. You'll find him.'"

"He says, 'Thank you, thank you' and says he'll send me a check for my commission."

"Are you right all the time?" I felt as if Aunt Merry and I were aliens, flying through the wheat fields in a space ship.

"One hundred percent of the time." She swiveled to face me,

the gold trim around the neck of her caftan glittering. "I can guarantee that somebody living with her grandmother just outside Santa Fe will answer that ad, and the happy couple will drive to New Mexico to pick up their dog. My little helper will hand over most of the reward money to me, keeping a bit for herself. All the time I'll be back in Ohio, so nobody can connect us. Not that these people ever try. They might suspect they've been had, but they've got a new dog. Everyone's happy. Even the dog."

I glanced down at the pavement racing underneath us. "I thought you had a gift."

"I do," she said. "I know how to make a living."

"I'm getting tired," I said. "My eyes aren't seeing very well."

"At the next rest area, pull over and take five."

"What if you can't find a dog that looks like theirs?"

"He's waiting at Mother's. Captain Crunch Junior." She swung her feet back up on the dashboard. "It'll be an adventure, sugar," she said.

MY GRANDMOTHER lived in a low brick house with tiny windows, surrounded by ramshackle outbuildings that looked like they were floating in a sea of red dirt. A few cottonwood trees punctuated the gray-green sagebrush. "This is a farm?" I asked Merry. "I thought you lived on a farm."

"We utilized an irrigation system," Merry said.

When we got out of the car, I saw a dog tied to the cornerpost of the front porch. He was yellow, but he looked part Lab and part something else. He was smaller than a Lab and had floppy ears. "They'll never believe this is their dog," I said. He strained at the rope and wagged his tail. "Is that the best you could find?"

"Now don't speak ill of our canine friend," Merry said. She took the two bags of groceries we'd just purchased out of the trunk of her car and thrust them into my arms. Then she leaned further into the trunk and emerged with a small TV set.

"What's that for?" I said.

"For you," she said, and grinned. Her teeth were too white.

Inside, while Merry unpacked the groceries, I wandered through the house. It was nearly bare of furniture. I could find no evidence that my father or Merry had ever lived there, not even a photograph. There were two rooms with single beds and small dressers in them, and one of those bedrooms was strewn with a woman's clothes. I tiptoed into another room where my grand-mother, balding and feeble, lay in a hospital bed under a pile of old quilts. There was a smell like sour milk. "Grandmother," I said. She lifted her head and yelled out, in a surprisingly strong voice, "Run, run—the Baptists are after you!" I backed away.

In the den, Merry was bustling about in the corner, unplug-ging a large TV set and hoisting it from a table onto the floor. A slight red-haired woman wearing a black jumpsuit leaned against the wall with her arms folded, watching Merry. Merry was talking to the woman but not looking at her. "I figured you really didn't need this fancy set," Merry said, "and we can really use it, what with Dick's poor vision." She lifted the little TV she'd taken from the trunk and set it on the tabletop. "There. That'll do fine."

"Does it work?" the red-haired woman said.

"Been working for years. Came from a motel liquidation."

The woman snorted. "I guess it's black and white."

"It's good quality," Merry said, patting the small TV like a pet.

A little while later I stood out in the driveway. Merry sat be-hind the wheel of her Lincoln, her elbow crooked out the win-dow. She'd only stayed long enough to unload my things and swap TV's, and now she was heading back to Ohio. I held on to her door handle. It was getting dark. "I can't do it," I said.

"It'll go smooth as silk." Merry winked her green eye at me.

"Read those want ads every day, sugar. Should be anytime. I'll be back before you know it."

I tried to think of something that would slow her down, if not stop her. "What should I tell Dad?"

"I wouldn't tell him anything." She started the car. "Considering your track record. And his."

"What'd he do?" I said, but she didn't seem to hear me. She stepped on the gas, flicking her hand in a wave as she spun out onto the dirt road.

I watched the red dust settling and thought about Iowa—our two-story white house with its porch swing and our sweet-smelling lawn that rolled under my treehouse down to the corn-field. At home, on a summer evening, the air would be full of humidity and comforting sounds—crickets, country music from passing cars, the distant voice of the baseball announcer at City Park. Daisy would be cooking my father's dinner—maybe pork chops and baked potatoes. I couldn't picture what my mother would be doing because she lived with Smitty, in his Victorian house across town. For years, Smitty and my mother had eaten breakfast together every morning at the cafe, and every afternoon she helped him with his business affairs. Finally, after she'd spent all of Christmas Eve and Christmas Day with Smitty, my father said to her in a joking voice, "You like him better than you do us. Why don't you just move in with him?" She called his bluff and did just that. Since Daisy had already taken over at our house, it wasn't that much of a change.

I stood there in the driveway till the sun had dropped behind the mountains. Then I untied the dog and took him inside.

I GOT INTO A ROUTINE right away. Every morning at breakfast I read the entire newspaper, saving the lost-and-found ads for last.

When I'd finished my Grape-Nuts I placed the bowl on the floor, and Captain Crunch Junior stepped up and licked the bowl clean and then some, causing it to roll around the kitchen floor.

"You kids stop that racket," my grandmother screamed from her bedroom.

The red-haired woman, who turned out to be my grand-mother's live-in nurse, sat across the table from me, reading *Silent Spring* by Rachel Carson. She was half Mexican, her name was LeeAnn, she was forty-two, and her hair, she told me, was natu-rally red.

The first morning I was there she'd said, "Aren't you going to get bored? How long are you staying?"

Merry hadn't warned me against telling Lee Ann about our scheme, but I knew I shouldn't. Besides, having a secret made me feel important. Merry had chosen me to help her, and since I was in a position to help, why shouldn't I? "I'm here on a rest cure," I told LeeAnn. "For my mental health."

"Well then," said LeeAnn. "You'll fit right in."

After breakfast I would grab an apple from the fridge and make three peanut-butter sandwiches. In the living room, which was totally empty, I tied a rope to Junior's collar and we set out for a walk down the dirt road toward the mountains. Strange-looking houses lined the road—adobe houses with scraggly yards from which dark-skinned people stared at me. Sometimes I pretended Lisa Lazar skipped along beside us, barefoot, in her silly green bathing suit. The air was clear and dry, and the sky was so blue it almost hurt to look at it. We strolled past cactus plants and lizards sunning themselves on white rocks. To the south were rounded hills with ribbons of pink running through them. The mountains loomed straight ahead. We walked and walked until I let myself realize we must be miles from my grandmother's house. Nobody knows me here, I thought, and nobody knows where I am. That thought was a signal that we'd gone far enough for one day. Junior and Lisa and I found shade under a pine tree and split the sandwiches and the apple.

When we got back, worn out and thirsty, we napped till dinnertime—frozen dinners and Purina Dog Chow that Merry had left. In the evenings I watched the little television in the den with LeeAnn, who was always doing something else at the same time, like sewing a hem or balancing her checkbook. At seven she spoonfed my grandmother her applesauce, and at nine she gave her a sponge bath. During commercials we talked about all kinds of things, including the existence of God. Neither of us believed, although we both wanted to. I couldn't bring myself to tell her about Lisa.

One night, while we were watching "Nightmare Theatre" and LeeAnn was knitting a Nordic sweater, she told me she thought Merry was a sleazebag. "She's sold off every antique, everything of value in this house."

"What's wrong with that, if nobody else wants it?" I said, realizing I sounded just like Merry. "Merry looks out for herself," I said. "I kind of admire that."

LeeAnn shook her head, clacking her needles together. "I think it's disgusting. At least wait till the poor thing's dead."

"So why do you work here?"

"I won't be here forever," she said. "Besides, I always liked Mrs. St. John. I grew up down the road."

"Did you know my father?"

"He used to let me ride his pinto pony." She held up the front of her sweater and admired it. "Merry used to make us kids march around in a parade just so she could be the majorette. Your father was always helping people, fixing things."

This didn't sound like my father. Whenever he was home from his job at the newspaper, he spent hours sitting in his chair, staring out the living room window at the cornfield behind our house, tapping his empty pipe on the edge of the coffee table. Daisy would bring him fresh glasses of iced tea and rub his shoulders, and sometimes he remembered to say, "Thanks, honey." Their behavior sickened and infuriated me, but I knew better than to let on.

LeeAnn resumed her knitting. "You seem like such a well-adjusted kid," she said.

"Young adult," I said, and we both laughed.

Later that night, Junior hopped up onto my bed, settled himself on my feet, and fell asleep. I lay awake, wondering what LeeAnn would think if she knew the truth about my family and the horrible thing I'd done. I wondered if she'd think I was crazy. Other people thought I was.

After the incident with Lisa, my father took me to a psychiatrist in Indianola. He wore a hearing aid and kept asking me how I felt. "Fine," I kept saying, feeling sorry for him.

He sighed. "Is there anything bothering you?"

"Well," I said, "I keep wondering where that girl's parents were when she went out into the deep water. Why weren't they watching her?" The psychiatrist wrote something down in his notebook, and I knew I'd disappointed him.

At night, after my father and Daisy were asleep, I would pace around our house, shredding tissues and gasping for air. During the day, while they were at work, I lay on the couch watching soap operas with the sound off. Once my mother dropped by, dressed in her pale pink suit, my favorite, the one she wore to the Garden Club meetings. She sat down beside me on the couch, trying to appear calm, but her eyes were fixed and tense, like a cat's. "The whole town knows what you did," she said. "Do you realize your father had to publish an article about it? In Smitty's paper?" My father had worked his way up to editor-in-chief, but my mother never let us forget that Smitty owned the paper. She grabbed my ankle and shook it. "Why would you attack the little girl? What were you thinking?"

I couldn't stand seeing my mother, the president of the Magruder Garden Club and Ladies' Literary Society, behaving like this. I couldn't stand her helpless hand-wringing. I said, "I hated that girl's frilly bathing suit."

My mother burst into tears. "What's wrong with you?" she said, but didn't wait for an answer. She got up and ran out of the room.

Junior, a hot weight at the end of the bed, let out a loud snore. I jerked my feet out from under him, but he didn't wake up. I knew what was wrong with me, and my mother did too, even though she pretended otherwise. I had become a delinquent because I did not intend to take my turn as Daddy's nursemaid. I did not intend to make myself useful.

AFTER MY FIRST DAY in New Mexico, I didn't go in to see my grandmother again. It was too depressing. I never called home, and when they called me I said I was having a very educational experience. I told my father that Merry was off on a short business trip—going to some motel liquidations—and that she'd left me in the care of Grandmother's nurse, LeeAnn, and that LeeAnn had taken me sightseeing on her days off. I mentioned some places I'd read about on the back of the New Mexico state map.

"How's Mom?" he asked me.

"Sweet," I said. "But kind of confused." I told Daisy I'd bought a square-dancing dress with the fifty dollars she'd given me and she pretended to be horrified.

Once my mother called and said that she'd seen Lisa's mother in the Jack and Jill, and that Lisa was doing fine. "Outwardly," my mother added. Every night Junior slept at the foot of my bed.

"The ad appeared after I'd been in New Mexico nearly a week. "Lost: Yellow Lab, from a convenience store near Española. 2 years old. Goes by Captain Crunch. Reward. Call Steve and Cyndi Richardson.""

That morning Junior and I walked past the horse pasture, past the school bus converted into a house. We kept following the road when it turned and climbed uphill through some pine trees. A hawk circled overhead, screeching. We'd never gone this far before. Lisa turned and ran back down the hill. I realized that the real Lisa no longer looked like the girl in the bathing suit. For one thing, the bathing suit wouldn't fit. She was a year older. She was bigger, taller, and smarter.

Junior stopped and gazed back at me, questioning.

"Lisa may not ever want to swim again," I said. "Did you know that?"

He sat down on his haunches, his eyes on my sack of sandwiches.

The phone number in the ad was busy till eight-thirty that night. "He showed up at my door hungry and weak, like he'd walked a long way," I told Cyndi. "Does your dog have a little white spot on the crown of his head?" Merry had coached me on what to say.

"Yes!" Cyndi shouted. "You're the first person who's mentioned the spot. I've gotten four calls already, and nobody's mentioned the spot. It's him, Steve. We found him!"

"I'll send you a picture, so you'll know for sure." I tipped back in my chair, feeling cocky. Merry had taken a picture of Junior, a tad blurry, and it was already in an envelope with the address and a stamp on it.

"You don't have to," Cyndi said. "I can tell by your voice that Crunch is right there in the room. We'll be there in three days."

"Three days?" I rocked my chair back down with a thud, which startled Junior, who was sprawled out in front of the screen door.

"Give him our love, will you?" Cyndi said. "Tell him we're on our way."

"Would you like to tell him yourself?" But she'd already hung up. "Jesus H. Christ," I said. Junior flopped his tail.

"What was that all about?" LeeAnn stood in the kitchen doorway with her hands on her hips. She wore gym shorts and a T-shirt that said ART WON'T HURT YOU. She said, "What are you and Junior up to now?" She pronounced "Junior" in the Spanish way, *"Hooneor,"* and I loved to hear her say it.

I said, "If you're a real nurse, how come you don't wear a uniform?"

She said, "If you're not a Christian, how come you're talking to Jesus? 'Twilight Zone' is on. Grave robbers. Right up our alley."

"DON'T LET THEM leave without him," Merry said on the telephone later that night. "And listen, sugar. About the reward money. Get cash. I'll give you a third."

"I don't want it." Talking to Cyndi, hearing her voice, had made me feel guilty about tricking her.

"I'll start a savings account for you," Merry said. "For college."

"I'm not going to college."

"Escape money, then. In case you get into another jam. You're impulsive, just like Brother."

So this could go on and on, I thought, this getting into one jam after another. "Okay," I said.

"See you on the weekend," Merry said.

"But what if they know I'm lying?"

"Remember. You're not saying he *is* their dog. You're just saying he *could* be."

I hung up and wandered into the den, where LeeAnn sat in the recliner, finishing up a crossword puzzle, her reading glasses perched on the end of her nose. "Whatever you and Merry are cooking up," she said, "I don't want to know about it."

"It's a losing proposition," I said.

"Six-letter word for 'nuts,'" LeeAnn said.

"Insane." I flopped down on the hairy brown couch. My bare thighs immediately started itching. "What was my father really like?" I said. "Was he some kind of rebel?"

She lowered her newspaper. "Because he held up the liquor store?"

I sank back into the couch, feeling queasy. After a while I said, "How long was he in jail?"

"Not a day," LeeAnn said. "Your grandfather got him and his football buddies off scot-free. They were drunk when they did it, but still. Worst thing that could've happened, him not being held responsible. He slunk off in the dead of night and never came back."

I closed my eyes.

"Didn't you know?" LeeAnn said. "Shoot, I'm sorry. You acted like you did."

"I knew," I said, and I felt like I had. My father had committed a stupid, public act, left his home forever, and was still waiting for his comeuppance. I might be doing the same thing, if Merry hadn't come along. It was much smarter to operate in the gray areas of life, like Merry did. She would never cower, and she'd never wait around for anything. And she'd never get caught.

CYNDI CALLED ME at noon from Española on the third day, and I gave her directions to the house. Afterward I sat on the front porch in my white sundress, drinking lemonade and telling myself I was the picture of trustworthiness. LeeAnn had gone to the Laundromat, and when she got back, I was going to tell her that Junior's rightful owners had shown up out of the blue to claim him.

I gazed down the road. With Junior gone, I thought, I'd be too afraid to go on hikes, and Lisa had grown up and left us. That's what I was focusing on then—how bored I'd be without them.

A dusty gray Volvo pulled into the driveway. Cyndi stepped out first, smoothing down her flowered smock. She was very pregnant. "Tabitha?" she said, starting toward me. That was the name I'd given. My alias.

I set down my glass and jumped up to greet her. Confidence, I told myself. Pretend you're Merry.

Steve climbed out of the driver's side. He wore a sweaty T-shirt and running shorts, as if he hadn't even bothered to change from his run before heading off across the country. He looked at me skeptically and didn't speak. I knew then that this trip was Cyndi's idea.

"Hello," I said, shaking Cyndi's damp hand. Her hair was long and wavy, pulled back in a messy ponytail. She had a large, pleasant face. I said, "How was the drive?"

"Horrendous," Steve said. "Illinois. And then Missouri."

"Would you like some lemonade?" I said.

"Where is he?" said Cyndi. "Where's Crunch?"

I'd shut Junior in my bedroom, because I thought they should see him first in a dim light. "Resting," I said. "It's his nap time."

When I opened the bedroom door, my knees were shaking. Junior reclined on my bed like a prince. He raised his head but didn't get up. Cyndi gasped and covered her mouth.

Steve crouched down on the floor. "Crunch. Come here, boy."

Junior stared at them. "He doesn't remember us," Cyndi said, swaying on her feet. "Is that possible?"

"He's not awake yet," I said. "Wake up, Junior." He leapt up and pranced over to sit on my foot. I said, "I've been calling him Junior."

"Junior." Steve patted the floor. Junior went to Steve, wagging his tail. I held my breath. Steve scratched Junior's ears and then inspected him all over, even examining his teeth. Finally Steve looked up at me, but I couldn't read his expression. "Thank you," he said gravely.

Cyndi plopped down on my bed, her face pale. "I still can't believe it. I haven't been able to sleep, my blood pressure's gone up. My due date's six weeks."

"Sit," Steve said to Junior. Junior licked Steve's face. "Lie down," Steve said. Junior jumped up and put his paws on Steve's chest. Steve said, "He doesn't remember anything I taught him."

"Dumb dog," I said.

"Crunch," Cyndi called in a soft voice, and Junior trotted over and hopped up on the bed beside her. "Now he remembers," she murmured, hugging him. "He remembers. Hello, Crunch."

What if it really is Crunch, I thought. It could be. Or Crunch reincarnated. I started to cry, and I imagined Merry shaking her head in disgust.

"Are you sad about giving him up?" Cyndi said. "I'm sorry. I've only been thinking about myself."

"He's not Crunch," I said. "He's Junior. *Hooneor.*"

Cyndi frowned at Steve. "Where are your parents?" Steve said.

"My grandmother," I gestured with my head. "She's senile." I wiped my nose on the back of my hand and then wiped my hand on my white sundress.

"I'm sure you're upset," Cyndi said. "You can get another dog."

348

"No," I said. "I'm trying to tell you. This dog came from the pound."

Cyndi and Steve exchanged concerned looks. "We're just glad you found him," Cyndi said, scooping up Crunch and handing him over to Steve. Crunch lay awkwardly in Steve's arms with his legs sticking straight out, and they both stroked him under the chin. They didn't care whether or not Junior was Crunch. They loved him no matter what.

"I almost drowned someone," I said. "I was scared and I took it out on her."

Cyndi patted my shoulder. "You'll be okay, Tabitha," Steve said.

"My name's not Tabitha, it's Sophie St. John," I said. "My parents sent me out here from Iowa for the summer, but my grandmother doesn't even know me." I stopped crying, and my heart began to pound. I could feel their generosity infecting me. "You're not suckers," I said. "You're good people."

"That's nice," Cyndi said. She turned to Steve. "We should get going."

Crunch began to squirm and Steve dumped him onto the floor. "I hate to leave Sophie here," Steve said to Cyndi. "We could give her a ride back to Iowa. It's on the way."

Cyndi slipped her arm around Steve's waist and sagged against him, but she didn't protest. I sensed they were playing some sort of game, a game in which they took turns leading valiant, ill-conceived rescue missions. One proposed a course of action most people would consider absurd, and the other went along as though it all made perfect sense. Their game, the kindness and futility of it, and the way it bonded them together, made me like them even more.

"Why don't you call your parents?" Steve said. "We've got room in the car."

I sat down on the edge of my bed and blew my nose, remembering the last time I'd been home. Merry and I had swung by Magruder on our way to New Mexico. She stayed in her Lincoln, listening to the radio, while I went inside. My mother was there for the occasion. One by one they came forward and kissed me, blank-faced, like I was in my coffin and they'd already cried themselves out. Daisy slipped me a fifty-dollar bill. "Buy yourself a summer dress," she said. My father hugged me with one arm, his face turned away. "See you soon," my mother said, opening the door like a hostess at a party. They seemed united, more like a family, with me gone.

Steve and Cyndi were watching me, waiting for my decision. "Thanks anyway," I said.

I followed them out onto the front porch, Junior trotting between them like their long-lost son. Cyndi and Junior climbed into the car, but Steve stopped in the driveway. "Is a check okay?"

I had forgotten about the reward money. "Don't worry about it," I said.

"That was the agreement," Steve said, turning toward the car. "I'll get my checkbook."

DURING THE NIGHT my grandmother died in her sleep. LeeAnn discovered her in the morning and called the funeral home. After the coroner pronounced her dead, the funeral-home men took her away, wrapped in one of her quilts. LeeAnn and I spent all morning on the phone. We couldn't reach Merry. She was already on the road somewhere between Ohio and New Mexico. My father said they'd come out to New Mexico as soon as they could get a flight.

In the afternoon I asked LeeAnn if she wanted to go for a

walk. The sky was clouding up behind the mountains, but we set out anyway. "We get storms every day in midsummer," LeeAnn said. "No biggie."

"I never got to know Grandmother," I said. "I wish I felt sadder. I'll miss Junior more than I will her."

LeeAnn, striding along beside me in shorts and hiking boots, just nodded. It had never occurred to me that LeeAnn would own a pair of hiking boots. It was odd seeing her outside, in the daylight, moving along with such assurance that she seemed to leave an impression in the air behind her, like an echo. I realized she'd been walking on this road for years. "What are you going to do now?" I asked her. "Where will you go?"

"I've got a husband in Santa Fe," she said. "I need to make amends and move on."

I waited for her to elaborate, but she didn't. "Me too," I said. Some day I would have to talk to Lisa, the real Lisa, face to face. A gust of wind kicked up the dust around us, sending a plastic cup flying past our feet. We bowed our heads and kept walking. Clouds rolled over us and I felt the first drops of rain. LeeAnn stopped and pointed to an adobe house with a rail fence around it. I'd gotten used to seeing it every day on my walks. "That's where I used to live," she said, and we stood there in the rain looking at the house, which was for me transformed into something mysterious. The windows in front were open, and white lace curtains whipped in the wind.

WHEN MERRY pulled into the driveway that evening, I left LeeAnn in the kitchen and went out on the front porch to get it over with. Merry nosed her Lincoln right up to the steps like she was docking a boat, then she climbed out, brushing her hair frm her eyes with a bejeweled hand. She was wearing the purple caftan, which was stained between her breasts. Coffee, or chocolate. "I'm beat," she said.

I sat down on the top porch step, wishing I didn't have to give her bad news.

She came up and sat on the step beside me. "Run get the money," she said.

I forced myself to look in her eyes, which were both brown. "I've got a check, made out to me. I think we should split it fifty-fifty." I'd practiced saying this in front of the mirror, but even so, my voice lacked authority.

She sighed dramatically and dropped her head. "And I've got a funeral to pay for."

"How did you know about the funeral?"

"I picked up negative vibes all across Missouri," she said, "but I didn't want to believe them. Finally I pulled over and called Brother."

We sat in silence, looking out at the sagebrush. My mouth was so dry I couldn't swallow. Merry glanced at her watch. "Holy moly." She stood up and jumped off the steps. "Help me get my stuff in, sugar," she said, dashing around to the rear of her car. "Then we need to carry some furniture out of the house. A man's coming for it in half an hour." She opened up the trunk and peered at me around the lid. "We have to do it before Brother gets here. He'll try to lay claim to the whole kit and kaboodle." Her face disappeared and I could hear her rummaging around in the trunk.

I remembered what LeeAnn had said about Merry the majorette, making all the kids march behind her in a parade. I could see there would never be a halt unless I called it. "You're on your own, Aunt Merry." I hadn't practiced saying this, but it sounded as if I had.

Just then LeeAnn yelled through the open window, "Fried chicken!"

Merry slammed her trunk shut and blew past me into the house. I went in behind her, walking at a leisurely pace.

THE FOLLOWING SUMMER, when I was sixteen, I got a part-time job at the Magruder City Pool. They put me down in the basement of the rec center, next to the locker rooms. I sat on a stool behind a battered wooden counter, collecting admission fees and handing out wire baskets and locker keys attached to large safety pins. Most of my earnings I put in a savings account I'd started with my half of Steve and Cyndi's check. Escape money.

One Saturday afternoon, after a heavy rainfall, when the pool was virtually empty, Lisa and her mother came through. Lisa's hair was cut in a bob and she wore a Speedo bathing suit. Her mother, a beautiful, haggard-looking woman, trailed behind her, wearing thongs with big plastic daisies on them, smoking a cigarette.

"Hello, Lisa," I said. My face flushed and I wished I'd kept my mouth shut.

Lisa looked up. She didn't recognize me or even seem to wonder how I knew her name. "Hi," she said. She grabbed her mother's hand and tugged. "I'm going off the high dive. First thing."

Her mother smiled at me and rolled her eyes. She didn't recognize me either. "We got a show-off here." She slid some change across the counter. "The diving board at the club isn't as high as this one."

I held out their baskets and keys, and Mrs. Lazar took them. I had to say something more to Lisa. "I'm the one who held you underwater. Two summers ago." I smiled idiotically. "Sorry."

Lisa nodded. "Okay." She started running down the hall toward the women's dressing room. "Cowabunga!" she yelled.

There was a line forming behind Mrs. Lazar. She glared at me, gearing herself up to give me a piece of her mind, even though, I could tell, she'd rather not be bothered. She took a drag of her cigarette. "I sincerely hope you got rehabilitated up in Des Moines," she said.

"I did," I said. "Completely."

Kids in line were pushing and shoving. Mrs. Lazar kept glaring at me, waiting for me to grovel. The ash on her cigarette was ready to drop onto my counter.

"But then again," I said, "I might do the same thing anytime. Or worse."

"I see," she said. She turned and addressed a suntanned woman behind her. "I guess they let anyone work here. This place used to have some class."

"Hurry up," barked the suntanned woman.

Mrs. Lazar shook her head in a world-weary way and flip-flopped off down the hall, flicking her ash on the floor as she went.

The suntanned woman handed me a crumpled dollar bill. "Some folks think they run the world," she said. "If you know what I mean."

"I do," I said. "I certainly do."

Charlotte

HOLIDAY REINHORN

THE DAY MRS. LINKABAUGH MOVED IN NEXT DOOR, I cracked my pubic bone in two places. It was 97 degrees, according to the giant thermometer Karl Bongaard had hanging on the side of his house. I was swinging at the time, watching the men from the moving company slide pieces of a fuzzy red water bed out of their truck, when my outgrown swing set pitched like a mechanical bull. A fire hydrant loomed, and I touched down somewhere along the curb. Through a small patch of consciousness, I looked up into the faces of four Mayflower movers as the sky ripped open and all of the clouds dropped to earth like wet rags.

At the Veterans Administration Training Hospital, I was in Room 503 with air-conditioning and a man named Victor Samuels, who pulled open the separating curtain every chance he got and started talking. He said he was originally from St. Louis and that last year his prostate had started hardening up into a little missile. My mother, Bobbie, said we had to be polite to Victor Samuels no matter what because he was probably tortured by the Vietnamese.

Dr. Maryland, the orthopedist, liked Bobbie right away. When he pinned up the X-rays and she asked whether smoking was all right if she held it out the window, he said, "Why don't the both of you call me Kevin, okay?"

This kind of thing happens all the time. My father used to say it was because Bobbie could never repulse a man no matter how hard she tried. From the time she was seven to nineteen and a half, my mother, Roberta Marie Peek, was Miss Glendora Heights Southern Division, Miss Teen Hideaway Cove, Miss Young Zuma Beach, Miss Autumn for Sunkist, and third runner-up to Miss La Jolla because she was skinnier then, and nobody could tell she was pregnant.

Even now that she's almost twenty-nine, all the men still like her, and it doesn't matter whether they find out first about the trophies and the train trips and the foot modeling. Jim Juergens, the softball coach from the community center, even came into the girls' locker room when I was changing once and said he had special dreams about making love to Bobbie and getting to be my father. That was the same week Coach Juergens got arrested for walking around the dugout without pants.

Kevin sat in a chair at the foot of my bed and took a long time showing us the X-rays.

"As you can see," he said, smiling over at Bobbie, "the fractures are on the left side of the bone. To prevent a limp, I had to actually rebreak the pelvis in the center, just to set the whole thing back in balance."

"This is unbelievable," Bobbie said, leaning over to hand me her last piece of spearmint gum. "I thought this kind of thing only happened to Denny."

Kevin looked at the tan line where Bobbie's wedding ring used to be.

"Who's Denny?" he asked, staring at her like she was the first woman he'd ever seen in his whole life.

Usually, we don't mention Denny to new people right away, because he has concentration problems and can't keep his hands off things. The last medical bill we had from Denny was when Bobbie took him to the Rub-a-Dub Automatic Car Wash and let him ride through it in the driver's seat all alone. He got into the glove compartment, where Bobbie left her purse, and swallowed three sleeping pills and a half-pack of wintergreen Certs and had to be rushed straight to the Poison Center.

"Denny's my little brother," I said, and Kevin looked relieved. He turned back to the X-rays.

"Actually, this was a really easy one," he said to Bobbie, pointing to the problem area in the center of the screen. "Once I had a clean break, I used stainless steel to stitch up the bone."

Bobbie held out her hand and I put the gum wrapper in it.

"Metal stitches," she said, shaking her head at the ceiling. "Holy Christ."

"It's better than a broken leg, though, isn't it?" Kevin said. "At her age, the bones are so soft, it's like sewing tissue. She doesn't even have to wear a cast."

Bobbie sighed into her hands, and Kevin looked like he might cry.

"Please don't worry," he said to her. "The incision will barely leave a scar."

I asked Kevin if he was married.

"Of course he is," Bobbie said, sliding the window shut and brushing her cigarette ashes off the sill. "And whoever guesses how much money Kevin makes in a year gets a free Jell-O."

I guessed a million dollars and Kevin smiled.

"I'm afraid we're only a government hospital around here," he said. "I guess I get the Jell-O."

Later, after Victor Samuels came back from his radiation and went to sleep, Bobbie scooted her chair up next to the bed and told me two things: I had to call my father collect right away to tell him I almost died, and that yesterday she had entered me in a preteen beauty contest. I reminded her that my pubic bone was broken, but she said she had already tracked down a sponsor who assured her I would not have to appear in the swimsuit section with any of the other eleven-year-olds or be required to go up or down the auditorium stairs on my crutches.

"They said they'd even put in a ramp if we want," she said, handing me the telephone before she went off with a nurse to sign more papers. "Isn't that terrific?"

My father was supposed to be living in Coos Bay by the water, and most of the time I was the one in charge of calling him. He wasn't usually at his house very much, but since we were in a hospital, I had the operator ring for as long a time as she could, just in case he picked up.

"How did his voice sound?" Bobbie asked when she got back from her errands.

"Okay," I said. "It sounded all right."

On my last day at the Veteran's, Peggy, the physical therapist, taught me how to use the crutches. My job was to practice limping up and down the hallway on alternating legs while she and Bobbie kept the rhythm going with loud claps. In the pharmacy on the first floor, I chose purple armrests for the crutches, and Bobbie bought me flower stickers to paste on the wood. Then, when it was time to go, Kevin walked us over to our car and gave Bobbie his telephone number.

"There are a few choices on here," he said, ripping her off an extra page from his prescription pad, "so give me a buzz anytime."

On the drive home, Bobbie told me everything she knew about our new neighbor. Her name was Mrs. Linkabaugh; her ex-husband, Bill Linkabaugh, was not allowed within 1,000 feet of her house by order of the Oregon State Police; and on the day she finally moved in, Mrs. Linkabaugh handed out at least fifty flyers with Bill Linkabaugh's picture on them just to warn everybody.

"And I want you and your brother to be very careful of characters like these," Bobbie said, cutting off a delivery truck on her way into the carpool lane, "because North Willamette is going downhill."

North Willamette is our street. When we were with my father, we lived on North Amherst, North Lombard, and North Mc-Crum. Now Bobbie says she'll never move again, not even if North Willamette becomes a slum.

Mrs. Linkabaugh's new house used to belong to Oliver Grevitch, who died trying to put up his storm windows. One Saturday he got out his ladder and climbed all the way up the side of his house and had a thrombosis. Bobbie's boyfriend Dale was in the driveway when it happened, and he says Mr. Grevitch hung on to his ladder the whole time and the two of them fell together, just like a chopped-down tree.

"Light me a cigarette, will you?" said Bobbie. "This bitch in the Gold Duster won't get off my ass."

When I got it lit, I tapped her, and she held out her hand so I could stick it between the right fingers. The woman in the Gold Duster leaned on the horn, but Bobbie ignored her and smoked with her tip out the window. When the honking got louder, she stuck her middle finger in the rearview mirror.

"This woman can eat me," she said, punching down the automatic lock button and pulling us back into the exit lane. "Now, roll up your window and hold on, we're taking Killingsworth."

I turned down the radio and kept my eyes on the floor mats, because Killingsworth and Alberta were bad avenues. The summer lifeguard at Peninsula Park used to tell everybody in the free swim that carloads of men from Killingsworth kidnapped girls like us all the time and did it to them over and over in the double-doggy style.

When we got to Lombard Street and into downtown St. John's, Bobbie drove past the Coronet store, where Dale was the assistant manager.

"Honk and wave!" she said, but I left my hands at my sides. The last time we visited Dale at work, he was refusing to give somebody a refund on a stuffed animal. The man asked for store credit, but Dale pulled a pencil out of his red apron and pointed it at the man's chest.

"That's not our policy at Coronet, buddy," he said. "No refunds. No exchanges."

Bobbie leaned across the gear shift, trying to see in through the big double doors. "Wave!" she said. "Why aren't you waving?"

"Because nobody will see me."

"Well, that is a really nice thing," she said, jamming down the gas and pulling us back out into the road, "considering Dale paid for your pubic bone."

"He did not."

"Oh yes he did."

I told her he didn't. My fractures were covered by our family health insurance, or paid for by my grandmother Peek.

"Oh, really?" said Bobbie, turning from the wheel and grabbing for another cigarette. "You better have a word with your father about that."

I didn't know what this meant, but there wasn't time to figure it out, because she was digging through her purse, and something large made of poured concrete seemed to be racing toward the car at a dangerous speed, and I said to watch out, watch out, but it was too late, because by then we were driving onto a parked island.

As the tow truck pulled us into our driveway, I saw Mrs. Linkabaugh for the first time. She was on her front porch in a velour mini-robe, sweeping the Astroturf doormat that used to belong to Oliver Grevitch. I stared at her thigh muscles flexing and her big chest swinging around in a nice sort of rhythm.

"Don't look at her!" Bobbie said. "God."

But everybody stared as Mrs. Linkabaugh bent over and shook out her mat, because she was a lot bigger than Bobbie. Everywhere.

"Jesus Christ," the two-truck driver said. "Get a load of that shit."

"Well, she doesn't seem too concerned about Psycho Bill today," Bobbie said, waving and smiling at Mrs. Linkabaugh through the tow-truck window. I waved at Mrs. Linkabaugh, too, and she blew me a kiss, shrugging her apologies as the chained Doberman in her yard lunged toward us over and over.

After he got the car unhooked, the tow-truck driver, whose pocket said *I'm Eddie—May I help you?*, didn't even talk to Bobbie. He walked right by the Bill Linkabaugh poster staple-gunned to the telephone pole and straight up onto Mrs. Linkabaugh's parking strip to introduce himself. While they were talking, Mrs. Linkabaugh retied her bathrobe two times, and Eddie kept teasing her Doberman with his elbow, making the dog jump up and down like a seal.

Pretty soon, they went into Mrs. Linkabaugh's house, and I imagined her putting on tea to boil and *I'm Eddie—May I help you?* coming up behind her like my father used to do with Bobbie when he lived with us, and while the kettle was screaming, the kitchen table would be bumping and scooting itself all the way across the floor and into another room. But Mrs. Linkabaugh's windows stayed just as dark as Oliver Grevitch's used to be in the old days, and there was nothing to see except the empty tow truck and the Doberman that kept on whining and throwing itself up against her front door.

Bobbie hung our picture of Bill Linkabaugh on the center of the refrigerator. She told Denny and me to watch for him at all times, and if we saw anybody that looked even a bit like him, we were to dial 911. Denny sat with his cap gun aimed out the window until it was time for dinner, and everybody looked at the Bill Linkabaugh poster while we ate. A refrigerator magnet was between his eyes, which made him seem even more threatening.

"I can't look and I can't look away," Bobbie said, staring at the poster. "He's got Son of Sam written all over him."

Denny dipped the tip of his gun in and out of his milk. "Son of who?"

"Sam," said Bobbie. "Son of Sam. And don't make people repeat themselves."

When we were done eating, Bobbie propped me on the couch with all six of her pillows and opened the windows and doors as wide as they would go. She paid Denny five dollars to go to bed early, and while she was watching him get ready, to make sure he didn't brush his teeth with just water or put his pajamas on over his regular clothes, I listened to the crickets and the swishing of the automatic sprinklers that Mrs. Linkabaugh had inherited from Oliver Grevitch. There were eight sprinkler heads in all, installed in two perfect rows of four on the front and back lawns and set to a special timing system that watered each section of the grass in wide, revolving fountains every night at nine-thirty. The night was so quiet, I could even hear stray drops of sprinkler splatter against the side of Mrs. Linkabaugh's house if I listened close enough, and I concentrated on the bright yellow light seeping out through her curtains, wishing they would open up and let me see if she and Eddie were inside listening to the sprinklers, too.

Even when I didn't have a fractured pubic bone, our living room couch was my favorite place to be. From our living room we had a view of the whole street, and especially of our left-side neighbor, because Bobbie had the couch placed right in the nook between two big picture windows at the front corner of our house. And since every house on North Willamette and North Amherst between McCrum and North Woolsey had the exact same floor plan, all the windows of our houses matched up perfectly, with only about eight feet in between. When Oliver Grevitch was alive, he had kept his curtains closed twenty-four hours a day, not like the Bongaards on the other side of us, who never close theirs, ever. The Bongaards were the reason Bobbie had Dale put our satellite dish up in front of her bedroom window, because she said she wanted to be able to let in some light once in a while and not have disgusting Karl Bongaard leering in at her constantly with his moon face.

By the time Denny was tucked in, my pelvis hurt so bad it felt like it might crack in half all over again, so Bobbie gave me an extra pain pill like Kevin told her to, and sat with me for a while on the couch. She held my hand, and we looked through some of her beauty-contest picture albums together. Most of them were of her winning, and not expecting to, and screaming, and having her eye makeup streak down, but tonight there was one I'd never seen before stuck in with all the rest. Instead of being up on a stage with a bunch of other girls, in this one she was totally alone, standing on a stepladder under an orange tree and reaching up to pick one. There wasn't any makeup on her face, and her bangs fell straight down into her eyes without curls. She had on a dirty white tank top with cutoff jeans, and the mosquito bites on her legs were scabbed over from too much scratching.

"What's that one?" I asked.

"Just me on a picnic," she said, turning the page, but I turned it back.

"With who? You look messy and nice."

"I don't even know with who," she said, smoothing down the plastic page where it was bubbling a little around the edges. "Let's check what's on TV."

After Mrs. Linkabaugh let in her Doberman, Bobbie went next door to get the bill from *I'm Eddie—May I help you?*, but nobody answered her knock. She came back after a while, and I lit her three cigarettes before she threw up her hands.

"What should I do?" she asked. "Call a tow truck to tow a fucking tow truck?"

Then Denny came back out wearing only his pajama bottoms, so Bobbie got her five dollars back and said we could both watch *Rat Patrol* reruns until midnight. She didn't go out with Dale, either, and we got to eat as many bowls of Honeycomb as we wanted, until my stomach pressed way out like a fist. Halfway through the second episode, Bobbie went into the kitchen and had a phone fight with Dale because he wouldn't come over. She told him to kiss her ass and then sat on the receiver.

"Go ahead, you prick! Come on," she said.

But when she put her ear back to the phone, we could tell from the look on her face that he'd already hung up.

Most of the time Dale doesn't spend the night over here because he has to be at the Coronet putting prices on things by nine A.M. He says he likes it better when Bobbie spends the night at his apartment over on Germantown Road so he can know exactly where all his stuff is and use his own shower and towels. Denny and I have never been over to Germantown Road, but Bobbie says the only thing Dale's got over there that we don't is a Water-Pik, and that his shower is probably where she got ringworm.

I was allowed to stay on the couch for the whole night and take one more half of a pain pill just in case. After I'd swallowed it with orange juice, Bobbie emptied the whole bottle onto the coffee table, chopped the rest of the pills in half with a butter knife, and locked all of them in the same drawer of her dresser where she keeps the pills Denny takes for his attention span.

Our old babysitter Crystal was the one who figured out he was hyperactive. One night when Bobbie was gone, she was talking to her daughter Crissy long-distance in California, and while she wasn't looking, Denny climbed up on the couch and started jumping so high he flew up and cracked his head open on the ceiling. Crystal hung right up on Crissy, and we screamed and screamed at him to stop, but Denny kept bouncing up and down, up and down, with the blood running into his ears until we pinned him to the carpet. Then, when Bobbie got to the emergency room, Crystal explained to her that Denny was at least as hyper as her son Ray used to be, and that we had better give him Ritalin. I know for a fact my father was the one who paid for all of that.

It was late by the time Eddie left Mrs. Linkabaugh's. By then everybody was asleep but me, because I like to watch the raccoons come up from Mock's Crest Marsh and go through the garbage cans in the back alley. Sometimes whole families come. I've seen them eat cake mix and raw eggs and Tender Vittles cat food. Usually, I get to put out a bowl of water for them, too, because we heard they like to wash their food. But tonight the alley was empty except for Eddie, who spit on Mrs. Linkabaugh's grass before he got inside his truck and peeled out, on his way to another accident.

On regular nights, I wake up two or three times, but because of Kevin's pill, I slept the whole night on the couch without waking up once. When I opened my eyes, Bobbie was sitting in the La-Z-Boy with Denny on her lap. She was smoking and staring out the window with the tow-truck bill in her hand.

"There's living proof that the *Penthouse* letters are true," she said, pointing the burning end of her cigarette at Mrs. Link-abaugh's driveway. "Bad timing for *you-know-who*."

"You-know-who doesn't want to live with us," said Denny, swinging his legs back and forth and making the chair bounce. "You-know-who wants to live in Coos Bay."

Bobbie reached up in the air and grabbed one of his ankles. "What did I tell you, Denny," she asked, "about sitting still?"

"You told me to try it."

"That's exactly right," said Bobbie, dropping his leg and looking back out the window. "So practice what I preach."

When my father moved to Coos Bay, Bobbie put all his *Penthouses* in a Hefty bag down in the basement next to the pup tent Denny and I got from saving Green Stamps. She said he only read them to torture her because of her small chest. Besides the *Penthouses*, my father also read *Hustler, Roadie,* and *Big on Top,* so I'm sure Bobbie was right about him liking Mrs. Linkabaugh.

After breakfast Bobbie gave me her July *Cosmopolitan* to read for the rest of the morning, and in the afternoon she taught me how to do the wave. She said the wave is the most important part of the beauty contest, twice as important as what a person says.

"The judges absolutely loved my wave," she said, cupping her hand and fluttering the fingers up and down in her famous way. "So you've got to do it, because everybody always waves flat-handed now."

I'd seen Bobbie doing her wave in pictures and to my father a hundred times because when he first saw Bobbie, she was riding a giant float shaped like a Sunkist navel orange in a parade through Rosemont, California. She had waved and waved at him and the big group of people he was standing with, not even knowing that he was going to follow her orange through the crowd, all the way back to the football field where the parade started, and that right after graduation, she was going to wind up in Oregon with him and me and Denny.

Because of how slow I was on the crutches, it took us a long time to get my wave right. We decided to add a wrist swing to my wave that made it more complicated than Bobbie's, and after an hour of waving at each other into the bathroom mirror, switching rooms, and alternating arms, Bobbie decided I ought to try it out on Mrs. Linkabaugh, who was outside in purple short shorts, hosing down her camper.

"Pick a point above her head to focus on," Bobbie said, standing beside me at the window and holding on to my extra crutch. "Then go through the whole thing one step at a time."

We tried all kinds of combinations to get her attention, but Mrs. Linkabaugh was too busy cleaning the inside of the wheel wells to notice.

"Those waves are looking totally perfect," Bobbie said, staring out at Mrs. Linkabaugh, who was bending down to spray underneath the cab. "She's just not the type to appreciate them."

After Mrs. Linkabaugh went inside, I thought Bobbie and I would keep working on my waves until dinner, but Denny came home from day camp, and Dale called to convince Bobbie to go out, so she took the phone into her bedroom. I figured they were talking about my pelvis money, too, because the phone cord was pulled as tight as it would go and I couldn't hear anything they were saying through the door.

Denny took off his socks and shoes and sat down next to me on the couch to wait for Bobbie, and we watched Mrs. Linkabaugh's camper drip-drying in the sun together. It was covered with hunting stickers, and a pair of mossy green antlers were bolted to the top of the cab that made it look weird and alive. It was easy to imagine Bill Linkabaugh dragging the dead owner of those antlers through the dark woods, home to wherever he and Mrs. Linkabaugh had lived.

"Check out the gun rack," Denny said, pointing at the window right behind the driver's seat. "It was his truck for sure."

He took off the house key on a string that Bobbie made him wear to day camp, and swung it around like a lasso. "Bill Linkabaugh is coming back to get it with a gun."

I stared at Denny and the horned half-animal camper, suddenly remembering the possible danger we could all be in, picturing Bobbie and Dale out playing pool while Bill Linkabaugh ripped down our screen door with the butt end of a hunting rifle.

"You better go get Bobbie off the phone," I said, keeping my eyes glued to the camper. "Now."

Denny threw down his house key and hit the floor at a dead run.

"*Bobbbbie!*" he called, slapping her bedroom door over and over again with a flat hand. "Bill Linkabaugh is coming over here tonight with a gun."

Bobbie's door cracked open slowly, just enough to let out her head. She covered the receiver and bent down to Denny's level, putting a hand on his shoulder and talking to him very slowly, right into the face like he was deaf, too, and not just hyperactive. "Denny," she said, nodding while she talked and looking him straight in the eye, "it only says that on a poster."

"Well, it's a police poster, Bobbie," said Denny, crossing his arms. "You better tell Dale that poster was made by the Oregon State Police."

Bobbie stood up and looked at the ceiling. She took a deep

breath and let it out in a long sigh. "Dale is very aware of that, Denny, thank you," she said, pulling her head back into the bedroom. "Thank you very much."

Denny came over to the couch and shoved the crutches into my hands. "It's a police poster," he said.

I stood in front of Bobbie's door for a long time and stared down at my feet. They were barely even touching the carpet at all, dangling like lead weights between the two fat rubber traction cups on the bottom of my crutches. Kevin had told us I was supposed to feel normal after the second day, but as my fist knocked on Bobbie's door, the whole top half of my body seemed way too loose and light all of a sudden, like everything on me from the waist up was rising, shooting up into the air with a rush, like a helium balloon.

"Bobbie," I said, in my calmest voice. "Open the door."

I heard the receiver click, and Bobbie was standing over me immediately. She was smiling, but everything on her face said that if Bill Linkabaugh or the blurry ache in my pelvis didn't kill me, then she definitely would.

"What?" she said.

Karl Bongaard's lawn mower started up outside, and I closed my eyes, listening to the horrible chopping sound it made, preparing for death.

"Bobbie!" I yelled over all the noise. "Bobbie?"

Bobbie looked over at Denny for a minute and then back at me as if we were crazy. "What?" she screamed back. "*What?*"

Through the window behind her, I could see parts of Karl Bongaard's body jerking by as he followed his lawn mower from one end of his grass to the other.

"Well," I said, focusing hard on her kneecaps. "My wave is not ready for the contest. And Denny and I think you ought to stay home tonight."

Bobbie leaned back against the doorjamb and crossed her arms, listening to the lawn mower roar practically up to the edge of our house, then move away.

"Really?" she asked, looking me up and down and straight in the eye. "That's what the two of you think, huh?"

"Yep," said Denny, before I could stop him. "That's what we think. Her wave sucks, and Bill Linkabaugh is on the loose, and you better stay home and get us dinner."

"Well, Denny," said Bobbie, walking past me into the kitchen, "you can tell your sister I'm not staying home tonight. For her information, this kind of behavior is called pressure, and I get enough of that from Dale."

"Then what are we supposed to eat?" I yelled after her. "If you're always going out and leaving us here?"

A cupboard door slammed, and another one opened.

"Tell your sister she's having Potato Buds and a green vegetable, Denny," she called from inside the refrigerator. "And that she had better stop rattling my cage."

Dale honked when the Potato Buds were still lumpy, and by that time, we had made Bobbie feel bad. She turned up the burners, dumped in the rest of the milk, and gave Denny a bigger spatula to stir with.

"Whip them, precious. Whip them!" she said, digging through her purse for the number of the pay phone at the Billiard Club. She leaned out the screen door and held up three fingers to Dale, which meant to wait three minutes before honking again.

"What you can do is call information for the number after I go," she said. "You know what to ask for—it's in St. John's."

She handed me each of our pill halves and twelve dollars for a cab fare in case of an emergency, but I didn't even look at her.

"Doors and windows are to be locked by ten," she said,

reaching back to zip up the rest of her dress. "But I'll probably be home long before then. Okay?"

I stared out the window and whispered that I didn't care. I might be calling Coos Bay.

"Excuse me, madame," Bobbie said, cupping her hand around her ear like she was hard of hearing. "Is that a threat?"

But I only shook my head and concentrated on the dirt patch in the front yard where my swing set used to be.

Dale leaned on the horn.

"Don't test me, either of you," Bobbie said. "Because Coos Bay is a fucking joke."

Denny stirred the potatoes without looking up, and I peeled a flower sticker off one of my crutches.

"Well, this is just great, isn't it?" Bobbie said, slamming a new stick of butter down in the center of the table. "I guess the sooner I go, the sooner he can bring me home."

"Yep," said Denny, continuing to stir. "And then Bill Linkabaugh can come over and kill us."

Bobbie marched over and grabbed her open purse off the coffee table. "I can promise you Bill Linkabaugh isn't going to be killing anybody, Denny," she said, checking the contents before she snapped it shut. "The swamp thing next door only wishes he was that desperate."

Denny brought dinner over to the couch, and we ate without mentioning Bill Linkabaugh or even looking at his poster. After dinner he got us water for our pills, rinsed the dishes, and made sure all the burners were off. I had him put some leftover Potato Buds out for the raccoons and was about ready to have him lock up early and turn on all our stand-up fans when we heard Otis Redding coming from next door. It was one of Bobbie's favorite songs, "(Sittin' On) The Dock of the Bay," and it floated in through Mrs. Linkabaugh's wide-open bedroom curtains, where she was sitting on the edge of her furry red water bed with a man.

Both of us could see that she was listening very carefully to him, nodding at whatever he said, understanding him perfectly. In fact, the strength of all her yesses was even rocking the water bed a little, making it seem like the two of them were riding in a boat.

Denny ran to lock the doors and brought the Bill Linkabaugh poster in from the refrigerator, but from the back of the head, we couldn't tell a thing about the man on the bed at all except that he slicked back his hair.

I slid down on the couch as far as I could go, and Denny crouched next to me with his chin on the sill. "Screw Coos Bay," he whispered, "we're calling the cops as soon as he turns around."

I nodded. "As soon as he turns around."

I stared down at the poster until my eyes started to swim, trying to memorize everything about Bill Linkabaugh's face and ignore the red words printed beside his left cheek: MAY BE ARMED. There was a buzz inside my ear, as if someone had turned on a tiny blow dryer. And I remembered Kevin's pill that was probably going to make me fall asleep long before the police could even get their squad cars to our house.

Denny closed one eye and aimed at the man's head with an imaginary gun. "If that's Bill," he said, "he's gonna be sorry he was ever born."

I covered Denny's mouth with my hand. "Stop talking," I said, "or I'll kill you."

Mrs. Linkabaugh was wearing the same shorts she'd had on earlier, but with a new halter top made out of yellow bandannas. Right near the end of the song, when Otis was sighing and breathing and humming, she grabbed the man's head, pushing it against her chest, and the two of them stood up and started dancing, swaying back and forth on each other like they'd had too much to drink.

"How tall does it say he is?" Denny asked, grabbing the poster out of my hands. "I think he's too short to be Bill."

"Bill is five-eleven, one-eighty," I said, grabbing the poster back and giving Denny a charley horse. "We have to look at him from the front."

The man flipped Mrs. Linkabaugh around and started dancing with her from behind. He reached around and put a hand across her eyebrows and pulled her head back to rest on his shoulder, burying his whole face in her hair.

Her neck was bent back at a bad angle, like maybe he was about to break it, but then, right after "Midnight Train to Georgia" started, Mrs. Linkabaugh said something to the man that made him let go, and they both started to laugh out loud, quietly at first, then deep from the belly, like what was happening in that room had to be the most hysterical thing in the whole wide world.

"We better do something," Denny said, but neither of us moved. All we could manage was to watch without breathing, pressing our faces closer and closer to the window screen until I was sure we were both going to smother.

It took them forever to get over laughing, but when they finally did, Mrs. Linkabaugh grabbed the man by the arm and dragged him out onto the back patio. She hooked her screen door to the side of the house, and a giant pool of buttery light spilled onto the lawn. Then she jumped down the steps and backed farther and farther out onto Oliver Grevitch's thick summer grass, gesturing for the man to follow, holding out both hands. But he didn't move an inch.

"Charlotte," he called to her from the top of the porch steps. "Charlotte, c'mere."

But Mrs. Linkabaugh ignored him and kept on going.

"Her name's Charlotte," Denny whispered, and we both ducked our heads below the windowsill for a minute and said her name out loud. "Charlotte Linkabaugh."

And in the fuzzy shadow glow that surrounded her, from the streetlight and the porch light and the light of the moon, Mrs. Charlotte Linkabaugh reached down and slipped off her slingback sandals, tossing them over her shoulders out into the dark, one at a time.

Once the man saw that, he came down the porch steps right away, but before he could get even halfway across the yard, she ran up in her bare feet and jumped on him, wrapping her legs around his waist and letting him dance her around and around in circles. The man arched his body backward to hold up all the weight, turning her faster and faster and faster like an ice skater, until everybody lost track of the time except for Oliver Grevitch's automatic sprinklers, which blasted out of the ground right on schedule.

Then, in the middle of the water that seemed to be spewing everywhere, in the middle of Mrs. Linkabaugh's terrible half-hyena scream, the surprised man froze just for a second, and he looked up at the sky as if he was very confused about where all the water was coming from, and as he stood there in front of us, with his eyes searching the air above his head, there was no disputing anymore who he was.

"Holy Christ," said Denny. "Bill."

I nodded. "Bill," I said. "It's Bill."

And while we stared out at the yard next door, trying to make our calculations about which police to call, and how many, and when, the Linkabaughs were running through their own sprinklers, illegally.

They had both started laughing again but sillier, dizzier, this time, uncontrolled. Both of them soaked through all their clothes, chasing each other around like they'd never figured out how good cold water could feel in the middle of July.

One time on the way around the yard, when Bill was chasing her with his belt, swinging it around his head and snapping it behind her like a wet towel, I saw Mrs. Linkabaugh jump through a burst of water like a track hurdler. Her hair was plastered to her cheeks and her arm was stretched way up above her head, reaching high like Bobbie in the messy white tank top, trying to grab for that orange on the ladder back in California, and as I waited for her to come back down, to land again on the slippery grass, I wished the hot night could stretch out forever, because I knew that, like Bobbie, she would probably never be up in the air like that again.

Contributors

George Saunders is the author of several books, including *The Brief and Frightening Reign of Phil*. He is a frequent contributor to *The New Yorker* and teaches at Syracuse University.

Jennifer Egan is the author of several works of fiction, including *The Keep*.

Victor D. LaValle is the author of *The Ecstatic* and the PEN/Open Book Award winner *Slapboxing with Jesus*.

Julie Orringer's stories have appeared in *The Paris Review*, *Zoetrope*, and several other publications. Her first story collection is called *How to Breathe Underwater*.

contributors

John Barth is the author of numerous works, including the National Book Award–winning *Chimera*. His most recent book is *Where 3 Roads Meet*.

Rattawut Lapcharoensap is the author of the bestselling *Sightseeing*.

Stanley Elkin received the National Book Critics Circle Award twice, for his novels *George Mills* and *Mrs. Ted Bliss*. He died in 1995.

Stacey Richter has won three Pushcart Prizes and a National Magazine Award, and her fiction has been published in *GQ*, *Granta*, and elsewhere. She is the author of *Twin Study* and *My Date with Satan*.

Jim Shepard is the author of *Batting Against Castro* and several other works of fiction. He is a professor at Williams College.

Alicia Erian is the author of a short story collection, *The Brutal Language of Love*, and the novel *Towelhead*. Her work has appeared in *Playboy*, *Zoetrope*, *The Iowa Review*, and other publications.

A.M. Homes is the author of several books, including the novel *This Book Will Save Your Life*.

Robert Boswell is the author of *Century's Son, Mystery Ride*, and several other works of fiction.

contributors

Kevin Canty's most recent novel is *Winslow in Love*. He teaches at the University of Montana in Missoula.

Mark Jude Poirier is the author of several books, including the novel *Modern Ranch Living*.

Amber Dermont's stories have been published in *Tin House, Zoetrope, Alaska Quarterly Review*, and several other publications. She teaches at Francis Macon College in Georgia.

Nathan Englander is the author of a story collection, *For the Relief of Unbearable Urges*, and the novel *The Ministry of Special Cases*.

Malinda McCollum's stories have appeared in *The Paris Review, The Pushcart Prize XXVII, McSweeney's*, and *EPOCH*. She lives with her family in Charleston, South Carolina.

Chris Adrian is a writer and physician. His novel *The Children's Hospital* was published in 2006.

Elizabeth Stuckey-French's most recent novel is *Mermaids on the Moon*. She teaches at Florida State University.

Holiday Reinhorn is a recipient of the Tobias Wolff Award for fiction and the author of the story collection *Big Cats*. Her work has appeared in *Ploughshares, Other Voices, Columbia*, and *Northwest Review*, among others.

Permissions

CPSIA information can be obtained at www.ICGtesting.com
Printed in the USA
BVOW04s1237020214

343600BV00001B/13/P